SILKWORM SECRETS

DARK SECRETS FROM A DISTANT PAST

RHONDA FORREST

Valeena Press

COPYRIGHT

This book was previously published by Valeena Press as, 'Silkworm Secrets' by Lea Davey (Rhonda Forrest)

Copyright © 2016 by Rhonda Forrest

First Edition Published 2016 - Silkworm Secrets by Lea Davey (Rhonda Forrest)

Second Edition Published 2021 - Silkworm Secrets - Dark Secrets from a Distant Past by Rhonda Forrest

All rights reserved.

The characters and events portrayed in this book are fictitious. Any similarity to real persons, living or dead, is coincidental and not intended by the author.

Disclaimer - Every effort has been made to ensure that this book is free from error omissions. Information provided is of general nature only and should not be considered legal or financial advice. The intent is to offer a variety of information to the reader. However, the author, publisher, editor or their agents or representatives shall not accept responsibility for any loss or inconvenience caused to a person or organisation relying on this information. A catalogue record for this book is available from the National Library of Australia.

Published by Valeena Press

Book Cover Design and formatting by Ethel Beckett and Rhonda Forrest

ISBN 9780645056303

SILKWORM SECRETS

DARK SECRETS FROM A DISTANT PAST

'When I'm up here, it's as if I'm floating and everything else has been left below. My mind settles as I climb the mountain and I feel at peace. The ancient trees with their rough bark wrap around me like silk cocoons. Their solid trunks and tendril roots grip the ground as if to say, I will hold you, I will not let go. The air is clear, not sticky or musty, and there's a breeze that wings its way through the branches, the leaves and across my face. The world below ceases to exist. If I close my eyes I float above the surface of the earth and ... I am calm.'

Bobby Carlon

PART I

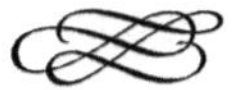

CHAPTER 1

There had been great excitement the day the silkworms first came to the treehouse. Walking knee-deep through the dense covering of ferns and bushes beneath the mulberry tree, Bobby had announced that he had a surprise for Ruby in his satchel. It was dim and cool under the tree, the knotted branches and canopy forming a shady, secluded area, only a few frilly-necked lizards and the occasional brown snake sharing the space with the two of them.

She had tried to get him to stop and open his bag, the suspense almost too much, but he kept walking, determined for once not to let her win.

'Wait, Ruby Rose. Just wait until we climb up and then I'll show you.'

'But what is it? Can't you tell me? I'll die of curiosity.'

Ruby liked to be in charge and know everything. The suspense made her climb erratically, stopping and starting, continually looking down at Bobby climbing steadily below her.

'Just get up there and I'll show you,' he said.

Standing on her toes, she balanced on the rungs leading up the tree. The bottoms of her feet were stained, dark purple colours mixed with dirt from the earth below. Her flowery cotton dress was also discoloured, purple from where she had sat on some of the thousands, perhaps millions, of berries that had dropped from the tree during the fruiting season.

Above them, the trail of timber blocks, like steps, wove their way up into the darkest reaches of the tree. Nails that had long ago been hammered into the rough, textured bark held the timber secure, and as they climbed higher, tiny glimpses of the sky became visible; a blue backdrop to the thick branches that reached upwards, their tops covered by the dense canopy of weeping smaller branches and leaves.

Perched amongst the thick foliage of the massive mulberry tree, the treehouse was obscured, a safe haven, a place no one else bothered with, tucked away in an over-grown corner of Ruby's backyard. The two best friends considered the spot to be the best place in the world, and its location among other large trees—figs, mangoes and a towering pine tree—provided them with their own secret corner, a safe house with no adults, just the two of them, talking, laughing; conspirators.

'Hurry up.' Ruby used her bossy voice, holding up the canvas for Bobby to enter the treehouse.

Once inside he had reached into his satchel and presented Ruby with a number of pieces of cardboard, all covered in multitudes of silkworm eggs. She was ecstatic and caused him great embarrassment by continually hugging him and then jumping up and down, making the treehouse creak and shake a little.

It had been school holidays and they had watched every day, Ruby recording in her notebook when the tiny, grey eggs stuck to the cardboard had lightened in colour.

Finally the day they had both waited so patiently for: tiny silkworms, hundreds of them, wriggling, squirming and climbing over each other, filling an old school port, safe in their new home.

Although Ruby had only been eight, she was fastidious about keeping records of events that occurred in and around the treehouse. She left her small notebook in the treehouse, only removing it when she needed to record major incidents.

Today she wrote: *143 healthy silkworms. All eating leaves.*

* * *

THE SILKWORMS GREW QUICKLY, fattening on the never-ending supply of leaves from the mulberry tree that was at its best, the thick canopy dripping with the heaviness of its foliage and fruit. The job of picking the greenest leaves from the tree and making sure that all the worms were fed had been allotted to Bobby. Bobby's other job was to clean the droppings from the boxes so the silkworms would have enough room to move around.

They had found extra boxes, the original school port now overflowing with fat silkworms that quickly ate through the leaves. Their droppings were bright green, an indication, Ruby told Bobby, that they were happy and healthy.

Once, when Ruby was not around, Bobby had carried the largest container, the school port, down the tree and into his bedroom at home. Plugging in the vacuum cleaner, he had tried—just using the pointy end of the vacuum and not the brush part as he later explained to Ruby—to suck up the droppings and give the container a really good clean.

Ruby had not been impressed and had efficiently recorded in her notebook:

September 24, 1968, 54 large fat silkworms.
   Now only 12 surviveing.
   Bobby and vacum encident.

Now she needed to make more notes regarding the latest incident. Bobby stood beside her as she recorded in her neat handwriting:

March 4, The accident, 1970.
   School port moths, 17 healthy moths, now only 7 surviveing, 2 of those are injared becous of falling from tree.
   Bobby and Ruby falling over encident acident.

'What?' Ruby said as she looked up at Bobby, his mouth opening as if to speak.

Perhaps it's not the best time to point out her spelling mistakes, he thought, as he closed his mouth, instead smiling and shaking his head. 'You're the best club president,' he said, 'and at least we still have some moths, even after the accident yesterday.'

The small girl rolled her eyes at him, an indication that she was not impressed with the situation.

He had long ago decided to ignore Ruby's habit of eye rolling, as well as to go along with most of the ideas she came up with. The time he spent with her was his only sliver of happiness in amongst the misery of home and school, and he would do anything to keep the peace between them, whatever it took to stretch out the time before he had to return home. Even though the happenings of the day before had been calamitous to Ruby, they hadn't even rated in his own list of personal disasters.

Ruby was oblivious to the situation at his house. Although he sometimes longed to tell her what was really happening, he had decided that for now it was better to keep it that way, to keep it all to himself. Just try not to think about it.

CHAPTER 2

The accident had happened the day before, on what had started out as a typical afternoon but had quickly gone wrong; a disastrous chain of events resulting in the moth tally decreasing to just seven.

As usual, they had both rushed home after school and made their way up into the treehouse as quickly as possible. They lay side by side, enjoying the cool of the rough timber flooring in their meeting area.

Bobby was happy to lie still and listen to Ruby as she chattered on about making a new area that she wanted to call the sitting area. Although there were many sections to the treehouse, designated and specified, it was, after all, not such a big structure. They had drawn boundary lines for the different areas on the floor with white chalk, the faint lines invisible in places where their bare feet or bodies had rubbed over them.

Now they sprawled out with their heads in the spying area, feet pushed up against the stump of the activity table, their bodies stretched across three areas—spying, meeting and activities.

Bobby, being the elder and taller of the two, lay contorted, with his knees bent high and his neck twisted slightly so he could fit across the largest flat area of the treehouse. He tried to stretch out his long legs, sinewy from years of school sport and running, before resigning himself to the cramped conditions. Turning his head, he looked through the slits in the timber walls. His intense brown eyes were set deeply, and his tousled dark hair, springy with the Queensland summer humidity, framed his squarish, still boyish face.

Ruby was stretched out fully beside him with her shoulder jammed up against his, her bare feet nowhere near the stump-table that hindered the comfort of the taller Bobby. Conspirators; two sets of eyes flickering back and forth, lying deathly still as if their lives depended on invisibility.

'I told you it was a good idea,' Ruby whispered, indicating the rolled-down canvas across the doorway. 'There's no way anyone can see in now.'

'You're smart for a girl. Sometimes.'

Bobby's chuckle was cut short by the cutting look, a savage glare as the small girl turned towards him, glinting green eyes scowling, her scrunched-up face willing him to remain silent. They stared hard at each other and Bobby concentrated on her face as he counted the biggest freckles, a smattering of cute brown spots across her nose that faded into each other as they ran across the top of her somewhat chubby cheeks. There were a couple of gaps in her teeth where adult incisors had failed to come through quickly enough to mask the fact that she was still young enough to be losing baby teeth.

Knowing better than to tease Ruby about still having teeth like a baby, he kept his quick words to himself rather than incur the wrath and sharp retorts that would flow forth from her; so young but already more than capable of sticking up for herself.

Wavy blonde hair spread out beneath her, so long that it reached below her red cotton shorts. Her thin brown legs were stretched out beside him as she tried to match the length of his own. Ruby didn't like to be far behind Bobby in anything, and she was always measuring her height, telling him that one day they would be the same size.

'But you'll never be as strong as me,' he would say, flexing his muscles, thinking that one day he would have muscles as strong as Popeye in the cartoon pictures.

'My dad says that I can do anything a boy can do,' Ruby said. 'Just because I'm a girl doesn't mean I can't do stuff. He reckons I can do whatever I want, and if I want to be the strongest person, well, I can be.'

'Girls can't do some things that boys can.' Bobby looked at her, suspicious of her confidence and confused about her ideas, so different from what was promoted in his house.

'Of course they can. I can be whatever I want. If I want to be a doctor, well, I can.'

'That's not right. Girls should be nurses or mums.'

'My dad says if I want to be an astronaut like Neil Armstrong then I can be. He says I'm really smart, and when I grow up I can be whatever I want.'

'Bet you can't be a concreter like him.'

'Bet I could.'

'Girls are supposed to get married and have babies. They look after the kids and cook, clean the house.'

'I don't like cooking and cleaning. I hate cleaning the bathtub. I'm going to do something else when I'm grown up.'

'Like what?'

'I'm going to be a lawyer.'

'You mean like on *Homicide*?' he said, referring to the popular television show.

'Yeah, you know, they solve crimes.'

'I thought you weren't allowed to watch those shows. How do you know what a lawyer is when you aren't allowed to watch it?'

'Silkworm secret,' Ruby said. 'If I lie in bed with the door open, I can see the TV screen reflected in the big mirror on the sideboard. My dad's a bit deaf so he has it up pretty loud. I get to see most TV programs, but you can't tell him or Mum.'

'Lawyers are always men.'

'I watch *Matlock Police* too.'

'Your dad would be angry if he knew you were watching those programs. You'll be in trouble if you get caught.'

'Bobby, I won't get caught. Besides, they're really scary, so most of the time I put my hands over my eyes.'

'You're lucky that your mum and dad care about you. I wish my parents were like yours. The other day Theresa asked me how you get a new mum and dad. She's tired of all the trouble at home and the way Sally doesn't get looked after properly. I didn't know what to say. I wish I was older, then I'd run away and take them both with me.'

The two best friends stared hard at each other as they talked. It was a game they often played: who could go the longest without blinking. Both blinked sharply, however, when a loud voice bellowed up from under the tree.

'Ruby, you climb down here this minute. I know you're up there. I wasn't born yesterday.' Footsteps scuffed through the thick layer of fallen leaves, moving closer, the voice booming out again. 'You get down here *now*. I've got jobs for you to do and you're not supposed to play until your homework's done.'

The two conspirators, who had no intention of moving or answering, pulled faces at each other, imitating the adult face below.

'Your father will clip you across the ears when you come down and there'll be no ice cream for you tonight.' Mary, Ruby's mum, waited for a reply. 'You're wasting my time, Ruby. I've got better things to do than look for you. I'm telling you now though, if you didn't change and you've got mulberry on that school uniform there'll be hell to pay.'

The exasperated voice faded away as Ruby's mum made her way back to the house.

'She's not really mad,' Ruby whispered. 'She just likes to sound like she is, making out she's the boss.'

Bobby looked worried. 'Are you sure your dad won't thrash you?'

The small girl's laughter resounded off the rough timber walls. 'Are you joking? My dad loves me too much. He would never hit me.'

'Does your mum ever hit you?' Bobby was trying to manoeuvre his neck, which was starting to feel like it would be attached sideways on his body permanently.

Ruby's little face scrunched up, her eyes narrowing. 'She loses it sometimes, especially when I keep going on about something. Because I'm more stubborn than her, she knows she can't beat me. I can always tell when she's really mad because her face goes red and her eyes … it's like she's a dragon and there're flames coming out of them, red flames licking out of her green eyes. And sometimes her lips go real thin and mean, like this.' Ruby sat up and gave a demonstration.

'What does she do? Does she use a belt?'

'Worse than that.'

'A cricket bat? A broom handle?'

'Don't be silly.'

'I know,' Bobby said, 'the whippy wire out of the curtains.' His curiosity was aroused as he imaged the horrendous punishment her mother might inflict.

'Way worse.' Ruby loved having Bobby's full attention. 'She goes all quiet, then she starts whispering all the angry things she wants to say to me.'

'You mean she doesn't scream or yell?'

Ruby rolled her eyes. 'No, she goes quieter and quieter, telling me off, saying she's going to tell Dad all the bad things I do.'

'Then what?'

'She snaps off a branch, a thin little branch from the wattle tree out the front. She sort of tests it in the air and then real quick, before I can run away, she twitches me with it.'

'Across your face?'

'No, stupid, across the back of my legs, and it stings like crazy and sometimes it leaves a red mark. If I rub it really hard I can make it stay there until Dad gets home and then I tell him that she whipped me with a thick tree branch.'

'Is that it? A bit of a whack from a wattle twig across your legs?'

'Well, it stings.'

'That's nothing, a little wattle twitch.'

'If I put it on real good and make out it hurts a lot,' Ruby said, 'when I sit with Dad at night he rubs it for me. Then he sort of lectures me, tells me how to get around Mum, how not to annoy her. You know the sort of stuff: "Your mother loves you, you need to be nice to her, don't bite the hand that feeds you." Dad reckons she's the boss.'

Bobby lay without speaking, staring up at the patchy tin roof.

'Bobby, are you listening to me? Do you reckon your mum's the boss?'

A lengthy silence followed before he spoke. 'There's no way Mum's the boss. You know my old man; you've seen what he's like. He's not kind like your dad.'

'Your dad's always nice to me,' Ruby said, 'and he gives me a little sausage when we go to your meat shop, and sometimes he makes Mum laugh. He always chats to her, tells her she has a pretty dress on, says he can smell her dinners cooking and that she must be the best cook in the street.'

'Ha.'

'Mum says that your dad has done really good to have such a big shop, and Dad reckons your dad is a good butcher giving us the meat cheaper, and he says that your sister Theresa works hard, she does good at school, and Mum and Dad think you're smart, and your Uncle Mike, well, Mum says, "Fancy having an uncle that knows the prime minister, real high up in the government he is, and he has so much money and—"'

Bobby cut her off, wondering how she could speak for so long without a breath. 'You know things aren't always what they seem to be.'

'Like how?'

'Just … never mind.' He stretched out his stiffening muscles.

'What do you mean? Don't start something and not finish it.'

'I mean sometimes things look good to other people, but they're only seeing what's on the outside.'

'Well, what's on the inside?'

'Forget it. I'm going to get your stupid records book so you can write up the tally.' Bobby sat up suddenly, signalling an end to the conversation.

'Hey, I'm the boss.' Ruby grabbed Bobby as he tried to stand up, his long legs wobbly and unsteady after lying cramped and still for so long. 'Just because you're older—'

And that was when, in a split second, it happened: 'the accident' as Ruby liked to refer to it.

It was like watching a slow-motion movie. Ruby gasped out loud as Bobby's legs became tangled, his body twisted, and he lurched unsteadily towards the table in the centre of the treehouse. The piece of fibro that made up the top of the table rested on the stump of a huge branch. Apart from the way the tabletop crumbled a little around the edges from time to time, it made a perfect flat surface for many of their activities.

That day a number of containers were lined up neatly across the table: an old school port with broken hinges, its stickers peeling; two shirt boxes, the colours on their sides faded and blurry; and two smaller shoeboxes. All the lids on the containers had been punched with multiple holes, providing air for the tiny creatures within.

Ruby's eyes widened as Bobby stumbled and fell forward, one arm reaching out to steady himself and stop his face smashing into the boxes on the table. His hand made contact and he grasped wildly at the closest object. Before their eyes, the largest container, the school port, turned over, the lid going one way, and the rest of the port flipping forward and landing upside down in the reading area.

'Shit.' Bobby gathered himself, standing steady, looking from Ruby to the school port.

They both knew. They knew that below that port, which was now lying lidless in the centre of the reading area, were gaps in the timber floor that opened to the ground far below. This was serious. Bobby registered the fact that Ruby hadn't reprimanded him for swearing; rule number five on the list of Silkworm Club rules.

Ruby crawled slowly over to the port and waited for Bobby. Together they lifted it, cautiously moving it straight up and not sliding it, or allowing it to have any more contact with the floor than necessary.

'Uh-oh.' Bobby pursed his lips and waited for Ruby's response.

'They've nearly all fallen through the gaps,' Ruby said. 'They won't live, they can't fly.' Her voice was shaky as she carefully tried to pick up the contents that had fallen from the container.

Bobby pressed his face to the openings between the floorboards, one eye closed, trying to spy any survivors of the fall.

Ruby's voice took on the steadiness and authority of the Silkworm Club president. 'I'll pick these ones up. Can you please go down and see if you can find any on the ground?'

She scooped up the mulberry leaves scattered on the floor, a few silkworm moths gripping to their surface, their delicate wings flapping wildly, their eyebrows furrowed. 'It looks like there are about five here. That means twelve are missing. This morning there were seventeen.

Hurry up, Bobby, they only live for a few days so we need to find them and put them back in the box. Then they can lay their eggs.'

As usual, Bobby followed her instructions. Even though he was older by three years, Ruby was the club president, and besides, she was good at organising everything and everybody. It was easier to just follow her directions and do what he was told.

He scrambled down the tree trunk, hanging onto the timber steps and hand guides that wound their way down to the ground. The thought of looking for white moths that had probably drifted off on the wind made him smile. He knew that the heavy leaf litter and dense ferns growing wild under the tree would envelop and hide a free-falling silkworm moth that had no sense of surviving in the wild.

But he would try; he would do anything to please Ruby because she was, after all, his best friend.

CHAPTER 3

'*D*ad says you've just got to get on with stuff,' Ruby said as she tidied the treehouse. 'Step forward and don't cry over spilt milk. I'll bring a mat up and put it over the gaps in the floor.'

The boxes on the table were now lined up straight. Everything had to be in its place and she cast her eyes over the timber boxes, squinted and then rolled her eyes when she noticed the ice-cream tin with a few large mouldy mulberries left in it.

'Got it.' Bobby tipped the few remaining mulberries out the window, replacing the container in its correct position on the shelf. Amused at how neat she had to have everything, he watched her move the crate chairs so they were even and straight.

They both ran their hands over the boxes that were full of cocoons. When the moths hatched, they would hopefully add to their now decreased tally.

'See you in the morning,' Ruby said to the silkworms.

Bobby held up the canvas for her as they made their

way out of the treehouse and into the real world below.

When they reached the bottom of the tree they sat for a while, balancing on the huge protruding roots that were covered in the same rough bark as the trunk; sections of the roots smooth however, due to the continuous movement of bare feet across them over the years.

'I have to go in,' Ruby said eventually. 'It's nearly night. Even Dad will go mad if I come in after dark.'

'I better go home, too. I still have to do all my jobs before Dad gets home. I'm sorry about the moths, Ruby Rose.'

'Best friends don't get mad with each other. It was sort of my fault, too.'

Emerging from the cover of the trees, they turned in the direction of their houses, both looking up at the horizon as the fading light threw an orange hue over the backyard. Ruby saw the light flick on over the back veranda and knew her dad would be starting to look at the clock, wondering if he should call her in to clean up before dinner.

'See you tomorrow.' Bobby sounded despondent, sad.

He never wants to go home, Ruby thought. He must really like the silkworms, and me, better than his own family.

The darkening light separated them, the clicking of the side gate indicating that Bobby was in his own yard.

Sure enough, Ruby's dad Francis was sitting out on the back steps, his work boots and socks kicked off to the side as he enjoyed a smoke in the balmy evening light. She ran towards him, her small legs going, as her dad would say at a million miles an hour. Placing his cigarette down on the brick stairs beside him, he held both arms out as she jumped onto him. Chubby arms wrapped around his neck, her kisses smothering his face.

'My Ruby Rose, my little mulberry fairy,' he said, squeezing her tightly, his face nuzzling into her blonde wavy hair.

'I'm never going to let go of you.' Ruby clung to him, her mulberry-stained face squashed into the hairs on his chest, her legs drawn up so she could nestle in, snug and secure.

'What have you been up to today, little one?' He moved her to one side so he could puff on his cigarette.

'Dad, Dad, you'll never believe what happ—'

Her mum's voice interrupted them. 'Right, you two, the pair of you, grubs. One covered in mulberry, the other in concrete dust. You need to clean up before you come in for dinner. Stop your story right now, Ruby. We'll listen while we have dinner and then I'll decide if you get dessert.'

Ruby recalled the earlier incident, when her mother was looking for her, calling out. It seemed so insignificant now. Wait until she told them about the moths, and how Bobby had rescued two of them, then surely she would get dessert.

Francis picked her up and she wrapped herself around the front of him, her arms around his neck and her legs wrapped around his waist. They looked at each other and laughed together.

Ruby's mum put on her cranky voice. 'Clean up, both of you, or else there'll be no dinner for either of you.'

Steam rose from the hot water as Ruby bathed, only her head above the water as she lay back in the old claw-foot bath. She loved the bathtub. It was deep enough for her to float in, and the warm water closed in over her, softening the mud and mulberry stains.

Her dad would be in the outside shower now, scrubbing hard, removing the dried concrete and dust, the remnants of a day of hard work. She knew he would wait until she had run the bath water, letting her get the hot water first in case it ran out. After he finished, her mum would send him in to get Ruby moving.

She hated getting out of the tub. Instead, she always drew out her time, leaving it until the last moment to take the small scrubbing brush from the wire basket hanging on the wall. Then she would scrub as hard as she could, removing all of the dirt and stains from her hands and feet. She knew her mum would inspect her cleanliness, and if she had missed any marks, Ruby would have to use the bucket and cold water outside to finish off after dinner.

The door rattled as her dad banged on it. 'Hurry up, dinner's out.'

Ruby emerged scrubbed and refreshed. Her dad hugged her, one hand ruffling her hair, both revelling in the freshness of feeling clean.

The three of them sat around the small dining-room table and ate their evening meal, her mum smiling and relaxed now, her dad talking about his day. It was the usual steak and mash, carrots, and of course the greens— beans and peas. This was their favourite time of the day. It was quiet, just the family, all tucked up together, ready to chat and catch up with what each other had done during the day.

Her dad beamed at both of them. 'Righto, Ruby Rose, now tell us what exciting things you did today.'

*D*appled light filtered through the canopy of thick green mulberry leaves that formed a ceiling over the splintered roof of the treehouse. Shafts of sunlight beaming through wider gaps exposed the blue of the Queensland summer sky above, which appeared to move, rather than the scurrying, puffy clouds throwing shadows as they passed.

An assortment of odd-sized floorboards attached to the tree's broad branches made up the base of the treehouse. Nails popped up out of the boards, ready for the first unsuspecting foot to rip across them. Over the years, different dwellers had added their own individual design or character to the treehouse. Discarded timber, nailed vertically, gave the structure its walls and rusty corrugated tin laid across convenient branches formed the roof. The entire structure was near waterproof, helped along by a collection of canvas off-cuts and fibro sheeting.

Ruby had added canvas rollups to the two small windows and the doorway that had been cut out of the wood. The canvas could be rolled up to let in the light and fresh air, or rolled back down when dim light or invisibility from the rest of the world was required. Wooden crates nailed to the wall held a few discoloured cups, a couple of chipped plates and two Norco ice-cream tins. Larger timber boxes served as seats, and three of these were positioned neatly around the centrepiece of the treehouse, the table.

Orderly signs specified different areas. There was a reading corner, designated by a wooden sign nailed to the wall saying so, and a spying corner where, if you lay flat, you could see through the gap in the timber that coincided with an open space in the sprawling, drooping branches of the tree.

Through this gap it seemed the entire world was visible. Not only Ruby's yard below, but also those of her immediate neighbours', and of the yards that adjoined them. Reaching out further, sharp eyes could spy over the farm that sprawled out beyond the houses, a green oasis, the black-and-white cows visible against the backdrop of lush pastures. Red-tiled roofs capped stuccoed low-set houses, their yards large, each one different, offering a patchwork of colour and a variety of matters: sheds, fences and people who went about their daily lives oblivious to the all-seeing eyes of those lucky enough to be privileged members of the Silkworm Treehouse Club.

To date there were two cards in the box; two members sworn to secrecy who—*hand on chest, cross my heart and hope to die, on my grandmother's grave*—had promised each other that the password and all that took place in the treehouse would remain secret. *Until I die, and amen, blood brother, spit sisters, pass the same piece of chewing gum around, cross my heart and hope to die again.* Their secrets were safe; they were in this together.

* * *

'WHO DO you love the most, Bobby?'

'What do you mean?'

'Well, I think sometimes I love my dad the most, but then if I had to choose, I couldn't pick between Mum and Dad. So now I know I also love Mum the most, it's just a different love.'

'I don't love anyone the most.'

'You must do. Do you love your mum or your dad the most? What about your sisters?'

Bobby sat up and peered through the canvas covering the window. 'I told you, no one.'

'You're not allowed not to answer properly.'

Bobby stood up. 'Only girls think about those things. I'm going. I don't want to play with the silkworms today.'

'You're not allowed to just go. Who will I play with?'

'I'm going.'

'Where are you going?'

'Home.'

* * *

RUBY TRIED to forget about being angry with Bobby. Although they'd been friends since before she started school, they had only been best, *really best* friends since she'd started in grade one. That was four years ago now, when she had been five and Bobby was eight.

On the first day of school, Mary had walked her

through the front gates, staying just long enough to hear Ruby's name called out and to be satisfied that her daughter had been put into the correct line of year-one students.

The next morning, the second day of grade one, Ruby had waited on the front veranda for Bobby. She watched as he rode his bike, a satchel strapped to the back, up the dusty driveway to collect her. Her rusty Bluebird bike was ready, her new school port clipped onto the rack behind her seat.

The year before she started school, Bobby had taught her how to ride using a smaller bike, holding it steady so she could mount it from the small porch at the front of her house. Once her feet had found the pedals, they had steered together, eventually the bike and her finding their own momentum as Bobby ran alongside holding onto the seat, helping to keep her balanced. After a while she only needed help getting on and off, and getting started, and he would hold her and the bike upright for a moment before giving it a good shove.

Ruby had tried to concentrate on the pedalling and steering as she hurtled down the driveway, but often a cloud of dust signalled that she'd been unable to maintain her balance. A couple of times she had focused so intently on the steering part that even though Bobby had yelled out and run towards her, she had failed to navigate around the wide juniper trees that grew down the side of the driveway. Luckily she had only incurred scratches and cuts, a telltale scar above her left eye showing the place where a sharp branch had ripped across her face.

Bobby was definitely her best friend. Although she knew she could usually boss him around, when something went wrong and she felt a bit out of her depth he was always there to help her out. Sometimes she would play with some of the other kids in the street, and often she visited Lynette, a girl the same age as Bobby who lived a few doors up the road.

Ruby was envious of Lynette, who lived in a large brick house and had fancy, expensive clothes. But the older girl's mum was fussy, and Lynette wasn't allowed to get dirty or visit anyone else's house. Her dad made Ruby wash her feet before she went inside their house. To add to this her strict parents had once told Bobby that boys weren't allowed over, so he had left Ruby there by herself and vowed never to return.

'She's not even allowed to climb trees,' Ruby had confided to Bobby. 'And can you believe it, she has to wear shoes *all* the time.' They had both looked down at their feet, as usual, blackened, dusty and dirty, their toes wriggling in the loose dirt of the driveway. 'Do you know, she's the only one in the school photo with shoes on.'

'She must have more than one pair,' Bobby said, amazed at the thought that not only did Lynette own perhaps two pairs of shoes but also that she wore them to school. Sometimes he and Ruby wore shoes to school in winter, but really, in summer?

Ruby soon gave up on Lynette, and although she had friends at school, at home she preferred to spend her time with Bobby.

'One day he'll seem a lot older than you and he won't want to spend time with you anymore,' Ruby's mum had told her after watching the two of them jumping up and down in the cut-off corrugated tank that served as their swimming pool in summer.

'He'll always be the same older than me.'

'I know what you're saying. He'll always be three years older than you, but as time goes on he'll change. He'll get older quicker than you.'

'He won't,' Ruby said. 'Besides, one day I'm going to marry him and we're going to live in a treehouse. But don't tell him, it's a secret.'

Mary had laughed, thankful that Ruby had such a close playmate, but she wondered what the teenage years would do to such a friendship. Ruby was their only child; they had tried for years to have children before she arrived. Sometimes Mary wondered what it would've been like to have more children, for Ruby to have a brother or sister. But she pushed the questions aside, forever grateful that she had been able to carry and deliver a healthy beautiful baby.

When the new family moved in next door, Mary had hoped that the children would be friendly and Ruby would find a playmate. The eldest girl, Theresa, was quite a bit older than Ruby, and then came Bobby, followed by his little sister Sally.

The dad, Vincent, bought and ran the local butcher's shop. Mary had hoped that she too might find friendship with the new lady next door, but she had only ever glimpsed Isobel a couple of times. Vincent had told Mary and Francis that his wife was not well, and preferred to stay inside and look after the family.

Occasionally Mary had spotted Isobel outside, but the other woman ignored any gestures or overtures of friendship, quickly making her way inside when Mary had called out.

Theresa also stayed in the house a lot, only emerging

to make her way to school and back, never going with any of the other children and rarely responding to any of their greetings. Sometimes Mary would hear the youngest girl, Sally, crying or yelling, but she too mostly stayed inside, her cries muffled and eventually silenced by the walls that closeted the lives of those inside.

The explanation from Bobby was that Sally wasn't normal. 'She was born different,' he told Ruby. 'Even though she's three years younger than me, she's only really like a two year old, you know, like a baby still.'

Ruby had only seen Sally once or twice, from a distance. 'Is that why she doesn't go to school?'

'Yeah, something's wrong with her brain. It happened when she was born. You can't teach her anything. She can't learn things like reading or writing. Dad says she's cuckoo and should be in a home, but Sally understands me sometimes. She'd rather be with me than Mum. Mum can't even look after herself, so she doesn't bother looking after Sally much. Mostly me and Theresa do everything for her.'

'How come no one ever visits your house except for your uncle?' Ruby had asked. 'Don't you have other family, like grandmothers or cousins?'

'Dad isn't friends with anyone. His mum and dad are both dead. I never even met them, ever. Dad's brother, that's my uncle, he comes and stays, but I wish he didn't.'

'What about your mum?'

'Her family never talked to her again,' Bobby said, 'after she married Dad, that is. I don't think she has any brothers or sisters, but I don't know because she doesn't talk to me about anything. She doesn't talk at all, well, hardly ever.'

'What's wrong with her?'

'Dad said she's mental, you know, like crazy in the head. I'm not sure what's wrong with her. I can't remember her ever being any other way.'

'Why can't you bring Sally over to play? I'd look after her. Maybe we could just play in the yard, not up in the tree, if you're worried about her falling. I could get some paper and books, and try and teach her to read and write. Can I please, Bobby? I want to help her.'

'Ruby Rose, you don't understand. Sally's brain, it just doesn't work right. She doesn't understand hardly anything. She doesn't speak, she just makes noises that no one but me can understand. Besides, she's not allowed outside. Dad wants her kept inside so no one knows we have an idiot in the house. That's what he says. He keeps saying he's going to put her in a home. When she gets sick he won't even get the doctor for her.'

'But she looks normal. I saw her once when she followed you into the backyard. I could see you both from up in the tree.'

'Hey, you're not supposed to spy on me.'

'I wasn't spying. I just happened to be up here, and you know I can see your whole yard. Sally followed you. She's pretty, and she looks normal to me.'

'Well, I'm telling you she's not normal. Her mind is like a baby's, and I don't think it'll ever change. Sally's never going to grow up, she's always going to be the same.'

'She's lucky she has you, Bobby. What would happen if you didn't look after her?'

'Dad would put her in a home. I've heard him talking to my uncle about it. One day he'll do it, I just know.'

A troubled look crossed Bobby's face; it came whenever they talked about his family. Sometimes he would start shaking, his hands first and then his legs. When that happened Ruby would sit quietly, just listening, knowing but not fully understanding why he had to talk, to tell someone—his best friend who he knew wouldn't tell anyone else.

They had a pact, silkworm secrets, and it calmed Bobby to know that he could tell Ruby some of his problems.

As much as Bobby knew Sally needed him, he couldn't wait until everything was done and Theresa was home. Then he could escape; he could run from the musty house with the stale smells that lingered in every room, and the oppressive air that filled his lungs, squashing him, making him feel small, confused and mostly sad.

Bobby always yearned to be outside; whenever it was possible he'd escape from his house and spent time with Ruby.

The two of them would pump up the tyres on their bikes and ride for miles, pushing down hard on the pedals, their legs aching as they traversed the steepest roads they could find. Together they followed stony tracks and trails, Ruby always wanting to find out what was at the end or how they could get to the highest point.

Once they reached their destination they would unpack the lunch Ruby's mum had made for them, which usually included a warm but still bubbly bottle of lemonade each to wash down the sandwiches and biscuits.

The two friends loved the places they discovered, and they would come home tired and dirty, satisfied that they had made some new discoveries, found a higher hill to climb, a different view.

Ruby always wanted to be at the front, the first to see what lay ahead, the first to pick up a kangaroo skull or spy a koala perched high in the towering gums. Bobby, slow and steady, always followed, his keen eyes taking in everything around him.

On one such day he called out to Ruby to stop.

She pushed backwards on the pedal, braking hard before turning to him, indignant. 'Why?'

'You always go too fast. You missed a big bunch of kangaroos back there lying in the grass.'

'Where?' Her face scrunched up in annoyance.

'In the paddock with the purple flowers.'

They had crept back on foot, silently, peering through the long grass at a big mob of kangaroos that were lying in the open paddock, soaking in the sunshine, oblivious to the fascinated onlookers.

'One day I'm going to live out there past those mountains,' Bobby told Ruby, pointing to the mountain range far to the west. 'Someone at school told me they'd lived out there and there's hardly any people, just a lot of horses and cows.'

'You're not allowed to move away from me,' Ruby told him. 'You're my best friend.'

On another day Bobby had needed to double her back on his rickety bike. Ruby had come off a beauty in her rush to be first and, as her dad would say, going like a bull at a gate.

The front tyre had hit a large rock, buckling the bike, twisting and wrenching the handlebars out of her hands and throwing her onto the hard rocky ground. She sat up, trying hard not to cry as Bobby used his T-shirt to wipe her face. One side of her face was grazed, with tiny rocks embedded under her skin.

For once she had stayed quiet and listened as Bobby took control of the situation and told her what to do. Both of her knees were bleeding and he used the tea towel from around the lemonade bottles to stop the flow of blood.

Trying to be brave, she stood up, assuring him that she would be fine and they could just ride home slowly. Then she had crumbled to the ground again, one ankle swollen and twisted.

Bobby told her to listen to him and that he'd get her home. Pushing her old Bluebird bike into the long grass he took note of the location so they could find it easily on their return. He then manoeuvred her small, light body onto the port rack behind his seat and told her to grab onto him as he pushed the bike back down the rocky trail.

Francis, who had been cutting the bushes out the front of the house, watched them come slowly up the road, Bobby still doubling Ruby as she held onto him tightly.

'Looks like you two have had fun,' Francis said as he lifted her off the bike and carried her into the house. 'Come in, Bobby. I'll get you a cold drink and biscuit. You must be knackered after lugging her all the way home.'

The smell of Dettol soon filled the air as her dad gently washed Ruby's legs, dragging the washer across the wounds, making sure all the tiny pieces of rubble were removed from under the skin.

She bit her lip, her face pale as her dad wrapped a cloth filled with ice around her ankle, assuring her she would be fine. There was no way she would cry while Bobby was there. He would think she was a cry-baby, a girl or, worst of all, a sook.

THE FALL from the bike had happened a long time ago. Ruby was older now, nearly ten, and Bobby would soon be a teenager. They still did everything together: bike riding, playing in the yard and down at the creek, looking after the chickens and ducklings when they hatched, and every season gorging themselves on the plentiful mulberries that hung from their tree.

Playing in the treehouse was still their favourite pastime. Every year they gathered as many old boxes as they could find and lined them up on the activity table. As the winter months passed, and new shoots and leaves appeared on the mulberry tree, they placed the carefully saved pieces of cardboard with hundreds of tiny eggs attached into the new containers with the utmost care.

Each day they checked the progress, watching the eggs hatch into tiny worms that wriggled around their new home, crawling over each other as they munched voraciously on the dark green leaves that lined the boxes. It was the same every season; their anticipation increasing as they tried to predict how many eggs would hatch and how big they would grow.

Before long the boxes overflowed with plump large

silkworms and Ruby and Bobby would divide them, finding even more boxes to house them in.

The curly white bodies grew bigger and bigger until the worms could eat no more. Moving sluggishly, the fully-grown silkworms manoeuvred into corners of the box or the gaps that formed under the wrinkled leaves. Then they began.

They spun fine golden threads, enveloping themselves in bright yellow cocoons, going to sleep tucked against the walls and corners of the boxes that housed them. For the next few weeks the boxes were silent, the cocoons and dried leaves stationary, the two carers relieved from duties for a while.

When Ruby and Bobby grew tired of waiting, they would gingerly lift the corner of one of the lids and peer into the dimness of the box, checking for movement. There was always great excitement when they spotted the first fluttering moth and the count would begin. They left the lids of the boxes open when they were up in the treehouse because the moths' bodies were too heavy for their fine wings, and there was no risk of them flying away.

Wings fluttering rapidly, the moths moved around the box until they found another moth of the opposite sex. Once they had mated, the male moth died almost straightaway while the female survived for a few more days, laying hundreds and hundreds of tiny eggs.

It was Bobby's job to remove the dead moths, and he stacked them together into the many matchboxes they collected for this occasion.

'Don't press them down too hard,' Ruby would always say. 'The poor little moths, you'll squash them.' It always upset her that these beautiful creatures, which had worked their way out of the tightly woven cocoons, only lived for a short while.

Bobby would dig a hole directly where Ruby pointed and together the numerous matchboxes were lowered into the earth. The hole would be filled back up with the damp red soil, a homemade cross consisting of two sticks tied together pushed into the earth to denote the final resting place of their beloved silkworm moths.

* * *

RUBY BUSIED HERSELF, neatening the treehouse, trying to work out why Bobby had been so angry and gone home when she had asked who he loved the most. Soon there was nothing left for her to tidy, so she lay across the floor, positioning herself in the spying area so she could peer through the gap in the wall out to the yards beyond. If she looked to her left, or what Bobby said was north, she could clearly see the next three adjoining yards.

They were all large, the smallest being half an acre. The largest was the Waltons' place next door at nearly an acre. The Waltons were rich. Mr Walton was a travelling salesman who spent most of the year working away from home.

If Ruby looked between the trees and into the Waltons' yard, she could see the large, white wooden house standing like a centrepiece in the middle of a bridal cake. Verandas that ran around three sides of the house could be reached by climbing the fifteen steps at the front of the house. Bobby and Ruby had counted the steps many times while watching Lewis, the Waltons' gardener, sweep them every day without fail.

Lewis lived under the big old house in a comfortable space with a bedroom, kitchenette and bathroom. Ruby and Bobby both liked the gardener, who had a big droopy moustache and a funny accent. They often took him an overflowing bucket of mulberries and he would invite them in, later sharing with them the most delicious mulberry pies they had ever tasted.

Mrs Walton obviously liked Lewis, too, and even though he was only supposed to be her gardener they had often seen him enter her house late in the afternoon, a bottle of wine tucked under his arm.

Lewis kept the gardens neat and brimming full of roses, camellias and other flowering plants, reminding Ruby of the English gardens she had seen in books and magazines. The skilled gardener had raised the garden beds and edged them with small concrete walls that were adorned with broken pieces of old crockery. Roses, lilacs and pansies painted onto once expensive plates and cups were now pressed into the concrete. Ruby and Bobby liked to run their hands over the pretty mosaic patterns, the smoothness and beauty of the painted pictures cool under their hands.

Spying from high up in the treehouse, Ruby and Bobby sometimes saw Mrs Walton and Lewis walking around the yard together, the tall well-dressed lady pointing out different flowers and plants, and Lewis accompanying his words with his usual hand gestures.

Lewis's passion for the garden was evident in the way he gently pruned the prickly roses, picking the most delicate unopened buds for Mrs Walton's antique vases that perched on every table and stand in her house.

One day Mrs Walton followed Lewis into his little home beneath the old white house.

Ruby asked Bobby what he thought they were doing. 'They've been in there for hours,' she said, 'and Lewis doesn't even have a television. They must like talking to each other.'

Bobby hadn't answered. He had just looked at her, blinked, and reminded her of their code of secrecy and silence. 'Remember, Ruby Rose,' he said, 'anything we see or say up here stays up here. You can't even tell your mum or dad.'

'I know that, they're silkworm secrets.'

Soon it began to get dark and Ruby had to go inside, so she never knew how long Mrs Walton had stayed with Lewis. 'She's still in there,' Ruby said, before they went to their separate houses. 'Maybe they're playing Scrabble or something.'

'Maybe they are,' he said.

She hated it when Bobby got that look on his face, a look that reminded her that she was still younger than him and he knew about some things she didn't. It annoyed her because, after all, *she* was the president of the club, the organiser. She was supposed to be in charge, it wasn't right that Bobby knew more than her just because he was older.

She thought back to the day she had fallen off her bike and he had taken control. She hadn't liked that feeling; she liked to be the one doing the bossing.

And now she was cranky. How dare he just walk out of the treehouse and go home. This was supposed to be a meeting. He was supposed to clean out the boxes, not get angry just because she had asked him a question.

She kept herself busy filling in the pages of the records book, taking note of all that was happening around her.

*D*ATE *1972*

Silkworm count 245, 132 big ones, 85 small ones, 28 tiny ones.

Ruby cleaned boxes.

Silkworm secrets, Bobby angry. Didn't clean boxes, Ruby had to do it.

Bobby ran home.

Lewis dug new rose garden and then visited Mrs Walton upstairs in her house.

Ruby going to look for Bobby.

CHAPTER 6

Peering through the treehouse window, Ruby looked down into Bobby's yard hoping to see him returning. He would need to say sorry and tell her what was wrong. Why was he so cranky? She knew she would forgive him; he was, after all, her best friend.

But Bobby's yard was empty. A couple of hens clucked loudly as they strutted freely around the dusty backyard, and a loose piece of tin on the chook house flapped in the breeze, creaking occasionally. Further down the yard was another shed that had been renovated and turned into a granny flat. Bobby's uncle Mike, his dad's younger brother, often stayed in the newly transformed shed for a couple of weeks while he had a break from work.

Ruby had seen him going back and forth from his car to the shed, carting in his suitcases and bags. Uncle Mike, as he liked everyone to call him, strutted around town in his swanky city suits like he owned the whole place. He dipped his hat to everyone he passed, and had a way about him that all the ladies seemed to like.

'He's very posh and well spoken,' Ruby's mum said after she first encountered him sitting behind the counter at the butcher's. 'Such a gentleman, and look how well he's done for himself. He's supposed to be very rich.'

'Bobby doesn't like him, but don't say that to anyone.' Too late, Ruby realised she had just released a silkworm secret. Luckily, her mum was so busy praising Mike Carlon and fluffing her hair in readiness to go out and buy meat that she hadn't heard what Ruby said.

Bobby cringed when Ruby repeated what her mum had said. 'Honestly, Ruby Rose, he's really horrible. Don't ever talk to him. If you see him, go the other way.'

'He can't be that bad. Why don't you like him?'

Bobby was cranky with her that day as well. She hated it when he said things without finishing them, making her feel like she was only getting half the story.

'It doesn't matter why,' he said. 'Just for once, listen to me. Like I said, don't go near him. I hate him.'

Maybe Bobby needs to hear what Dad talks about a lot, Ruby thought. 'Tolerance is what people need,' her dad always told her. 'Everyone's different; you're not always going to like everything about a person, and it'd be boring if we were all the same.'

Recently she had tried to discuss this with Bobby, figuring that he needed some helpful advice. 'You need to be positive about people, Bobby, not always so grumpy. He's your uncle. Besides, he brought you all presents, you told me.'

'I threw mine in the bin.'

'You threw the Meccano set in the bin?' She was horrified, 'I can't believe you did that. Why didn't you give it to me if you didn't want it?'

'I don't want to talk about it.'

'Why not? What's the matter with you? We always talk about everything. Why don't you like him? Mum said he even helped old Mrs Corrigan up the road bring the cows in the other day. She says he's a really kind man.'

Looking back now, Ruby remembered that Bobby had walked out on her that day as well. Boys, she thought. As soon as you ask them too many questions they just walk away. Well, she'd had enough of that. She was going over to tell him off, to tell him that he couldn't start saying something and not finish it just because she was younger than him.

She made her way down the winding ladder steps, jumping past the last few, her toughened feet quickly finding their way along the narrow dirt path that ran through the thick undergrowth. It was lovely and cool as usual, her feet familiar with every tree root as she skipped lightly across the dampened ground, moist from the covering of fallen mulberries that squished between her toes when she trampled on them.

When she got closer to the fence she wondered what Bobby's response would be when she appeared at his house.

It had always been like this, ever since they first became friends. He never wanted her to come to his house. Once on his birthday years ago, they had sat outside on his veranda while he opened the present she had given him. When he had fallen sick with the measles, even though he had caught them from her, she had only been allowed to sit outside his bedroom window to talk. But she had only been there for a little while before he asked her to go home.

It was an unspoken rule now, and had been for years. He would come to her house, he would play all day in her yard, they would spend hours in the treehouse, but she was not to come to his house.

'Why not?' she had asked him several times over the years.

The conversations were always the same.

'Dad hates people coming over. I'm just not allowed.'

'What about your sister? Doesn't Theresa have girl-friends over?'

'She's not allowed either.'

'Is that why your mum doesn't have friends? That's stupid. How come your mum is never outside? She only ever comes out to hang the washing. Doesn't she like being in the yard?'

'She gets sick a lot.'

'What with?'

'I don't know, she just gets sick. That's why it's my job to look after Sally during dinner and at night.'

'Why don't you bring Sally over? She's not much younger than me. She could be part of the club.'

'No way, Mum doesn't like her going outside. She wants her inside. Ruby Rose, I've told you all this before. Sally's not normal. My parents don't want people seeing her.'

'I bet your sisters love your dad. Dads love their daughters, my mum says. She sometimes reckons that my dad loves me more than her and that I can twist him around my little finger.'

Bobby didn't say anything, letting her prattle on, forever amazed at how much she talked.

'Every night Dad reads me a book. Sometimes he

makes up his own stories and he's really funny. He listens to all my stories, too, and every night he tells me he loves me. He's the best dad in the world. Does your dad read to Sally?'

'Nah.'

'Why not?'

'Why do you have to know everything? He just doesn't, okay? Not everyone has a dad like yours, or a mum who looks after them. When you get older you'll realise that. My father's not very nice, Ruby Rose. You only have to say one word wrong and you cop it.'

'What about Theresa?'

'He says she belongs in the house, and that she has to learn to cook and clean so she can help Mum. Theresa wants to be a nurse, but Dad says she should get married and have kids, not worry about looking after sick and dying people.'

'My dad says I can be whatever I want to be. He says girls these days can do the same as boys and that he wants me to have a really good job so I can look after myself.'

One day Bobby had surprised Ruby.

'Silkworm secret, Ruby Rose,' he said.

'What?'

'I think Theresa's going to run away from home and become a nurse.'

'But she's only fifteen.'

'I know, but she reckons next year she's going to go. The hospital will take you once you're sixteen, and you can live there and get trained really good.'

'But your mum and dad would be upset if that happened.'

'Dad would just get cranky because Theresa does a lot that Mum should do, but Mum doesn't do any of the work because she's in bed most of the time.'

The two of them were lying flat on the floor, the discussion going back and forth, with Ruby getting more confused about the way that Bobby's family functioned, or rather didn't function. She wanted to be friends with Sally. Sally was Bobby's sister, after all, and Bobby was one of her favourite people in the entire world, after her dad and mum. She knew he had to help a lot looking after Sally and she wanted to help him.

Once when she was in the spying area by herself, Ruby had watched Bobby sitting with his little sister on the back veranda, brushing her hair, cuddling and holding Sally like a baby doll, picking her up and hugging her when she cried. It was a different side to Bobby. She knew he loved Sally a lot, maybe even more than his own mum and dad.

'You love Sally, don't you?' she asked him.

'Of course I do, she's my sister. Besides, us kids have to stick together, look after each other.'

'Don't your mum and dad do that? Your dad doesn't seem that mean.'

Bobby didn't answer, he just stared straight ahead through the gap in the spying wall.

Ruby gazed down to the yard next door. 'Oh look, it's your uncle, going for a walk with Theresa.'

Bobby's uncle had arrived last week and was staying in the granny flat, spending most of his time out and about. Ruby's mum had seen him at the back of the butcher's shop, and she told Ruby and Francis. 'He has a lot of important functions to attend,' she said. 'He's very much in demand.'

Ruby and Bobby watched now as Uncle Mike walked with Theresa down the backyard. Bobby's eyes were as big as saucers. He sat up quickly and moved towards the treehouse doorway.

'Dad's working late and Mum will be asleep,' he said. 'I've got to go, I've got to look after Sally.' His face was red and his hands shook as he undid the canvas covering that concealed them high above the ground.

'Are you okay?' she asked.

There was no answer. Bobby descended so fast that Ruby was sure he had jumped over the last seven or eight steps. She decided she would never understand Bobby and the way he acted sometimes.

That night, she told her mum and dad what had happened. Francis and Mary were well aware of who Bobby's uncle was and listened to Ruby as she talked about the uncle's visit.

Recently Mike Carlon had been elected to quite a high position in government and they had listened to him interviewed on the news the night before. As well as gaining the prominent role, he had also been elected to the board of a large charity group run by the church in the city. Mike Carlon had talked about all the work he was going to do for those who needed help, and how his role in government gave him that extra opportunity to give back to the community.

Mary had also heard glowing reports about the handsome politician after visiting the hairdressers in town. She said how everyone was talking about Mike, the brother of the butcher Vincent. Mike was a bachelor and all the young single girls were chasing him. What a catch!

Ruby listened to her mum, thinking how wrong Bobby was about his famous uncle. She decided that Bobby needed to grow up, and she would tell him so the first opportunity she had.

CHAPTER 7

As she made her way through the Carlons' backyard and onto the veranda, Ruby thought about all the strange comments Bobby had made about his family. Boys were so silly sometimes, and she was going to let him know this time. She was older now; she was nearly ten, and he had to stop treating her like a little kid.

Knocking softly, she poked her head through the open back door, squinting as her eyes adjusted to the dimness that cloaked the inside rooms of the house. All the curtains were drawn. She looked down the hallway, noticing that the bedroom doors were also shut. The only sound came from a television in a back room. *Gilligan's Island*; she recognised the music.

She knocked a little louder and then peered around outside once more, before taking a bold step into the house. Step by step, she followed the sound of the television, calling out Bobby's name as she walked down the dark hallway. Eventually she reached the room the music was coming from, her eyes adjusting to the lights as she looked in through the open door.

Bobby sat on a small wooden stool brushing Sally's hair, his back to the doorway. He didn't notice Ruby standing in the doorway and only turned around when Sally started waving at something behind him.

Ruby opened her mouth to speak, but couldn't. She stood wide-eyed, mouth open, aghast at what she saw. Red welts formed a criss-cross pattern on the bare skin of Bobby's back. Some of the wounds had partially healed, but were still covered by thick crusty scabs, distinct on his pale skin.

Bobby stood up, grabbed a shirt and threw it on quickly to cover his back.

'Hello, Sally,' Ruby said, trying to regain her composure and process what she had seen. She smiled at the tiny girl, noting the thinness and pallid complexion of a child who obviously did not get out in the sun much.

Sally held up her hairclips to show them off, and Ruby noticed the awkward, stilted movements of the small girl's limbs.

'Sally, say hello to Ruby Rose.' Bobby's voice was shaky. He told Sally to watch the television, adding, 'I'll be back soon.'

Gently he took the hairclips from her, pushing them back into her hair. He talked quietly to her and then passed her the hairbrush, which immediately became her entire focus. It was as if Ruby and Bobby no longer existed. Sally's entire attention was riveted on the brush. They watched in silence as she turned it over and over in her hand, as though she had never seen a hairbrush before. The background music of *Gilligan's Island* hung in the air between them, adding to the confusion and surreal mood of the moment.

For once, Ruby was silent as Bobby guided her back down the hallway and out the back door. He had a tight grip on her arm and propelled her straight towards the side gate, neither of them speaking until they were on her side of the fence.

Bobby's eyes were wide and when he spoke, he sounded desperate and close to tears. 'Don't ever come over here again. If you come again, we can't be friends.'

'What happened to your back? Why is your house so dark inside?'

'I have to go back in. Mum will be awake soon and I have to help Theresa cook dinner.' The words were tumbling out of his mouth, his face now angry. 'If you tell your dad, I won't be your friend. I won't ever come over again.'

'Sally's really thin, Bobby. But she's so pretty, like a little doll. But she looks too small, like she doesn't eat enough.' Ruby ignored his anger, overwhelmed by her concern for Sally and what she had just seen.

'I know. It's part of her condition and that's why I have to be the one to feed her. That way I can make sure she gets the right food and that she eats it all. Sally will do things for me, like eat. She won't do that for anyone else.'

'She's lucky to have you.'

'Mum used to look after her, but I have to do it now because Mum's always sick. Theresa helps too,' he said, 'we both look after her. Sometimes we take days off school because when we're not here Mum leaves her in the cot most of the day.'

'But Bobby, she's the same age as me. How come she gets treated like a baby?'

His voice was nearly a whisper. 'She has a lot of things wrong with her, things that can't be fixed. You have to remember that her brain is just like a baby's and that'll never change. The doctors didn't want Mum to bring her home from the hospital. They said she should go straight into a home, and Dad wanted to do that but Mum wouldn't have it. Now Mum doesn't even care about her.'

'What about when your uncle comes, does he help?'

He nearly spat at the words. 'Are you kidding? He wouldn't help with anything. Besides, Sally doesn't like him and she won't go near him. I think that's part of the reason he doesn't stay in the house. That's why he has his own flat down the back.'

As usual, Ruby wanted to help, to try and fix things, to make everything right for Sally and Bobby. 'I'm sure there are people who can help, doctors who come around and check on people who have things wrong with them.'

'Ruby Rose, you can't fix everything. Sally was born that way and nothing can be done about it. I know that when we're up in the treehouse you think I just follow everything you tell me to do, but at home I have to take over. It's like I have to be in charge, because if I don't everything will be a mess and my dad will send Mum and Sally away. I have to go back now. You should never have come over.'

'Right, Bobby Carlon, but next time you will talk to me, you will tell me things, because I am not a baby.' She stood on her tiptoes, her shoulders pushed back to look taller, but Bobby had walked away. Her last words were directed at his back, the wounds now hidden under the thin cotton of a worn-out T-shirt.

Angry and confused, she climbed into the treehouse and took the records book off the shelf, venting her thoughts by writing onto the ruled pages everything she could remember. She added drawings showing the marks on Bobby's back, and she tried to draw a picture of Sally holding up her treasured hairclips.

In her mind she went over everything that had happened. It wasn't just what she had seen that day; it had also been the eeriness of Bobby's house, and the strange feelings she experienced when she was inside. A lump had formed in her throat the minute she walked through the back door. There was something odd about the house. The rooms were all dark and musty, the curtains always drawn. And where was Bobby's mum? Why was she always in bed?

Eventually Ruby climbed down from the tree, spotting her dad sitting on the back stairs. She reminded herself that she had been sworn to secrecy, that Bobby trusted her not to tell anyone. Running into her dad's arms, she was smothered by his kisses and she giggled.

She felt a strange sensation and realised that it was guilt. Maybe Bobby was right. Maybe his mum and dad weren't like hers.

Clinging onto her dad, she looked into his dark, kind eyes and spoke the same words she did every afternoon. 'I love you, Dad, you're the best dad in the whole wide world.'

A broad smile lit up his face and his eyes twinkled, making her feel like the most loved little girl in the world.

'Ah, but I love you more, Ruby Rose,' he said, 'my little mulberry fairy.'

They rubbed noses, their own secret code, before snuggling into each other and discussing who was the dirtiest, who was the muddiest, and whether mulberry stains were better than concrete stains. She felt safe and secure when her dad's strong arms wrapped around her and she inhaled the smell of sweat and tobacco ingrained in his clothes. It was as if Francis sensed that Ruby needed an extra cuddle that night and for a long while they sat on the stairs until the mosquitos became too fierce and they knew it was clean-up time.

That night Ruby felt even better after sitting with her mum and dad. She listened to them talk about how they had met, and then laughed along when her mum told a funny story. Ruby's dad also laughed, and Ruby thought his deep chuckle was the best sound in the world. Her dad hugged them both and told them he must be the luckiest man in the entire universe to have two such beautiful girls to look after.

After seeing the marks on Bobby's back, and the way that Sally lived, Ruby knew she was also very lucky; there were things going on next door that weren't right.

Next meeting, she decided, there would be silkworm secrets that must be shared.

CHAPTER 8

'Confucius says that thousands of years ago, Empress Leizu of China was sitting under a mulberry tree sipping a cup of tea. She was fourteen years old. As she sat and drank her tea, a golden silkworm's cocoon fell into her china cup. Leizu picked out the mysterious cocoon and began to unravel the golden thread that wrapped around it. She gently pulled out the strong thread and stretched it further and further, right across her garden, watching as the rays of the sun bounced off the golden strands. The beautiful Leizu unravelled more and more cocoons until she had made a thick thread, which she then spun into a shiny piece of silky cloth. This first piece of cloth she made into a beautiful cloak for the very, very famous emperor of China. Leizu became the legendary goddess of silk.

'The Chinese kept the secret of how to make the silk cloth for thousands and thousands and thousands of years. To reveal the secret of making silk from the cocoons of little silkworms would result in the penalty of death. However, many other countries all over the world that traded the silk from China wanted to know how the Chinese people made such beautiful, colourful cloth. The jealous Japanese kidnapped four beautiful Chinese girls, along with some mulberry shoots and silk-moth eggs. Another Chinese princess, who married a very handsome Indian prince, carried the eggs of the silkworms and shoots for a mulberry tree inside her fancy headdress when she travelled to faraway India. She also, like the four young kidnapped girls, knew how to raise silkworms and weave their silk. Finally, two monks told the emperor of Constantinople the secret of how to make silk.

'And that's how,' Ruby said as she closed her eyes dramatically, 'the whole wide world came to know about the beautiful, clever silkworms and the incredible silk they could create.'

She closed the records book, in which she had written the history of the silkworm, placing the book like a valuable treasure on the table. Choosing her cleanest hand, she pressed it down over her cotton shift dress, pushing the creases out, flattening the bright yellow sunflowers that adorned the cool cotton material.

Watching her, Bobby smiled, knowing that she loved it when she could sound all grown up, trying to keep up with him as the years poked more and more gaps between them. He knew their friendship would probably change when he went to high school after Christmas. Some of the boys at school were already teasing him about spending so much time up a tree, with a little kid, and even worse, a girl.

But Ruby Rose, had been with him from the start. She hadn't even started school when they first became friends.

For years they had counted the eggs, the worms and the moths, and then stored the cocoons, waiting for the first sign of the unravelling of silk as new life began, and they could once again search for the biggest, greenest leaves, watching to see which worm would become the fattest of the season.

The treehouse had become like the moth's cocoons: his haven, a safety net, high above the rest of the world and free from the turmoil, anxiety and misery of home. Until recently Ruby had been too young to suspect or notice certain issues in his life. She hadn't asked any tricky questions; she had just been there, his best friend, soul mate.

Some nights he would sneak into the darkness of his side yard and watch through the gaps in the curtains as Ruby sat at the table with her mum and dad.

Ruby's dad was always cuddling her, lifting her high in the air, squeezing her until she squealed with delight. Their house emitted a warm glow at night, the three of them all tucked up together, happy, peaceful and content. Sometimes Bobby joined Ruby's family during the day. Mary always insisted that he have some cake and a drink, and sit with them at their table where he had enviously watched them so many times at night.

Their kitchen was similar to his own, with painted wooden drawers and cupboards, basic kitchen bowls and cups, and lino lifting at the edges, scratched and worn from use over the years. The walls were painted yellow and Bobby loved to look at the faded, framed prints that hung on them. His favourite decoration was a line of painted china ducks, five of them positioned on the wall, biggest to smallest, as if they were going to fly away through the kitchen window.

A collection of small ornaments filled a shadow box that hung on the wall above the wooden kitchen table. Mary would dust them and then pass them to Ruby and Bobby, who took turns to carefully stand each piece on the table. Ruby's favourite was a tiny porcelain teapot while Bobby loved to wind up the miniature grandfather clock, holding it up to his ear to listen for the sound of it ticking. Once the assortment of trinkets was lined up on the table, they would invent stories about where the ornaments had come from.

One day Ruby declared her teapot had come from the Queen's house in England. 'A servant maid stole it and brought it back to Australia with her,' she said. 'She sold it and had enough money to buy her own mansion overlooking the beautiful Brisbane River. The owner of an antique shop bought the teapot and gave it to his beloved wife, who just happened to be my great-grandmother. It's been passed down through the family, and one day it will belong to *me*, Ruby.'

Bobby decided his clock had come to Australia across the wild seas, with a convict, an Irish convict. 'It was his only belonging, and he wound it each night and lay with it next to his heart so he could remember someone he loved that he had left behind in England. He was a good man and he was pardoned.'

Ruby interrupted Bobby's story with questions, and he had to explain about convicts sometimes being given their freedom for good behaviour and hard work. He waited patiently for her to be quiet before he continued.

'The convict, who was now a free man, kept the clock

over the years, believing it brought him luck. This man was responsible for building many factories and houses, and he soon became very rich. He, too, passed his favourite ornament down through his family, always to the eldest son.'

Ruby frowned at this idea, but before she could open her mouth to protest the unfairness of the gender based decision, Bobby continued.

'The original man, the convict, who became a freeman, always said that one day it would be passed down to a great man, a gentle man who was very kind and had a great spirit. This man would leave it to his daughter who he loved very much. And that daughter, Ruby Rose, is you. That clock will one day belong to you because your father is the man that the convict, who became a freeman, was talking about.'

Ruby clapped her hands with delight. 'Perfect story, Bobby,' she said. 'Maybe one day the clock will be mine and then I'll be able to give it to you.'

'I'm lucky to be able to look at it when I'm here. One day, Ruby Rose, you might have a boy or girl and then you can give it to one of them.'

'How would I know which one to give it to? Maybe one could have the teapot and one the clock. Or maybe they'll like the ducks on the wall.'

Bobby wondered how one person could talk so much. Ruby always spoke her thoughts out loud, trying to work out everyone's problems, wanting to help out, to make everything right. Just like everything had to be in the right place. He watched as she put back all the ornaments precisely in their same spots in the shadow box, talking the entire time.

Sometimes if it was cold they would sit together on the old genoa lounge, tucked up under colourful crocheted rugs, excited when Ruby's mum brought them cut-up fruit, or, if they were really lucky, Bobby's favourite, ice cream and jelly. If Ruby begged hard enough, they would be given a lolly each, the wrappers usually ending up stuffed into the holes and gaps of the old lounge chairs.

On rainy afternoons, Francis would come home early from work and join them, sitting in his designated chair, a rug thrown over it to protect the cloth from the dust that was always attached to his work clothes. He'd ruffle Ruby's hair as he passed, a quick kiss to her cheek and kind words of protest as her little arms tried to hold him down for a hug. 'I'm filthy, Ruby Rose, cuddles later.'

Watching this, Bobby always shrank back. As much as he wanted to talk, he couldn't, well, not at the beginning anyway.

Sensing Bobby's disquiet Francis would ask him questions. 'What are you learning about at school, Bobby? How many cocoons have hatched? Shush, Ruby Rose, let Bobby answer.'

Soon Bobby would find himself talking, at ease and comfortable in the homely, unfussy household. Together they'd watch the afternoon show on television, Francis usually asking Ruby to get up from her comfort to switch the channel to the one he wanted.

One afternoon Francis said, 'No, no way are we watching *The Brady Bunch*. Turn that channel to *Hogan's Heroes*. Outvoted today, mulberry fairy, I have the support of another young man. *Hogan's Heroes* it will be.'

Ruby got up and changed the channel, the three of

them settling down to laugh at the antics of the characters in the popular comedy show.

Ruby strutted around the room, a tin bowl on her head, imitating the bumbling Sergeant Schultz. She finished in front of her dad, saluting dramatically. In her gruffest German voice, she said, "I know nuffink! I see nuffink! I hear nuffink!'

'*Jawohl, Mein* Colonel,' Francis replied, his finger under his nose to imitate a moustache.

Bobby laughed along with them. The familiar theme song, blaring from the treasured black-and-white television, signalled the end of the show, bringing Bobby back to reality. He had to get home before dark.

Francis stood to shake his hand, treating him like an adult, as someone important. 'You're always welcome here, Bobby, you come over whenever you like.'

'Thank you, Mr Bradley, but I'd better be off because my dad'll be home soon.' Bobby heard his voice fading inwards as his confidence and the sense of fun disappeared. A knot of pain in his stomach heralded the end of the day and the beginning of the evening routine that was standard pattern at his house.

'See ya, Ruby Rose, I'll try to be on time in the morning.'

'She's a stickler for times, young Bobby,' Francis said. 'Everything has to be in its place, and always on time. Little Miss Organised.'

Ruby walked Bobby out, noticing that he'd gone quiet. He never wanted to go home. 'Come early in the morning,' she said, trying to cheer him up, 'and we can play on the pogo stick before school.'

He walked through the squeaky side gate, ducking

under the overhanging bougainvillea vine that threatened to close over the hole linking the two houses.

* * *

AFTER FINISHING the story of how silk came to be, Ruby thought about Bobby's quietness and the look that came over his face whenever he had to leave her house and go home. Lifting the lid from the closest shirt box, she peered wondrously at the wriggling, chomping worms, their small black droppings scattered over the dark-green mulberry leaves that made up the bed of the box.

'My dad helped me look that up in the encyclopaedia and then I copied it into the records book. It looks like silkworms have always been attached to secrets.'

'Pass me those new leaves, Ruby Rose,' Bobby said. 'I'll clean the boxes tomorrow.' He placed the new leaves gently on top of the old chewed-up ones. 'How amazing that a worm can spin silk that turns into cloth.'

'Dad made us this.' Ruby held up a small wooden stand with a flat piece of wood that turned on nails positioned in the centre. 'When our cocoons are ready this year we can pick the thread and spin it out on this to make silk.' She flipped the centre around, watching it as it spun, envisaging reams of yellow thread unravelling from the cocoons, ready to be made up into silk.

'How will we turn it into silk?' Bobby said. 'It'll just be a long thread.'

'I'll have to ask Dad again. It'll probably tell us how in the encyclopaedia. Bobby, what happened to your back?' She turned back to him after carefully placing the spinning-stand on one of the shelves.

'It doesn't matter, it's nothing.'

'We're best friends. I thought we shared all our secrets, silkworm secrets.'

'If I tell you, you have to promise that you'll never tell anyone.' She could see Bobby's mind ticking over, assessing the risk of her repeating his story. 'Trouble is, Ruby Rose, I know you tell your dad lots of things. You have to promise me that everything I tell you, and I mean *everything* … you can't tell anyone, especially not your dad.'

'You know I won't, I never have before.' Ruby grabbed his hand across the table. 'You have to tell me.'

'The marks on my back …' He hesitated, looking around as if there could be someone else listening in. 'It's where my dad hits me. He, um, well, he belts me. He has a thick, leather shaving strap that used to belong to my grandfather and, well, he belts me with it. How long he hits me for depends on what I've done, or sometimes it depends on … it depends on how much he's had to drink.'

Ruby's eyes were wide, transfixed on Bobby's face. Not only was she shocked at the information, but she also had never heard Bobby talk for so long at once. 'Why doesn't your mum stop him?'

'Because then he hurts her,' Bobby said. 'Sometimes he hits her anyway. Not with the belt, though, he just uses his hands, his fists, to hit her.'

Ruby moved off her chair, dragging it closer to Bobby, who was bent over the table, his hands grasping the sides of his face, the tears streaming down, falling steadily, making splotchy marks on the tabletop. She had never seen him cry so much, not even when the sharp stake went through his leg and her dad had to pull it out. There hadn't even been a tear when her dad poured yellow anti-septic liquid into the gaping hole that was left.

'He hits your mum? Is that why she stays inside so much?'

Bobby nodded. 'When she has a black eye, or bruises, she never wants anyone to see her. But there's more than that, Ruby Rose. Mum's sick. I'm not sure what it is, but she cries all the time, and she doesn't talk. Most days she only gets up for a little while, and then she goes back to bed, back to that horrible dark bedroom.'

'We have to go to the police.'

'Didn't you listen to me? You can't tell *anyone*. This is why Theresa's going to leave as soon as she can.'

'He hits her as well?'

He nodded again. 'She cops it, too. Even if she just leaves one dish unwashed, or hasn't swept the floor, he's into her. He calls her a fat pig and then he hits her.'

'We have to tell someone.'

'He says that if we tell anyone, next time he'll use his knives. He has all his butcher's knives in the house. He says he'll slit our throats and no one will know.'

For once Ruby was speechless, her eyes wide as she tried to take in what Bobby had just told her. 'You have to come and live at our house.'

'It's not that simple. I have to look after Sally. There's other stuff going on.'

'Does he hit Sally too?'

'No, he ignores her. He says Sally's simple, just like Mum. I'm just glad he doesn't hit her, because I think I'd kill him if he did.' Now that Bobby had started talking it was as though he couldn't stop. 'You know ... he likes other women too.'

'What?'

'He takes up with other women, him and my uncle at the back of the butcher's shop. I walked in one day when they had two strange women in there.'

'What were they doing?'

'Rude stuff, stuff you don't need to know about. My uncle's a pig as well. They're both evil. That's why I'm telling you. Don't ever come over to my house again.'

'But what are we going to do?'

'Nothing. It's just the way it is. I try and keep out of trouble, and look after Sally. I don't know what to do about Mum, though, because she won't talk about anything, she hardly speaks at all.'

Both of them were quiet, Bobby staring down at the table, Ruby trying to work out how she could fix the problem.

'I overheard him telling my uncle something,' Bobby continued. 'He said he's going to get Mum and Sally sent away to a home for the cuckoos. That's exactly what he said.'

'What are you going to do?'

'There's nothing I can do. If I tell anyone, he'll … I think he'll kill someone. I know it, he has it in him.'

Mary's bellowing voice sounded from below the tree, making them both jump. 'Ruby Rose and Bobby Carlon, come down from up there. It's past dark.'

'Shit. Remember, Ruby Rose, not a word,' Bobby said. 'This is the biggest silkworm secret ever, and if you tell anyone I promise I'll never see you again or be your friend.'

'I promise, Bobby.' They pressed their thumbs

together, the gesture signifying the highest degree of secrecy possible in the Silkworm Club.

* * *

THAT NIGHT RUBY tossed and turned, visions of the marks on Bobby's back, his tears, and the thought of what really happened next door reeling in her head. Timidly she got up to close the old wooden hopper window, the creaking swing of it adding to her rising fear. Shadows long against the wall of the house swayed and moved, the rustling of the bushes and trees adding to her fear. She could hardly move.

A moment later her small bare feet padded quickly in panic across the lino, down the dark hallway and into her parents' bedroom. Standing at the edge of the bed, she touched her dad on the shoulder until he turned, eyes barely opening, to face her.

'What's up, mulberry fairy?' he mumbled before lifting her over him and placing her securely in the middle of the bed.

'I had a bad dream.'

'You're safe now, go back to sleep.'

Ruby lay awake for a long time. She liked to fix things, to help people, especially Bobby, but she had made a promise. Listening to the soft breathing from her mum on one side, offset by the usual snoring from her dad on the other, she felt safe.

Guilty thoughts of Bobby alone in his room filled her head. The idea of telling someone went over and over in her mind, but the thought of his dad threatening Bobby's family with knives scared her, and she knew she couldn't tell anyone. She just had to try and help Bobby as best she could.

Snuggling in, she relaxed, and soon her gentle, childish breathing matched the softness and rhythmic sound of the human walls on either side of her. She slept soundly, secure and content.

CHAPTER 9

As the year drew to a close, Ruby realised that life, as she knew it was changing. One day she had overheard Martha, the woman who drove the van and delivered their bread, talking to her mum.

'Mary, what do you know about the butcher's wife next door?' Martha had whispered.

Ruby's sharp ears picked up the question, as she lay hidden, curled up in the woven round chair, her idle fingers picking at the red vinyl that wove its way up and under the white strips that held the chair together.

'She's never outside,' Mary said. 'I've tried so many times to talk to her when I do see her, but she hardly speaks. Ruby is best mates with the boy, and he's a nice kid. The girls I rarely see either.'

Martha looked around, making sure no one was in earshot. 'People are talking about them. Of course I don't like to gossip, but they say the butcher and his brother have women down at the butcher's shop after it closes. I don't see anyone when I drop the bread off, but the milkman, he says that the kids are neglected. The door was open one day and he reckons it was a mess inside, real dark and stale.'

Concealed behind the back of the wicker chair, her darting eyes peering through the gaps in the weave, Ruby could clearly see their faces and hear their conversation, watching as the bread lady put the loaves of bread into her mum's tin.

'You know,' Martha continued, 'years ago Vincent and his brother, well, I used to think they were the bee's knees. Vincent was always polite and would often give me a compliment. I thought he was a nice man. He still chats and spends time talking to the customers. But now I'm not so sure about him. I don't like the way he acts. His eyes roam everywhere, you know, when you're in the shop. The brother Mike, though, he's nice. He's a politician and he's also involved with the church. I think he's a really good man.'

Ruby stiffened, nearly giving away her hiding space as Martha continued. 'I don't think you should let your Ruby play with that boy because you don't know what he's seen or done. She's getting older now. Do you think perhaps she should stay away from him?'

'Bobby is a nice boy and they've always been friends. They're just kids.'

'They say the mother belongs in the crazy house and that the younger girl's the same.'

'Look, I don't know much about them and, really, it's their business,' Mary said. 'I don't want us to be sticking our noses into other people's affairs.'

Straightening up Martha adjusted her apron. Mary picked up the bread tin, signalling an end to the conversation and clearly showing she didn't want to be gossiping any further about the neighbours.

'Well, it's just strange, that's all,' Martha said. 'Those two Carlon kids are never out playing with the others in the area.'

'Sometimes I see them out the back here,' Mary said. 'They do go outside a little.'

'Ah well, each to their own, I guess.' Martha closed the back of the bread van, shaking the flour from her apron. 'See you in two days. Remember what I said, though, you keep an eye on that Ruby.'

'Thank you, Martha, see you again soon.'

* * *

THE CONVERSATION HAD GONE ROUND and round in Ruby's head for days, making her feel like a traitor when she saw Bobby.

Anticipating an afternoon of play, the following Saturday Ruby scratched hopscotch squares into the dusty driveway that led from their post-war timber house to the main road in the distance. Saturday afternoons were when she and Bobby could spend time together; his dad worked late on Saturdays, often far into the night. The ten squares were clear in the dirt of the driveway and ready to be hopped upon, two stones ready for the markers.

Filling in time while she waited for Bobby, Ruby wandered down the driveway and opened the squeaky lid on the tin that was their mailbox. Then she remembered: Saturday, so no mail today. Standing on the fence, she peered in. As usual, a huge green frog, its protruding eyes closed, took up the entire bottom of the tin. Closing the lid carefully, she looked up and down the road before returning to sit on the low front veranda.

There was trouble from the start. Bobby came flying up the driveway on his rusty old bike, skidding across her neatly drawn hopscotch and scattering the markers, covering most of the marks with twirling dust.

'You're late,' she said.

'I had a lot of jobs to do. I went as fast as I could.'

He apologised and patiently helped her redraw the squares before allowing her to go first. For once she was happy to let him be the boss and take control.

They looked up from their game at the sound of a car turning into the driveway next door. The black, official-looking car with the round emblem on the bonnet zoomed up the driveway and made its way straight to the granny flat at the back of Bobby's house.

'That's your uncle's car, isn't it?'

'Yep.' Bobby's face had paled and he stood still, not worrying about hopping now, both feet planted firmly in one hopscotch box.

Ruby glanced down at his feet, noticing that he wasn't in the least concerned that he had broken the rules of the game. 'Do you want to go up to check on the moths?' She could see that the arrival of his uncle had left him disinterested in the game.

'Yep.'

He followed her without hesitation. Their bare feet moved quickly towards the coolness and seclusion that lay beneath the huge trees in the corner of the backyard. Both were oblivious to the squelching mulberries underfoot, focusing on climbing quickly up the tree into the safe cocoon of the treehouse.

Bobby went straight to the window opening, the drawn curtain allowing him to look straight down onto his own yard while Ruby busied herself with the boxes, checking for new cocoons and ensuring there was water in the lids they left for the moths. Sweeping the floor with the small brush they kept in the treehouse, she looked up at Bobby, who continued to peer silently through the window.

'How long do you think he'll stay?' There was no reply. 'Bobby, I asked you a question.'

'I don't know. I didn't know he was coming. He's taking in his suitcases, and that usually means he'll stay for a while.'

'At least he doesn't stay in your house. Look, he's going out already. Sit down, Bobby, you look sick.'

'I can't breathe.' Gasps came out between his words. 'My stomach hurts.'

Ruby pushed him down onto one of the chairs, telling him to take deep breaths. 'Bobby, I'm here. Breathe properly.'

Although Bobby's eyes still darted nervously around the treehouse, his breathing slowed as he listened to her, eventually matching his breaths with hers, the pains in his body diminishing.

'What do you need to do? What are you worried about?' Ruby asked him.

'He'll be going down to the shop. I'm going to go home. I need to look after Sally. I've got to go.' Gulping down the tumbler of water that Ruby had placed in front of him, he looked up at her, taking in her questioning, worried look. 'Thanks, Ruby Rose. It's okay. I just need to go home now. We'll talk tomorrow.'

THE NEXT DAY RUBY WAITED, but Bobby didn't come. She spent the morning in the treehouse cleaning the boxes, renewing the leaves and collecting mulberries so her mum could make the pies that her dad loved to eat. Through the spying window, she watched the weekly ritual next door.

Bobby and Theresa sat in the back of Vincent's big car and, just like a chauffeur in a movie, drove slowly down the dusty driveway before turning right in the direction of the church where they went each Sunday. As usual, Mrs Carlon and Sally weren't with them. Ruby could see the blinds pulled tightly across the windows of Mrs Carlon's bedroom. She knew that Bobby's mum usually got up for a little while in the morning for breakfast before taking the medication that allowed her mind to rest and her body to sleep.

Ruby knew that every day was much the same. The family was used to it, Bobby said. His dad rarely entered his mum's room, instead sleeping outside on the daybed on the veranda. At night his dad filled himself full of rum or beer before stumbling to bed, kicking things out of the way, cursing them all, his snoring soon echoing through the closed-in veranda.

Bobby always stayed with Sally until she was asleep before curling up on a small bed in the same room. The dark circles that were under his eyes each morning when he came to collect Ruby for school were testament to an ingrained pattern of disturbed sleep.

Lately Bobby had opened up more than usual, and Ruby was starting to get real insight into the life of his family; a life that was unknown to the outside world, hidden by drawn curtains and silenced family members.

Sometimes, instead of arriving on his bike to collect her in the morning, Bobby would call out over the fence, peering nervously around as he told her he would be staying home with Sally instead of going to school.

'But you should be going to school,' she would say.

'I just need to stay home today, there's a lot to do.'

Other days Ruby noticed the paleness in his face, and a distinct thinness in his gangly teenage body. Gathering food from home, she would make up a package for him, filling the brown paper bag full of biscuits and fruit that she knew he would share with his sisters. It troubled her to see how sad Bobby often was these days, and no matter how much she tried to cheer him up, he rarely smiled.

For the millionth time Ruby wondered if she should tell her mum and dad, but Bobby had made her promise, a silkworm promise that she knew could not be broken.

Sometimes she overheard her parents talking about the family next door. *Something's not right. Those kids should be at school. Bobby looks terrible. Do you think they're getting enough food? You never see the mother. If she's not well, why doesn't the doctor come for visits?*

Conversations followed, with the usual answers to the many questions her mum and dad asked each other. *We need to mind our own business. Mrs Carlon is sick and can't cope with talking to people or going outside. The uncle's always there, and he's wealthy so surely he's helping with their problems. They all go to church, they're good people.*

Ruby thought about her parents' concerns now and

realised that at some stage she may need to ask for help. Bobby was, after all, her best friend … but there was the complication of the silkworm secrets.

Her mind tumbled back and forth as she looked out through the gap in the treehouse curtain. Rambling paddocks sprawled out behind their backyards and an old farmhouse perched crookedly on the hill beyond. Small human figures moved around on the hill, just visible in the far distance. Cows chewed on the thick green grass, and a dog ran across the paddocks, its bark echoing as it chased a scurrying hare heading for the safety of the nearby bushes.

Ruby peered to the left. She could see Lewis leaning on his pitchfork. He wiped his brow with a handkerchief, the midday sun beating down as he tended to Mrs Walton's vegetable patch. Maybe Bobby could talk to Lewis about his family. Repositioning herself so she could watch Lewis fully, Ruby thought about this as a solution.

Biting her lip, she was stumped once again as she recalled a conversation over the fence between Lewis and her mum last week. Ruby had strained to listen; Lewis's accent made his words sound strange and as usual, he had thrown his hands around dramatically to emphasise his words.

'That Bobby,' Lewis said, 'not good way. Yes, just other day I see bruises, arms, and burn mark on leg. He tell me he had fall from his bike, but …' Lewis had twisted his nose in that funny way he had, his moustache moving in unison. 'He is, what the word, nervous, like telling me a lie.'

'It's a funny household,' her mum had said. 'I never see Isobel and I rarely see the girls. Bobby's a lovely boy but we don't really want to get involved and it's best not to interfere. As we say, each to their own.'

'I know.' Lewis nodded in agreement. 'Very should mind my business. I don't think mother is well, how you say, father say to me she is crazy in head. Probably good people, trying to do their best. Bring kids up and put roof over their heads.'

'They reckon the little one is a bit, you know, slow, sort of simple.'

'Aaaghh.' Lewis let out a long sigh. 'That explain it. Probably all looking after mother and girl.'

With that, the conversation had changed to other, really boring things, and Ruby had tuned out. She wasn't interested in how much water had been in the rain gauge or what month was best to plant watermelons.

'You must plant on exhibition Wednesday,' Lewis had told her mum. 'That show day. Not day later or day earlier.'

Lewis was the expert on everything to do with plants, and her mum always listened intently, working out where and when to plant the next round in the veggie patch.

Ruby thought about what Lewis had said as she looked over to the yard next door. At that moment Bobby's uncle came out through the door of the granny flat. She lay flat, hardly breathing as she watched him look around the dusty yard before sauntering over to the back fence. Leaning on the wooden rail, he peered over to the farm beyond, his manner relaxed as he casually lit a cigarette, dragging deeply and slowly, flicking the ash over the fence as he took in the paddocks beyond. Eventually he turned around, tucking in his shirt and smoothing his hair before looking across the backyard again. He circled the fence line until his eyes seemed to be looking straight at Ruby.

She let out a little gasp, certain that he could see her staring down, spying on him, watching his every move. Lying perfectly still and holding her breath, she waited until his gaze left the mulberry tree and returned to the cluttered yard next door. His foot swivelled in the dust as he squashed the end of his cigarette into the dirt before heading up to the back porch of the house that sat silent and empty.

He came back out only a few minutes later with Theresa. The young girl walked slowly, hesitantly, carrying a bucket and mop, hurried along by her uncle, who carried a dustpan and broom. They both disappeared into the granny flat, Theresa's uncle taking one last look around the yard before shutting the door behind them.

Ruby thought about Bobby's mum, left alone in the main house. For one moment she thought about sneaking over, maybe picking some flowers. Perhaps she could read to Mrs Carlon, talk to her, keep her company.

She sat up, the idea of helping Bobby's mum turning over in her mind; that obsessive desire, always her longing to make things right, to help someone, to make them happy.

Maybe Sally would like to see the silkworms. Ruby could tell her the story about the history of silk, perhaps they could play together or she could clean Sally's room. While Theresa was cleaning the granny flat, Ruby could clean the main house. That would be a big help.

And then she remembered Bobby's words. *Don't ever come over here again. If you come again, we can't be friends.* An unbreakable code between two best friends. Not only were there silkworm secrets that she couldn't tell, but there was also the promise she had made to Bobby that she would never come to his house again.

She sighed loudly, resigning herself to the promise she had made. Instead she busied herself neatening the shelves, sweeping crumbs through the gaps in the floor, and filling in the records book.

When everything was in order and up to date, she looked through the treehouse window towards the back veranda of her house. She could see her mum and dad sitting on the metal chairs, waiting for her. Her mum's feet were stretched out, positioned on her dad's lap, and his hands were rubbing them, twisting her toes, massaging, strong hands pushing this way and that. Even from a distance Ruby could see that her mum's eyes were shut, and a look of sheer bliss was on her face.

Ruby looked harder, taking in the food that was laid out on the metal table in front of her parents. Pancakes! In the blink of an eye she had pulled up the canvas covering the doorway and scurried down the rickety timber pieces, jumping over the last few as usual. In her haste, she lost her balance and landed flat on her backside in the ferns and long grass.

Thank goodness Bobby isn't here to see me, she thought.

The pancakes, and the relaxed family Sunday breakfast beckoned. She brushed the grass seeds and dead leaves from her sunflower dress, and ran as fast as she could towards the smell of freshly brewed coffee, pancakes and cooked bacon.

CHAPTER 10

$\mathscr{L}$ife for Ruby was always much the same. Weeks turned into months that flew past quickly. Her thin, short legs stretched out and hems of dresses had to be constantly let down. These days she plaited her hair herself, a huge wad of twined blonde hair hanging down the middle of her back.

Her dad said she was still small enough to sit on his lap, and in the afternoons the two of them sat together on the back stairs, cuddling and talking. Ruby listened intently, hanging off every word, the connection between them deepening as Francis watched his chubby baby turn into a young lady.

Ruby's mum had given her more jobs to do around the house. 'You're twelve now, Ruby, you need to earn your pocket money,' her mum told her. 'The scraps have to go to the chooks, and make sure old Daisy has water in the trough. I can't believe you'll be at high school next year. You won't be able to be late then because that bus won't wait for you like your mate does.'

Even though Bobby was now at high school, he still picked her up each morning, the two of them riding together as far as her school before he continued by himself to the high school further up the road.

Ruby loved the closeness between the two of them. She pretended that Bobby was really her brother and Sally her sister. Daydreams filled her head: Bobby and Sally living with her in their house, her parents adopting them, Bobby in the spare bedroom and Sally sharing with her. She'd look after them and help them with their schoolwork, make cakes for them and read Sally books every night.

Visions of the three of them cuddled up on the lounge with her mum and dad filled her head as she skipped down the shady path, excited and in a hurry, her already dirty feet pushing through the layer of wet leaves; the coolness of the fresh air awakening her skin.

She had heard the click of the side gate earlier and knew that Bobby was ahead of her this morning. He was probably already up in the treehouse, cleaning out the silkworm boxes. Rushing through her jobs, she impatiently completed her mum's requests, the rest of the day planned in her head.

She was looking forward to the carefree summer holidays, with weeks and weeks of freedom, sleeping in, no schoolwork and more time with Bobby. Hot summer days, the beckoning swimming pool—well, really a cut-off water tank—toads to chase at night with sticks, and savage summer storms to watch in the afternoons.

Thank goodness for Dad, Ruby thought. Even though her mum was good company, it was her dad who gave her the companionship of missing siblings at night. When they sat together on the back porch, he taught her the patterns of the stars; the science of the planets, the moon and sun; and how the trees made the air clean.

She listened to his stories from long ago, his childhood, the farm he had lived on, the night he had met her mum, and the excitement for both of them when a baby girl had arrived in their lives.

Ruby prattled back to him about what was happening at school, what Bobby and she were up to with the silkworms, and what she had planned for the holidays. Conversation flowed as they talked about the different jobs she would like to do, her dad always telling her how smart she was.

'All A marks on that report card, Ruby Rose,' he said one night. 'You might be prime minister one day.'

'She'd be better than the one we got now,' her mum chipped in when she came to sit with them on the steps.

Together they watched the sun sink into the horizon, the fading light sending the blues and yellows into washes of pink and orange, kookaburras high in the trees heralding the end of the day.

'Okay, you two,' Mary reminded them. 'Clean-up time and then dinner.'

Night after night Ruby and her dad cuddled together, the warmth from his body washing over her, his dusty muscly arms wrapping around her body as they sat together as one, watching the light of the day fade into the balmy darkness of the night. The racket of cicadas filled the air and bats flew overhead, their wings flapping noisily. Sometimes they stopped for a feed in the mulberry tree that looked even larger, looming in the dimness, outlined against the darkening sky.

There was less noise in the back corner of the yard during the day, the quiet haven shaded and hidden under the cover of the massive trees. Ruby's ears rang with the silence now as she ran down the leafy path, eager to be with Bobby and up in the treehouse. She was so eager that she nearly ran straight into the fat yard cow that stood steadfastly blocking the path.

Large brown eyes circled by prominent long eyelashes stared hard, a curly tuft of white hair in the centre of the cow's forehead drawing Ruby's attention as the cow swung her head wildly, cranky at the intrusion into her quiet, shady rest area.

'Daisy, shoo,' Ruby said as she waved her hands at the annoying cow.

The cow swung her head angrily. She took a step towards Ruby, showing her who was boss this morning, unbending and threatening in her pose, front hooves set stubbornly in the leaf litter. The steps of the treehouse beckoned just behind the tiresome cow, but Ruby knew better than to antagonise her.

It wasn't the first time Daisy had stopped Ruby from entering the treehouse. It was worse when she came down the ladder and the cranky old cow was standing solid beneath the tree, refusing to move. Often Ruby would have to yell out for her dad. Of course, Daisy went with him placidly and willingly; she was after all, his cow.

Today, though, Ruby had to run all the way back to the house and get the scrap bucket, then entice the cow far enough away from the ladder so she could quickly run in behind, jump nervously onto the ladder and clamber up quickly into the treehouse.

'Where've you been?' Bobby stood in the doorway of the treehouse, taking in the scene of the cow and the scrap bucket now being tossed around as Daisy tried to lick every remnant of food from it.

'That stupid cow, I swear she's jealous of Dad and me. She doesn't throw her head at anyone else like that except me.'

Ruby stood on one of the top rungs watching Daisy glare up at her, as if she was thinking of climbing the ladder.

'The other day Dad was milking her and I hit his shoulder to get rid of a mosquito,' Ruby said. 'Daisy went crazy and kicked the milk bucket trying to get to me. There was snot coming out of her nose and her eyes were rolling back in her head. I swear she wanted to kill me. Dad had to throw me over the fence because there was no way she was going to stop. After all that, she came back to

Dad as if nothing had happened, and just rubbed up and down on him like a cat.'

Bobby laughed, used to Ruby's back-and-forth relationship with her father's favourite cow. 'Someone else is here today,' he said hesitantly, blocking her way in.

'Who?'

'Well, I said they could come in. I know you've always had a rule about it, but she needed to go somewhere. She's running away from home.'

'Theresa?'

'No.'

Ruby stepped inside, expecting to see Bobby's sister hiding out, escaping from the situation at home. She gasped, a look of shock on her face. Lynette Smyth, the girl from two doors down, was sitting at the table, and not only sitting there but also drinking water from their cups and looking around as if it was accepted for her to be there.

For once Ruby said nothing.

Bobby spoke quietly. 'I told her it was fine, that you'd be all right with her being up here. She's got nowhere to go and she needs to hide.'

To Ruby's dismay he sat down on the seat right next to Lynette, passing her his very own brown handkerchief to wipe away the tears on her face. The fact was not lost on Ruby that he was very attentive towards the crying girl, and she looked closely to see if it was the same handkerchief she had given him last Christmas. It was, and here he was, handing it to Lynette, who used it to blow her nose as if it belonged to her.

Ruby looked at the two of them, taking in the situation, the close proximity of Bobby to the pretty, dark-haired girl, who … Ruby stared hard. Lynette was wearing a bra. She had breasts, big bumpy ones, bulging from her chest and filling out her red T-shirt. And if Ruby wasn't mistaken, Bobby was looking straight down Lynette's top as he passed her another glass of water.

Ruby straightened up, very aware that she still didn't need to wear a bra herself. As her mum said, not much use wearing one when there's nothing to put in it.

Lynette sniffled, wiping her nose with the hankie. 'Thanks, Ruby,' she said, 'Bobby said you wouldn't mind. I need somewhere to go. I can't go back home.'

Ruby sat down across the table from them. Had she missed something over the last year? When did these two become friends?

As if he had read her mind, Bobby said, 'Lynette and I see each other at school. She's in the year below me.'

'I know that.'

'We thought you might be able to help, perhaps let her stay up here. No one will know.'

'How come you're running away?' Ruby asked Lynette.

Lynette looked at Bobby, who nodded. 'Bobby said you can keep a secret,' she said.

Ruby scowled, they had obviously discussed this previously and not included her. 'Of course I can.' Her eyes flashed indignantly.

'Promise.' Lynette and Bobby spoke at the same time.

Ruby sat up straighter. 'Of course I promise.'

'I'm not going back home. My grandfather lives with us and I need to get away from him.'

'That's why you're running away?'

Lynette looked at Bobby again, who reassured her. 'She won't tell anyone, we have a pact, silkworm secrets.'

Lynette looked down at her feet. 'He touches me.'

'What do you mean he touches you?' Ruby said.

'He puts his hand down my pants, and then he makes me do foul, really rude things to him.'

'What?' Ruby looked straight at Bobby, waiting for him to speak. 'He touches you down there?'

'He's sick, he won't stop and I can't take any more.' Lynette started to cry, great gasping sobs that echoed throughout the old wooden treehouse.

Wrapping his arm around Lynette's shoulders Bobby tried to comfort her. Ruby jumped up and sat close to Lynette on the other side, taking her hand in her own.

'I don't want him to touch me any more. I hate him. I wish he was dead.'

'Have you told your mum or dad?' Ruby asked.

'I tried to tell Mum. She slapped me across the face and said if I ever tell such lies again she'll send me to one of those girl's homes and I'll have to scrub toilets and never see my friends or brothers again.'

'How long has it been happening?'

'Since I was about ten. Because he lives with us it's really hard. I can't get away from him and he just waits until everyone else is out of the house and then he finds me. I've tried to lock myself in the bathroom, but he can take the lock off and then he says if I don't do what he says he'll kill all of us.'

'What should we do, Bobby?' Ruby said. 'Dad will do something. He'll go to the police and then they'll arrest Lynette's grandfather. It's against the law; they send those people to jail. He'll go to jail.'

'And then what happens, Ruby?' Lynette said. 'Mum

and Dad will hate me. They'll think I made it all up. They'll say I'm the bad one.'

'No, they won't,' she said. 'It's easy, you just go to the police and they'll put him in jail.'

'My grandfather's friends with all the policemen. He used to be one, remember.'

'It's true, Ruby Rose,' Bobby said. 'It's not as simple as you think. You don't have to live with it. Not everyone is good like your dad.'

'What would you know, Bobby?' Ruby said. 'How would you know what it's like for Lynette? We have to help her.'

Ruby was shocked to see the look on Bobby's face, the way he twisted towards her and spoke to her in a way he had never done before, his words angry.

'Don't ask me what I'd know. What do you think that fucking *Uncle Mike* does in the shed in the backyard? What do you think Theresa's had to put up with for years from that bastard? And what do you think happens when I try to say something to my father? What do you reckon happens? Do you think he goes to the police? Of course he doesn't. He just says I'm a liar and I'm the one with the dirty mind. Last time I said something he nearly killed me. He told me to keep my dirty thoughts to myself.'

Ruby's mind was in turmoil and her stomach twisted. Visions of Bobby's uncle walking Theresa down the backyard. Every time he visited. Watching them enter the granny flat, yet never seeing her come back out. Thinking that Theresa cleaned for a very long time. The way Bobby hated him so much.

'I can't believe you've never told me this before,' Ruby said.

'What's the use of people knowing? There's nothing anyone can do about it. My uncle's a very powerful person, and just like Lynette's grandfather he knows a lot of important people. They'll just say we're lying.'

'We need to tell *someone*.'

Bobby's voice was strained. 'We can't tell anyone. They'll send us away. No one will believe us. We've tried, both of us.'

Ruby was perplexed. She felt left out. The two of them had talked about this for ages and not included her. Bobby watched her, reading her mind.

'We've talked to each other a lot at school, Ruby Rose. Lynette needed someone to talk to and I understood straightaway because of what happens in my house. You have to keep it a secret, you can't tell anyone, first because no one's going to believe it, and second because my uncle and Lynette's grandfather are dangerous people. They're the sort of men who could do anything.'

Lynette started crying again. 'My grandfather is crazy. He says if I tell anyone he'll kill me.'

Ruby listened carefully as Bobby's voice dropped to a whisper. 'Lynette and Theresa are going to run away together. Tomorrow they'll get on the train down to Sydney. They need to get away. I have some money, and we thought you might have some as well that you could help them with. Are you in? Silkworm secrets?'

Her mind kicked into gear. 'Of course I'll help. Maybe I could make up some packets of food tonight. I'll give you enough to eat until you get a place to stay. Where are you going to live?'

'Um, we don't really know yet,' Lynette said, 'but I'm sure once we're in Sydney there'll be someone to help us. I told my mum I'm staying at a friend's place tonight, so they won't notice me gone until tomorrow afternoon.'

'Are you sure it's the right thing to do?' Ruby said.

'I have to get away. I've put up with it for so long and I …' The gulping sobs returned. 'I want to make it stop.'

'Please don't cry, Lynette. I've got about ten dollars saved up at home.'

'I'd come with you if it wasn't for Sally,' Bobby said.

Ruby was shocked that Bobby would even think of leaving her when he was supposed to be her best friend. How had she missed all of this? Why hadn't he told her before? She looked at both of them. The beautiful, dark-haired girl, her face streaked with tears, sad eyes reflecting the terror, the years of torture. And then Ruby sensed the shame. She could tell from the way Lynette talked that she thought some of this was her own fault, that she was the bad one.

Bobby's face also reflected his hurt and shame; the fact that he knew about what happened to his sister but couldn't do anything about it. The constant suspense, the waiting, the fear of what his uncle might do next.

'Why hasn't Theresa told someone?' Ruby asked Bobby.

'She did. She told one of the nuns at the church, who took her to see Father Edward.' Bobby took a deep breath and looked down. 'He told Theresa she was a dirty slut and that she had to go to confession more often. Girls like her should be remorseful, he said, and if she didn't cleanse herself of her lies and fantasies she was likely to end up in hell.'

Lynette's sobs had stopped, and her voice was now calm and resolute. 'No one wants to help or know about what's been happening. The only way out is to run away. I just need to stay up here until first light tomorrow morning, and then Theresa and I are going to the train station. We're leaving on the first train. She's got the tickets and knows where to go once we get to Sydney. We just need help from you, Ruby. We need some money, and for you to let me stay up here the night. I can't go back. I won't. I'd rather be dead than for him to touch me again.'

Confused and bewildered, Bobby looked beseechingly at Ruby. Why was life so bad, so difficult? He wanted to be out of his own situation also, but there was no way he could leave Sally. His mother was declining even further into a state of nonexistence, only coming out of her room on occasion to eat or attempt to do some of the household chores. She usually only lasted a short while before silently slipping back into the darkened bedroom. He and Theresa were the only ones caring for Sally. And now Theresa was going, and it would all be up to him.

'Of course I'll help,' Ruby said again. 'I'll bring up a blanket and pillow, and we'll make up a bed for you. Why don't you come and sleep in my room?'

'Thanks Ruby, but I know your mum and she'll ask too many questions, plus she might check with my mum. They'll work out something's going on. I'll be fine up here.'

'I'll do anything to help you too, Bobby. You need to tell me what I can do. We'll work it out.'

'You're my best friend, Ruby Rose. I knew you'd help with all this. That's why I brought Lynette here.' To her surprise, Bobby gave her a hug; it was a rarity for him to display any sort of physical contact, with her or anyone.

'I'll be back soon and I'll bring the blankets and food.'

In her mind, Ruby was running through a list of all the things the two older girls needed. It scared her to think of them running away, leaving the safety and comfort of home, but obviously their homes were not safe. Lynette was right, there was no option. They had to get away.

Lynette's grandfather had always been around when Ruby went over to play. An old grey-haired man, he had always seemed nice, funny, making jokes. Now, when she thought about it, Lynette had always been quiet when he was around.

Once the two girls had stayed locked in Lynette's bedroom when they were home alone with him. Ruby remembered how the grandfather had knocked on the bedroom door and asked what they were up to. Lynette had put her finger to her lips to signal Ruby to be quiet. He had knocked again, and when there was no response he had tried the door handle, which of course being locked wouldn't turn. After jiggling the handle for a while, he had muttered something and given up.

Ruby hadn't thought anything of it at the time, but now it made sense. Lynette's pale face and stillness, the way she told Ruby they had to play in the locked room, only coming out when her mum and dad came home.

Ruby felt sick. Should she tell someone? What would her dad do? What *could* he do? Lynette's mum knew already and hadn't believed her, and for heaven's sake, the priest ... why hadn't he gone straight to the police? But Lynette's grandfather had been a policeman and Bobby's uncle was a famous politician. Who was going to believe them?

Ruby knew she couldn't tell anyone about this. This was the biggest silkworm secret ever. She needed to help the girls, organise food and money, and make sure they got away from the situations in their very own homes. A grandfather, an uncle, how could that happen?

Pushing the confusion to the back of her mind, she concentrated on gathering the items, methodically ticking off the list in her head, nothing forgotten, glad that she was at least some help to Bobby. That would be the next thing once Lynette had escaped, she would need to think about how to help Bobby protect Sally. And Bobby had to protect himself too. Remembering the marks on his back, the stories of the beatings, the strangeness of his mother, she knew she had lots to do and this was only the beginning.

CHAPTER 12

It took until the next afternoon for Lynette's family to notice she had disappeared. Her parents had knocked on Ruby's door, their voices solemn when they asked Francis if anyone had seen their daughter. Ruby's dad had called her out from her bedroom and asked if she had seen Lynette.

For the first time in her life she had lied to him. 'No, I haven't seen Lynette.'

A short statement that made her dad's eyes squint and look suspiciously into her own.

When Lynette's parents had gone, her dad called out to her, rousing her from the security of her bedroom where she had quickly retreated. 'Um, could you come back out here, Ruby Rose? Are you sure you haven't seen Lynette? Look me straight in the eye and tell me the truth.'

The silence between them was an obvious sign that she was lying.

Francis looked suspiciously at her. 'Ruby Rose, I want the truth. Where is she?'

'I can't tell you, I've promised not to tell.' Her voice wobbled, but the look on her face was determined and strong.

'Are you telling me you know where she is? This is important, Ruby Rose. If they can't find her they'll call the police. They've checked all her friends' places and now they think Theresa next door is missing as well. If you know something you need to tell me, because this is serious.'

Silence again. Torn between revealing the truth to her dad and keeping her promise to Bobby.

'There must be a very good reason why you're not telling me.'

'There is. I can't say.' Tears welled. She hated not telling him, but she couldn't betray Bobby's trust.

Her dad was the only person in the world she would cry in front of. No one else could make her cry. She'd bite her bottom lip when the teacher used the little ruler on her fingers, and be more determined than ever not to show tears when anyone else upset her or when she hurt herself. She had nearly cried the day her mum slipped over on the back stairs and split her head open, but she had held it together, knowing she needed to be in charge, managing to not only hold a towel on her mum's bleeding head but also call the ambulance.

The feeling of being in charge, in control, and stronger than others sat well with her; she taught herself to be the leader, to try new things, not to be afraid and to always work hard at everything.

'Don't give up, keep going, you can do anything,' her dad had told her over and over again. And now, for the first time ever, she felt like she was going against him.

'Are they safe?'

'Yes, they will be. I'm sorry, Dad, but I can't tell you because there's a reason they've gone and they'll be safer where they are than at their homes.'

'What? That doesn't make sense.'

'Please, Dad, please trust me with this. You always told me that trust is one of the most important virants.'

'Virtues, Ruby Rose, not virants.'

'Well, this time you have to trust me. I can't break a promise.'

'As long as you can promise me they're safe.'

'I promise.'

INTERROGATIONS HAD NOT GONE SO WELL for Bobby, whose father, on discovering that Theresa was missing, had headed straight for the leather belt, knowing full well that Bobby would know where she was. The fact that the other girl from up the road had also disappeared, well, obviously Bobby knew. He headed angrily to where Bobby was cutting wood in the backyard.

Ruby watched from the treehouse where she had fled to, worried that further pressure from her father would lead to her revealing where the two girls were headed.

'Get inside now!' Vincent yelled at Bobby.

Bobby kept cutting the wood.

'Fucking get inside, you little bastard.' Vincent, a giant of a man, pushed Bobby roughly, grabbing the axe from his hands, pushing him towards the back stairs of their dilapidated house, his voice angry and loud, clearly discernible to Ruby in her distant perch high in the tree.

She didn't remember moving, but the next thing she

knew she had descended from the treehouse, feet landing solidly in the mushy leaves and mulberries below. Looking up from her landing position, she glared straight into the ominous, unblinking eyes of Daisy the cow. It took only a second for Ruby to gather herself, standing as tall as she could before looking the menacing cow in the eye. It was almost as though the cow had sensed the unfolding drama and decided to complicate it further.

'Bugger off, you bloody cow.'

Swearwords previously unused but stored in her mind burst forth, her panic at getting help for Bobby overcoming her usual terror of Daisy putting one of those horns straight through her body.

Daisy's head swung wildly, her eyes rolled, and a snort came forth from her wide, flaring nostrils.

'Piss off, I'm not bloody scared of you.' Ruby's voice was deep and loud as she yelled straight into the cow's face. 'Get out of my way.' Her arms flew around wildly and she clapped her hands. 'Piss off.' Ruby used the strongest swearwords she knew, staring straight at Daisy, no longer scared.

The cow stopped its menacing behaviour and took a couple of steps backward, clearing the way for Ruby to pass. The animal looked at her once more before putting its head down, sniffing the ground, now uninterested in Ruby and instead looking for shoots of grass amongst the thickness of the shady undergrowth.

Ruby's bare feet flew over the pathway and she jumped over the brick stairs running into the kitchen, where Francis and Mary were sitting.

'Dad,' she shouted, 'you have to help, quickly. Bobby's father's going to kill him.' Her words came out in short gasps, formed from panic and loss of breath due to the quick descent from the treehouse. 'Please, Dad, hurry, you have to help. He's made him go inside, I know he's going to kill him. He has an axe.'

Francis stood up and placed his hands on Ruby's shoulders. 'Start again, calm down and tell us what the hell is going on.'

'I was up the treehouse.' She took a deep breath, her chest heaving. 'I saw Bobby's dad push him inside. He was cutting the wood. He's really angry about Theresa. I know he'll beat Bobby up, make him tell him where she's gone. Please, Dad, you have to stop him.'

Francis looked from Ruby to Mary.

'Please, Dad, please.' Ruby tugged at his shirt, trying to get him to head towards the house next door.

Mary spoke firmly. 'Go, Francis. I think you should help. Ruby, you stay here with me. That's right, don't you dare move.'

Francis moved quickly, his wife's direct response spurring him into action. Unlatching the side gate, he took long strides towards the back door of the house next door.

As Mary shut the back door Ruby threw her arms around her mum's waist, holding on tightly, her heart beating wildly against Mary's stomach. They stayed wrapped together, the still of the afternoon pounding in their ears as they strained to hear any noises coming from the Carlons' house.

'It'll all work out, Ruby. Your dad will make sure Bobby's safe.'

Ruby was terrified at what she had seen, knowing full well what Bobby's dad would probably do. She wanted it all to go away, all the turmoil, the stories, relatives touching girls, the marks on Bobby's back, his sad face.

For a long while Mary and Ruby clung to each other, waiting for Francis to return. When he finally did, he sat down at the small kitchen table, the shock evident on his face. He asked Ruby to get him a beer out of the fridge. She opened it as he had taught her and placed the bottle and a glass in front of him, both her and Mary pulling out the old wooden chairs to sit with him.

With shaking hands Francis poured himself a beer. Ruby waited, allowing him to take a couple of long swigs from the glass before the questions tumbled from her mouth. 'What happened? Did you stop him beating Bobby?'

'Bobby's all right, Ruby Rose, he'll be okay.' He pulled her over onto his lap, holding her tightly, patting her blonde hair before kissing the top of her head.

'Give your father a minute,' Mary said, her hand resting on Francis's shoulder while he took further gulps from the glass that was now nearly empty. Francis hardly ever drank, and it was usually only after working in the hottest days of summer that he finished off the day with a couple of glasses of beer.

What had happened? Ruby waited, giving her father time, watching his hands that were still shaking.

'Bobby told his father where the girls have gone, but Vincent had already laid into him before I got there. Vincent made Bobby tell him where they were headed.'

Ruby's hand went up over her mouth and she felt sick again, worried for Bobby, not believing that he had forsaken the secret that she had so guiltily kept from her own parents. She was also worried about him being hurt. 'What did Bobby's dad do to him to make him tell?'

'He's got a swollen eye, and I think, well, Bobby's father had a heavy leather strap in his hands. I reckon Bobby had probably copped a few of them across his back before I got there.' Francis looked up at both of them. 'He had that younger sister lined up next to Bobby. He told Bobby if he didn't tell him where Theresa was he was going to flog her as well.'

'Those poor kids.' Mary's face was stricken, horrified at the thought of what had happened and what had obviously been going on for god knows how long.

'He was so upset, crying, really upset, young Bobby was,' Francis said. 'Look, I don't want to say much more.' He looked at his wife, indicating that he had said enough in front of Ruby.

'I've talked to Bobby's father,' he told Ruby. 'I've said I'll go to the police and that he can't hit the kids like that. It's against the law. Bobby's all right at the moment and he's looking after Sally. Vincent's taken off. He said he was going down to the police station himself so he could tell them where the girls were headed. He's a violent man. You're never to go over there, Ruby Rose. Who knows what he's capable of.'

'Bobby has never let me go over. That's why he always comes here.'

Francis drained the last of the beer, his hands calmer now. 'I'm going to ring the police. It needs to be reported because he can't flog the kids like that. He told me that it's his business how he disciplines them and I needed to mind my own business, but it's not right. I've seen bruises on Bobby before, the poor kid. Problem is, I doubt the police will do anything.'

'They could put him in jail, and then Sally and Bobby could come and live with us. We could look after them,' Ruby said.

'It doesn't work like that, plus their mother is over there. It's very strange that even with all the noise and commotion she didn't come out of that room. It's an odd household, all right. And now the girls running away.'

'We have to fix it, make it right, Dad, please.' Ruby looked pleadingly at Francis.

'Bobby's father was pretty wild. He stopped, though, when I intervened. He said his kids have to be taught a lesson and I should understand, being a father and all. He reckons that all he does is work his guts out, and that Theresa had gone behind his back, stolen his money and pissed off down to Sydney. He said he was going to drag her back by the scruff of her neck and throw her into the girl's home in Brisbane.'

Ruby's dad's usually calm manner was disturbed, his steady brown eyes flashing, his hand clenching the empty glass. 'I'm going to ring the cops now, while it's still fresh in my mind.'

Francis and Mary exchanged a look.

'Time for a bath and then bed, Ruby,' Francis said. 'Everything will straighten out in the morning.' He spoke quietly and she knew better than to argue with him.

* * *

RUBY'S MUM stayed in the bathroom with her, helping her scrub the stubborn mud and stains from her feet and legs.

'When I'm big I'm going to be a police or a judge, and I'm going to lock people like Bobby's dad up,' Ruby said.

'There's a lot of bad people out there, Ruby. Don't be too quick to trust anyone, and never let anyone treat you badly. Decent men don't thrash their kids or their wives. They look after them and love them, just like your dad does.'

'He's the best dad in the world. Bobby always tells me that. Why can't he come and live with us? We have a spare room.'

'His dad wouldn't let him for a start, and that's his family over there, his mum, his sisters. They're all in it together.'

Ruby's mum hugged her closely, the two of them nestling together, Ruby loving the feel of her crisp clean pyjamas against the warmth of her mum's body.

When her dad returned from making his phone call he wrapped his arms around them both.

'The cops aren't really interested. I didn't think they would be. I tried to tell them what went on and what obviously goes on over there at other times. They said Vincent's already down there, pressing them to locate the two girls, and they're more interested in that. They said he'd told them he'd belted Bobby to get the information out of him. They sounded pretty pleased about it all. Sorry, Ruby Rose, there's not much more I can do. Time for bed for you.'

'Will you tuck me in, Dad, maybe talk for a while?'

He tousled her hair lovingly. 'There's nothing I'd love more.'

CHAPTER 13

The two of them lay next to each other, the floorboards of the treehouse a cool, solid mattress for their bodies. Bobby lay on his side, the painful welts on his back causing him to flinch each time he moved. Ruby looked straight into the dark pools of sadness that filled his eyes. One eye was so swollen and black he could hardly see through it.

He spoke slowly, quietly. 'They brought them back this morning. They weren't even gone for two days.'

'How did they know where to find them?'

'They got them when the train reached Sydney. They were headed straight for King's Cross. Theresa had arranged somewhere for them to stay there, but they never made it.' His one good eye never left hers, and sadness and guilt was written on his face. 'I shouldn't have hinted where they were going. I thought Sydney was a big place, that they wouldn't find them.'

'It doesn't matter, they would've found them anyway.'

'Lynette's dad picked her up from the police station, just after they got back.'

Ruby passed him a hard-boiled lolly. 'What about Theresa?'

'The police brought her back in their car. Dad made Mum get up and pack Theresa's bags, just a few things, and he didn't let her take anything valuable. She won't need much where she's going. That's what he said to Mum.'

'What did your mum do?'

'She was like a robot. My dad pushed her a few times with his hand. "Hurry up," he said, "don't take all day." She never looked at any of us. Didn't look at Theresa or the police. Theresa was begging her.'

Bobby started to cry, the tears squeezing through the slit of one eye and running across his face before joining others falling freely from his good eye. The tears left a damp stain, a small puddle on the weathered boards of the treehouse.

Ruby pulled a lacy hanky from the pocket of her shorts and gently dabbed Bobby's face; for once he let her comfort him, not moving.

'Theresa tried to shake Mum,' he said, continuing with his story. 'She was begging Mum not to let them take her. I tried to stand in front of the door. I yelled at the policeman and I tried to tell him she's not the one doing the bad stuff. He said she needed help, that there was only one place for girls like her and she needs some time to straighten out. They took her away. She was sobbing, Ruby Rose, sobbing like her heart was breaking. I pulled on the policeman's arm. I tried to stop him. I tried to tell him that she never did anything wrong.'

Tears flooded Bobby's face, his words coming out in between huge sobs, his body shaking with fear and distress

Ruby sat up and pulled him towards her so she could wrap her arms around him. She could sense the anguish, the sorrow, the hidden secrets and she rubbed his arms, her touch calming him a little.

His arms were wrapped around his knees, and his feet perched on top of Ruby's. 'Mum just went straight back to that filthy dark bedroom and never said a thing.'

'What did your dad say?'

'He sort of smirked, with that look he gets when he's drunk. He said, "Good riddance to bad rubbish." That's all he said. Then he went outside and drove off somewhere in his car.'

'What are we going to do?'

'There's nothing we can do. They've sent her to the home for girls in the city. They lock them up, make them work and teach them to follow rules. That's what the policeman said, and that she'll get out when she can behave.'

'You know my dad rang the police the other night, but your dad was already down there.'

Bobby looked up. 'He's brave, your dad. He stood between my dad and me. He stopped him from hitting me again, and grabbed the arm that was holding the belt. I wish he was my dad.'

The tears stopped flowing as Bobby calmed, just an occasional gulping sob broke the talk between them.

Ruby wanted to cheer him up, to get his mind off what had happened. 'What do you want to be when you grow up, Bobby?'

'I don't know, nothing, I guess.'

'You have to be somebody. You must want to be something.'

'Nothing.'

'That's stupid. What do you want to be? Or where do you think you'll live?'

'I want to live somewhere where everything is bright, where the sun is always shining in every room. I want a house with lots of windows that the sun will always come in. I'll paint all the chairs yellow. Bright. Sunny.'

After expertly changing the topic, Ruby said, 'I want a big house. It's going to have a lot of rooms, and a toilet and bathroom inside the house. It'll be up a tree, though, like a treehouse, and my kids will have to climb down to go to school.'

'You can't live in a treehouse. That's not real.'

Ruby ignored him. 'When you look out all you'll see will be the tops of the trees and the leaves. You'll be able to see everyone's houses below, and the people, they'll be like tiny ants scurrying around, so far below. Some days I'll even be able to touch the clouds from my treehouse. My kids will all jump out the windows and bounce around on the clouds. Like a trampoline.'

'Clouds aren't solid and you can't jump on them. They're made of water droplets, like crystals hanging in the air. Your kids will fall straight through.'

Ruby scowled at his practical words. 'Bobby, does your house have kids?'

'No. Just lots of sun and yellow furniture.'

'I'm going to have a lot of kids and my husband will be the best dad in the world.'

Bobby smiled now. 'Who'd marry you, Ruby Rose? You're too bossy.'

'My dad says that someone has to make the decisions. He says I'm good at looking after other people and sorting out their problems.'

'You always make me feel better. You can't fix my problems, but I'm really glad you listen to me.'

'You're my best friend in the entire world. Of course I listen to you.'

'I hope you get your treehouse, Ruby Rose, and lots of kids.' Bobby sat up gingerly, the welts on his back stiffening, not moving in tune with his skin.

'I hope you get your yellow house and lots of sun. You can get whatever you want,' she said, 'you just have to keep telling yourself you can do things. Don't ever give up. If you want something bad enough, you can get it.'

'I know, determination, you tell me all the time. Sometimes it's easier for some than others. I just want things to be right. I don't really think about anything else much. I just try to get through each day without getting belted or sent away like Theresa.' His face fell at the reminder and he put his head between his knees, lost in his own thoughts.

Ruby had learned to sit without talking. She knew now that Bobby's problems were so big that sometimes he needed to just sit with her. They didn't need to talk; he just needed her to be there, to listen.

She so desperately wanted to help him, for him to come and live with them. Her dad had talked to her every night since Theresa and Lynette had run away, describing different family situations and explaining how other kids lived. He told Ruby that he and her mother had always tried to protect her, always being careful about who was around her. But he couldn't tell her why the police wouldn't do anything about the beatings next door. She still didn't know why people told her she had to mind her own business, that she couldn't fix everyone's problems, that some kids just didn't have nice homes or families.

Her mum had sat with them, the three of them in a house full of love and security, calmness and the simplicity of an everyday household.

'Remember, Ruby Rose,' her dad had told her when he tucked her in bed the night before, 'it's not money or big houses that make people happy. It's love, and being surrounded by good, honest people. Be happy with the simple things in life and don't want too much.'

'I just want you and Mum to be with me forever,' she mumbled, already half asleep.

Her dad had kissed her goodnight, his hand, as usual, ruffling her hair, before pulling the mosquito net around her bed. 'Goodnight, Ruby Rose, sleep tight.'

'When I'm up in the treehouse it feels like I'm floating. Everything bad is left below. When I climb up the tree, the branches make me feel safe, like the moths in their cocoons. The trunk of the tree and its roots come up from the ground and tell me that they will hold me safe and not let me go. The tree and Ruby Rose make me happy and I like the clean air and the wind that moves through the branches, the leaves across my face. The world below stops and it isn't there any more. If I close my eyes I float above the earth and for a moment I am calm.' Bobby Carlon, August 1975.*

Ruby gently closed the records book, returning it to the rough crate shelf. For once she was silent; her mouth opened twice, but no words came out. Her hand reached out to take the ice block from Bobby.

'I watched you the other day, Ruby Rose,' Bobby said, 'last week when you were all playing cricket in the back-yard.' He sucked hard at his own ice block, the red colour transferring from the ice to his lips.

Ruby slurped noisily, orange juice running down her

chin. 'You should've run faster, they're melting too quickly. You were up here? Why didn't you come and join in?'

The solitude and peace had been a welcome relief for Bobby, who had lain in the treehouse for hours, blocking off his mind from the escalating worries at home. A clear view of the yard had allowed him to watch and enjoy Ruby's family playing and laughing, the backyard cricket match nearly luring him down from his lofty, spying perch.

Cousins, grandparents and other family members who had come for the day all joined in. Young and old spread out across the yard, taking positions, vying for the best hit or bowl. Older ones encouraged the little ones, helping them hold the bat, throwing an easy ball, all in, jostling and laughing, aiming to get the kids the most runs possible.

Ruby's Uncle Tom had hoisted her high on his shoulders and done a jig before sprinting around the yard, running faster each time Ruby squealed with delight. Bobby watched Ruby's uncle as he played tag, and red rover. He waited for him to do something wrong, but he was like Ruby's dad, just a younger version, much like a big kid himself.

Immersing himself in the picture Bobby had imagined that he was part of it. He watched as everyone feasted on huge slices of watermelon, the men joining in with the kids to see who could spit the seeds the furthest. They had all gathered together for a family photo, Ruby's dad pulling silly faces for the camera, her mum pretending to be cranky with him for spoiling the photo.

The daylight faded, the air cooled and still he watched.

Men nursed babies, mothers held toddlers on their hips, older kids bounced little ones on their laps or pushed them on the old swing set. Shadows grew long over the backyard and Bobby had to squint to see, as the visitors piled into the collection of cars that lined the driveway. There were lots of hugs, handshakes and kisses, the laughter and tired happiness drifting up into the treehouse, audible remnants floating on the early-evening air.

Ruby broke into Bobby's thoughts. 'Why didn't you come and join in?' she asked again. 'My dad would've loved it if you had.'

'I just enjoyed watching it all. Besides, your uncle was there.'

'Uncle Tom? He's the kindest man. I just love him. He's my favourite uncle in the world.' Ruby echoed her father's words when she said, 'You know there are lot of good people in the world, Bobby. Not all uncles are bad.'

'There's not many good people in my world.'

Rustling noises in the bushes below the tree made Ruby look down through the slits in the floorboards. Daisy stood in the shade beneath the tree. The cow often heard them or sensed when they were up in the treehouse, and stood guard below, her actions depending on whether it was Bobby or Ruby who wanted to pass.

'It looks like her leg's caught in something.' Ruby peered closer, watching as the cow attempted to lift her leg, trying to move out of the thick shrubs.

Bobby sat up and moved towards the door of the house. 'She's stuck, all right. No use you going down, it'll only make her angry.'

Ruby pulled a face. Even though she had bluffed the cow once, since that day the relationship between her and

Daisy had returned to normal. More than once she had had to run quickly for the closest fence or tree to escape the head swinging and snorting of the angry cow.

Descending effortlessly through the branches, Bobby's hardened feet found their mark quickly on the smooth, worn ladder stairs. He held out his hand and let Daisy smell it before moving slowly, talking softly to the distressed cow, whose leg was held fast with wire that spiralled out of the undergrowth.

'Shhhhh, Daisy, it's me, Bobby. I won't hurt you. I can help you, but you'll have to stand still. Don't struggle because you'll only make it worse.'

The cow's huge brown eyes held still, framed by the longest eyelashes Bobby had ever seen. He looked into them as she stared at him calmly, talking to him without a voice.

Her nose was wide and he patted it, his voice soothing, running his hands along her silky neck. 'Daisy, we can fix this easily. Stand still, though, don't move or you'll pull it tighter.'

Bobby looked carefully, taking in the twisted wire, the way it was caught around the hind leg. He knew that if she decided to panic the wire would tighten, causing all sorts of extra problems.

'SShhhh, Daisy, I can help you, just hold steady.'

He reached down, suddenly a little nervous at being so close to her hind legs that he had so often observed kicking out at flies or other annoyances. Running his hand down her rump and then along her back leg, he used both hands to loosen the wire, wondering how it had managed to twist its way so securely around her leg.

'It's all right, Daisy, this is easy to fix.'

Trying to convince himself as much as reassure the entangled cow, he spoke softly, realising that the wire was not going to come away easily. The old jersey cow stood solidly, only occasionally flicking her head sideways at a fly, or peering around slowly to observe the dark-haired boy crouched in the coolness of the huge tree, working deftly to pull the wire away from her leg.

'Got it, Daisy, just one more bit.'

He twisted and tugged, holding her hoof up to bring the wire under her leg. Standing upright, he tossed the twisted wire into the bush on the other side of the fence, making his way to the front of the cow. Still talking to her, he rubbed the top of her nose, his gentle hands caressing Daisy's wide flat brow. Bobby played gently with the twisty white hair in the centre of her forehead, rubbing hard up behind her ears the way he had often watched Francis do.

'You're a good cow, Daisy. You stood still for me.'

He called out to Ruby, looking upwards at her as she peered down from her safe perch high in the tree. 'You should see her eyes. She has the most amazing brown eyes, and the middle bit looks like a piece of bark.'

Ruby giggled as Daisy bent her head low and pushed her head up and down Bobby's body. The cow rubbed up and down gently, using the side of her head, ensuring that her horns never touched him. His hands scratched her head again and they looked deeply into each other's eyes.

'She understands what I think,' Bobby said.

'I can't believe it. How come she's so nice to you?'

Ruby had descended from the tree, amazed by what she was seeing. Coming up behind Bobby, she spotted a slight flicker in the cow's eyes as the animal turned her gaze from Bobby's face to her own.

'Uh-oh.'

'Holy dooley, Ruby Rose, make a run for it.'

Daisy turned from rubbing up against Bobby's body, her eyes now focused squarely on Ruby's shocked face. The cow's head swung low, saliva flicking through the air as she sidestepped Bobby and made a beeline for Ruby, who was now standing on the shady pathway.

Familiar with the glaring evil in the cow's eye, Ruby started running. Her small bare feet skipped over every tree root and rock as Daisy followed in hot pursuit, head swinging wildly, the gentleness and kindness of the previous moments undone in the blink of an eye. The cow's stare was firmly fixed on Ruby's backside, and the swinging motion of her head, with horns on top, made clear what her motives were when she caught up with the fleeing child in front of her.

The barbed-wire fence and large iron-rung gate loomed ahead, Ruby's last chance of escape. Like something out of a wild-west movie, Ruby straddled the gate and threw herself over it. She turned back, her wide, frightened eyes taking in the cow that was only seconds behind her.

Daisy planted her feet firmly as she came to a sudden stop in front of the gate and let loose a bellowing moo. Her stomping hooves caused a cloud of dust to rise up and spittle flicking from her nose skimmed through the air, landing very close to Ruby, who was thankfully protected on the opposite side of the fence. Ruby lay in the safety of the long grass clutching her stomach, gasping for breath after her panicked sprint.

Minutes later, Bobby's grinning face appeared behind the cow. Daisy turned slowly and looked at him calmly before munching on the long green blades of grass that grew under the gate, only inches from where Ruby lay, glaring angrily at the cow now grazing contently.

Bobby jumped the gate, landing squarely beside her. 'I wouldn't have believed that if I hadn't seen it for myself.' He was trying hard to keep his composure.

'She hates me. I'm sure she wants me dead.'

Bobby couldn't contain his laughter any longer. It was a rare moment, and one that Ruby would never forget. His entire face crinkled up, his eyes were alight, and the most amazing laugh came forth. He laughed loudly for so long that he ended up sitting down in the grass, buckled over, tears streaming down his face, loud guffaws, hoots of laughter ripping from within, belly laughs Ruby had never heard from Bobby before. He rolled in the long grass, trying to talk, but no words came out.

It was infectious, and before long the two of them were laughing together, one stopping to try and recap the event before looking at the other and starting all over again.

Ruby tried to explain it that night to her dad, but the laughter started again and all she could see was Bobby rolling around in the grass, delirious, happy just to be a kid. It was as though all his woes had vanished and it was only Bobby and her, happy and trouble free.

Daisy had not even lifted her head and had only continued to chew the grass noisily near their feet, taking in the scene. As if she understood.

CHAPTER 15

The school year was already off to a terrible start for Bobby. He swore a lot when he talked now. 'That bastard math teacher Mr Mac has it in for me,' he told Ruby. 'If he canes me one more time, I'm going to get the cane from his hand and break it over his fucking head. I'll see how he likes that.'

Ruby, unsure of what to say, looked down, scowling at what she thought were unnecessary swearwords. She watched Bobby warily as he cleaned the silkworm boxes, his gentle hands lifting the munched-up leaves with the tiny white worms clinging to them onto the treehouse table. He stopped to pick up one that had dropped from its precarious perch, carefully sliding a fresh leaf under its delicate body, before placing it back with the other grazing worms.

'Why does your teacher hit you?'

'He says I'm stupid, that I'm dumb and I should be kept down. Some of the girls laugh at me. Not the boys, though. They all think it's pretty cool that I get caned.

One of them even bought me a bottle of soft drink at lunchtime. He said I must be pretty tough 'cause I don't even flinch when Mr Mac canes me.'

'Do you think when I'm a judge I can arrest teachers who cane kids?'

'It's not against the law, Ruby Rose. They can do what they like to us, just like all adults can. They can do whatever they want to kids and no one will stop them. It's the same for Theresa.'

'Have you seen her?'

'One of the boys at school knows another girl who's in the home. It's supposed to be real bad, with some really mean girls there. This girl reckons that Theresa has run away and been caught twice since she's been in there, and she just keeps getting into more and more trouble.'

'At least she's safe, away from your uncle. Is he staying long this time?'

'He seems settled in and he's got a lot of bags with him but I'm not sure how long he's staying. He's out working during the day and I don't know where he goes at night. Sometimes he goes out with Dad. Who knows, who cares?'

This was a new side to Bobby and Ruby was having trouble getting used to it. He pretended that he didn't care about anything much any more, but she knew he did.

Ruby and Bobby had always talked about everything. She had sat with him and listened when he talked and cried over Theresa. And then there was all the upset over Lynette and her perverted old grandfather. Bobby had been so angry and upset with all of that, but now when things happened he just shrugged his shoulders and told her he didn't care about much any more.

He told her the boys at school were his friends, and no, he hadn't told them anything about what happened at home. 'Lots of them have shit happening, too,' he said. 'I'm not the only one, Ruby Rose. One day you'll grow up and see what really goes on. I don't give a shit about much anymore.'

Ruby had tried to put on her most adult voice. 'I don't think you should swear like that, Bobby, and I can't believe that you're hiding cigarettes up here.'

'Hey, Ruby Rose, silkworm secrets. We have lots of secrets now, never to be told to anyone. Not that it'd matter, no one gives a shit anyway.'

* * *

BOBBY HAD BEEN at school the day they took his little sister Sally and his mother. He arrived home in the afternoon to an empty house. Tight-lipped and cursing the filth that had built up in the darkened main bedroom, Vincent, the head of the now disintegrated family, informed Bobby that neither his sister nor his mother would be returning. Bobby was now in charge of looking after himself.

'Where did they go,' he asked his father. 'Where? I didn't even get to say goodbye. When can I see Sally?'

His father towered over him. 'We took them away to the crazy house, both of them, locked them up. They aren't allowed visitors, either, so don't even try to find them. I called the ambulance this morning. Luckily your uncle was here to help out.'

Bobby's head spun around as he heard the familiar

voice behind him. His uncle blocked the doorway, standing solid.

'Where are they?' Bobby spat the question at him.

'Take it easy, young Bobby,' his uncle said. 'I know it's a shock. Vince, why don't you leave this to me.'

Mike Carlon put his arm tightly around Bobby's shoulders. 'Your poor old mum, the courts have committed her. They say she's criminally insane. And Sally, well, we always knew, didn't we? Not quite the full quid, eh. She's better off where she is. Both of them are. There's no visitors allowed where they are, no family even. They'll look after them real good, give them all the right tablets, and make them better. They'll look after both of them, let them be together.'

Mike's fingers dug into Bobby's shoulder. 'Those places are used to caring for girls like Sally,' he said. 'They're both better off in there. It's supposed to be a really nice place, but no visitors are allowed. You hear me, Bobby? Don't go trying to find them because no one's allowed in. They say it upsets them too much to have visitors and they want what's best for them. Now you just have to get used to being the only one left here. Think yourself lucky you haven't been cursed with all the ills and problems the others had.'

Bobby felt the coldness of his uncle's fingers through his shirt. He stood silently, still in shock.

Mike put both hands heavily on his shoulders, facing him, his cold eyes inches away from his own. 'Remember this. They're staying where they are. No fuss, because you're a man now, so it's about time you started acting like one. Got it? No carrying on, just life as usual. And if you try and visit or find them, the home will make it worse for them. They'll lock them up separately and won't let them see each other. They said that if anyone tries to visit, they'll lock Sally in a dark room away from your mother. So just forget about that.'

Vincent used his formidable height and his angry, twitching face, to intimidate Bobby and shout orders at him. 'Clean this shit up, Bobby,' he said, looking around the dark bedroom. 'I want it spotless. It stinks in here. Your uncle and I are off to the shop because it's going to be a busy day tomorrow. Lots of prep. Let's go, Mike.'

Vincent grasped Bobby's arm. 'Remember, no complaints, it's the way it's gotta be. I should've had your mum committed years ago.'

Bobby stood silently, his head reeling, the words bouncing around in his head. The two men walked out through the back door, and moments later he heard the car take off down the driveway, tyres squealing as it made its entrance onto the main road.

Walking through the empty rooms, the echo of his footsteps resounded through the hollow shell that had once been their home. Something shifted in him, like a pain, a tingling that started in his fingers, moving through him until it filled his entire body. An unbearable ache, a dullness, a heaviness that spun in his head, like a claw had reached in and taken every memory, cutting a frayed, jagged family thread that had bound him to the others.

He stood in the doorway of Sally's room. Blurred visions, like ghosts, appeared in front of him, and he slumped onto the small bed where he had lain so often cuddling his little sister, protecting her, keeping her safe. Her clothes, her belongings, her few treasured toys had all disappeared. He looked at her pillow. Her little Twinkie doll that she loved so much was underneath it, and her hairclip was lying on top. He pushed his face into her sheets, breathing deeply, taking in the smells from where her small body had last lain.

If only he hadn't gone to school today. Could he have stopped his father and uncle sending his mother and sister away? His father had always said he was going to put them in a home. 'That's where they belong,' he used to say, 'with all the others just like them.'

The 'cuckoo home'; he had said it often enough. First Theresa had gone, and now Sally.

To Bobby it felt as though his mother had been missing for a long time; had she ever really been there? He searched his memory, but there was nothing. Only the dark, damp smell that still permeated the house from the horrible cheap scent she sprinkled on her clothes, trying to mask the odour of illness, or whatever it was that pervaded her bedroom.

It was over. He felt the finality of it, the breaking of his mind, the tautness, the ongoing fear that had been with him forever. Now he had nothing. He knew he couldn't stay; he had to go and leave this evil house forever.

So many times he had planned his escape in his mind, only to be stopped by the thought of leaving Sally. Now she was gone. He knew that between the two men—his father talking for years about getting them both committed, and the contacts with important people that his uncle had—there was no saving her.

He had seen his uncle cover things up before, using his influence to make things go the way he wanted. Only last year Mike had bragged about how he had stepped in and helped the man who delivered their meat.

Gus Smithfield, a good friend of Bobby's father, who often drank with Vincent and Mike out the back of the butcher's shop, had been drunk when he ran over old Mr Parkinson who was riding home on his pushbike. The collision had broken both of the old man's legs, smashed his bicycle and put him in hospital for a couple of months.

Mike had bragged about how knowing all the right people in high places had paid off, and Gus Smithfield had been back behind the wheel of the delivery truck that same week, grinning and waving like nothing had happened. Mr Parkinson's hospital bills were all taken care of, new furniture was delivered to his home, and life returned to normal.

Mike loved telling Bobby and whoever else was listening that Mr Parkinson had even had a new bike delivered to his door. 'All ready for when his legs are fit for pedalling again,' Mike said. 'It's not what you know, young Bobby, it's who you know. You just remember that. When you need your good old Uncle Mike to drag you out of trouble, you need advice about the ladies, or you get yourself in trouble, you come and see me. I know everyone.'

Bobby felt sick every time Mike spoke to him. He'd sit silently, sullenly, never replying until his father thumped him.

'Your uncle's speaking to you,' his father would say. 'Answer.'

'Yes sir, I'm listening.'

And Mike would reply, 'Good for you, young Bobby. You're the only sane one in this whole family.'

Now, as Bobby lay looking at the mess around him, he wondered if he was actually insane too. Voices bounced around his head, and everything in his mind felt tight, like his head was about to explode. His heart thumped and his body reverberated with each pulse, like his insides were banging from one side of his body to the other. His eyes flitted nervously and he looked through blurred vision at his surroundings: wooden floorboards, flaking paint on the ceiling, a print on the wall, Mary holding the baby Jesus, confusing smells, tattered heavy curtains, a sliver of light coming through the window.

He had to get away. Leave. Get out quick. Now. Before they came back. He was nearly sixteen, they couldn't stop him, and besides, where he was going no one would find him. The plan had been in his head for years; he had been waiting for this day to come. A day when there was no Sally at home. The threats had always been there: the 'cuckoo house' for both his mum and baby sister.

His small bag was ready now and everything he needed was in it. Taking the money earned from odd jobs from its hiding place, he took one last look at the small bed where Sally had spent so much of her life. Tears pricked his eyes, but he willed them away. There was nothing to cry about now. They had taken everything from him. He had nothing left.

* * *

SLOWLY HE CLIMBED up the old mulberry tree into the treehouse, his legs heavy. Ruby had gone out with her mum and he knew he would be alone for one last time in the only place where he had, just sometimes, been able to catch rare moments of peacefulness. He stayed for a short while only, leaving a small item and a note.

He knew Ruby would be angry with him, and sad because he had left. But time would move on and she would find her own path, her own life. Ruby had lots of people to care for her and she would soon forget him.

Lying on his back, the coolness of the breeze and floorboards beneath him, he peered through the layers of glossy dark leaves that hung heavily with the fruit that had so often stained his clothes, feet and hands. He would leave all his secrets here, and the wind would take them, scatter them over the paddocks beyond: his childhood, gone. Tears welled up again, but he held them back. Through the windows he could see the clouds scuttling across the sky, willing him to follow their direction.

He descended slowly until his feet were planted firmly on the track below, the dirt and leaves speckled with shadows formed by the sinking sun in the western sky.

Daisy stood like a farewell sentry, her eyes never leaving his, silent and still. The last touch of his childhood was his hand on her forehead, twirling her white forelock hair, scratching and rubbing her face. The eyes of a young boy peered deeply into the endless depths of the cow's dark brown eyes, understanding as they looked back into his. It was as if she knew that one person could endure only so much. That sometimes it was a good thing to run away from problems—evil, insurmountable, unfixable and dangerous problems.

The cow rubbed gently against Bobby's side. He opened his mouth but no words came; instead, his thoughts rattled around inside his head. *Goodbye, Daisy, be nice to Ruby Rose.* And with that he was gone.

CHAPTER 16

No one came looking for him. There was no knock on the door from Vincent or Mike. They knew he had gone, but they also knew there was no use looking for him.

Vincent let Francis know in no uncertain terms that he wasn't going to search for Bobby. 'I couldn't care less,' he said. 'He's big enough to look after himself and he'll be miles away by now. If he wants to go, that's his problem, not mine. He's nearly sixteen. If he gets in trouble it's his fault. Let's see how big a man he is without us to help him. Bugger him, ungrateful, lazy little bastard.'

Francis tried to talk to Vincent. 'I think you should report it to the police. He's only a kid.'

'You can report it if you want, but I'm telling you now, they won't care. They already know I'm not chasing him. By the time we find him he'll be sixteen anyway and then he can do what he wants.'

Vincent was right; the police were not interested.

'His uncle, he's a good man,' the constable said to

Francis when he headed down to the police station to report the incident. 'He came and told us what happened. The mother and sister are better off in care. That's why they have those places for people like them. And boys, well, we all know what they're like, they leave home all the time. He'll get work somewhere and then have to figure out his own life. It'll be good for him. Young people these days, they just don't appreciate all the things their families do for them.'

'I don't think he was treated very well at home,' Francis said.

'What, just because Vincent disciplined him? That poor man, what with the crazy wife and daughters. Jesus, he works his guts out down at that butcher's shop and not one of them appreciates it. He's lucky Mike stands by him and works with him. He'll help him out.

The constable leaned towards Francis, the front bench of the police station separating them. 'We're his mates, and we all have to stick together, help each other out. We all have a few ales together, you see. So it's probably best if you keep your nose out of your neighbour's business. Maybe tighten the reins a bit on your own wife and daughter instead of wasting time on others. Next your daughter will be running off like that eldest of Vince's did. Girls, they just need to know their place; to know who's boss.'

Anger simmered and bile rose in his throat as the policeman stood up straight and gave him a wink. 'Gotta keep them in line, isn't that right?'

Francis turned away, angry words on the tip of his tongue but knowing it would be a waste of breath. There were so many like the constable, still with the overriding prejudice that women were inferior, that they should be treated as such, and that their main role was to look after the men and keep the house.

It was useless. He had tried but the police didn't care; they were on Vincent's side and considered him the victim, not his children or wife. It was the poor butcher who had been hard done by, unlucky with family, but lucky to have his brother to help him.

Francis headed home, knowing that he had to talk to Ruby Rose. She had to stop going down to the police station because it wasn't helping. Perhaps Bobby was better off away from it all. He was pretty smart, resilient. He would survive; perhaps do well. But how was he going to convince Ruby? So headstrong, always wanting to solve problems, and outraged that Bobby had just left without talking to her.

* * *

A MONTH PASSED, and Ruby still hadn't shown her father the note or item that Bobby had left her.

'He didn't really have a choice, did he, Ruby Rose?' Francis said to her one day. 'What did you want him to do, keep copping it? What with his mum gone, and Sally, he really didn't have anything to stay for.'

'What about me? We were best friends. Why didn't he ask me for help? He could've stayed here with us. You could've put him on at work. We could've helped him. I would've taught him his schoolwork. Why didn't he ask me for help?'

'He's nearly sixteen, for goodness' sake. I wasn't much older than that when I went off to war. Sometimes boys just have to grow up quicker, stand on their own two feet. It's time for you to accept that he's gone, Ruby Rose.'

'I want him to come back.' Tears streamed down her face as she held onto her dad, who hugged her tightly.

'I know you do, but it just isn't going to happen. Sometimes things are hard to accept, but you have to get on with it.'

'Do you think he's found somewhere to live? Somewhere to sleep? What about food?'

'He's pretty tough, and he's had to deal with a lot in his life already. Maybe he's found a treehouse somewhere, a quiet safe place. He'll be all right. He's better off out of here, and besides, they're moving out anyway.'

'What? When?'

'There was a van there today,' Francis said. 'I think the house is empty. They emptied the sheds and the flat down the back. Vincent's closed the butcher's shop and Lewis told me the two of them, Vincent and Mike, are moving down south. Down near Melbourne.'

* * *

THE WOODEN STEPS leading up the tree trunk were a bit loose as Ruby climbed up to the treehouse. Stopping halfway, she rubbed her hand over the spot in the bark where they had carved their names. The distance between the steps were shorter and she realised it was because her legs had grown; they were so much longer now than years ago, when she and Bobby had first established the Silkworm Club.

A noise above her caused her to look skywards. Perhaps he was up there, waiting for her, holding ice blocks for the both of them, waiting to tell her about his adventures. But today, like every other day, the treehouse was empty—apart from the red-eyed possum perched high in the furthest, darkened corner.

The container lay untouched, the food still intact. No one had opened it; no runaway had been so hungry that he'd eaten the Vegemite sandwiches. The small lemonade bottle, still unopened, was also standing in exactly the same position she had left it.

Peering through the spying gap, Ruby watched the two brothers next door as they walked around the backyard, picking up shovels, tyres, metal drums, anything left and throwing it all into the trailer attached to Vincent's car. How many times had she watched them, hating them both?

The last time she had watched them was the afternoon that Bobby had run away. It had been late, and she'd been upset and confused about the letter and package he had left for her up in the treehouse. The light had been fading, but she was drawn to watch the two brothers in the back-yard next door. They were arguing. Vincent had been extremely agitated, pacing up and down, waving his hands in the air and yelling at Mike. A few words drifted up to her, and later that night she wrote them carefully in the records book, along with a description of what she had seen.

Her keen eyes tried to take in the situation and events that had passed, but everything had become blurry and mixed up. The note from Bobby, the panicky feeling she got when she thought the two men next door might spot her up in the tree, the package he had left her. She had lain in the dim light, her stomach churning, confused and upset at what was happening.

Now the two men were going, their trailer full of rubbish for the dump, the yard raked clear, the veranda empty, and the house and sheds devoid of any furniture or belongings. Walking around the now empty yard, they checked behind the sheds, making sure they had left nothing. The smell of the cigarettes they both smoked constantly wafted through the still air.

Wishing she could hear all of their conversation she strained to listen as they stopped walking but continued talking, standing close together. Their body language indicated that they were still agitated and angry and her stomach churned as Mike spat on the ground before taking out his handkerchief to polish the rounded emblem on the bonnet of his car.

Vincent closed the back door and took one last look around before they both got into their cars and drove slowly down the driveway, Mike exiting last. His car tossed up clouds of dust, the tyres squealing loudly as he reached the bitumen and sped off down the road behind Vincent.

Ruby lay still on the floorboards watching the clouds. Each day the sky was becoming more visible as the mulberry tree dropped more of its leaves in preparation for the colder months ahead. The silkworm boxes were all gone, the spinning block her dad had made for her and Bobby the only sign left that there had once been a thriving silkworm hatchery here in the lofty treehouse.

Peering down at her, the possum watched intently, waiting for her to leave. Bobby would have liked to see him.

Last year she had helped him hand-rear a baby possum he had found, its mother more than likely the squashed carcass out on the road in front of their houses. Together they had fed it milk through an eyedropper until it was big enough to eat pieces of apple and pear. Bobby had named it Ringo, and sang the hit song 'You're Sixteen' over and over to it. Ringo sometimes nuzzled into Bobby's neck, and liked nothing better than to climb inside his shirt, pressing up against his skin.

Ringo had survived, and when he was big enough they decided it was time to set him free. When they had first pushed him out onto a branch, the possum didn't want to go. He stood still, his big eyes staring at them until Bobby gently prodded him along with his hand. With one last look, the possum scampered off, climbing high into the tree, big and strong enough now to fend for itself.

Sometimes, if they sat quietly, Ringo would make his way down the tree and sit on Bobby's shoulder, taking pieces of fruit from his hand, before quickly exiting the treehouse and returning to his own spot further up in amongst the smaller branches.

Ruby knew that this was Ringo watching her, not coming close, just following her every move.

A voice from below called up to her. 'Come down, Ruby Rose, it's getting dark, the mosquitos will eat you alive.'

'I'm coming, Dad,' she called back, taking one last look around the empty treehouse, one last look at Ringo. She wiped away the tears with the back of her hand and made her way slowly out the small doorway and down the huge trunk.

Her dad stood at the bottom of the tree, his feet

sunken in the thick leaf litter. Squeezing her shoulders, he kissed the top of her head. 'Time for dinner and clean-up.'

They walked slowly up the overgrown path, Francis' arm around Ruby as they headed towards the warm lights of the house and the aroma of dinner cooking. There was no need for words, each knowing what the other was thinking. There was nothing left to say.

PART II

Ruby drove carefully up the windy dirt driveway, the car struggling, tyres sliding and spinning in the mud with the weight of the heavily laden trailer bouncing along behind. She reminded herself that on this first day of the new millennium she was starting a new life. It was a new year.

She wound down the windows, the cold air refreshing on her skin. In the rear vision mirror she could see her dad grinning in the car behind, enjoying watching her try to traverse the steep, heavily rutted pathway to her new home. His old four-wheel drive travelled slowly but steadily, well used to the ruggedness of off-road driving.

Eventually the vehicles reached flatter, level ground, both drivers slowing, allowing time to take in the amazing view stretched out across the western reaches of Ruby's new property. Grass grew in the middle of the track and cowpats blotted the earth, some unavoidable, squelching under the tyres, the tread firmly imprinted in their shape.

As they rounded the last corner, the bushes and trees

hid what lay ahead, and the valley view was concealed. Ruby knew already that this was her favourite part of the property: the heavily timbered grove, with lush knee-deep kikuyu grass offering a carpet of green leading up to the towering trees that formed the boundary of the house yard. The cars passed under a massive cassia tree, its trunk chunky with rough bark reaching up to branches that stretched out in a wide circle. Pink flowers weighed down the limbs, sagging, pointing towards the brightly coloured spread of fallen flowers covering the ground below.

Other large trees, in no particular line or order, helped form the thick canopy, creating a tunnel entrance to the yard, the driveway curving and finding its way in through the shady entry. Huge jacarandas, leopard trees with dappled smooth trunks, and pepperinas with red berries lighting up the green foliage towered over smaller flowering trees. The air was cool and fresh beneath the foliage, sunlight filtering sporadically through a few small gaps on the edges of the cluster. After a while the trees thinned a little, revealing the old worker's cottage perched on a small hummock, facing the expansive view across the valley.

The two cars pulled up next to the back stairs and Ruby jumped out. Excited, she quickly walked back to the four-wheel drive, opening the driver's door for her dad.

'Jeez, I thought I was going to have to get out and give you a push,' Francis said, shoving a tattered hat on his head. He swung his legs slowly around to the step of the car before easing himself gently onto the ground.

Ruby had the walking stick ready for him and held his

arm, steadying him on the uneven ground. 'Bloody hell,' she teased him, 'you're starting to look like an old man.'

'You're so funny, Ruby Rose. Wait till you're eighty-four, you might need more than a walking stick. Yep, we're all getting old. No complaining, though, because the alternative is not good.' He gave a small chuckle, throwing his spare arm around her shoulders, squeezing tightly.

'Thanks so much for helping me bring all my stuff up here, Dad. I'll be able to get in and sort everything out now.'

'It's good to drive again, even if it is only up your windy driveway, and the old Land Cruiser still goes like a rocket. How about we have a walk around before you take me back down?'

Slowly, arm in arm, they walked around the side of the house.

Francis stopped constantly, using his stick to turn over the numerous pieces of wood and concrete that littered the yard. 'You're going to be busy cleaning up, Ruby Rose. What a ramshackle old property. I'm still a little surprised.' He turned towards her. 'You've always gone for modern, concrete houses with neat ordered yards. I'd say this is just about the opposite of your last place.'

'Exactly, Dad, this is the big change for me. I need to get my life in order. The yard and house will keep me busy, and I intend scaling back a little at work. I need to get my stress levels down, make changes, and lead a different life than the last twenty years. No more hustle and rushing, this is all about what I want to do.'

'I'm not saying it's a bad thing, and this place is amazing. It's just that it's so unruly and overgrown, with mess everywhere. You've always had everything in straight lines, ordered, and your days follow such strict routine.'

'I know, isn't it exciting? Finally, and I don't have to answer to anyone.'

'Do you miss him? Do you miss Ben, Ruby Rose?' The old man had stopped walking and stood gazing out across the valley.

'Sometimes at night I think it would be nice to have some company, maybe just someone to chat to, talk about the day at work, projects to do around the house, just the general things in life. The point is, Dad, Ben stopped talking to me properly years before it all ended. He was really only there in body, not spirit. If it wasn't about his work, money or investments, he just wasn't interested.'

'Or other women.' Francis scowled. 'I could never work out how he had us all so fooled.'

'I think that was one of the hardest things for him, at least when he came clean about it all. He really did think a lot of you and Mum. He didn't want to hurt either of you.'

'He should've thought about that before he went prancing around all over the place like a single man. And besides, never mind us, you were the one he hurt the most. Seeing that woman behind your back and then coming home, acting like everything was normal.'

'I know, I know. I was so caught up in my career, though. Working late, pushing myself and letting myself get so stressed all the time. Sometimes I wasn't the easiest person to live with either, Dad. And like he said near the end, I'd stopped needing him. I'd become so independent and he'd started to feel like there wasn't any reason for him to be there.'

The old man's voice was gravelly. 'Perhaps he

should've spent more time at home instead of flying around the countryside chasing criminals.'

'It's part of his job. I knew that when we got married. Honestly, when I look back now I can see I was just as much to blame as he was. I was by myself so much that I just started to not need him anymore. I was so caught up in work—'

'And he wasn't?' Francis interjected.

'It just got messy, too routine, and by the time we realised, it was too late. Neither of us was in love with the other, and by then he'd met Sue. I don't hate him, Dad. We had a lot of good years together.'

'You pushed yourself too hard. You can't always fix everyone's problems. Those kids you let yourself get hung up over, well, a lot of them anyway, were just too damaged. Unfixable.'

'I know, Dad, and I've learned to accept that over the years. I guess it was also not being able to have my own children. I started to think of the kids I was helping as my own. I wanted to bring them home and fix all their problems.'

'You should've adopted. I never wanted to ask at the time, but how come you didn't?'

'Ben refused. He said it was fate, it just wasn't meant to be, and he didn't want a kid that wasn't his. I tried to talk to him so many times. You know how badly I wanted kids. And now look at him, two of his own he absolutely dotes on. I always knew he'd make a good dad.' Ruby smiled at Francis. 'He's a good man, Dad.'

'It's not too late. Your mother was nearly forty when she finally had you, and I was a bit older, as you know.

God, I think of all those years we tried, waited. I used to look to the heavens and pray: *Just let us have one.'*

'Jesus, you, Dad, praying?' Ruby stifled a laugh. 'It's a wonder the sky didn't fall in on you.'

His hand rested on her shoulder, stopping to get his breath. 'I know, it's the only time in my life I ever prayed. Well, then, and when your mum was dying.'

Ruby patted his hand. 'No, I've decided it just wasn't meant to be. It's okay, I'm happy, probably happier now than I've been in a long time.' She shaded her eyes, looking over the valley below, so green, its undulating hills dotted with cows. 'I know I'm going to love it here. It's a lot of work, but now I have more time. The only problem is, you're not here with me.'

'Now, we've been over this a million times. I'm good where I am. Your mum and I decided a long time ago we didn't want to be a burden to you. Okay, so everyone in there is old, but, hey, most of us are still pretty active. It's nice and flat to go for a stroll, and I look forward to playing bowls each week. Besides, it's a good size, that little house, and I'm still surrounded by all of your mum's things.'

'I guess you're not really that far away, either. As long as I can see you each week,' She took a breath and squinted suspiciously. 'And as long as you ring me when you need something, or if you're not well.'

'You don't need to worry because we all look out for each other. There's always someone walking past, calling out, checking to see I'm all right. Your mother and I had it all planned, that's why we moved there years ago. We knew that if one went the other would be settled and looked after. You have to be practical, Ruby Rose. We can't live forever.'

'Don't talk like that.' She cuddled in under his arm. 'You'll live until you're one hundred and one.'

'I doubt it, not the way I feel sometimes. Some days I already feel like I'm a hundred years old.'

Ruby pulled an old wrought-iron chair out for Francis, leaving him to sit quietly for a moment while she got them both a cool drink from inside the house. Watching him through the dusty kitchen window, she thought how much older he looked since her mum had died. Mary's illness had taken a toll on both of them, but more so her dad, who had cared for her up until the end. They had both been there with her when she took her final breath, Francis sitting for hours afterward, lingering by Mary's body, not wanting to let her go.

Ruby had begged him to come and live with her in her big home on the canal, using the argument that she was now by herself, the house was huge, he'd have his own space in the separate granny flat downstairs, it was close to the water. She had gone on and on, but Francis had become more stubborn with age and he had stuck to his decision to stay in the retirement village, claiming he enjoyed his bowls, there was plenty to do and he felt settled. It had been his and Mary's home.

'Cold fizzy lemonade.' Ruby placed the two glasses down on the round table and sat down, the shade from the house providing a cool spot. 'It reminds me of when I was a kid.'

Francis's shaky hand lifted the glass, his bushy eyebrows lowering as he closed his eyes and enjoyed the first cold sip. 'Remember the ice blocks your mother used to keep stocked in the freezer? What a treat. I liked having one of them myself on a hot day. Where have the years gone, Ruby Rose? Sometimes I have to stop and think about how old I am. When I wake up in the morning, before I move this tired old body or look in that blasted mirror, I swear I'm still a young man. It just feels like yesterday. I don't know how it's gone so fast.'

Ruby watched his shaky hands. 'It's a bit scary. I feel the same, like I'm still eighteen. The years rush by, and the busier I am the quicker time passes. I'm really looking forward to just working part time, hopefully slowing it all up.'

'As they say, take time to smell the roses. I think that was one good thing about growing up when you did—life was a lot slower and we weren't so rushed. When you were a kid you spent the entire time playing. The days drifted by, they didn't *fly* by. Now it's so different. People are always busy and rushing. Us oldies, we often have a bit of a chuckle as we watch you young ones rushing around, trying to make so much money.'

'Well, you have to make a good wage these days, Dad. Living is not cheap.'

'I know, but you ought to know'—he looked down, eyes nearly closing—'you know now that money does not buy you happiness. Look at all the money you two had, and what good did it do?'

'You're right, as usual.' She rolled her eyes at him. 'My happiest days were when Ben and I were first married and we lived in that tiny little cottage, actually just a bit smaller than this one. We were really happy there. We didn't have much, but it didn't matter.'

'It's true. Look at the little house we lived in as a family all those years.' His eyes became misty. 'Happiest days of my life, sitting out on that back step, waiting for you to come in from playing.'

'Some of my best memories are from when we sat around the table at night, talking, laughing—you, Mum and me. God, I was lucky, Dad, you two were just the best parents anyone could ever ask for.'

'Ah, we got by. We didn't have a lot. Not much money and we thought we were just the best when we bought that big black-and-white television.'

They sat reminiscing, laughing together, recalling the many funny incidents that had occurred over the years.

'God, it's great to have a good belly laugh.' Francis's laugh was so loud that some of the cows in the paddock lifted their heads to peer at the two of them. 'I think you should call that cow Daisy.' He pointed with his craggy old finger.

Ruby laughed. 'No way, she might take a disliking to me. These cows are friendly. They like me.'

'I need to get up, Ruby Rose. The old bones are stiffening up and you still need to drive me back down the mountain. I'm glad you can use my old ute up here because it's not much use to me these days.'

Francis grasped the walking stick, using it to push

himself up out of the chair. He moved slowly, his body riddled with arthritis, the consequence of old age as well as the damage done by decades of working with barrows and concrete. With their arms linked, leaning on each other, they walked slowly to the grassy area in front of the house.

'You'll never get sick of that view.' He waved his stick across the air in front of them.

From where they stood, they could see the grassy bank sloping down; a huge jacaranda tree filtering the sunlight, creating a shady area in front of the house. Other large trees framed the view: pines with leaves that hung like long needles, the bark glowing pink, their tiny cone-like seeds littering the ground below. Further to the right, three massive bunya pines posed a symmetrical stand, their dome-shaped crowns rising over the top of other trees, acting as lookouts, the elders of the forest.

'They must be over one hundred and twenty, probably a hundred and thirty feet tall.' Francis shaded his eyes, looking high up into the lance-shaped leaves that formed a thick barrier around the trunk and far-reaching branches.

'How high is that, Dad?'

'Oh, in your language today, roughly maybe forty metres.' He gazed up into the branches. 'I'd love to know how old they are.'

'They're beautiful, but you can't climb them or walk under them without shoes on. Their leaves are so spiky. The real-estate guy told me that they drop huge nuts that you can eat.'

'Yeah, that would be right, Ruby Rose. When we were kids we cooked them up. I think my dad used to roast them over the coals of the fire. The nut's about as big as a football,' he said, using his hands to demonstrate the size, 'but if it hasn't broken when it hits the ground you'll need to pull it apart. You have to rip into the large part and get all the small nuts out.'

'What do they taste like?'

'Much like a chestnut,' he said. 'They're pretty good, but you'll have to watch out for when they drop because it's only certain times of the year. You'll know it, though. Make sure you don't get hit on the head by one, and watch out for those bloody spikes. We used to try and climb those trees, but like you say, it's near impossible. Spikes everywhere.'

They stood peering up into the horizontal branches of the biggest bunya tree, the dark green foliage highlighted by the brilliance of a clear summer sky.

'These trees are sacred to the Aborigines,' Francis said. 'My old man told me once that he could remember them all coming together for some sort of festival, a dance ceremony, those singing parties they have.'

'Where was that, Dad?'

'You know, it probably wasn't that far from here. He came from around here, maybe just a bit further inland. He said there were hundreds of these trees and that before the white fellas cut most of them down, the Aboriginal people would come from faraway places. They'd meet and gather around the trees, pick the fruit and have a big party, all around the fire.

'Can you imagine it? I wonder if they did it here.' Ruby closed her eyes, trying to visualise what it must have been like a hundred years ago, when Aborigines perhaps sat in the shade of the older trees here on her property, feasting on the bunya nuts.

'We stuffed them up, we sure stuffed them up.' Francis started moving again, hunched over, his once fit and agile body now struggling with the effort of walking over uneven ground. 'I've got to keep moving, Ruby Rose. I'm worried that if I stop I won't start up again.'

He walked further, determined to have a look around, breathing in the clear hilltop air, the country aroma of cowpats mixed with the smell of the bush. Stopping once again, they sat down on a log seat, positioned by the previous owners to take in the best part of the view.

'Look at that, it takes your breath away.' Francis looked out to the east.

'I love it, it's like I'm up in the trees looking through the foliage at the world below.' Ruby shaded her eyes, gazing out across the valley.

'Now, have you learned the names of those mountains yet?'

'I know the biggest one is Mount Tibrogargan and that they're volcanic plugs.'

'You've always known that, that's not a new fact.'

'I'm going to look them up when I get a chance. By the time you come up here next I'll be able to tell you the whole history of the area, and I'll know the names of all the mountains.'

The volcanic plugs known as the Glasshouse Mountains rose up from the floor of the valley, creating a spectacular backdrop to the rolling hills that dropped off beyond the huge trees in Ruby's front yard.

'Are you sure you won't come and live up here with

me?' She put her head on his shoulder and wrapped her hands around his arm as she cuddled in.

'Don't start that again. I'll be fine. I'll come and stay sometimes. You'll see plenty of me.' The old man rose from the seat, shaking his head at the scenery. 'You do have the best view in the world, though.'

Francis would have settled in nicely up here, with the country air, always something to do, but he knew he would end up being a burden to Ruby, and he needed to be near that blasted doctor. The pains and aches in his bones weren't the only problem. Lately there had been a few secretive visits to the doctor about the chest pains he had started experiencing. There was no way he was going to tell Ruby, though. What could she do anyway? She had enough on her plate, what with being by herself and sorting out this place. If only there had been a brother or sister for her.

Francis worried that when he went, Ruby would be alone. She wouldn't have any close family to lean on. There were cousins, whom she saw sometimes, but that wasn't the same as having a brother or sister. He looked at her, a young, beautiful woman, and his heart swelled with pride as her gorgeous green eyes held his. There was still a small smattering of freckles across her nose, which he knew she hated and often covered with makeup. Her wavy hair, just like her mother's, was no longer blonde but brown, and today it was pulled back into a bouncy ponytail, revealing her smiling face.

'Face of an angel,' he muttered, starting to walk unsteadily around the back of the house. 'Just one look at the grove out the back before we go, Ruby Rose.'

They stood for ages looking upwards at the canopy

that joined together above them, forming the entry to the house yard.

'Look at that, Dad.' She pointed up into the high reaches of a massive poinciana tree, its horizontal branches as thick as a man's body, stretched out and entwined with the branches of other nearby trees.

Francis walked under the tree to get a better look. 'Looks like there's been a treehouse up there at some stage. Not much left of it now, though. Those trees, they were always great climbing trees.'

'Do you remember the treehouse Bobby and I had, Dad?'

Of course I do, it's where you spent most of your childhood days. You two were great mates. Did you ever hear what happened to him after they all left?'

She shook her head. 'I ran into Lynette. Do you remember Lynette Smyth, who lived near us?'

'Ah yes, about three doors up the road, next to the Corrigans.'

'Yes, that's them. Well, I saw Lynette at a funeral.'

'Whose funeral?'

'One of the kids we went to school with, Jimmy Blunt, but I don't think you'd remember him. Mum might have, but he never came to our house so I don't think you'd know him.'

'What did he die of?'

'I think it was suicide. They said it was drugs, but from what I heard I'm pretty sure he committed suicide.'

'Never can understand that. Life is so precious, there's always a way around everything. Nothing should be that bad.'

'I know. The drugs get them, though, then depression,

and then it spirals out of control. Jimmy didn't have a great life. His family life was terrible when he was a kid.'

'What about Bobby?'

'Lynette said she'd made contact with Theresa, but years ago, mind you. Do you remember Theresa, Bobby's sister? She and Lynette ran away together when they were teenagers.'

'I'll never forget that. Christ, that father of theirs was evil. A brute of a man, not one speck of kindness in his soul.'

'He's dead now, died years ago, as did the mother. Lynette filled me in on it all. She said Theresa's had a pretty hard life. Apparently she lives near Brisbane in government housing and has five or six kids.'

'Where does Bobby live?'

'We talked about that, but it seems like no one ever heard from him again. Theresa said that she once talked to a guy we knew from school who'd worked with him out west. A property, she told me the name of it, way out near Mt Isa, or somewhere like that. Theresa's tried to track him down a few times over the last twenty years, but she's never been able to find him. Lynette said she's given up. She reckons he must be dead because there are no records of him living anywhere.'

'He had it tough, that kid. Never really stood a chance.'

They stood together, holding hands, Ruby feeling like she was ten years old again, her dad's worn and wrinkly hands clasping hers, warm against each other.

Francis winked at her. 'Okay, Ruby Rose, time to take this old man back down the mountain. I'm supposed to be making up a four with the ladies for cards this afternoon.

It's the first day of the new year, so drinks and all. I don't want to be letting them down now.'

They walked back to the car together, both turning to get one last glimpse of the trees that had evoked so many memories—memories of a different place and time.

CHAPTER 19

Usually Ruby got out of bed as soon as she opened her eyes, but this morning she lay on her back, taking in the different sections of her new bedroom. The walls, floors and ceiling were all timber slats. The floor a mixture of embedded dirt and stains scattered across the worn boards. Through the French doors she could see across the wide veranda, and she perched up on her elbows to gaze at the view, looking out across the valley towards the mountains far to the east.

The room was large, and at the moment stacked high with the boxes she had carried in from the cars yesterday. A light hung above her, the bare bulb dangling on a long black wire that hung from the ceiling, circled by a decorative ceiling rose, lending a spot of elegance to an otherwise tatty, peeling ceiling.

Ruby thought about the conversation with her dad yesterday, going back over his desire to stay in the retirement village in nearby Noosa. She realised he was thinking about her more than himself, but she also knew he was probably right and that it was better for him to be near everything he needed. He looked good, she thought, and even though he was unsteady on his feet, he seemed fairly healthy, his mind still sharp as a tack. She didn't want to think about when he was no longer around because he had always been there; she had never lived more than half an hour away from him, both now and when her mum was alive.

Recalling her conversations with Lynette, she felt a little guilty that she hadn't elaborated on the details to her dad, not telling him that she and Lynette had met for coffee a few times over the years. To this day, Ruby, Theresa and of course Bobby, who didn't seem to exist anymore, were the only ones from Lynette's past who knew what she had suffered.

Lynette would talk openly when they met, possibly because Ruby was a trained social worker and knew when to listen and when to interject, but probably also because Ruby knew the truth. She knew what Lynette had suffered and that no-one had helped her. Lynette had told her mother and the local priest, and had also confided in a teacher at school. But as she often said to Ruby, for what? It was all to no avail, because none of them had done anything. They all knew, but they hadn't believed her, saying she was making it up, trying to get attention.

'Why would I make that shit up?' Lynette had been upset when she and Ruby had last talked. 'The old bastard, right up until I was about fifteen. It happened again and again, until the day I'd had enough—'

Ruby interrupted. 'How did you stop him?'

'He always waited until we were alone, when no one else was around. As much as I tried to avoid it, staying away from home a lot, there were times when I couldn't get away from him. This one day, I just couldn't take anymore and I stood up to him. We were in the car. Mum had asked him to drop me off somewhere but I said I'd walk. But she wouldn't listen. It was like she'd completely forgotten or chosen to wipe what I'd told her from her memory. She was close to her dad, so obviously my grandfather never did to her what he did to me.'

Ruby felt angry as she listened intently. 'So what happened?'

'He stopped the car in front of where I was going, well, a bit further down the road, sort of near a bush area. Usual story, no one around.'

Ruby shook her head. She had heard so many similar stories over her working years.

Lynette's voice was shaky as she continued. 'Tried to put his hand up my skirt. "How about it, Lynny?" he said. He always called me that and he'd put on this sickly-sweet voice. I can't stand the name to this day. I trapped his hand as hard as I could and pulled it away from my legs. I told him to fuck off. I swore at him so hard and looked him straight in the eye. I told him if he ever touched me again I'd kill him because I wasn't scared of him, and if he ever came near me again I'd make sure he suffered and I'd tell whoever I could.'

Lynette was trying hard to stay composed, to hold it together. 'He laughed at first and said something about how now I had a boyfriend I didn't need him anymore. It was as if he actually thought I liked him. I swore at him again and got out of the car. He started to go all weird, pleading with me, asking me to get back in the car, saying he wouldn't do bad things to me again. Spoke to me like I was a little kid. I was fucking fifteen! It didn't stop until I was *fifteen*!'

Ruby passed Lynette a tissue to wipe away the tears that were streaming down her face.

'Sorry, Ruby,' Lynette said, 'but you're the only person I can talk to about this. You and Bobby were the only ones who knew about it, I could always trust you two.'

'Those bloody secrets we had, Lynette. We should have told someone. Someone should have helped you, Theresa and Bobby. Poor Bobby, copping it all the time, trying to protect everyone.'

'Fucked-up lives, that's what we had. I got married at seventeen. Anything to get out of that house. Married to Joe Turner, still a kid, what hope did we have? Lucky he was a decent guy and we had a few good years together. I've been married twice since then. I'm not great at relationships, always needing someone, usually choosing the wrong guys. I never find it easy to settle.'

'These things have a terrible effect on families and relationships. I've worked with so many adults, Lynette, both men and women, who were so badly affected by both physical and psychological abuse when they were kids. You really should get some help.'

'At this stage, I'm not doing too badly. Better than Theresa is. The fella I'm with is really the best. He's gentle and understanding, and he's the first partner I've ever talked to about what happened. He understands. He picks me up when I'm down and gives me space when I need it. I think this time it's the real thing.'

'God, I hope so, Lynette. You deserve so much.

Everyone deserves to be happy.' Ruby found herself choking up, unusual for her. 'All kids deserve to be treated right. We all deserve to have happy childhoods, to live safely, to be loved and cared for.'

'You did. You had the perfect life. Theresa and I used to talk about your family.' Lynette grasped Ruby's hands over the small table. 'We used to imagine that we lived in your house, with your mum and dad. We longed to sit outside all together like you did, talking, laughing. God, the fun you used to have at the family parties in your backyard. It was what our dreams were made of. And we wanted your mum and dad to be our mum and dad.'

'I was so lucky and I was surrounded by good people, loving family. I feel guilty now because sometimes I used to be jealous of your family. You had so much money. You always got the best clothes and new bikes. Sometimes I wished I was you!'

'Ha, you would never have wanted to be me. I hardly have contact with my parents now. I just can't forgive them for what happened.'

'I wanted to adopt you all, Bobby's sisters and you. I had it all worked out. I'd dream about it, where you could sleep in my house, where all your clothes would go. I guess that's what I've always liked about the social work— the fact that I can help people. I can't always solve their problems, but I can lighten the load just by talking and listening to them.'

'I think talking like we have today does help,' Theresa said. 'All those secrets, so many secrets we kids had.'

They both stood up to leave, hugging firmly with an understanding and trust that ran deep, fostered by child-hood connections.

'Bloody silkworm secrets.' Ruby sighed and shook her head.

Lynette laughed at the term from so many years ago. 'I always knew I could trust you, Ruby. We'll meet again.'

Ruby allowed herself a few more minutes of luxury. Sleeping in. She closed her eyes and tried to remember what Bobby had looked like. All this talk about childhood had made her think about him; wonder what had happened to him. She knew that somewhere among all those boxes were photos, taken by her mother in their backyard. They were small black-and-white photos. Her and Bobby hanging off each other, more photos showed them sitting on the back veranda eating ice blocks. She would find them when she unpacked.

For years after Bobby had gone she had worried about him, wondered if he was being looked after and where he was. Did he have somewhere to sleep, someone to talk to? As she moved into her senior years at high school, her school work had been her priority, and time had marched on as she studied for her social-work degree, honours and then masters.

There had been boyfriends, parties, travel and

marriage to Ben, whom she had met during her time spent with clients in the courts. A busy life filled with a variety of work and family commitments had left little time to dwell on childhood events, and as time went by she rarely thought of the people who had made up such a major part of her life as a child. She had focused on her mother and father; they came first, along with Ben and her clients.

Life had been busy, and it was only when she met up with Lynette or her dad reminisced that she found herself wondering what had happened to Bobby and questioning if he was still out there somewhere.

Her decision to buy the ramshackle property set high on the hills near Maleny had been instantaneous. She had never contemplated this lifestyle before, previously embedded in the busy, social life of the Sunshine Coast. A visit to the hillside area after a friend's wedding nearby, had aroused her interest, and before she knew it she had haggled a little, signed a contract and become the owner of a rustic cottage on a very rundown property.

She smiled to herself, amused at the spontaneity of her choice. It had probably been the first—perhaps the only— unplanned, impulsive significant decision she had made in her life.

The large house on the canal, with the white glossy tiles and grey shiny kitchen, had been sold, along with most of the furniture that didn't meld with the rustic floorboards and 1920s style of the new house. She had placed many of her belongings in charity bins. Bags full of extra clothes, along with what she decided was a vast array of frivolous and unneeded shoes and handbags were picked from their neat lines in her walk-in robe and given a new home at the local charity store. She didn't care about them anymore, couldn't be bothered selling them and just wanted them gone.

It was a cleansing of both house and soul, a new beginning, and now there was so much to keep her busy. Sitting up, she decided that lying in bed wasn't going to get anything done. It was time to start.

CHAPTER 21

'A cup of tea, that'll get me going.' Ruby flicked on the jug, rummaging in the nearest box to find her favourite cup.

The non-conformity she had tried to achieve when she moved into the house had not extended to her kitchenware. The ordered and neat plates and cups from the previous house had come with her and only a few mismatched favourites had found their way into the boxes.

The kitchen was going to be her starting point. It was the room she'd probably use the most to begin with, the fridge and new gas stove already in place and all set to go. There were plenty of timber cupboards to store every-thing, and underneath the dirt the doorknobs were white porcelain, matching the chunky, white basin and drying racks set into the timber bench. Shelves, which would be great for displaying her bowls and plates, lined one wall, with hooks underneath perfect for hanging mugs and cups.

Dirt and grime covered everything and cobwebs smothered with dust hung from every corner or ledge. Start with a small area, she told herself. Get the kitchen done bit by bit, and then move onto the bedroom and the rest of the house.

The floor she would leave until last. Scuffing it with her shoe she realised that she would probably need to get someone in to fix it. She was excited, imagining how the wide knotted timbers would look once they were cleaned and polished.

Outside was going to have to wait. It was overgrown, but it didn't matter. There were a few sheds dotted around the property and she couldn't wait to explore them, as well as the many other corners and hidden areas that existed on the twenty acres of overgrown trees and grass. Grabbing a bucket and some cleaning tools, she began.

SHE SPENT the next week scrubbing, scraping and cleaning the entire kitchen, knowing it had to be done while she was off work. When she returned, even though it would be part time she knew she wouldn't have any spare time. There would be papers to look over at night and clients to think about, solutions to be found.

Every day she woke early and returned to where she had ended the day before. At night she fell into bed exhausted, waking in the morning with her arms and body aching from the exercise the day before. Previously well-manicured nails were now broken and scratches and bruises dotted her arms and legs, the consequences of dragging furniture around as well as cleaning every corner and crevice she discovered.

Sugar soap and scrubbing brushes, along with as much muscle power as she could muster, soon removed the grime from the ceilings and wall. The panels of glass in the old hopper windows were soon gleaming, and large spiders sent running for their lives, flicked unceremoniously outside.

Nothing changes that much, she thought. Once I start something I become obsessed with it and can't stop until it's done, until everything is in its place.

Looking around the neat kitchen, she felt very pleased with herself. Apart from the floorboards, everything was clean. It was starting to look like a real kitchen. The cupboards now hung evenly, the small tool bag her dad had given her coming in handy. He had taught her how to use a hammer and nails, the different screwdrivers and the basics of fixing things around the house.

She had screwed the wooden shelves back into the walls and filled them with bright plates and bowls. Cups hung from the hooks, and canisters and jars filled with food lined the benches and tops of the cupboards. She had even hung the five china ducks, flying in sequence, largest to smallest up on the wide timbers that made up the kitchen wall. Enamel cake and condiment tins stacked together had also been around forever, and looking at them now, Ruby felt a nostalgic tug, like she was back in her mum's kitchen, a simple kitchen like this one.

She poured herself a congratulatory glass of wine, taking it outside to sit on the brightly painted yellow chairs she had positioned on the veranda. It pleased her that most of her furniture now, the pieces she had wanted to keep and placed in the cottage, came from her child-hood, family home. This was what she wanted. Not the fancy, glossy, expensive furniture that had filled the house on the canal, but instead old wooden chairs and tables her dad had made, the silky oak sideboard and beds, the old genoa lounge and the big Persian rug she had loved lying on when she was a kid.

Much of it had been stored in their shed, her dad unable to part with it. He had asked Ben and Ruby to store it and she had been unable to say no. It had always annoyed Ben. 'All that old shit,' he used to say, 'you'll never use it. You don't even like that sort of thing.'

'I know,' she would tell him, 'but it's Mum and Dad's stuff. They don't have room for it and you know what he's like, he can't bear to throw anything away. I can't say no. Just leave it there. It's all covered up, the shed's huge, what does it matter?'

Ben had given in, as he often did with her. She knew she was bossy and always thought she was right. He had found it easier to go along with her, just keep the peace and let her run the show; instead, he threw himself into his work, the distance between them growing wider by the years. 'You couldn't care if I'm here or not,' he would say, 'you just do your own thing anyway.'

The arguments had started, and deep down she knew he was right. Sometimes she did want someone to lean on, to help with the hard decisions, but it was no longer him she wanted. The distance was too great. They had tried counselling and going away together, but they drifted further and further apart. Ben had fallen in love with someone else and had been seeing her for a while before he came clean about it.

At first she had been angry, hating him for cheating on her. How could he be with someone else, love them, make love to them, look at them the way he had once looked at her? But, sensible as usual, she had to be honest with herself. Deep down she knew she had driven him away.

He had tried to talk to her, taken her away on romantic weekends, brought her flowers and attempted to get her to slow down at work. But she had been busy, too independent and wrapped up in her own work.

The break-up five years ago had been amicable. She had stayed in the big house, buying his half out and everything else they had split down the middle. The last time he had come to collect some of his belongings, they had sat and talked and shared a bottle of wine.

Ben had been open about his feelings. 'We were in love once, Ruby, and it was good for a lot of years. We shared so much.' Watching her he realised that he knew every inch of her face and he thought how her eyes looked sad, without the usual sparkle.

'It was good, Ben. I have lots of fabulous memories and I don't regret any of the time we spent together. I just regret the way we became in the end, and I know now that the person I had become contributed to that.'

'You're a beautiful soul, Ruby. You have so much compassion, wanting to help people all the time. You're a much better person than I am. I really hope you find happiness, because you deserve to be loved.'

'Thank you, Ben.' She had kissed him gently on the cheek, sad that this part of her life was coming to an end and that today was the final chapter of her married life.

She had sat in the same spot long after his laden-up car had driven out of the shiny tiled driveway. Stars began to fill the sky and the humid night air swirled around like the thoughts in her head. There was a heavy sadness, but a weight had also been lifted. When had they fallen out of love? How had she let that happen?

That was almost five years ago. Ben had moved on with his new partner, Sue, a teacher who stayed home and looked after their two kids. Ruby hated to admit it, but Sue seemed to be a genuinely nice person. They had run into each other a few times over the years, and she had surprised herself at how well she'd handled the meeting each time they crossed paths.

The children were adorable, and Ben, well, she had to admit that he was relaxed and content. He always chatted happily with Ruby, and Sue would just smile. She never said much, and Ruby wondered if she felt guilty. After all, they had been having an affair when she was still Ben's wife. Sue didn't seem to mind Ben talking to her, though, or passing her one of the kids to hold.

They were obviously very happy together and she knew that Ben had found what he wanted in life. He had moved on and was leading a very different life to the one that they had shared for all those years.

After she talked to him the last time, she had questioned herself. There was no animosity, no bad feelings, so why had seeing him upset her? She was doing fine, she had always been able to cope by herself, and she definitely didn't love him anymore. Her career was where she wanted it to be, she had friends to travel with, a beautiful home. So why did she feel like there was something missing? The only time she felt absolute contentment was when she was with her parents, the three of them together.

After her mum had died, she had spent even more time with her dad. They had gone on road trips together, driven across the Nullarbor, visited Western Australia and come back through the Northern Territory. She had coerced him to travel by plane, and they flew to Europe where she had driven him through the countryside, along rugged coastlines, over the Alps, exploring ancient cities and villages that hung off steep cliffs overlooking the ocean. They had visited war sites from both world wars, and travelled through France, Germany, Austria, Belgium, Holland and Scandinavia before crossing to the United Kingdom and winding their way through Scotland, England and Ireland.

Francis had loved every minute of it. He was interested in the different ways that people lived, and the countryside and cities that were so different to what he had known all of his life.

'I didn't think I'd ever travel out of Australia,' he said to Ruby. 'Who would have thought it? I wonder what your mother would have made of this, driving on the wrong side of the road. There's no way she would've got on one of those huge planes.' He still talked about the places they had been to, the sights they'd seen. At the end of their trip Francis had been ready to come home, and he had happily returned to his life at the retirement village.

Ruby, however, had been unsettled after their travels. The big house that she had to get people in to clean because it was so large and had so many bathrooms suffocated her. The pristine lawn and neat square gardens, planted with matching and symmetrically placed plants, annoyed her. She wasn't sure what it was that she wanted.

And then one day she had been persuaded by a real-estate agent she had met at a friend's wedding, into having a look at a property he was trying to sell. She wasn't sure whether he was more interested in getting to know her so he could ask her out, or just wanted a sale. The dating wasn't successful at all, but his marketing skills, coinciding with her unsettled attitude, led to her agreeing to look at a property that he touted as a 'renovator's delight'. She wasn't really into renovating; all the previous homes she and Ben had owned had been brand new or close to it. When something needed fixing they paid a tradesman. Why waste time when someone else could do it?

Joe, the real estate guy, who had been the worst kisser in the world, had been cunning and prompted her to view the property when it was at its best, when the sun was coming up over the eastern reaches, throwing its majestic light over the mountains. The vision had taken her breath away, and from then on she viewed everything else through rose-coloured glasses: the trees, the paddocks, the stillness in the air, the isolation. As soon as she laid eyes on the dirt driveway winding its way under the massive shady trees, the property was sold. She had loved the look of the house: the wide verandas, the tin hoods over the coloured-glass windows and the rusty red roof.

The steps could be easily fixed, he assured her, along with the other broken parts of the house. 'Nothing that a hammer and nails won't fix,' he said.

The trees at the front of the property were towering and shady, and she could picture herself sitting under them reading a book, sipping a wine. The possibilities were endless.

Joe said there were other structures around the place and he showed her the closest one, not far from the house, a small rustic shed with a squeaky door hanging loosely on its hinges. Inside were small rustling animals, fleeing from its darkened corners, that he assured her weren't rats. 'Must be possums,' he told her.

'Don't possums normally perch up high? I don't remember seeing them running along the ground. They looked like rats to me. It doesn't matter anyway. I love this shed. You could do it up, have it as a cabin. It has an outhouse out the back.' She pointed to a huge rusty, shower rose that hung from the trunk of the nearest tree. 'And look, I'm sure that's what it's been used for before.' Ruby could envisage the dilapidated old shed done up. Her dad could come and stay, maybe he'd live up here with her.

Joe had turned to her, putting on his best persuasive, real-estate voice. 'What do you think then?' He added extra words that blurred into the background. 'Investment … money … bargain … fixer upper … portfolio … security—'

She interrupted. 'I love it, even though it's really rundown and there's so much work to do. But I could do some of it myself and pay workmen to come in and do the big stuff.'

'The electricity and water are fine, the owners have just had that all fixed, so it's all ready to go.'

Ruby had made an offer and by the next day the contract was sealed. The property was hers.

DRAGGING her mind back to the present, she smiled at the memories of the day she had bought the house and subsequently, gently, rid herself of Joe, the real-estate man.

'Cheers,' she said out loud, clinking the full wine glass up against the rough weatherboards on the outside wall of the cottage. The wind in the trees whistled back at her and she smiled, the pristine view as usual taking her breath away. She wondered if she would ever get used to it. The changing vista, the way the mountains peaked, thrusting upwards through the low-lying fog that so often settled across the valley floor.

She practised the names: Mount Tibrogargan, Mount Tibberoowuccum. No wonder the area, and particularly the mountains, had significant cultural importance for the Aborigines. She could sense it as she looked out: there was something spiritual, calming, a soothing presence that soaked across the landscape and drifted softly through the branches of the trees, rising up sharply and dramatically on the slopes of the mountains. Taking a deep breath she closed her eyes, feeling content and at peace for the first time in years.

CHAPTER 22

*P*aint smells wafted through the cottage, accompanied by the voice of Freddie Mercury bellowing from the sound system. Every window was flung open as wide as possible, the breeze flowing through the house, cooling the humid summer air. Tarps and blankets covered the furniture and floor where Ruby stood in the middle of the main bedroom, surveying the freshly painted room. Her arms ached, the roller and tin lying on the floor while she waited for her energy levels to return.

Her dad had tried to talk her into hiring a painter. 'Don't be so bloody stubborn,' he had said, 'it's a huge job and you have plenty of money. You'll get a better job done, plus you have no idea how hard it is to do ceilings and walls, especially in these old places.'

'I'm fit and young, besides it'll be an achievement if I do it myself.'

'Hold your arms up in the air, yep, that's it, both of them. Now hold them there for as long as you can.' He laughed when she admitted it didn't take long for her arms to ache. But it hadn't stopped her; as usual, she was determined and wanted to do it all herself.

She gazed around the room. She had achieved a great deal, but her body ached. Five days of painting and her arms felt like they were going to fall off, her legs throbbed from going up and down the small ladder, and her back and stomach, well, they felt like they were bruised all over. I suppose I got a workout, she thought. It beats going to the gym. Maybe she could get a painter in to do the rest, considering there was still most of the house to go.

Looking at the old hopper windows closely she realised that she had flicked specks of paint on the glass when she had painted the adjoining walls. She was going to have to spend more time on some parts of the house, areas she had already covered. Annoyed with the imper-fections of her work, she headed to the freshness of the air outside.

Going outside was always rejuvenating. Although her body still felt like it had been run over by a steamroller. Washing out the roller and brushes, she sang softly along with Freddie, wondering if she was - similar to the message in the song - actually escaping from reality. The lyrics suited her mood and purpose, and soon she was singing along at the top of her voice, the kookaburra perched on the wide railing of the veranda cocking its head to the side to listen.

Revitalised, she laid the equipment out on the grass to dry, and neatly folded the drop-sheets and blankets and put them away. I can do it, she thought. I can do anything. 'One room done,' she said out loud.

She collapsed into the hammock, which was positioned to take in the best of the view while she rocked back and forth. Ruby dozed off, the moving clouds and cool breeze sending her from a state of exhaustion into a deep sleep.

THE SOUND of the phone ringing caused her to open her eyes, and she forgot for a moment where she was. Shaking her head, she realised she had collapsed in the hammock, and yes, that was her phone ringing, perhaps for the second time because she might have heard a ringing noise in her sleep. She jumped up and headed inside, her aches forgotten until she moved.

She sat down on a chair next to the bench where the phone was, her legs in pain, as though she had run a marathon. 'Hello.'

'Hi, Ruby, it's Ben here. You sound a bit puffed. Sorry, did I make you run?'

'Hi, Ben.' She laughed. 'I've been doing some painting and I'm just a bit stiff and sore. I don't know how Dad did all that concreting for so many years.'

He laughed also, the banter familiar to both of them. 'I know, I moved some dirt the other week with the wheelbarrow and I felt like I had stretched myself, like an ape with long arms.'

'I think I'll get someone in to do the rest, pay someone to do a proper job. I just won't want to admit it to Dad, though. He tried to get me to do that at the start.'

Ben asked how her dad was and they chatted for a while, Ruby curious as to the reason for the phone call. He had only ever rung her a few times over the years and that was usually to sort out something from the settlement.

Finally he got to the point of his phone call. 'Ruby, do you think we could get together for a coffee? I've got something I want to discuss.'

'Ben, is everything all right, the kids, Sue?'

'Oh yeah, no, everything's fine. It's nothing like that. It's just something to do with one of the cases our firm's been involved with. I think you may be interested, but I don't really want to talk about it over the phone.'

'You know I can't talk about client details, Ben.'

'I know, I know that. And the same goes for me. But, well, how about we meet and I'll fill you in. I do think you'll be interested.'

'Sure, sure.' She thought about what she had booked in. 'I'm going down to see Dad on Friday. I'm still on leave so I have some spare time at the moment.'

'That would be great. Say eleven, at Bistro on Main.'

'Lovely, I'll see you then. Um, Ben, Sue doesn't mind you meeting me, does she?'

'No, it's all okay, I've already mentioned it to her and she's fine with it.'

Hmm, glad he's honest with her, she thought. She felt a little stab of jealousy. 'Great, see you then.'

Ruby tried on three different outfits before she decided on the right one. Why was she so nervous? She was at ease with Ben. There was nothing left between them. Looking in the mirror, she brushed back her hair, letting it hang loosely over her shoulders. Ben had always liked the more structured, neat look, with her hair tied back, nails painted and immaculate clothes with shoes and bags to match.

Now, as she peered into the old crazed mirror, she was surprised at the difference in her appearance since she had moved to the cottage. Brown, wavy hair flowed down to the middle of her back, with a small clip holding one side back behind her ear. Her face, arms and legs were tanned from the work she had been doing outside. Her nails short but neat with not a hint of nail polish.

Stretching her body, she surveyed her image in the full-length mirror, smiling at her reflection. Her well-rounded backside was bigger than she wanted it to be, but thankfully her waist was still tiny; she had an hourglass shape with long, slender legs. The loose, colourful dress she had chosen showed off her figure. She reached down, groaning at the aches in her body as she tightened the strap on the casual flat sandals she was wearing.

Looking all right, she thought to herself. It was funny that she didn't need all the makeup or heavy jewellery she used to wear. Maybe she would soon start to look like a hippy, which would sort of go with the area up here. It felt strange to get dressed up. Goodness knows how I'll be when I go back to work, she thought. Around the house she only ever wore tiny old shorts, a singlet top and had even started going without a bra. What's happening to you, Miss Prim and Proper, she thought.

She looked around the bedroom and raised her eyebrows at all the items out of place.

Although the bed was made, with the sheets tucked in hospital tight, the chair in the corner had clothes left on it, and books and papers lay strewn across the floor. Her eyebrows went higher. The books weren't even stacked; they were, yes, *strewn*. Chuckling to herself, she realised that the thought of the mess in the rooms didn't bother her. In fact, she liked it. The house felt lived in, comfortable and relaxed. It reminded her of home when she was a kid.

Back then there had always been newspapers scattered over the kitchen table, items stacked on the floor, and her dad's shoes or a shirt he had taken off and thrown in the corner. Her mum had been clean but not very tidy. That's why the house had always been so relaxed; no one had to worry when they visited. Everyone always liked coming there because they could unwind, feel at home.

How had she become so structured, ordered? Why the neat-freak thing?

Now life had changed. She thought of this place, the cottage, and the overgrown yard with the unruly huge trees that threw their leaves and branches down to mess up the grass. The unkempt surroundings calmed her and her worries disappeared. She could be herself, or whoever she wanted to be. And she liked it. She liked it this way. She liked the new her.

Heading down the steep driveway, she felt alive, like there was a change in the wind. Something big was going to happen. She was in control. What did Ben want to talk to her about? Money? Family? In an hour or so she would find out.

* * *

Sitting opposite Ben, she could see his eyes appraising her.

'Wow,' he said, 'you look terrific. Like a different person.'

'Thanks, Ben, you look good too.'

'No, Ruby, I mean, you *really* look good. You just get better with age. Have you been working out? You look so fit.'

She laughed out loud, that infectious light laugh that he remembered so well. 'I told you I've been doing some painting. Seriously, I haven't stopped since I bought the new place. I've been working in the yard and on the house. I've even been up on the roof fixing the gutters.'

'You would never have done that years ago.'

'I know. I don't know when I lost the plot—the pleasure of simplicity, the most important things in life.'

'It's true. You and I were both so tied up with our jobs, money, all the flash things in life.'

'We lost sight of reality.' Ruby's voice was wistful; there was so much water under the bridge. 'Dad tried to point it out to me several times over the years. He threw out hints constantly. "Money isn't everything, Ruby Rose,' he would say. "It won't make you happy." I can still hear my mum's voice. "Do you really need such a big house? It just means more bathrooms to clean. Look how happy we were when you were growing up and we only ever had that little house." You know Ben, they weren't too far off the mark.'

Ben looked down, his voice quiet. 'Let's not look back, Ruby. It was what it was and we're both happy now. You are, aren't you?' He looked her in the eye.

'I am, Ben. The last couple of months since buying the property, I really feel like I've come home. It's as if I have a connection to where I live and the things I do. I'm close to Dad and he comes and stays with me. Really, he's the most important person in my life.'

'He's great, isn't he? I've run into him a few times. Last time I had Sue and the kids with me. I could tell he was genuinely pleased to see me and to be introduced to the family. I have so much respect for him, and your mum. I suppose Francis has never forgiven me for what I did, though.'

'He knows, Ben.' Ruby's voice had gone quiet. 'I've told him. He always knew there were two sides to the story.'

'Thank you, Ruby.'

'Now, what's the reason for this meeting? I must admit you've made me curious.' She took a long sip of her coffee.

'Well, where to begin.' Ben lowered his voice. 'Do you remember years ago there was a politician arrested for a case of child abuse? You said at the time that you'd known him when you were a kid. He lived next door to you, or something like that. He went to jail. Only a short stint, but he was put away for a while.'

'Mike Carlon.'

'Yep, that's him. Good memory.'

'Oh, I'd never forget his name. He was the uncle of the family next door. He didn't live with them all the time but he used to spend a lot of time there. There was a little self-contained flat down the backyard that he lived in when he came to stay.'

'He was charged back in the late eighties on one case of child abuse. There was a small write-up in the papers at the time and then it was hushed up. Do you remember?'

'Yes, absolutely,' she said. 'I asked you to look it up, to see what happened. You had to do a fair bit of digging to find out what the end result was, which I think you said was a few months in jail. Remember, at the time you thought there was something fishy going on, though, like there'd been some sort of cover-up or a payment made.'

'He had some pretty high-ranking friends, both in politics and in the justice department.'

'I need another coffee,' Ruby said. 'It's too early for a wine, isn't it?'

Ben looked at his watch before gesturing to a nearby waiter. 'How about a light lunch with a glass of wine? I do have a lot to talk to you about.'

Ruby ate quickly, the large glass of wine finding its

mark. Just the mention of Mike Carlon set her nerves on edge. Sometimes she would deal with a case of child abuse through her work, often working with the kids involved, but more often counselling adults who had been abused as children. At least these days kids spoke up, they told someone, and parents acted, reporting what happened and often seeking help from someone like Ruby. They were prepared to let families be torn apart, sit through arduous court sessions and to face family members who so frequently were the perpetrator.

'Okay, go on.' She looked at him over the top of her glass.

'Well, there's two points of interest, two separate but connected issues.'

Ruby leaned forward, her full attention focused on Ben and what he was about to say.

'I interviewed a guy the other week who's been in and out of jail over a number of years, with charges of robbery, assault, the usual crimes. Years ago he met this guy in jail who was a politician up on child-abuse charges. He said this guy wasn't in there for long and they'd had to move him into solitary to safeguard him from the other prisoners. They guy I spoke to used to run a few paid favours for the man and sometimes they would talk together.' Ben raised his eyebrows. 'My guy told me some interesting information about this politician, things he'd bragged about. He said the guy's name was Mike Carlon.'

Ruby was speechless as Ben continued to reveal the details of the confidential information, only occasionally shaking her head, her eyes wide as she listened carefully. Her face portrayed her shock. 'That's unbelievable, but then again, you know what? It could also be correct.'

'There's more. Mike Carlon was convicted of further offences.' Ben's voice dropped to a whisper. 'He was charged with molesting two young girls, and from what I can gather they were friends of his family. The thing is that the girls' father is a wealthy businessman, so I'd say that Carlon wasn't able to pay him off. This time he didn't get away with it. I've read some of the files, not that I'm dealing with it personally, and it was pretty bad. What he did to them. It's serious shit.'

'Those poor girls,' Ruby said. 'He's such a creep. God, I always hated him. I hope he's been locked up and the key thrown away. What a vile creature.'

Ben took a steady gulp of his wine, his eyes looking straight into Ruby's. 'This businessman, the father of the two girls, he dug around a bit more, or rather his legal team did because they want to really go for Carlon, push it further even though he's already been locked up for molesting the two girls. The father wants his blood. They've contacted another victim from the past. I think you may know her. She used to be Theresa Carlon but she has a different surname now. The info I came across says she's Mike Carlon's niece.'

Ruby's hand went to her mouth. 'Oh my god, yes, Theresa, she's his niece. She's a bit older than me, the eldest girl of the family that lived next door. I can't believe it, after all this time.'

Ben continued. 'Remember years ago, when we'd get into those discussions, and you told me about Carlon, about the family next door. You said that he had abused the eldest sister and another girl who lived up the road.'

'No, the other girl up the road was separate. That was her bloody grandfather, a completely separate issue.'

Ben took a long sip from his wine, waiting for Ruby to continue.

'Mike Carlon was horrible, evil, yet he came across like butter wouldn't melt in his mouth. He charmed all the women, and at first they used to think he was just it. Really good looking, a smooth dresser, had the gift of the gab, and of course the flash black Mercedes Benz and all the connections. Looking back, I can see he was laying the groundwork for a career as a politician. He was an absolute bastard, though, and poor Theresa, she suffered years of torment because of him.'

Ruby's mind flashed back to the scenes she had witnessed in the backyard. Bile rose in her throat, and she took a big sip of wine to wash away the memories of Theresa and the isolation of that backyard flat.

'Anyway, it's going back to court,' Ben said. 'Carlon was still in politics before the last conviction and has some connections, but not like years ago.'

'You'd think the girls' father would have been careful around him. You know, because of the past offences,' Ruby said.

'That past conviction left a stain and many of his friends deserted him. But what often happens over time is that people forget and new acquaintances wouldn't have known anything about his past.'

'And you know what?' Ruby's eyes flashed. 'None of this would have happened if those bastards had done something about it twenty years ago. They all knew. The cops, the school, even the bloody priest knew. Dad tried to take it up with them down the cop shop, about the beatings that the younger brother Bobby was getting. But they didn't want to know about it. They were all mates, in business together. Bloody cover-ups. The girls, Theresa and Lynette, they tried to get help from quite a few different places, but for what? Theresa ended up in a home and Lynette came back home to suffer further. And I knew; I knew for all those years. The only person I've ever told was you.'

'How come you never told anyone? It's a wonder you didn't tell your dad.'

'We had a code, a code of silence. They swore me to secrecy. Besides, looking back now I don't think it would have mattered anyway.'

Ben looked at his watch and lowered his voice. 'I do have some other details that this guy in jail told me. I've kept it until the last to tell you because it's disturbing and I'm only going to say it once.' He leaned forward, his voice a whisper. 'I want you to remember that often these guys lie or exaggerate, but this information has been passed on and shortly there'll be another trial with new evidence and charges.'

Ruby was unable to move. Her eyes transfixed on Ben's face as she listened intently to him repeating the last conversation he had had with the criminal, a man who had sworn that his story had come from Mike Carlon.

When Ben finished, Ruby's head was spinning. She reached for a glass of water, taking large sips, trying to think straight. 'Are you telling me they're going to charge him with *murder* as well?' Her voice was small, her mind reeling.

'Look, I can't say any more, but they're sure they've got a case. The crim I interviewed was adamant about what he'd been told by Mike Carlon. The information's been passed on. And I think that's all I'd better say.'

Ruby was speechless. She sat silently as the waiter cleared their table.

Ben looked at his watch again. 'They're building up the case now, so you might find that at some stage someone will contact you. I'm sorry to dump this all on you, Ruby, but I wanted to give you some of the background information.'

'Thanks, Ben, I appreciate you filling me in.'

Ben stood to leave. 'I have to go. I have a meeting at one.' He passed her a piece of paper. 'This is Theresa's contact details. From the looks of it she doesn't appear to have a partner or anyone close to support her.'

'Thanks, Ben.' Ruby slipped the piece of paper into her bag.

'If you don't contact her, I'm sure you'll read about the case in the papers. Either way, I thought you'd want to know. Remember, you didn't hear any of this from me.'

'I really appreciate it. You're the only one I've talked to about any of this.'

They hugged, Ben giving her a soft kiss on her cheek. 'You look great. Keep up the work around the house, it's obviously agreeing with you.'

'Thanks, Ben, until next time.' She turned and walked away, her head churning with all the information Ben had shared.

Two squatter's chairs sat next to each other, timber arms touching, positioned to look across the small, neat garden that formed the backyard of Francis's unit in the retirement village. The back fence was covered in a bright array of flowers and greenery. A dark pink bougainvillea vine entwined with the bright yellow of an allamanda vine. Heavily scented jasmine crept lightly over the two vines, the mixture of aromas and bright flowers a pleasant backdrop for the lush green lawn.

'Not as good as your view.' Francis took a sip of the icy cold beer, the froth lingering, settling on his thick grey moustache.

'But it's still all right, Dad. You always say you don't want more than this to look after, and besides—'

Francis interjected before she could start. 'Ruby Rose, don't start. I know I can come and live with you.' He smiled warmly at her. 'I did enjoy that last week up there and it's certainly a beautiful place, but this is home, and besides, I feel your mother here. Sometimes I'm sure I can hear her voice, especially when I can't find my glasses or the remote for the television.'

He chuckled, looking at the small backyard. 'It's not a bad outlook, although the best part's that beautiful river down the bottom of the street. I'm lucky I can still walk down there, because it's not far. I like to sit on the bench seats and watch the water go past, nice and slow. Sometimes there are a few little boats out there, people having a fish.'

Francis looked down at his feet, his voice suddenly sad. 'I'm glad you've filled me in on all this Mike Carlon business. God, I always knew he was evil, but I never realised just how bad he was. Do you think you'll get called to give evidence?'

'I think it's only a matter of time.'

Francis turned to look at Ruby, placing his large craggy hand over hers where it lay on the arm of the chair. 'When I sit here I think about all the years I've had, Ruby Rose, all those wonderful years with you and your mother. I know, I've been the luckiest man in the world. You and your mother, all those years.' He wiped a tear from his eyes.

'Dad, are you okay? What's brought this on?'

'Well, I'm getting old, you know. I'm not going to be around forever. I want you to know how special you are to me and how wonderful all the years have been. How lucky I was to have you, and still have you in my life nearly every day.'

'I know, Dad, I know.'

'I know, you and I, we don't normally talk about these things. But I want to say it, I want you to know that I love you and you've been the best daughter anyone could ever ask for.'

Ruby had turned on her side, and was trying hard to stop the tears from brimming over. 'I love you, Dad. I'm the lucky one; I was the one who had the best childhood. You and Mum, you gave me so much love, and you spent so much time with me. The beliefs you brought me up with, the fact that you always told me I could be whatever I wanted to be.'

'And you did, didn't you? A social worker,' he said, 'and with extra degrees. We knew you were capable of doing whatever you wanted, what with your kind heart, always wanting to help others. I'm happy for you, Ruby Rose, you're in the career you wanted and you're good at it.'

'It was my calling and I do love it. Mind you, I haven't minded this time off either and the option's there for a couple more months if I want. They're in the process of revamping the office, and they say it's a good time for me to take some of my long-service leave. I think I might take some more time, maybe finish off the house.'

'And get a painter in.'

'Yes, Dad, I'm going to get a painter in to finish the house.'

'Hmmph.' He nodded his head. 'Do you think you could do me one more thing?' She turned to him, worried. It was not like him to be so melancholic. 'Could you get me another beer? That was just the best.'

Ruby chuckled and before long returned with another two icy beers. They clinked their glasses.

'Cheers,' they both said, laughing out loud together.

CHAPTER 25

Although Ruby had already decided to make contact with Theresa Carlon, she didn't have to start searching because Theresa's solicitor contacted her the week after she met with Ben. This morning both of them were coming to the house to talk to her. The solicitor's name was Joe Biddich, and Ruby knew from Ben that he was well respected and very successful with the cases he had taken on in the past.

She heard a car coming up the dirt driveway. It slowed, as most vehicles did, when it entered the tunnel of trees, the shade and cool area enticing visitors to appreciate the effect of driving through an archway of beautiful trees.

An area in the shade on the front veranda was prepared, the coffee and biscuits ready. It was just her nerves she needed to keep in order. He's going to be hot in that shirt and tie, she thought, as she shook hands with Joe Biddich and gestured for them to take a seat.

Theresa had dressed for the occasion. Her obvious

attempt at looking well dressed did not pass Ruby's discerning eye. She had sat in on too many court cases observing people dressed in suits and ties, people who had obviously never donned formal attire before. Theresa looked totally uncomfortable in her tailored shirt, and pulled at it constantly, straightening, fidgeting, looking like she was ready to rip it off. The shirt only went halfway towards covering up the odd array of tattoos that adorned most visible parts of her arms and legs.

Ruby was dressed casually in comparison to both of them. A flowing wrap skirt coupled with a bright tank top gave her a Bohemian vibe, accentuated by the single strand of bright beads she wore around her neck.

Theresa was unrecognisable from the young girl who had dreamed of becoming a nurse and who had worked so hard at home helping her mum and looking after Sally. Hardened lines ran outwards from her eyes, and dark shadows beneath them added a rough gauntness to her face. Her lips were thinner than Ruby remembered, and numerous vertical lines were scrunched in above her top lip, even more so when she dragged incessantly on the cigarettes she smoked one after the other.

The solicitor filled Ruby in on the details of the case against Mike Carlon. He explained the charges of child abuse and then carefully outlined some details on the murder charges. Some of it Ruby already knew, although she didn't let on and had to emit forced, fake gasps at the news he was conveying.

Theresa's voice was raspy. 'You remember, Ruby, eh? Don't you? You and Bobby, yous were best mates. I bet he told you. You would've seen the marks on him. You must've known.'

'What happened to your mum?' Ruby asked her.

'She's dead.'

'What about your dad?'

'The old bastard's dead, too. I told him once about all that stuff, what was happening down in that shed in the backyard. He slapped me across the face, said I was just like my mother, cracked in the head. I told a few people, the fuckin' priest at church. No one gave a fuckin' shit.' Theresa's hands shook and Ruby wondered if cigarettes were the only substance she relied on.

'Um,' Joe said, as if reading her mind, 'you probably need to be aware that Theresa is dealing with a drug addiction, ma'am.'

'Please, call me Ruby.'

He nodded. 'It started when she was placed in the home for wayward girls in Brisbane. Life was tough in there and it all just went from bad to worse.'

'It's okay, Theresa. I've worked with lots of adults and kids who were in similar institutions. I can imagine what you've been through. I think I've heard every story there is and I know the homes were horrendous places, particularly for a young girl. And you hadn't done anything wrong.'

'Thank you, Ruby,' Theresa said. 'I knew you wouldn't judge me. You was always kind. Always looking after Bobby. You had a nice family.'

The three of them sat silently. The pain and years of abuse were written on Theresa's face; her eyes were hollow, her body thin and pock-marked, her mind jumpy, edgy. Ruby knew that nothing was going to make up for what she had been through.

'Theresa wants to pursue this, Ruby,' Joe said. 'She

wants to add this to the list for Mike Carlon because they're trying to get him locked up for good. He got off lightly years ago and he still has a bit of clout, but this time he needs to stay in there for a very long time.'

'It's so sad. Kids, they just deserve to have a normal life, not to be hurt.' Ruby got up and paced along the veranda. 'It's the courts, the judges, the laws … these bastards need to be locked up for good. But they get let off, paroled, given short sentences. And then, well, we all know what happens. They reoffend.'

Theresa started to get fidgety again and began picking at a sore on her arm. Realising that the meeting had gone on long enough, Joe stood up. 'I'll get to the point of our visit today.'

Ruby had been waiting for it and she listened carefully as Joe spoke. 'We need you to help us with something.'

'What is it?' she answered cautiously.

Theresa stood up, flicking her cigarette over the veranda. 'We need you to find Bobby.'

'What?' Ruby was shocked. 'I haven't heard from him since the day he left home. No one has. Anyone I've seen from school, they all say he disappeared. He might not even live in Australia, or, and Theresa, you may have to face it, you may be the only one left alive in your family. I think you're asking the wrong person.'

'He's alive, I know it,' Theresa said, 'and he can testify for me. He saw stuff, probably more than he ever told you. He saw things that happened up in the house as well.' Theresa was too upset to continue and started walking away, down across the grassy slope, looking out at the view.

Ruby felt nauseous. There was more that Bobby hadn't told her about?

Joe spoke. 'How old were you, Ruby, when he told you what was happening?'

'Oh, only young,' she said, 'probably about eleven or twelve. Looking back, I guess he may not have told me everything. At the time I thought he did, but now, I guess not.'

Joe passed her a page of writing. 'We've tried everything. The police can't find him and I've done all I can to track him down. We think you'll have a better chance because he might just come out for you. We've followed every lead, especially that one I've just given you. But it always ends up the same. No trace of Bobby Carlon.'

'I doubt that I'll have any luck either. It's been years. He probably hasn't thought of me since he left. Life was really tough for him and I'm thinking he's either ended up much the same as Theresa'—they both looked at Theresa lighting up another cigarette—'or I don't know, he might not have made it. He might not have copped the sexual abuse, but he witnessed it and he couldn't protect his little sister.'

'Will you help us?' Joe asked.

'Actually, I'd like to meet with you.' Ruby spoke quickly, wanting to talk before Theresa returned. 'There's some information I'd like to discuss with you, in private and as soon as possible. It's in relation to the murder charge.'

Joe raised his eyebrows. 'Sure, sure thing, here's my card. You have me intrigued.'

Ruby took the card, smiling at Theresa when she returned to where they were seated.

Theresa spoke loudly. 'I need to go, the kids are all at home so I gotta get back. Are you going to look for him, Ruby?'

'I'll try. I will try to help.' She hugged the agitated woman, holding her firmly until eventually Theresa's arms wrapped around her, the hug reciprocated.

Theresa looked her in the eye. 'We need the bastard put away. I want justice for us three kids and for Mum.'

'I'll try. I'll do my best.'

Ruby stood on the front veranda, staring out across the valley for a long time after they left, wondering where to begin. Should she do what they wanted? She was involved anyway, and she had an idea that once she met with Joe again she would be right in the thick of it all. There would be no more secrets; everything would be out in the open.

Unfolding the piece of paper Joe had given her, she read the words, *Astral Station, via Boulia. Robert Carlon registered for work November 1975.*

The date he had registered for work at Astral Station was over twenty-five years ago, and where the hell was Boulia? She folded the paper in half, looking up into the trees as if the answers were going to be there. Of course there were no answers and she still didn't know where Boulia was. As she walked slowly inside, she had a funny feeling she was going to find out.

CHAPTER 26

For the past week Ruby had used every research technique she possessed. After she met with Joe she travelled to Brisbane and scoured through old records, completed various searches through different agencies and read through lists of missing persons. A few days in and she decided to ring through to the station where Bobby had first enlisted for work.

At first Merlene, the old lady who owned the station, had been defensive. 'I can't just give out information to anyone. How do I know if you're an honest person or not? Someone's already rung here about him and I told them I'd never heard of him. You city people, you're probably chasing him for something he didn't even do. He's not here now anyway.'

Ruby had kept talking to Merlene; she could tell that the old lady knew more than she was letting on. 'Come on, Merlene, it's over twenty-five years ago. Surely it won't hurt if you give me some more information. I really need to contact him.'

'Why?'

'I'd rather not say.'

'Hmmph.'

'But he's not in trouble, I promise. It's just a family matter that we need his help with.'

'Hmmph.'

Ruby hadn't been able to get any further with the stubborn bush lady and so, going with her instincts, she had agreed to fly out and talk with her in person.

'Once I meet you then I'll decide if I want to talk to you or not.' Merlene had been very definite.

And so Ruby found herself stepping off the tiny, four-seater Cessna onto the dusty runway at Boulia. Before she left the coast she had discussed the trip with Francis, pondering over the ridiculous idea of travelling to the tiny township about an hours flight south of Mount Isa. She told Francis she had a gut feeling she could track Bobby down, and that finding him was going to provide a link, and support Theresa and the case. 'I can't not go,' she told Francis, who now also knew most of the details of the events that had happened so long ago.

Now that she was here, she questioned the notion of this trip turning up any clues. Sure, Merlene was still there on the property where a Bobby Carlon had worked so long ago, but was it the same Bobby Carlon? And would Merlene know where he might be now?

She squinted into the glistening sunlight, red flat plains stretching out as far as the eye could see, the dry dusty ground broken only intermittently by a straight track or road leading to somewhere: somewhere that was too far away to see. Patches of green were rare, with only the occasional lonely cluster of trees under which a few cattle stood. The vast landscape was overwhelming; the earth was never-ending, stretching out and beyond into nothingness, with only a lone windmill or feeding area where cattle gathered, breaking the landscape.

Merlene was waiting for the plane to land, leaning against an old rusty Toyota. She had dressed up for the rare trip into town and sported neatly pressed jeans, shiny boots and a checked shirt, topped off by the typical Akubra hat. A keen pair of blue eyes peered out from under the dark-grey hair that was bunched up under a hat. Her handshake was firm, and to Ruby her calloused hands felt a bit like her dad's.

'My husband Jack couldn't come' Merlene said. 'He's got too much work to do at the moment. The land's dry out this way, as usual. I guess you would've got a good view flying in over the ranges. Much green on the way?'

'No, not a lot,' Ruby said. 'I'd forgotten how huge the outback is. The sky is so much bigger out here than at home.'

Merlene led Ruby towards the pub in the wide main street.

'Australian Hotel-Motel,' Ruby read out loud.

'Yeah, thought this would be the best place to have a chat. It seemed a waste to take you out to our place. It's another three hours from here.'

'I really appreciate you driving in, Merlene. I didn't realise it was that far.'

'No, all good, love, I needed to come in anyway. You've flown a long way so I hope I can help you.'

Ruby decided to be honest with Merlene, and over a tasty counter lunch and a frosty beer she filled the older lady in on some of what had happened to Bobby's family and why she needed to contact him.

'That uncle! What a bastard! I'd love to put a twenty-two to his head and pull the trigger. You know, it doesn't only go on in the city or the suburbs, like where you grew up. It goes on everywhere, people from all walks of life. Believe me, I've heard some stories over my eighty-odd years. I think if you didn't experience something of it, you were bloody lucky.'

'I know.' Ruby nodded, not wanting to rush Merlene or push too hard about her knowledge of Bobby, but knowing that her time was limited and tomorrow she would be flying back out. It had been a long trip, and the fact that she hated flying at the best of times, never mind in a tiny plane, played on her mind. She needed to know if Merlene was going to be able to help her.

The barmaid brought over another two beers and Merlene settled back in her chair. 'I guess what you're really wanting to know is, can I help you track down Ringo? Or Bobby, as you call him.'

'It is pretty urgent.' Ruby pulled an old black-and-white photo from her bag, showing Merlene the picture of herself and Bobby eating ice blocks on her back veranda. 'I think he would've been about twelve, and I was nine.'

Merlene peered over her glasses, her face lighting up into a smile. 'That's him, my dear, no mistaking that cheeky face. He was, of course, a bit older than that when he came to us. He arrived at Astral Station in'—she pulled a piece of paper out of her pocket—'November 1975.' She pointed with her bent, arthritic finger to a name listed among others on a page titled *Worker's Register*. 'The name was Robert Carlon. Later on, he asked me to change it to Ringo Carlon. I didn't ask any questions. It was clear when he arrived that he was on the run, but it was also evident,' she said, tapping his name, 'that he was a good kid. If Jack were here, he'd tell you the same thing. We took to that boy from the day he arrived. At first he was pretty quiet, you couldn't get much out of him. A few of us tried to get him to talk about why he'd come out as far as Boulia. I mean, stone the crows, you couldn't get much further from civilisation. But he'd clam up. He'd lied about his age, we knew that; he told us he was eighteen. But we'd had sons of our own and we knew we were lucky if he was sixteen.'

'He would've been nearly sixteen. His birthday is the twenty-first of December and he was born in 1959.'

'Uh-huh, that would be right, then.' The old lady nodded. 'We always reckoned he'd added on a couple of years; I guess it stopped everyone asking so many questions. We tried to get him to stay up in the house with us, that's how much we took to him, both Jack and I, we would've taken him on as our own. But he wouldn't have a bar of it. He lived in a little humpy by himself that jutted off the workers' quarters. There was plenty of space in with all the others, but he always kept to himself, he didn't like to mix that much. The Chinese cook we had back then, Ah Ling, they got on great. Often he'd help him with the cooking and we'd hear them laughing and talking. Ah Ling probably didn't understand all Ringo said and vice versa.'

Merlene stopped and took a large swig from her beer. 'After a year or so he asked to go out with the fellas on the fences. Back in those days they went out on horses and spent weeks, sometimes months, away from here, fixing the fences, finding lost stock, all the while surviving the snakes, weather, fires and isolation. It was a tough job, especially for a young fella who was, after all, a city kid.'

Ruby was enjoying hearing about her childhood friend. 'Yes, he didn't even have a horse growing up.'

By now Merlene was enjoying Ruby's full attention. 'He loved the job. I think he liked being out by himself. He told me once that the outback was his home and that he felt a connection to it and would never leave it. I tried again to get him to talk, thinking that if he talked about his problems we might be able to help him.'

Merlene's eyes narrowed. 'I saw his back once. He walked out of the shower, it was an outside shower and he must've forgotten the soap or his towel. He had his little shorts on.' She took another long sip from her beer. 'He still had skinny legs, kid legs. But I saw his back, all right. I never forgot it. Scars all over it; reminded me of photos I'd seen of convicts or those black slaves in America.'

'What happened to him, Merlene?' Ruby was starting to feel exhausted. She wasn't sure if it was from the flight, the beers or the information about someone she had once cared so much about.

'He left us after about eight years. We were never really sure why, because he'd been with us for all those years. Occasionally he'd go and work for a season with another mob. One time he was gone for nearly a year. But he always came back in those days.'

'So what happened?'

'Well, he'd started coming into a few functions in town, mixing a little bit. Not a lot, mind you, just a little. We brought him into the rodeos. He'd sit with us at the bar, but he didn't drink much. He was a gentleman and the girls loved him. He was a real good-looking fella by then, in his twenties, tanned, muscles bulging from all the work. I think he came into town a few times. Word was that him and one of the girls who worked in the local shop were keen on each other.' Merlene stopped, nodding at the girl behind the bar, signalling another round of drinks.

'Did he have partners before that?'

'Not that we knew about,' Merlene said. 'That's what happened, though, all good one day and the next moment he'd taken off. Packed his swag and left for good. Ah Ling saw him walking out through the gate with his two dogs. He wrote me a beautiful letter. Such a lovely boy, he thanked me for everything, said we'd been good to him and it wasn't anything we'd done. It was just time to move on.'

'What about the girl in town? Did she go with him?'

'Nope. I asked her next time she served me when I came into town. She was upset because she'd really liked him, and he seemed to like her, but she got the same as me, no reason for leaving, just a letter and a goodbye.'

'Nothing else?'

'She did tell me that he'd talked about going to the Northern Territory. He wanted to check out some of the huge cattle properties up that way. Otherwise she didn't know either.'

'Where do you think he went, Merlene?'

'I reckon that little girl in town was right. I think he headed further up north. He wouldn't have gone back towards where he came from. He was always trying to get further away. One thing I can tell you is that I think he would've got a job working with animals because he had a special way with them. We saw it so many times here. Mongrel dogs that would snap and snarl at everyone, well, normally we'd shoot them, get rid of them. They'd always be the ones he'd pick as his own. He'd take one of those older mongrels, and he always had a pup to train as well. He had a way with animals like no one else did. He could calm a stressed horse, soothe it, talk to it until it was rubbing up against him. I reckon he headed off somewhere remote, and with animals. Probably with horses and dogs. Fencing, maybe. They were the things he knew.'

'Is there anything else you can think of, anything that might help?'

'If I was you, I'd head right up north. I'm guessing around the Katherine region, that's where the girl in town reckoned he was headed. He had plenty of money to get him there, not that he would've needed it. Sometimes I'd do his banking for him when I went to town, deposit some money for him. He didn't spend much, because he didn't drink a lot like some of the others.'

'The bank account, Merlene, what name was in it?'

Merlene thought hard, her face scrunching up as she visualised the bankbook. 'I remember the name on the top, from memory it was a little grey book. Commonwealth Bank, the name on it was Ringo, Ringo Smith. I remember now. The name on it was different from the one he gave me. He started off as Robert Carlon, then he changed that to Ringo Carlon. But the name on that book was Ringo Smith.'

'Do you remember what branch it was? Where he might've opened the account?'

'I think it could've been Mount Isa. We didn't have a

branch here and you had to put your money in through the post office.' Merlene's face lit up. 'I tell you what. I have a friend, Nora. Well, Nora used to live around these parts, but she moved into Mount Isa years ago. We still keep in contact by phone, or sometimes we write letters to each other, just every so often.'

Ruby waited patiently, knowing now that she had to listen to all the local information about who was who before the important details surfaced. She sat still, nodding politely at the flow of information about Nora and her family. Eventually Merlene got to the important part.

'Well, Ruby, bottom line is that Nora has a grand-daughter who works for the bank in Mount Isa. I bet they'd still have records there. Back in those days it was all handwritten. Who knows, it might be worth a try.'

The next day, after a good night's sleep, Ruby found herself hopping on another small plane and heading back towards the larger town of Mount Isa. Merlene had phoned her connections in the town and Ruby had an address where she would meet Suzanne, granddaughter of Norah, friend of Merlene.

It had been hard to say goodbye to Merlene. She had so many stories to tell, recollections of Bobby that matched up with the distant memories Ruby had herself. It was strange to think of him as even a twenty year old, much less an older a man of forty-two. All she could visualise was the lanky kid who used to spend his life up in the treehouse with her. She thought about how patient he must have been to put up with a bossy girl much younger than himself.

Her hands gripped the seat armrests as the small plane landed, its wheels bouncing across the uneven strip of concrete that was the Mount Isa airstrip. A blast of hot air met her as she stepped from the cabin and said goodbye to the pilot. She would be making her own way home from here.

Suzanne laughed when Ruby told her how excited Merlene had been to help her track down Bobby's bank account. 'It's not really allowed,' Suzanne said, 'what with the privacy laws and all the rest. But I know you're not after his money and I never really liked following the rules anyway.'

They spent the morning following up the leads Merlene had given Suzanne over the phone the night before. It didn't take long for her to pull up the right entry in the large, handwritten ledger books that showed the transactions and balance for each customer.

Merlene had been right: the name of the account they were looking for was Ringo Smith. Suzanne showed Ruby the date that Robert Carlon had closed his account, which showed a balance of $2513.85. She then flicked to another page further on, to a new account opened on the same day. The name this time was Ringo Smith and the account was opened with the amount of $2513.85.

'Going on Merlene's information, I would guess that this is the same guy and that he now goes by the name Ringo Smith.'

Ruby nodded, amazed at the ease with which Suzanne flicked through the huge books with their pages covered in notations and numbers; records of each person's banking in a time before computers or autobanks.

Suzanne traced the line of transactions with her finger. 'You can see here every time he withdrew or deposited money. It looks like he banked his wage every week, see how these dates are always about seven days apart. He only ever drew out small amounts. I'd say he was a good saver, particularly for a young fella working out here in those days. Most of them drank all their pay or lost it playing cards.'

Ruby pointed to the different names stamped next to the transactions: *Katherine, Camooweal, Kununurra, Weipa* and then *Cooktown*. 'Is this where he went?'

'Yes, it looks like he moved around a lot after Boulia. He certainly didn't stay put. These transactions were made at post office agencies. Usually only the bigger towns had a branch of the bank, and the smaller places just had agencies in the post office. He would've filled in his green deposit slip or red withdrawal slip at a post office. Signatures were at the back of the bankbook, visible only under a special light that most of the post offices had. Once they identified him they would fill in the amount, deduct or add, write in the balance, stamp it all up to make it official, and either give out or take the money. These forms they'd send back to us in Mount Isa because his account was still here with us. A clerk in the bank here would fill in this ledger book and that way make sure the balance in the ledger agreed with the final balance written on the bottom of the form sent through.'

Suzanne peered over the top of her glasses, looking closely, turning the pages, searching for the final entry in the ledger. 'I'm thinking that this last entry coincides with when the computer system came in. Look, account transferred to Cairns. End of entry and balance.'

'Jesus. Cairns? Why couldn't he stay in one place?'

'You're not from around here, are you?' Suzanne smiled knowingly at her. 'We get a lot of drifters in these parts. All out west here, right through the Territory and over beyond to Western Australia, there are thousands of miles of nothing but desert, huge properties, and people who don't ask too many questions. If you want to hide out from someone or something, well, these are the places you go.'

She pointed to the names of the towns where Bobby had been. 'Always plenty of work for a fella like him, and people in these parts are used to drifters, coming and then just going when they want. No questions about the past or present.'

'Thanks, Suzanne, you've no idea how much you've helped me.' Ruby stood up, ready to leave. 'At least we're up to the time when he would've entered the system somewhere. That's if he kept that name. There's no reason he would have changed it, well, not that I know about.'

Suzanne closed the ledger book. 'I'd say he would've kept it because during these years. Unfortunately they tightened up on identification, that is, what you needed to open a bank account. You had to have all sorts of documentation, like a driver's licence, birth certificate or bank account. He probably didn't have anything except the bank account in that name, so he would've used it for ID. I hope you find him, Ruby. Let's hope he didn't get the bug to go overseas.'

Ruby laughed. 'God, I didn't even think of that. As if Australia's not a big enough area to search.' She shook Suzanne's hand. 'I'll be in contact and let you know how I go.'

Suzanne helped Ruby carry her bag to the Greyhound bus that would transport her across the state to the northern city of Cairns. 'Good luck,' she said.

. . .

'THANKS, I think I'm going to need it.'

Ruby boarded the bus, sat down and pressed her face to the glass, the last dusty lights of the mining town fading into the distance as the bus began its long journey towards the coast.

CHAPTER 28

*R*uby's visit to Cairns was not a huge success. She turned up some information on a Ringo Smith regarding temporary employment for the council as a cleaner at the dog pound. Another search revealed a short stint on a sugar-cane farm north of Cairns, which had lasted for a couple of years, but the owners had changed and the people she contacted did not know of anyone called Ringo, or Bobby, so they weren't much use.

It was almost like she'd come to a dead end, and after the success of finding records and information out west she started to feel deflated. It's like searching for a needle in a haystack, she thought. Obviously Bobby never wanted anyone to find him, and he'd certainly never looked for anyone in his family.

The trouble was now that she had started on this search she didn't want to give up. It had become more about proving to herself that she could find him, that her research skills were the best and she would succeed. Her dad's old motto came to mind: *If you want to do something bad enough then you'll do it.*

She had to admit, though, that there was no use staying in Cairns. She was better off heading back home and searching on her computer. Although it was often sluggish to use, at least it did offer up websites that she could search through, hopefully revealing some leads to follow.

Completing what seemed to be a circle of the state of Queensland, she caught the Queenslander train from Cairns back to Brisbane. Splurging a little, she enjoyed the luxury of a small sleeper cabin all to herself. No more flying for the time being: she was going to enjoy being close to the ground, moving at a slower pace.

Lying on the bunk bed, Ruby watched the countryside slide past her window; darker hills and lush cane fields giving way to the wider open spaces of Central Queensland. The chugging, rattling and swaying of the train was soothing, and she lay on the bed for hours enjoying the scenery. She watched the colours of the landscape, the way the afternoon sunlight lit up the plains, the warm, orange light filtering across the dusty paddocks as far as she could see.

Flocks of cockatoos flew alongside the train, and large kangaroos bounded across everything in their path, jumping easily over the barbed-wire fences in their haste to get away from the noisy, clanking train that moved across their territory.

As darkness came she watched the stars, so bright away from the glare of the city. Her eyes closed and she slept easily, the train rocking gently as the red carriages wound their way down the Queensland coast, towards home, towards the cottage on the hill.

CHAPTER 29

Ruby had been home a couple of weeks and was once again enjoying the work both inside and outside the house. Francis stayed with her for the first week, and she had enjoyed filling him in on the trail that had come to a bit of a dead end in Cairns. After Francis left she had begun again, obsessively following the leads she had discovered so far. Using her slow internet connection, as well as visits to archives and the state library down in Brisbane, she now had a few more clues to look into.

She called Francis. 'It looks like I might be off to this property way out in western Queensland.'

Francis picked up on the excitement in her voice as he sat down with the phone for what he knew would be a lengthy conversation.

'Where is it and how are you getting there?' He was intrigued by her commitment to search for Bobby.

'It's a huge cattle property on Cooper Creek. It's not easy to get to and it's taken me a while to arrange the transport to get there. I'll drive down to Brisbane and then catch a plane to Birdsville. From there it'll be another small plane out to the property. I've talked to the manager out there at the station and given him a bit of an idea what I'm doing. He's not a talkative man and he wouldn't tell me anything to start with, but he did say he knew someone called Ringo. He said he'd have to talk to me first to see what it's all about. It sounds like a huge property, with lots of workers who come and go. He said I could stay there, that there's plenty of room. I'm leaving here at four o'clock tomorrow morning. I'm just putting some things in my bag now.'

'What's your lead this time? Is it recent or from decades ago?' Francis chuckled, shaking his head at her persistence.

'No, it's recent, well, a couple of years ago. But it's a photo, a photo of a group of stockmen, a few leaning on a fence, some on horses, a yard full of cattle. There's a bit of a write-up with it, about the drought, the price of beef, tough conditions on the land.' She was skimming the photocopy of the clipping, outlining to Francis the most important parts.

'How do you know it's him?'

'Well, I'm not a hundred percent sure because it only gives their first names. But there's a man in the photo called Ringo. It's only side on and I can't see that it's definitely him, but he looks around the right age.'

She waited for her father's response before continuing. 'I know it's a stab in the dark, Dad, but at the moment it's the only lead I've got and I have to chase it up. Also, I have a feeling about it. The guy in the photo, I can't see his face, but I feel like it's him.'

'If it's a couple of years ago, what makes you think he'll still be there?'

'I know, I realise he may have moved on. But you know what it's like, unless I meet face to face with the people who might know him they don't want to talk. Talking over the phone has proven to be pretty useless. I just think that if I go, there might be someone there who knows where he is.'

'You're pretty determined to find him, but even if your hunch proves right, I don't think he's going to be happy about being found.'

'I have Theresa and her support team on my back. They want him as a witness. It's all getting closer and they want to put that bastard away. We all know Bobby's crucial for the case, and besides, I promised Theresa.' Ruby sighed. 'I said I would find him if he's out there.'

'A man like that who hasn't ever settled down … Look at how many moves you've tracked him through and that's probably only skimming the surface. He doesn't want the past, Ruby Rose. I'd say he's pushed it all behind him.'

'I know. Look, I wouldn't go to all this bother if I didn't think it was so important. Plus, I don't really think he's got a choice in the matter. He's a crucial witness.'

* * *

RUBY FLEW across the width of southern Queensland the next day, watching in awe from the window of the small place as the hazy dawn hues lit up the flat plains of the fertile Darling Downs. As they flew further inland to the west, the sun rose higher above the horizon and the day awakened. The earth below changed dramatically, fertile patchworks of green crops replaced by the aridity of the dusty dry interior. Distance between towns stretched further apart, and the roads became straighter and longer.

She hung on tightly as the plane descended, circling a couple of times before lining up and eventually making a bumpy landing on the Birdsville runway.

The only motel in town offered comfortable accommodation and she enjoyed the air-conditioned rooms, lying in the cool that night listening to the noises from the pub next door. She smiled at the cheering and typical drunken talk that drifted across the carpark to her room. There was an occasional sound of a bottle smashing before the night finished off with an out-of-key singing performance by what were obviously the more lively members of the group. The bouts of laughter had stirred her from her deep slumber, but she had enjoyed the singing and had smiled to herself at the sound of people having fun.

The hung-over choir had been at the motel's cafe for breakfast the next morning and had smiled politely, nodding as she took her seat at the table next to theirs. She said hello and chatted to them as they sat down, commenting that they'd sounded like they were having fun last night.

The young man nearest to her said he hoped their racket hadn't kept her awake. 'We're on our way back from the ball.' He spoke slowly in a typical country drawl. 'B&S Ball, further down the track.' He indicated the vast desert.

Even though the party of men were a bit bleary eyed, they were all dressed neatly and she admired the stockman look of faded jeans and western-style shirts, well-worn riding boots and jeans topped with thick leather belts.

The food had arrived and Ruby and the stockmen quickly demolished the huge breakfast of bacon, eggs and tomatoes. The men washed it down with copious cups of coffee. Passing her as they left, they dipped their hats, the last one in the line leaning in towards her, a cheeky wink directed straight at her.

Finishing her coffee, she had smiled. It had been ages since she'd bothered with men. The last episode with the real-estate guy had put her off completely. Smoothing her hair, she reminded herself that she wasn't quite forty yet, which wasn't really that old and it certainly felt good to have someone pay her even that little bit of attention. Cheeky bugger, she thought, smiling and waving back at them through the cafe window.

The morning had passed quickly and before long she found herself boarding an even smaller plane than what she had flown on yesterday. This would take her to her final destination.

For someone who hated flying, she wasn't doing too bad, and she felt quite proud of herself as the tiny plane circled the dusty runway before straightening up to make its final descent. Ruby felt like she had travelled halfway around the world to get this far and was pleased to be finally reaching the property. The motion of the plane coming to a bumpy grinding halt dragged her mind back abruptly to the present and the task ahead. She watched a ute drive alongside, pulling up next to the now stationary plane.

* * *

'G'DAY, Ruby, it's a pleasure to meet you,' Dave said.

She shook hands with Dave and Edna Frost, the managers of the vast property she had

flown across and now landed upon. Ruby was taken aback at the heat that pressed down on her body; the dry, dusty atmosphere that was different once again from the heat she had experienced in other areas of the state.

'Wait till the wind blows in a couple of hours, missus,' Dave said. 'Then you'll know you're alive.'

When they arrived at the sprawling homestead, they sat out on the veranda of the main house on the property. Ruby enjoyed chatting with the middle-aged couple, who quizzed her on the coastal weather and then told her about the huge differences in temperatures and seasons living somewhere as remote as where she was now.

'Gets up to forty-seven degrees here sometimes, and that can last for a week,' Dave said in his languid country drawl.

His wife chipped in, pouring Ruby another cup of tea. 'Never mind that, what about the bloody winter? Some-times it's below zero.'

'Edna's done up a room for you, love,' Dave said. 'I hope it's all right. It's the best room in the house and looks over the southern reaches of the property.'

Ruby looked around, able to gain a good view from the veranda. She didn't say so, but she really thought it looked the same in every direction. 'Thank you,' she said, 'I really appreciate you putting me up. I do need to talk to you about why I'm here, though.' She pulled the paper clipping from her bag.

'I know,' Dave said. 'Edna filled me in on what you've told her and why you're chasing Ringo. You seem honest to us, otherwise we wouldn't be helping you.'

'We believe you're genuine,' Edna said, 'otherwise we wouldn't be telling you where he is.'

'So you know Ringo?'

Ruby's spirits lifted when Dave said, 'Yeah, of course we do. We wouldn't have let you come this far if we couldn't help you.'

Edna sat back, her glasses hanging loosely on the lower end of her nose as she sipped her tea. 'That's Ringo Smith, the fella there in the photo. He worked for us for a number of years. We never knew where he came from. He literally came walking in through the front gate one day. No car, no horse, nothing.'

Edna slowly poured herself another tea and Ruby started to realise just how unhurried everybody and everything moved in these parts. There was no rush.

'Just a couple of mangy dogs with him,' Edna said. 'We reckon he'd walked all the way from Windorah. He was after work. He said he'd take anything but preferred to work with the animals, especially the horses. Dave put him to work straightaway, mustering, fencing, branding, whatever we gave him he took it on. He was especially good at training the young dogs, teaching them to work with the cattle.'

Dave looked out across the paddocks. 'He's also one of the best for working with the horses. No rough heavy-handed ways for him, instead he's gentle, and I can always tell which horses he's trained. They're calm, steady, and you've only gotta guide 'em with your reins, they just know what to do.'

Ruby gulped out loud as Dave added, 'I wish he'd stayed, there's always work here for someone like him.'

'Are you saying he's not here anymore?'

'Well …' Dave put his cup down and stretched out on his chair, his long legs crossed at the ankles as he continued. 'Ringo always got a bit restless. You could always tell that he wanted to keep moving around. I'd keep him going for a while, send him out for weeks at a time, mustering, driving, letting him get away from it all.'

Edna had been watching Ruby and laughed as she noticed her roll her eyes.

'Sorry, Edna, but surely just being here is getting away from it all,' Ruby said. 'I mean, this is the most remote area I've even been to. How much more isolated can you want?'

'It's true, but when you're a drifter like him …' Edna shook her head. 'We get them here from time to time. I'm not sure what they're running from, but they just want out. They keep moving, all over the state, over the country, always headed somewhere remote. Occasionally they'll take off into town, you know, lots of them getting on the booze. But not Ringo, he was never a big drinker. Just the odd beer sometimes.'

Edna's eyebrows came together as she leaned forward, looking Ruby in the eye. 'He was on for a while with one of the women who worked here.' She looked at Ruby again, testing her, seeing if the words affected her.

'Edna, he doesn't mean anything to me, well, not like that. I'm after him to help his sister. I promise you I'm not chasing him for anything else.'

'Hmmph.' Edna leaned back. 'Just checking, you can never be sure. There are a lot of men running away from wronged women, or women who've done the wrong thing by them. We are a long way from anywhere.'

Satisfied now, Edna didn't hold back, filling Ruby in on the relationship that had developed. 'She was a jillaroo, tough as nails and a great little rider. She used to go out with him sometimes when he was away for a while and they got on really well. I reckon it went on for close to two years. Ringo seemed happy with the situation, even cleaned himself up a bit. Sometimes we'd ask him how they were going together. I think her name was Amy. He'd give you a smile or a bit of chatter back.'

'Come on, Edna,' Dave interjected, 'this'll take all night. Cut the story short, she doesn't need all the details.'

Edna threw a dirty look Dave's way, turning back to Ruby. 'She took off, the rotten bitch left him, and from what the other fellas told us, apparently he didn't even get a warning, she just up and left with the new Kiwi cook we'd employed only the month before. Big ugly bastard, covered in tattoos. Word was they went over to Western Australia, both working in the mines.'

'Oh, dear.' Ruby didn't quite know what to say.

Edna was clearly upset over the situation and followed with a few choice words about wayward women and how they treated men.

'Spare the dramatics, Edna, get on with the story.' Dave was getting bored; he had heard it all before. They were, after all, in a very isolated spot and he would have been the chief sounding board for Edna, who seemed to know all the personal details of the men and women who worked on the station.

'I knew he wanted to go, to get away from everyone here. I talked to Dave about it and we made some arrangements and told him about Augro Downs.' She waved her hand to the west. 'It's about another six hours that way. Well, we told him they wanted a stockman to look after the most remote areas, way out, months away and then just a few weeks back in and then out you go again.'

Dave lit a pipe, puffing quickly to get the tobacco going. 'He grabbed the opportunity with both hands. We said we didn't want to lose him, but that he could work between the two properties. When they wanted him he'd be out there and then when we needed him he'd come back to us for short stints.'

'And that's what happens,' Edna added. 'We don't see him for months on end and then we'll let Ed know, he's the manager on the other property, and he'll get him in and back to us for a while. Then he's back with them, they restock him and out he goes again.'

'And, um, whose property would he be on at the moment?' Ruby closed her eyes, comprehending now the distances, not only in between the tiny towns out these ways but also the massive areas that cattle stations covered. This was not like trying to connect with the person working on the farm next door at home.

'Well, you're in luck, and that's why we wanted you to come straightaway. Ringo's due in to us on Friday, four days away. There's some horses here I want him to work with.' Dave looked pleased with himself, puffing boisterously on his pipe as if the entire situation was resolved.

CHAPTER 30

The next few days passed quickly. The heat of the sun beat in through the window early each morning, waking Ruby. She lay in bed listening to the hundreds of noisy galahs flying above, squawking their presence, the noise echoing across the vastness of the outback. She had been surprised the first day, when she went for a walk and encountered some of the men who had been at the cafe back in Birdsville.

'Small world,' she said to them.

She chatted with them, not sure what they'd been told about her presence at the isolated property. Edna told her later that she had informed them that Ruby was a visiting tourist from the city keen to get a glimpse of rural life for the week.

One of the men, Neville, not surprisingly the cheeky one who had winked at her over breakfast, seemed to pop up wherever she happened to be. It was as though he was following her, waiting for the chance to chat.

He followed her down to the wide muddy creek on

Tuesday, catching up with her as she sat under the shade of the weeping gum trees that leaned out towards the centre of the water.

Keen to talk with someone new after spending most of her time with Edna and Dave, she started the conversation. 'Do you fish here?'

'Yeah, ya can get silver perch in there.' He pointed towards the water, just as something splashed in the shallows.

'Do you think that was a fish?' she asked.

'Nah, lots of turtles there.'

'Do you get crocodiles here?' Ruby eyed the water warily.

He laughed. 'Nah, not here, gotta be a way up north further for them.'

He held his hand out. 'Nev's my name. I hear your name's Ruby.'

'That's right,' she said as she shook his hand. 'Nice to meet you, Nev.' The good-looking stockman was not in a hurry to take his hand from hers, and eventually she smiled and pulled her hand away.

'Long handshakes out here.' His deep voice was friendly.

She was aware that he was looking her up and down. 'Well, time to get back. I promised Edna I'd look through all the old photos she has of the property.'

'I could think of something better to do.'

They started walking back, Ruby's new boots she had bought for the visit now covered in the fine dust that kicked up wherever she walked.

'Why don't you come and have a drink with me? I

could show you around a bit, see what life's really like out here.'

'Thanks, Nev, I'll see how I go.'

Ruby was taken aback as his arm rubbed hers, his dark, tanned skin a sign of the many hours he spent in the sun. His face was handsome, and a new cowboy hat was balanced in just the right manner on his blonde curls, visible when he tipped his hat as they parted ways.

'I'll expect you at sunset tomorrow afternoon,' he said. 'Meet you back here and I'll bring some drinks and food. It'll be a lovely afternoon.'

Confidence, she thought, as he strode away; the swagger of a man she decided was a few years younger than her. Perhaps she would meet him tomorrow. What could it hurt? She was only here for a few days and she needed something to fill in the time. Besides, he was very good-looking, and although she knew she was probably the only single female within hundreds of kilometres, it felt nice, good for her ego, she decided.

Her boots sank into the powdery dust, and she walked slowly, curious now about the date that had just been arranged. At least it would give her something to think about, something to fill in her time before the meeting with Bobby.

Wednesday afternoon came around quickly and Ruby felt a little nervous as she put on her jeans and a bright floral shirt. The reflection in the mirror pleased her, and she fluffed her hair a little, splashing a tiny amount of perfume around her neck. She was going to enjoy this: drinks and dinner on the banks of the Cooper Creek with a very good-looking young stockman.

Nev was true to his word and was waiting for her with wine glasses and a basket of food.

'I bribed the cook, told him not to tell a soul. We don't want every Tom, Dick and Harry to gatecrash our little party, do we?' He leaned across her, once again brushing his arm against hers and sending a pleasant sensation through her body.

Together they watched the sun sink low in the west, the silhouette of the coolabah trees black against the vivid orange-and-red sky, a spectacular sight as the air cooled and the moon came out high in the sky to the north.

'I brought some candles, eh, but I don't think we'll need them, the moon's bright enough,' Nev said.

'I must say I'm impressed. I can't remember the last time someone went to this much trouble for me.'

'You look like you'd be worth the bother. You're one amazing-looking lady.' He bent over and kissed her, surprising her, his lips finding hers, pushing down with a long passionate kiss.

'Thanks, Nev, but I really just came for a drink and some company. I'm not sure I'm, um, up for the romance straightaway.' She moved his hand away from her back, a little surprised by his forward manner.

'Jeez, sorry, I just got carried away. You have the most beautiful eyes I've ever seen, and your lips, I just had to kiss them. Here, I'll move away a bit so I'm not so tempted.' He flashed her a mischievous smile with the whitest, straightest teeth she had ever seen.

Smiling back at him, she tried to regain her breath, his hands on her back and his seductive kiss leaving her feeling a little confused. It had been so long since she felt close to someone. She tried to think straight. Was she attracted to him, or was it just the moment—the sunset, the wine, alone together in a beautiful setting in the middle of the Australian outback?

Get your act together, she told herself.

Changing the topic, she asked him about the river, where it went, did it flood, did he ever swim in it? Nev was a slow talker, but he was interesting and knew so much about Birdsville, the mighty Cooper Creek and the areas adjacent to the property. Ruby sipped her wine slowly, careful not to drink too much. She wanted to be in control and aware of what was going on. Nev, meanwhile, went through beer after beer, the cold liquid amber flowing easily down his throat.

The time passed quickly, until Ruby pointed out that it was late and that she should be getting back to the house.

'Dave and Edna aren't around tonight,' Nev said as he drained another stubby, tossing the empty bottle into the bush beside them. 'They won't be back till the morning.'

She was well aware that the older couple had taken a trip into town. They had informed her they would be back before Friday, to organise the linkup with Ringo.

'I know, Nev, but it's late and it's time to go back.' She packed up the bag he had brought, stacking the empty bottles inside.

'Don't worry about that shit, it's just a few bottles.'

Ruby watched him carefully as he staggered a bit, luckily walking in front of her so she could watch what he was doing. Not that it was very far back to the house, but she was starting to get a funny feeling about Nev and the way he kept looking at her. She was thankful she had put a stop to the kissing from the start, and was relieved when the homestead and outbuildings came into sight.

'Here, just bring that bag back in here for me,' he said. 'This is my little hut here.'

They had come to where Nev lived; a timber-slab building with a rusty iron roof.

A row of huts made up the accommodation for workers on the property. Nev's was second furthest from the main house, only one other hut that was on a lean standing on the other side of it.

Laughing and tripping on the doorsill, Nev pushed the old wooden door open, gesturing for Ruby to enter. Standing outside in the dark, with only the moon lighting the dusty area at her feet, she simply held the bag out to him, knowing she didn't want to set foot inside.

'Thanks, Nev, it was a nice night, but here's the bag. I'm off, see you in the morning.'

'Now, Miss City Girl.' He took hold of her arm, manoeuvring himself so she was between him and the outside wall of the hut. 'I think you should come inside with me. I can show you the best time you ever had. I'll give you the ride of your life.' He pushed himself up against her, pressing her back against the timber of the outside wall.

'Not tonight, thanks, Nev, and you need to get off me.' She pushed him away, her hands on his chest.

'Baby, baby, you know you want me.' He leaned forward, kissing up and down her neck as she tried to squirm from under his arms.

'Let go of me, right now!' She could feel her temper rising, his hands tight on her arms. 'Let go *now!*'

'Baby, just let me show you a good time.' He was starting to sound serious.

She thought about the fact that there probably wasn't anyone close enough to hear if she screamed out. 'Okay, that's enough, Nev.' She tried to wriggle away from him. 'You've had too much to drink, now bloody let me go.'

Nev wasn't taking any notice of her and continued to try and kiss her, his body moving so she couldn't push past him. Just as she was about to bring her knee up hard into his groin, a dark shadow loomed over both of them.

'I think the lady said to let her go.' A man stood behind Nev, obviously one of the other workers who had seen what was going on.

'We're just having a bit of fun.' Nev didn't stop, his hands moving up along her back, inside her shirt.

By now Ruby was struggling to get away, concerned about the fact that there were now two men and herself, alone in the dark with no one else around.

One minute Nev was right in front of her and then the next minute he appeared to lift off the ground and fly backwards through the air, landing on his back with a resounding thud. He lay sprawled out on the hard dusty ground. 'Sorry, miss, Nev here doesn't always have the best manners.' The tall man who had thrown Nev backwards spoke slowly, anger apparent in his voice as he watched the young stockman trying to locate his hat before attempting to stand back up.

'Jesus, you mad bastard. What'd you do that for? You could've killed me.' Nev's words were slurred together, his feet unsteady.

The man grasped Nev's arm and, opening the door to his hut, pushed him roughly in through the doorway, closing the door soundly behind him.

'He'll sleep it off. Don't worry, he won't hassle you again. He'll have some explaining to do tomorrow, though.'

'Thank you, I appreciate your help. He was getting a bit persistent.'

''Night, miss.' The stockman, obviously not wanting further conversation, dipped his hat and entered what Ruby had thought was an empty hut next to Nev's.

''Night,' she replied, before adjusting her clothes, which Nev had pushed in all different directions.

Her feet carried her quickly past the other darkened huts and up into the main house. Locking her bedroom door securely behind her, she lay on the bed, going over the events of the night. Although it had been dark and she had only briefly seen the face of the stockman who had just thrown Nev to the ground, she knew deep down that it was Bobby. The gravelly voice was not familiar, nor was the tall, muscular body or the face that was nearly completely hidden by a beard.

But the eyes … for a split second their eyes had met and she knew straightaway that the person she had been searching for was standing right in front of her.

Dave and Edna would be back tomorrow; she would wait and talk to them first before going to meet Bobby. She had to make sure she didn't send him running in the opposite direction. Excited now, and also a little nervous, she thought about how he might react. Obviously he hadn't recognised her, and as she snuggled down between the covers she went over what she was going to say to him.

For now, no more dates with good-looking stockmen. She had plenty of other ways to fill in her time, rather than drinks and dinner on the banks of the Cooper Creek.

CHAPTER 32

The day after Nev's candlelight dinner Ruby stayed around the house most of the day. She could hear the sounds of the men working over in the big shed and the paddock just behind the main house and wondered if Nev had recovered from last night. Edna and Dave returned late in the afternoon and chatted to her before busily attending to jobs left undone in their absence. They were happy to leave Ruby to her own devices for the rest of the afternoon.

She was curled up in a huge wicker chair on the veranda, watching a couple of dogs fighting over a bone, when Dave came up the stairs near to where she sat.

'Do you like the view?' He took off his hat, wiping his hand across the top of his head and flattening down his hair before replacing it.

'The clouds are amazing and the sky is huge,' Ruby said. 'It's the colours out here that I find so beautiful. The red of the earth is very different from the land near the coastline.'

'Yeah, too right, we're a long way from your beaches. It's beautiful, but it's also bloody cruel sometimes. You're seeing it at not such a bad time. Sometimes it's so dry and hot that the cattle start dying, the kangaroos come in plagues and you feel like tomorrow's never going to come. And then after a few years the rain comes, and it buckets down so much that everything floods and no one can move anywhere. Cattle drown, bridges and roads get washed away and farmers lose their fodder to the waters.'

'But you love it here,' Ruby said. 'You stay, and you've been here for so long.'

'Aye, we do, it's in our blood. Once you've lived out in these parts for so long, you never really leave. Most of us die out here. We wouldn't have it any other way.'

Dave leaned with both hands on the veranda railing, looking out across the dusty paddocks, the endless flatness, the red of the earth reaching out in uninterrupted stretches, broken only rarely by a fence or a crooked windswept tree. 'I believe you had a run-in with Nev last night.'

'Word travels fast. He'd had too much to drink.'

'I'll deal with him later. He's out with a mob at the moment, but he'll be sorry when he comes in. Ah, your mate told me what happened. He's down there now, in the last hut, the one next to Nev's.' Dave pointed down to the last hut. 'I told him you wanted to see him. He thinks you just want to say thank you, he doesn't know who you are. I'm guessing you knew who he was.'

'It was dark last night, and he obviously had no idea who I was. It's been over twenty years since we saw each other and we were both kids.'

'Did you recognise him?'

'Even though he wasn't supposed to be here until Friday, I knew it was Bobby, or Ringo, as you know him. He doesn't look anything like he did as a kid, though.'

'He's pretty rough, and he spends a lot of time out in the middle of nowhere by himself. That's what he likes. Nev'll be feeling sick today when he remembers who pulled him off you. They're sort of in awe of Ringo around here, the other fellas. He's pretty much a loner, although there've been quite a few occasions when he's surprised Edna and me and taken control of difficult situations. He steps up and becomes the boss when it's needed and then he just drifts back into the background. He doesn't put up with any shit. Nev's lucky Ringo didn't snap his neck.'

Ruby hopped up from her comfortable position, still watching the clouds hanging in the sky. There was a small amount of dark colour on their underbelly but very little promise of rain. They stared out at the teasing clouds.

'It can look like that for months,' Dave said, 'doesn't mean a bloody thing.'

Edna joined them. 'Here's some payslips for Ringo, Miss Ruby. Take them down for us and pay your visit. Get it out of the way. It sure is going to be interesting seeing what he thinks about being found after all these years.'

* * *

SOFT DUST SPUN around Ruby's boots, whirly-winds tossing the loose red dirt and a few stray leaves in a circular motion before petering out into the air. Stepping hesitantly out into the yard, she suddenly felt nervous. It was as though the past months had been all about the chase, but now that she was so close to meeting Bobby she wasn't so sure. Would he even remember her? Why would he want to be dragged back into the past when he so obviously had spent his life avoiding any connections to his childhood?

The dust spiralled higher, throwing up anything loose in its path and an eerie orange glow threw its light across the property. Her nose and eyes watered from the dirt in the air, her clothes now covered in a fine powder. She knocked loudly on the door of the last hut in the row. The wind picked up, and she knocked louder, holding her hat over her face as the light dimmed with the arrival of a dust storm.

'Come in, come in quickly.' The door opened and she was beckoned in, the heavy door closing rapidly behind her to keep the encroaching dust out. 'It's blowing up a beauty. Dave said you'd be down with my payslips. Let me turn the light on.'

Ruby listened to his voice carefully, the character familiar, but the words delivered so much slower and deeper. It was dim in the hut due to the blanket of dust pushing up against the windows, the tiny specks tapping like rain against the glass. Ruby waited for him to turn, watching him, looking for the characteristics of a boy she had known so long ago.

His bushman's hat, one corner bent, was low over his eyes. Dark unruly hair poked from beneath and a long beard covered most of his face. When he turned towards her she recognised the chiselled cheekbones, the familiar brooding brown eyes, now set in the rugged, darkened face of a man who had lived his life in the sun, hardened by the dirt and heat; he had the look of a bushman.

His eyes held hers for only a moment as she stood frozen, not sure what to say, where to begin. They stood staring at each other, for a second his eyes narrowing, searching her face before he turned away, his tall frame moving towards the window, looking outside.

'Uh, I think this is going to last for a little while. Can I offer you a cuppa, a cold drink?'

He seemed uncomfortable with her company. She was sure that if not for the thick blanket of dust outside he would have taken the payslips from her and ushered her out. In fact, he probably wouldn't have let her in.

'Thank you, I would love a cup of tea.' She found she couldn't quite begin to say what she had come for; the words were stuck in her throat. 'Do these storms blow up very often? I've never seen one before.'

'Ah, yeah, we get them a lot out this way. It's best to be inside when they hit.' He busied himself with the jug and cups, the inside of the hut filled with silence in stark contrast to the howling wind and banging of loose tin outside.

When he turned to put the cups on the table, her back was to him, trying to no avail to look through the window at the continuing dust storm.

'You won't see anything,' he said, 'that dust will be thick for a while yet.'

She turned to face him, the payslips held tightly in her hands. He had removed his hat and she could now see him properly, the knotted dark curls framing his face, a few silver threads of grey both in his hair and beard. They stood staring at each other, both looking curiously at the other.

'Do I know you, miss?'

'It's Ruby. My name is Ruby. Bobby, it's me, Ruby.'

His eyes closed and then reopened. 'The name's Ringo.'

'Bobby.' She walked closer to him. 'It's me.'

He looked down, his hand grasping the edge of the table as if to steady him. 'Ruby Rose?'

'There's only two people on this earth who call me by my full name,' Ruby replied, her voice excited, 'my dad, and a boy who was the best friend I ever had.'

'Ruby Rose?' He looked perplexed, studying her face before looking her up and down. 'The little mulberry fairy?'

Ruby smiled, her face lighting up, her grin widening. She had found him. She had found Bobby. 'You look so different. You grew, um, big, I mean tall.' She stumbled over her words; now that she had found him she wasn't sure what to say, where to start.

Bobby hadn't moved from where he stood. He shook his head and closed his eyes as if she wasn't really there.

'I've had a lot of trouble finding you. You've moved around a lot over the years.'

'You looked for me? You mean you came here because of me?' His eyes narrowed, and he looked confused and suspicious.

'It's a long story. But Bobby, it's great to see you. It's been such a long time.'

He closed his eyes again. 'It must be over twenty-five years.'

'I'm not thirteen anymore.'

His words so soft she could hardly hear him above the noise from outside. 'No, you're certainly not.' He shook his head again, trying to clear his mind. 'That was you last night, then, with Nev. What were you doing with Nev?'

'Filling in time until you came back. I was waiting to see you. Nev asked me for dinner on the riverbank and I thought it would be fun. Thank you for intervening last night. I think Nev had a very different idea of dinner than I did.'

'I can't believe that was you, is you … Ruby Rose.' Bobby kept running his hand through his hair. 'I'm confused about why you're here. I haven't seen anyone since I left home, when I was a kid. I … I've never seen anyone. You look great, you're so grown up.' He shook his head again, a faint smile on his face.

Ruby held her hand out and Bobby reached out to shake it. His huge hand gently clasped hers, the rough calloused skin warm and firm as he held her hand, shaking it slowly.

'My god, what the bloody hell are you doing here? Why have you come looking for me? I've spent my life tucking away from everyone and everything.' His voice, still slow, now sounded stern and admonishing. 'What is it that you want?'

The dust outside had long settled and the swinging bulb above the table lit up the inside of the small hut. They sat opposite each other, Bobby occasionally shaking his head, amazed that it was actually Ruby sitting across from him.

He searched in the back of the hut and found a bottle of wine. 'I don't normally drink, but I think tonight I'm going to need one.'

Ruby was thankful for the calming effect a glass of wine might bring. Bobby wasn't giving much away with regard to where he had been for the last twenty-five years, but he was intrigued to know she had followed his tracks around the huge state of Queensland.

'I can't believe people let you in on my details,' he said. 'Talk about no confidentiality. And wait till I talk to Edna and Dave.'

Ruby was still getting used to the slow pace of his speech, the many times he stopped in between words, the trouble he had communicating, saying what he really thought. She knew the close bond they had once shared was gone. This was a different Bobby; he was a bushman, used to isolation and the rugged Australian outback, rough living in humpies in the most remote areas of Australia, going weeks, sometimes months without talking to another person.

A life spent working with men, dogs and horses had built an invisible barrier around him, and sometimes when he spoke there was hardness in his voice. He'd had to fight for survival more than once, with men and animals. And women, well, she couldn't get much out of him at all. He was a man of few words, although Ruby knew there were many thoughts and words inside his head. She also realised that he didn't want to look back and wasn't that keen on looking forward either. As he said, he just lived day to day. Nothing wrong with that, and it was how it was going to stay.

He asked Ruby to get to the point, wanting to know the reason why she had tracked him down, listening carefully as she tried to remember all the important details about his uncle's past trial and what she had on the upcoming case. He didn't speak as she filled him in on the facts of both charges. No facial expression, no questions, nothing, just a stony silence.

A couple of times she asked him if he was okay. Did he want her to stop, have a break? He sank further back in his chair and nodded for her to continue with the story.

Now, as she neared the end, Bobby leaned forward, his eyes shut before his hands came up around his face, almost as if he couldn't bear to hear any more.

Ruby spoke softly. 'They asked me to find you because they'd exhausted every avenue and couldn't turn up anything on your whereabouts. Theresa was right—I was probably the best one to locate you. She wants him to stay locked up this time, Bobby. They need you to testify. We all want him done.'

'You've wasted your time.' He hadn't spoken for ages, just listened.

'Theresa needs you. She's a mess. Her life's been filled with turmoil and she tracks a lot of it back to him.'

'Well, we all choose our paths. I've come to learn that.'

'We need to make sure he gets the maximum sentence,' Ruby said.

Bobby was pacing, the bottle of wine long finished, the third cup of coffee steaming in his hands.

'I can't go back,' he said. 'I've, well, I've been thinking about going further out. I've got a job over in Western Australia to go to. Further out than here. Nothing but dust and flies. I'm sorry, Ruby Rose, but I don't do people and places. I'm a sole runner.'

He was slipping through her fingers. All her searching, travelling and finally finding him was going to come to nothing. He was going to bolt the other way, run so far that no one, not even her, would be able to find him. She could see it in his face, his eyes that now wouldn't look directly into hers. He was frightened and didn't want the past dragged up.

He knew he could disappear. The outback was a huge place and people in those isolated, far-flung areas weren't too worried about where you came from. They didn't ask many questions. As long as you were a good worker and kept your head down, you were okay.

Ruby took a deep breath. There was something else she needed to tell him. She had left it until the last, and now it was time to tell him what she had witnessed so many years ago. Evidence that was so sinister it could change the direction of the trial.

'I'll have one more cup of coffee, please, Bobby. One more cup and then I'm off.' Ruby looked up towards the ceiling, choosing her words, thinking carefully about what she was going to say to convince Bobby and change his mind.

CHAPTER 34

*L*ight was just beginning to appear in the eastern sky when Dave and Edna helped Ruby put her bags into the Toyota ute. A plan for Ruby's return to the distant eastern coast had been mapped out in the early hours of the morning, and she now waited hesitantly, nervously rubbing her hands together as she chatted to the elderly couple.

'Thank you so much for all your help.' She hugged them, sincere in her gratitude. 'I would never have found Bobby if it hadn't been for both of you.'

'We thought he'd probably run the other way, but hey, it was worth a try,' Dave said. 'Sometimes you just have to go with your gut instincts and forget the rules. Often these fellas need a shove, a bit of a shake-up.'

All three looked up as the door to the hut at the end of the row swung open and Bobby appeared. His hat was low across his face and a rolled-up swag with some belongings strapped to it was flung over his shoulder, the dust kicking up he walked towards them.

'Good morning,' Ruby said.

They all looked at him as he spoke; his words directed at Dave and Edna. 'The dogs are around the back, tied up so they don't follow. No good taking 'em into the city. Shouldn't be gone too long. Take care of them for me, will you?'

Dave stepped forward and shook Bobby's hand. 'Will do. You're doing the right thing, Ringo. Sometimes you've just gotta face up to the past.'

Bobby nodded before throwing his swag in the back of the ute. 'Thanks for the use of the spare ute.'

'Just drop it into my brother's place in Brisbane. He's coming out here next week, so he can load it up and drive it back out with some furniture Edna wants. Good luck and take care.'

Edna and Dave hugged Ruby again, watching as she hopped in the ute, Bobby taking the driving seat.

As they drove away, Dave turned to Edna. 'What a bloody mess,' he said. 'You never know the stories these fellas keep inside them. He's been carrying that around for all these years, never talking about it, just doing his thing out here.'

'I hope he doesn't give her a hard time. I know he's a decent fella, but he's not happy about going back in there and dealing with all that. The court case will be difficult for him, seeing his sister after all this time. He'll also come face-to-face with that mongrel.'

Dave put his arm around Edna's shoulders, years of wisdom between them. 'Sooner or later you've gotta face up to your demons. Maybe it'll be good for him, hopefully there'll be some sort of ending to it all. Closure.'

They watched as the car disappeared, leaving a trail of red dust behind it as it headed on its long journey east.

* * *

Ruby fell asleep before they had reached the bitumen road. She had been unable to sleep when she returned to the house the previous night; the exhaustion of repeating the story to Bobby leaving her emotionally and physically drained. Now the steady movement of the car, as well as the silence from Bobby, left her unable to keep her eyes open.

He watched her as she slept. She was curled up, feet tucked up underneath her, a cushion padding the side of the door where her head rested. It was the first time he'd been able to really look at her, and he kept sneaking glances in between watching the bitumen that faded into a hazy mirror image far into the distance.

The first night, when he rescued her from that idiot Nev, he had recognised something in her eyes. Just a glimpse in the darkness outside the hut, but something … something he couldn't quite put his finger on at the time. He had sensed a familiarity about her, but the feeling was gone as quickly as it had come. He was focused on the fact that Nev was annoying her terribly, if not coming close to pushing her into something she obviously wanted no part of.

That night, as he lay in his narrow bunk, he had tried to think who she reminded him of. Maybe he'd met her at one of the functions in town. He often went into town when the rodeos or shows were on. He'd tried to fathom that strange feeling when their eyes had connected, but he had eventually given up, unable to place her or think where they might have previously crossed paths.

Sleep had come eventually and he dreamt, as he had so many times before, of running, running hard, his feet moving, legs aching, lungs screaming at him. But his feet never left the hard rocky ground; he was running on the spot, not getting anywhere, not escaping whatever it was that was chasing him. The dream went on forever, and then, as usual, he drifted, almost like flying, his feet coming unstuck from the rocky ground, lifting off the earth, coming down to rest on soft mossy ground covered with ferns and undergrowth.

Instead of the heat and pain in the beginning of the dream, there was now a cool, shady area, a tunnel lined with enormous trees, the foliage covering him and keeping him safe from whatever had been chasing him. He never saw what it was he was running from.

Most nights he woke up well before he drifted onto the safe shady area. The dream would end with pain in his legs and feet, rocks poking into his skin, and often his legs moving even as he woke. Sweat would pour from his body and he would lie awake for hours after, unable to sleep, powerless to prevent his mind from replaying events that had happened over the years.

He preferred not to look back, as he had told Ruby Rose the night before. What was the use? There was no changing anything. It was what it was.

For years after he ran away he often thought of Ruby Rose and the lofty hideout in the mulberry tree. But as the years went past, he found it harder to conjure up an image of what she looked like. Sometimes he could picture her face, with her bright-green eyes and long wavy hair, and there was always a serious look of concern on her face. The picture in his mind dimmed with time as he purposely pushed the past behind him, making a conscious effort not to look back.

Today it was difficult to comprehend that this was the same person he had once spent so much of his childhood with. She was after all, now a grown woman. She still maintained the same sense of compassion, righteousness and, he remembered, her bossy, very bossy, ways.

Like a baby, he thought, looking at her, nice and quiet, docile now she was sleeping. A different story when she was awake, though, and he had no doubt that she would have been able to get herself out of trouble with Nev had he not intervened. Who would have thought that the little skinny girl who had followed him around for most of his youth would turn into a beautiful, headstrong woman who could track him down and talk him into returning to somewhere he had vowed never to go?

She stirred a little, nestling her head further into the cushion, her long slender legs manoeuvring to find the most comfortable position. He liked the way she looked; not too much like a city girl. She was relaxed and confident, and her clothes were feminine, fitting closely to her slim figure. Even asleep, squashed up in the corner of the dirty old ute, she was the picture of elegance.

Bobby's mind drifted back. Looking at her wavy brown hair and the way it fell on her shoulders, he remembered how it looked when they had lain on the treehouse floorboards together. Her hair had been long, wavy and blonde back then. Sometimes he would accidentally lie on it and then watch her try to get up.

He chuckled at the memory, thinking also of the

purple stains that were always around her mouth and smudged across her face and clothes.

Memories of her parents came back, and the house that he had visited so often, with its smells of cakes baking and cookies in the oven. He remembered her mother slipping him a biscuit while Ruby was getting changed to play. 'No, Ruby,' her mum would say. 'No biscuits or cake for you now, it's late. It'll spoil your dinner.' Bobby would turn the other way so Ruby wouldn't see him quickly chewing the last of the large biscuit Mary had given him.

He remembered those green eyes now, the same ones that had stared at him the night before, years ago squinting at him, her little mouth screwing up as she suspiciously checked his face for biscuit crumbs.

There had been some good moments and he thought of other times he hadn't thought about for many years, people and places from the past that had disappeared with other memories, ugly memories, he had left buried under a rock.

Watching her from under the brim of his hat, he thought how unchanged some aspects of Ruby were. Her tenacity to set everything right, to fix problems, her stubborn determination, like a dog with a bone; that had been her character even as a small child. He used to be in awe of the way she wouldn't allow herself to cry in front of him. How often had he sat and bawled in front of her, letting it all out, sobbing and using all her little handkerchiefs until they were wet through.

There were also happier memories; lemonade ice blocks, and little fizzy bottles of soft drink her mum would pack for them as treats when they went on their adventures.

Ruby stirred and shifted in her seat, stretching her long legs, her eyes opening and peering through the window. 'Wow, how long have I been asleep for? I have a habit of doing that.'

'About three hours.'

'Um, is there a town coming up soon?'

'We'll stop just up here a bit further. There's a garage there, a toilet.'

'Thanks, that's exactly what I'm after. Maybe a cup of tea and something to eat.'

Bobby just nodded.

Ruby's thoughts tossed around in her head. Jesus, he doesn't talk much. Funny how people change, it's as if we don't know each other at all.

* * *

VERY FEW WORDS were spoken as they sat opposite each other, both thankful for a strong cup of tea and half-toasted, potentially day-old sandwiches. They sat away from other diners, Bobby leading the way over to the shade of a large tree on the other side of the carpark. A heavy timber picnic table and bench seats provided a cool place to sit.

'You don't like being around people much, do you?' She smiled, hoping for some sort of conversation in return.

'Told you before,' he said, 'I don't like people much. Not my thing.'

'Don't you get lonely when you go so far out, away from life in general?'

'My dogs are with me. I love the bush. Being by myself.'

'Well, you realise that you're going to have to cooperate, perhaps open up a little once we meet Theresa and the legal team.'

'Yep, I'll do what I gotta do. The quicker the better, then I can get back to my life.' He stood up, letting her know that the break was over and it was time to get back into the ute.

To Ruby's dismay, once the car started churning over the miles, the motion of the vehicle made it difficult for her to stay awake. 'Sorry, Bobby, are you okay to drive? I can't keep my eyes open.'

She saw a glimmer of a smile; perhaps he was happy that he didn't have to make conversation if she was asleep.

'All good, sleep away. I'm used to it, the long distances. It's nothing for me. Get the cushion from the back again, make yourself comfortable.'

Wriggling into the corner, with her head comfortably up against the cushion, she closed her eyes and fell fast asleep.

She woke hours later, when Bobby stopped the car.

'Last stop before the final run of the afternoon. We're making good time,' Bobby said. 'We'll get to the next town before the sun goes down.'

'Oh, you're not going to drive at night?'

'Nope.'

Unconsciously she rolled her eyes, only realising she had done so when she saw his bushy eyebrows raise up in surprise at her gesture.

'That was a flashback,' he said, as he gave her a firm look, remembering well how she would always roll her eyes when she disagreed with him.

'Well, I thought we'd travel until late,' she said, 'perhaps cover as much distance as we could in one day.'

Shaking his head, he pointed towards the sides of the road. 'See all the big 'roos lying alongside the road around here? I don't feel like hitting one.'

'Oh, I hadn't thought of that.' It was as if she could read his mind: *City chick. No, you wouldn't think of it, would you?*

* * *

THE SUN WAS a ball of orange fire behind them, sinking quickly under the horizon, the colours brilliant against the red of the soil and the starkness of the huge open spaces. A few stars appeared high in the sky as they pulled into the tiny motel just off the highway. A vacancy sign hung crookedly, one side of the chain dangling loosely, unattached to the sign.

'Grab your stuff. You can get a room here for the night. I'll come back in the morning for ya.'

'What? Aren't you going to stay here with me? Where are you going? We don't have to stay in the same room. I'm sure there'll be two bedroom ones available, it doesn't look like there's anyone around.' Ruby looked at the empty carpark.

'Nah, don't do motels. Got a swag.' He walked back to the car, turning the ignition. 'See ya in the morning. Be ready by sunrise.'

Ruby stood in amazement by herself, her arm weighed down by her bag. Mumbling to herself, she could feel her anger building. Even though they'd been friends when they were kids, that didn't seem to mean anything to Bobby. He obviously didn't think much of her. She could feel the vibe, like he thought she was just a useless city girl.

Perhaps he wasn't too far off the mark, she thought. She definitely knew nothing about the outback, cattle or horses, but she wanted to yell out after him: *I never pretended to!*

What did he want? And who did he think he was? After all, she had made all this effort for his family. Travelled around the state, been accosted by a wayward stockman, and sat or slept in a car all day until her body ached. He was the one who had never bothered to contact any of them, hidden away, running away from all his problems.

She was dusty, tired and disgruntled, and annoyed with his attitude. The way he hid under that hat, and the scruffy beard and messy hair. Well, she'd had enough and tomorrow she was going to let him know, tell him what she thought. She would talk to him about how he needed to behave, to help Theresa, to do the right thing.

Thinking about the past twenty-four hours, she wasn't even sure if she liked him at all. There was the distinct possibility they weren't going to be friends, because this was not the Bobby of old. This was a big scruffy stockman called Ringo who hardly spoke and seemed to blame her for the fact that he was on his way to the big smoke. And now he'd left her to stay by herself in a musty little motel room in the middle of nowhere.

To make matters worse, when she went to the adjoining diner, which was the only food place open, the choice for dinner was a dried-up chiko roll or a pie that looked like it had been reheated ten times over the course of the day. Choosing the pie, she covered it in sauce, scraping the mushy peas from the top before biting into it, praying she wouldn't get food poisoning.

Falling into bed, she lay between the scratchy sheets, alone and a long way from home. It was annoying that Bobby, or Ringo, wasn't what she had expected him to be. Trying to ignore the bugs that were biting the parts of her body not covered by the sheets, she drifted off, the loud clanking of the air-conditioning unit a noisy addition to the muffled television noise from the unit next door.

Hopefully Bobby was having a comfortable, quiet night in his swag, because tomorrow she was going to give him a piece of her mind.

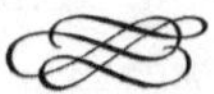

good night's sleep had calmed Ruby down a little. Surprisingly, the noises and smells of the motel hadn't been enough to keep her from sleeping. Packed and ready to begin the day, she sat on the motel doorstep watching the first rays of the sun peep over the horizon, the dark hues of the sky lightening as Bobby drove into the carpark.

Things went much the same as the day before. Ruby chatted for a while and Bobby nodded politely, not adding much to the conversation. He hadn't asked her anything about her life or what she'd done over the last twenty-five years.

After a while she found a CD to play, the soft music of Norah Jones filling the silence and relaxing both the passenger and the driver. Miles of bitumen panned out behind them, the road taking them closer to the city and the impending reality of why they were actually making this journey.

'We're scheduled to meet with Theresa and her legal

team the day after next.' Ruby had decided it was time to get some plans into place before they reached the busy outskirts of the city. 'You can stay at my place while it's all going on.'

'Nah, I'll find somewhere to stay, don't want to put you out.'

'You won't be putting me out. I'm not going to argue about this one, you're staying with me so I can make sure you're at all the required meetings and court dates.'

He frowned at her, unused to anyone telling him what to do. 'I'll be fine. Now I'm here I'll see it through. I can find my own accommodation. I told you, I don't do people and places, particularly not here in the city.'

'You're going to stay with me.' Ruby glared at him, her temper rising again. 'There's a separate cottage on my property so you'll have your own space.'

'Are you in the city?'

'No, I'm a bit north of Brisbane on twenty acres. It'll be better for you. It's out in the country and not so noisy.'

'What about your family, won't they mind?'

'My dad's in a retirement village down in Noosa, and he only comes and stays sometimes. I know he'd love to see you, if you feel up to it.'

'What about your husband, kids?'

'My marriage ended about five years ago and I never had any children. They're not sure why, but they think it's the same condition Mum had. Anyway, we couldn't have any.' She looked out the window, watching the scenery change as they neared the city.

'Oh, I just assumed you were married with kids. That's what you always wanted.'

'Well, things don't always work out how you expect

them to. Dad's the only family I have. Mum died a few years ago, so it's just Dad and me now.'

Bobby went quiet again, and Ruby figured he just wasn't that interested. She thought the mention of her dad might have raised some questions from him. Surely he would have liked to know how her father was going. But there were no questions, the only positive point being that he stopped arguing about where he was going to stay. He followed her directions until finally they were turning right into the gravel driveway leading to her house.

As so many of her visitors did, Bobby slowed under the towering trees, the shade darkening and cooling the air, the arch of foliage beckoning, welcoming silently as the car travelled along the winding path.

Ruby watched him, intrigued by the melancholic look on his face. 'They're beautiful trees,' she said. 'This is one of my favourite parts of the property. Hopefully you'll have some spare days while you're here to have a good look over the place.'

'I'd forgotten how green the hills could be, and the air, it's ...' He was lost for words for a moment as he held his hand out the open window, the cool breeze crisp on his skin. 'It's so fresh and clean. No dust.'

'It's a bit different than out your way. Wait till you see the view.' She could see that he was surprised.

Although it felt like an eternity before he spoke again, she could tell that he was not that unhappy with the cottage situation, and there weren't any further arguments about staying in the separate building.

Opening the door of the cottage, she pointed to the back door that led to the outside bathroom. 'The shower's out the back, and there should be towels. I had a friend,

Lesley, look after the place while I was away, stock up on food and keep the place clean. If I know her, yep, here we go, she's laid out fresh towels and soap for you.'

Bobby was watching her while she looked him up and down. 'There's shampoo there as well. Maybe if you wash your hair twice you might get out the dirt.'

She wondered how he was going to get a comb through the mass of curly hair that coiled out from under his hat, which he hardly ever took off. Between the hat and the thick beard, the only visible parts of his face were his cheekbones and his eyes, dark and brooding, looking at her now, daring her to comment on his appearance.

'Uh, I do know how to wash my hair. Thanks for the advice, but I think I can manage.'

'Oh, Bobby, I'm sorry, it's just, well, you look like a wild man from the bush.'

His eyes didn't waver and he continued to stare at her.

'You're going to have to clean up a bit. Maybe trim your beard, get some decent clothes. You need to look fairly neat and tidy for the trial.'

'They take me as I am or not at all.' He gave her one last cutting look. 'Thanks.'

She realised he wanted her to leave and that perhaps she had said enough. He *was* going to have to clean up his appearance, though. Out west he fitted in; he was just another rugged, dusty stockman wearing stained clothing, his tattered hat and well-worn boots adding to the wild look created by the long beard and mess of curly hair, but here it was a different story.

'Come up to the house when you're ready, Lesley said she'd have a meal prepared for us.' She walked out the door before he could reply.

CHAPTER 36

*R*uby showered and changed out of the jeans and shirt that had been her attire for the last couple of weeks, surprised at the amount of dust that came off her own clothes and body. She slipped on a loose floral dress, enjoying the cool fabric against her skin, clean and free of the dust and grime she had been covered in while sitting in the car.

Setting the table on the veranda, she saw Bobby, a lone figure under the massive trees at the side of the house. Still as a statue, he stood gazing out across the valley. His head moved only slightly as he perused the scene below before bringing his gaze back to the massive boughs of the bunya trees.

She went back inside, and from the kitchen window saw him stroke the rough bark, peering up into the highest reaches of the tree, lingering, before walking slowly towards the house.

'What are those trees?' he asked her when he reached the veranda.

Ruby beckoned for him to sit at the table, which was laid out with dinner. She poured them both a glass of red wine. 'Bunya-nut trees, aren't they magnificent?'

'They must be old.'

As she served the dinner, Ruby related the history of the trees and their significance to the local indigenous people.

'I often sit here and close my eyes, trying to imagine what this place looked like when the Aborigines used to come for their get-togethers. What the valley looked like down there. What they talked about. What their lives were like. I don't even know many aboriginal people. You must've had a fair bit to do with them, out west.'

'They're different fellas out there, a different mob to these ones. All different languages, different clans.'

'What are they like, the ones that live right out there where you work?'

'They're good blokes. Best horseman you can ever get. They're sorta one with the land. They'd have the same values as the tribes that once lived around here. The land is everything to them. Land and kinship.'

'What's important to you, Bobby?'

It took him a long while to answer. At first his eyes narrowed suspiciously, before turning away from her, looking out instead at the view. 'The bush and my dogs.'

'What about Theresa? She's the only real family you've got.'

By now Ruby was familiar with the wall Bobby put up as soon as she tried to get him to talk about family or reconnecting with the past.

'I stopped caring and thinking about the past a long

time ago. I don't look back, there's nothing good there. It don't mean a thing to me.'

'Theresa could do with some family,' Ruby said. 'She's not in a great place. She has mental health issues, probably from the drugs.'

His voice was unwavering, steady and slow as usual as he leaned forward and said, 'I told you, I'll do what I have to get the bastard locked up. Soon as I can, I'll be gone. No one will find me again. I don't do people and places.'

'Okay, okay, don't get so hostile. Can't you just loosen up a bit while you're here? I'd really like you to look over the place and um, actually, I do have one favour.' She paused, waiting to make sure he was listening. 'Dad would really like to see you. He doesn't ever ask me for anything and he never complains. He's told me so many times that if I could get you to come back he'd love to have a chat with you.'

'Of course I'll see your dad. I'm not a mongrel, you know. I'm just not used to having other people around, having to talk to a, um …'

'What? A woman?'

'Well, I work with men mainly. We speak the same language.'

Ruby mumbled under her breath.

He raised his eyebrows. 'What? What did you just say?' She looked at him; her wide eyes an innocent denial. 'I couldn't quite hear you.' He took a sip from the wine glass, enjoying the fruity taste of a hearty red wine.

'The same language, yep, you certainly do speak the same language,' Ruby said. 'It's called not able to communicate, let's bottle up our feelings and just pretend everything's all right.'

'No good whinging about anything.'

'What about talking about things, getting your problems out in the open? If we'd all done that years ago maybe we wouldn't be going down this track so late in the game. Maybe your bastard uncle would've been locked up.'

'We were kids, what else could we have done? The police knew, the priest knew. Who else were we supposed to tell?' Bobby filled up both their glasses.

'I often think about how Lynette even told her mother about her grandfather. And I remember her calling Lynette a slut.'

'I wonder what happened to Lynette.' The red wine had loosened Bobby up a little and he relaxed for a moment, interested in the conversation.

'I still see her sometimes,' Ruby said. 'We meet for a coffee. She's doing all right now.' She leaned back, smiling. 'I thought you might've had a crush on her when we were kids.'

Bobby's lips curled a little at the ends, not quite a smile. 'I did think she was pretty nice. She was sort of well built.'

Ruby laughed out loud, an infectious bubbly laugh that seemed so familiar to him. 'God, all that time when I just thought you were being nice to her, you were probably looking at how well built she was.'

'No, never, I was just a kid.'

Now he was definitely smiling, and Ruby felt a little of the connection of old, just the two of them laughing and talking. 'Do you remember the cow, Bobby?'

He thought hard. 'Daisy, the beautiful big jersey with those knowing brown eyes. Jesus, I'll never forget the day she chased you and you had to run for your life. The snot that used to come out of her nose when she sensed you were around.'

'That bloody cow, I don't think I ever got over her. Even now I get nervous when I have to walk through a paddock around here. One of them only has to look my way and I make a run for it.'

'That cow loved your dad. They say animals can sense a good person. Not that you weren't.' He smiled again. 'It's just that your dad was an extra good person.'

'That cow loved you, too. Remember how she used to rub up against you.'

Bobby stood up suddenly, his face sombre. 'Gonna turn in for the night. Thanks for dinner.'

''Night, Bobby.'

He was already halfway down the stairs, his back to her, just a wave of his hand signalling that he'd heard her.

The blackness of the night swallowed him up as she watched him leave, eventually a light appearing in the hut where he was sleeping.

'Goodnight, Bobby.'

CHAPTER 37

The following weeks consisted of meetings and interviews, visits to solicitors, briefings and discussions with both of them going over and over the events of so many years ago. Then, finally, a brother and sister re-uniting, coming together.

Bobby barely recognised Theresa. As usual she was nervous, twitchy, a cigarette moving constantly from her hand to her mouth. They hugged briefly, awkwardly, just going through the motions, doing what was expected of siblings who hadn't seen each other in a very long time.

A bench seat outside the lawyer's office provided a quiet place to sit, and for over an hour Ruby left them to themselves. She sensed that Bobby wouldn't go into detail with her about what Theresa and he talked about and neither sister nor brother showed any emotion as they came back in together. The solicitor briefed them, gave them advice and answered their questions.

* * *

Ruby had organised for Francis to come to her home for a couple of days over the weekend. She wanted Bobby to ease up, enjoy a little of his stay and, most of all, catch up with her dad.

Francis sat waiting under the huge trees that lined the gravel driveway. A crude log bench seat, situated under the far-reaching boughs of a huge cassia tree, provided him with a comfortable place to wait patiently for his much-anticipated meeting with Bobby.

Ruby drove up the driveway before stopping the car opposite the bench seat, shaking her head. 'I asked him to wait up at the house,' she said to Bobby. 'God knows how he managed to walk down the hill by himself.'

The old man stood slowly as the car stopped, straightening his stooped body, trying to stand tall. Gnarly weathered hands clutched at the walking stick as he used it to lever himself up, his other hand raised in a wave to the two arrivals.

'He's really excited to see you.' She hoped Bobby would be a little friendlier than he sometimes was to her.

'I'll get out here,' he said. 'You drive on, I'll walk up with him.'

Ruby hesitated, about to give her own instructions, but Bobby was already out of the car, the door shutting firmly behind him. She watched as her father stood still, his hand reaching out to Bobby's before they hugged each other.

* * *

That night the three of them sat on the veranda, the huge trees silhouetted against the sky, lit by a full moon.

Stars twinkled across the vast expanse, and the valley floor was dotted with the lights of the numerous farms, like firefly specks across the paddocks.

'Here's to old friends.' Francis lifted his glass high, clinking loudly with both Ruby's and Bobby's.

Ruby had been unusually quiet.

'Cat got your tongue tonight, Ruby Rose?' Francis asked her.

'Just enjoying the moment, Dad, that's all.'

She thought about all the short conversations that had taken place between her and Bobby over the last couple of weeks. She was always the one who initiated the talk, asking questions, trying to get him to open up, usually with little success. But it was different between the two men. Her old dad, stooped over, listened intently, nodding as Bobby talked to him. They had long conversations, Bobby listening, responding and asking questions in return, his tanned face changing expression as they broached a range of topics.

As the night wore on, the two men continued talking, picking up their conversation from the afternoon.

Francis asked Bobby about life on the cattle properties and the different places he had worked. 'It must be strange, coming back to the city after all these years. Having us come and track you down.'

'Well, I guess it's something that had to be done. I've blocked it all out for so long. Now, when I see Theresa, well, there's only her and me left. She needs the closure and something for the years of suffering.' Bobby took a long swig from his beer, his words slow, his voice deep and gravelly.

Ruby turned around from where she was leaning on the veranda. 'And do you need closure too, Bobby?'

Francis scraped the chair noisily as he rose from his seat. 'I'll leave you two to it. I'm going to bed. Jesus, those beers will set me sleeping.' He kissed Ruby on the cheek, his hand squeezing her arm. ''Night, my beautiful Ruby Rose.'

'I love you, Dad. Goodnight, sleep well.'

Bobby jumped up from his chair and held the door open, nodding politely to Francis.

Francis gave him a cheeky grin and a conspiratorial wink. 'Goodnight, Bobby, enjoy the night.'

The noise of the cicadas hidden in every tree and shrub filled the night air, the sound echoing in Ruby's ears. She was trying to quell the anger she could feel rising; anger at being shut out, on the outer. She had tried hard to reach out to Bobby, to renew the friendship they had once had, but he put up brick walls for her at every turn.

Since the first night, when she had filled him in on the evidence of the case so far and what Theresa and her team wanted from him, he had hardly spoken to her at all. General chitchat, as though she was a stranger, not someone who had gone to a lot of trouble to track him down and who wanted to help him.

Ruby filled up her glass again, watching him out of the corner of her eye as he walked past her and sat down on the stairs, looking out across the valley. She wanted to go and sit beside him, talk to him, have him talk back to her. Bobby had been the closest thing to a brother she had ever had, and now he was here she wanted that relationship to return. More than anything, she wanted to help him. Talk to him about getting through the upcoming trial; tell him that she was there for him and Theresa, that she was trained to help people.

She couldn't help herself. 'I asked you before if you wanted closure.'

Bobby didn't turn around; he just kept staring out into the blackness of the night. 'Closure, I had that a long time ago.'

'Do you think so? You're not really good at talking about it for someone who's had closure.'

'I guess it'll be closure to see him stay behind bars.'

'Bobby, I'm trained in this sort of thing. My job is to help people recover from trauma, abuse, events that happened in their childhood.'

'I don't need help.'

'I think you do, you just won't admit it.'

Bobby turned around, his face barely visible. 'I don't need help. You can't change what's happened, so you just gotta get on with it.' His words came out slowly but were delivered in a tone that signalled Ruby not to push it any further. 'It was good to talk to your dad. He's a good bloke.'

She wanted to ask why he was able to talk to her dad but not her. So many questions, things she wanted to tell him, to help him in the weeks ahead. Let him know that he wasn't alone dealing with it all.

'I'll cope by myself. I'll get through it all fine.'

It surprised her that he could still fathom what she was thinking without her speaking any words.

He came up the stairs, placed his empty glass on the table and dipped his hat. 'Goodnight, I'm gonna turn in.'

Ruby didn't answer him. He disappeared into the

darkness, and after a while the door of the cottage closed behind him. She sat for a long time on the veranda, sipping the wine, watching as the lights of the farmhouses in the valley below slowly turned off, one by one.

CHAPTER 38

The weeks before the trial had flown past and the days were filled with meetings and trips, back and forth to Brisbane in readiness for the upcoming court case. The most confronting day for both Bobby and Ruby came when, accompanied by a team of detectives they had to go back to Bobby's old house. There had been legal representatives and others there to support them, but the visit was emotional and exhausting, as well as challenging when required to remember the events of so long ago.

Francis stayed the night after that visit and the next morning he and Bobby took off early, before Ruby had risen from bed. She could hear the ute up on the ridge behind the house; no doubt they were checking on all the different areas and buildings on the property.

Both men seemed to have taken on a new energy, and during the day the conversation flowed between them. Ruby left them to their own devices, enjoying listening as they talked. Safe subjects, she thought, nothing too intrusive or close to what was about to unfold during the court case. Still, they seemed to be at ease and content.

'How come he opens up to you but he won't talk to me, or even show any interest in my life?' Ruby had cornered her father when Bobby had left for a shower.

'He just hasn't been around women for a long while,' Francis said. 'It's a man's world out there. He's used to talking to blokes, about, you know, bloke topics.'

'Well, it's not as if I'm some fancy delicate princess. I can talk cattle and dogs.'

Francis laughed, both hands resting on his wooden cane. 'Well, sometimes people just don't want to be helped. Regardless of what they've been through, they just don't need help. They've learned to deal with things in their own way. They climb over obstacles, kick them out of the way and make the most of what they've got.'

'I know, it's just …' She twisted her mouth a little. 'We were such good friends. It would be nice to talk like we used to, to confide in each other.'

'You're not that little kid anymore, and even more importantly, neither is he. Sometimes you can't get childhood relationships back. You might just have to accept that.' Francis put his hand on Ruby's knee. 'He's appreciative of what you've done, finding him, talking him into coming back, and especially for helping Theresa.'

'He is?' Ruby was surprised; she certainly hadn't seen any evidence of gratitude.

'He is, he told me so, plus a few other things. He did offload a little,' Francis said, 'he's just not a big talker. It takes him a while to get it out. He knows it's going to be tough and that he's going to have to face that bastard in court. He knows he has to stay calm and deliver, and remember the facts. It's a lot of years ago.'

'He talked to you about all that?'

'Sure, he's told me lots of things.' Francis chuckled. 'I don't need your fancy social worker's degree to talk to people. Sometimes it's just the practical ideas that people want to hear. Maybe my life experience counts a bit—you know, a degree in life.'

Ruby pulled a face. She could always count on her dad to bring her back down to earth, keep her feet planted firmly on the ground. The two of them bantered back and forth, the conversation growing livelier as they joked with each other as they had so many times over the years.

Bobby watched them from under the shade of the huge trees, their laughter and the sound of their chatter carrying on the breeze to where he stood. After a long while he joined them.

Ruby looked relaxed. Her wavy hair was tied back, and her piercing green eyes didn't miss a thing as she fussed over her dad.

'You're a good cook,' Bobby said when she served the steak sandwich.

Finally Bobby had acknowledged something. 'I enjoy it now I have the time.'

'She makes a mean curry, fish curry,' Francis said. 'You'll have to make it for Bobby one night.'

'I will if he'd like me to.' She turned towards Bobby, waiting for a reply.

'Thanks, that'd be good.'

Francis winked at Ruby, who didn't look that impressed; she was still waiting for a conversation longer than just a few words.

* * *

THAT EVENING RUBY said to Bobby, 'I've got your clothes ready for the morning, Bobby. The ones we picked out. They're all ironed, and I picked up a tie for you.'

She had tried to get him to trim his hair and beard, but was met with silent opposition, a resolute expression on his face that let her know in no uncertain terms that she should leave him alone. He didn't need to say it; she felt that she could read his mind, which was telling her to butt out and stop bossing.

'Bobby, could you help me into the house?' Francis stood up, ready to turn in for the night. 'It's all right, Ruby Rose, Bobby can help me.' He closed his eyes as she kissed him on the cheek. 'You make an old man very happy. I'm a lucky man.'

'Goodnight, Dad, I love you.'

Francis held onto Bobby's shoulder as they slowly made their way into the house, talking as they went.

Ruby was about to go and check that they were all right when Bobby came back out onto the veranda. 'Is he okay?' Ruby quizzed him. 'He doesn't usually ask for help like that.'

'He just wanted to give me a few tips for the weeks ahead.'

'Do you want to sit and talk for a while? I could make us a coffee.' Ruby was hoping for a final chance to talk to him before the trial began.

'No. Thanks for dinner. I think I'll turn in. Early up tomorrow.' He nodded before once again walking off abruptly, leaving her by herself on the veranda.

Ruby sat for a long time after he left, the moths and

bugs fluttering around the hanging light bulb the only movement in the still of the evening air. She sipped her drink slowly, the facts of the case turning over in her mind. Bobby's attitude towards her over the last few weeks had not been what she had expected when she set out to find him. But at least I was able to talk him into coming back here, she thought.

She knew, though, that once the trial was over he would head back, as far out west as he could go. He obviously didn't feel a connection to her, or the past years they had spent together as best friends, like kindred spirits, sharing so many sad and happy moments of their childhoods.

Maybe boys are different, she pondered, gazing out into the dark. Perhaps they don't hold onto the treasured memories of children. It was like Bobby only thought about the present, only wanted to look at the world one day at a time. Neither looking too far forward nor caring about looking back on the past, even the happy times.

She hoped that once Bobby left to go back out west they would still keep in contact, maybe catch up occasionally, ring each other or email, stay friends, knit back the threads that had once joined them together. But the barrier Bobby had put up between them, the distance and silence he reserved for her, was definite, solid, and she knew that once the case was over it was likely she would never see him again.

Ruby reassured herself that she had done everything she could. Not only had she found Bobby in the middle of nowhere, but she had also talked him into coming back and testifying. But that was as much as she could do.

She sighed, hating the fact that she couldn't fix the

problems, the invisible wall he put between himself and others, and his obvious inability to deal with the real world or, for that matter, to identify that someone cared about him, cared about being his friend.

Flicking off the light, Ruby stood, the silence and still night air wrapping around her as she watched the sky flashing savagely far across the valley to the south.

Across the grassy slope, hidden by the darkness of the night and the towering trees, Bobby stood also, watching the lightning flicker and zigzag across the distant horizon, the light of the strikes revealing the puffy dark clouds of the faraway storm.

He glanced towards the veranda, Ruby visible as she watched the same storm, unaware that he was standing not too far away. He watched her for a long time before walking slowly back inside the hut, shutting the door silently behind him.

CHAPTER 39

The three of them were all up early the next morning and soon the smell of bacon and eggs wafted out from the kitchen. Ruby set the table on the veranda and squeezed fresh orange juice, a favourite of her dad's. Steam rose from a pile of toast and a curly string of vapour spiralled out of the spout of a large enamel teapot in the centre of the table.

'Grub's up,' she said.

Francis's shaky morning legs made for a slow journey across the veranda and Ruby watched as Bobby pulled out a chair for him, settled him in and leaned his walking stick in its set position, out of the way against the timber wall.

'I love a big breakfast, Ruby Rose, that looks fit for a king,' the old man said, his weathered face scrunching up merrily as he winked at Bobby. 'She's a good cook, young Bobby, taught her myself.'

'You never did, Dad. I don't think I ever even saw you

make a cup of tea. Mum used to even put the sugar in and stir it for you.'

'I can cook, young lady.'

'What? Toast?'

'Well, I could cook if I had to. Just as well they bring those meals around at the village, though. I'd probably live on baked beans and toast if they didn't.'

Bobby smiled at both of them, enjoying the lively banter that always flowed between the two of them. 'It's a good breakfast,' he said, his words as usual slow and limited.

'Thanks, Bobby, enjoy.' Ruby had given up trying to get more conversation out of him and felt satisfied that he at least was enjoying the breakfast. 'Is there anything you want to go over in readiness for today?'

'No.' He shook his head. 'Everything's fine.'

'Good.' She looked at her father, who was closely watching the interaction, or lack thereof, between the two of them.

'Well.' Francis raised his orange juice. 'Here's to putting the bastard behind bars for good.'

At least he looked me in the eye, Ruby thought, as she and Francis clinked their glasses.

* * *

WHEN BOBBY CAME BACK from the cottage, Ruby and Francis were deep in conversation, their chatter stopping as they looked up at him. Bobby was wearing long pressed trousers and a collared shirt and tie.

'Holy shadooley, hey, you scrub up all right.' Francis looked Bobby up and down, laughing at the neatly dressed but obviously uncomfortable man who stood in front of him.

'You look good, Bobby,' Ruby said.

She stood up, moved towards him and, without thinking, straightened his tie and turned part of his collar to the correct position. She stood back, aware of his deepening scowl, his dark eyes meeting hers before he looked away. His thick, unruly dark hair still hung down to his shoulders. She bit her lip. His hair was clean but it was still a bit scruffy looking. And the beard, well, as much as she had persisted he had been just as stubborn, and only a tiny bit had been trimmed off, the majority of his face still hidden.

'It'll do,' he growled. 'It's as good as it's going to get.'

'You look fine, young man. Besides, it's not you who's on trial. They're not going to judge you.' Francis stuck out his chin, determined to be on Bobby's side.

'That's true, Dad, but there's going to be a jury, a judge, and it's a court of law, so you can't get much more formal. There's no way I was letting him go in there in his work clothes. Sorry, Bobby, I know it's caused some arguments, but seriously, sometimes I just wish you'd let me decide these things.'

Francis mumbled something. Bobby stopped scowling and gave the old man a quick smile.

'What?' Ruby said. 'What did you say, Dad?'

'Nothing, my love, nothing.' Francis's eyes opened wide, and his bushy eyebrows were pushed high into the deep wrinkles on his forehead.

'Bloody conspirators,' Ruby muttered. 'I'm going to get ready.' She glared at both of them before stomping off into the house to the sound of the two men talking, with a chuckle from her dad every now and again.

Men, she thought. I don't know why I try and organise them. She was starting to feel like she had no control over anything anymore. No one seemed to listen to her, and to add to her frustration, Bobby still treated her like a kid sometimes.

Focus, she told herself, concentrate on the task ahead. Think about the day, what to wear, the time—she looked at her watch—the drive to the city, which folders to take. She gathered up signed documents, drink bottles, snacks, tissues, Panadol and a kit containing every emergency item that might be needed.

'Right, let's go.' She walked back out, rousing the two men who were deep in conversation and tapped her watch. 'Time to go.'

This time there were no arguments or comments as they followed her, Bobby helping Francis down the stairs, Ruby strutting out ahead of them, glancing around to ensure they were behind her.

'Have you got everything, Ruby Rose?' Francis winked at Bobby before looking innocently at Ruby.

Ruby's eyes narrowed and she tilted her head to one side, looking at her dad without speaking.

'Just a joke,' he said. 'You need to lighten up, my love. And might I say you're looking splendid this morning. A beautiful sight for an old man's eyes.'

Shaking her head, she took his arm, planting a firm kiss on his weathered cheeks. 'I don't think I need anyone to help me be organised, but thanks for asking.' Finally her face broke into a smile. She could never be cranky with him for long.

'Move 'em out,' Francis said as he leaned forward and tapped Bobby on the arm.

Ruby started the car, glancing only quickly at Bobby, who sat quietly in the passenger seat. 'Ready?' She smiled at him.

'All good.' He nodded, looking straight ahead.

* * *

Bobby didn't speak again until they dropped Francis off at the retirement village. He had taken the old man's arm and walked him slowly to his front door where the two of them hugged, shook hands and exchanged words before Bobby returned to the car. Ruby waved and blew kisses to Francis, who stood leaning on his walking stick in the doorway, watching them as they drove away.

It's going to be a long trip into the city, Ruby thought, as she changed the channels on the radio, filling the silent void in the car with some upbeat music.

'Are you all right?' Ruby looked over to Bobby, who sat still and quiet as they weaved their way in and out of the heavy traffic that welcomed them into the boundaries of the city.

He nodded. 'All good.'

Ruby took a deep breath, realising that a couple of words were all she was going to get. She parked in the maze of the concrete jungle that was the underbelly carpark of the courthouse.

'Right,' she said, 'let's go.'

During the next week Bobby stayed by himself at a motel near the courthouse while Ruby stayed with friends on the outskirts of the city, her role as a witness disallowing her from attending court until she had given evidence. The media attention had increased with each day of the trial, reporters hounding the different groups as they made their way into the courthouse.

Several times on the news, Ruby had glimpsed Bobby or Theresa as they were hurried away by their support teams; Theresa beginning to show signs of anxiety as the days wore on. Mike Carlon had been a prominent politician, and the case was attracting a lot of attention.

It was hard to see from the television footage what effect the trial was having on Bobby. He appeared to be the same as usual. His long thick hair and bushy beard covered most of his face, and often his head was down as he pushed through the throngs of cameramen and journalists who waited outside the court each day.

Finally it was Ruby's day to appear in court. She sat waiting nervously for the bailiff to escort her into the courtroom. Sweat stuck to her hands and she took several deep breaths, preparing herself for what lay ahead.

Before she knew it she was guided to the witness dock, the court official prompting her to place her hand on the bible and read out loud the oath, affirming that her evidence would be truthful.

She was surprised at the shakiness in her own voice as she responded. *Breathe, breathe,* she told herself, pressing her shaking hands firmly on the dock in front of her.

The questioning from the prosecutors began and she steadied her voice, recalling her childhood living next door to the Carlon family. Ruby glanced over at the jury as she spoke about her friendship with Bobby over those years and the events that she had been aware of. She kept her eyes averted from Mike Carlon, who sat stony faced, his eyes mostly looking down at the dock in front of him.

'Can you tell me when you first became aware of the abuse that Theresa Carlon was suffering at the hands of the accused?' the prosecutor asked her.

Ruby recalled the day that Bobby had blurted out the information. 'I was only ten at the time,' she said, 'but I can still remember his story to this day. Bobby was distraught. He was only thirteen, but he knew what was going on and that it was wrong. He told me he'd told his father about it, and pleaded with him to make it stop.' She looked over at Mike Carlon. 'But Bobby copped it himself then. His father used to beat him. So many times I saw the marks on his back. He used to belt him with a leather belt.'

'And please tell the court why you didn't report the abuse inflicted on Theresa to your parents, whom you apparently had a good relationship with. You told them about Bobby's beatings, and a couple of times your father went to the police about it. He'd tried to help. Why didn't you tell your parents about the sexual abuse of Theresa, that Bobby had outlined to you?'

'We were kids, bound by secrets. We'd taken vows, the sort of oaths that kids make. Secrets that we swore to each other we would never repeat. I wanted to tell someone and I often thought about it, even years later, especially when I heard about similar cases. I'm a social worker and I've dealt with many clients similarly affected. I'd always think back to what had happened to Bobby and Theresa.'

'So when you were a child you never reported it or told anyone?'

'No.'

'Did you ever think Bobby was lying to you? That perhaps he had made it all up?'

'No, never,' she said.

'And why was that?'

'Bobby never lied. He wasn't dramatic.' Her voice become shaky again and she took a deep breath to compose herself. 'He was stoic. He just wanted to protect Theresa, and most of all his little sister, Sally.'

'Were there other reasons why you never doubted him? Did you ever see anything that supported his words?'

'We had a treehouse.' She noticed Mike Carlon's head lift and felt his eyes upon her. 'Bobby and I spent most of our free time up there. We could see out, yet no one could see us. If we kept quiet no one knew we were up there.'

'Could you see next door,' the prosecutor asked. 'That is, into the yard of the Carlon family?'

'Oh yes, you could clearly see into their yard. There was nothing to block the view.'

'And can you tell me what you saw that supported the facts that Bobby had told you with regard to the abuse Theresa was being exposed to?'

She took a deep breath, her eyes making contact with the members of the jury before turning back to the prosecutor. 'Mike Carlon used to come and stay with the family next door. He would arrive in his black Mercedes with his bags.'

'How long would you say he usually stayed?'

'Often for a couple of weeks,' Ruby said, 'sometimes a bit longer.'

'And where would he stay?'

'In the granny flat-type building in the back of the yard. It was self-contained, with its own kitchen and bathroom. He would sometimes go into the house, well, only in the afternoons when Bobby's father was at work.'

'How would you know if the father was at work or not?'

'He was a butcher,' she said. 'He owned the local butcher's shop. He never came home much before six o'clock.'

'Why do you think Mike Carlon went up to the house in the afternoons?'

Ruby looked confused. 'I'm not sure. Bobby never really spoke about that. It wouldn't have been to talk to Bobby's mother because that was the worst time of day for her. She never left her room much after midday.'

'Ms Bradley, did you ever notice Bobby acting strangely, perhaps anxiously, around that time of day?'

Her eyes widened. 'If Mike was there,' she said, 'or if he happened to come home before the father was home, Bobby would panic. That's if Bobby was over at my place. There were many times when we were playing, and in the middle of something, when we heard Mike's car pull up. I remember clearly how Bobby would panic, throw down his bike, jump down from the tree and start running back to his house. He'd yell back to me that he had to go home. Later on he'd tell me that he'd run back to look after Sally, to make sure she was looked after.'

'Did you ever find that odd?'

'Well …' She scrunched up her face, trying to think back. 'I thought about it a few times because Theresa looked after Sally in the afternoons, so usually Bobby was free to be at my place.'

'Did you ever ask him why he rushed home like that? Did he ever talk about why he was so anxious?

The judge intervened. 'Take your time, Ms Bradley. We realise the events are from many years ago.'

Ruby racked her mind. It was obvious that Bobby or Theresa, who had both already testified, had told the court something she might not be aware of. She answered honestly. 'No, he never talked about anything that happened in the afternoons, not in his house. He just used to say that he needed to look after Sally.'

'So you're not aware of any instances of abuse that may have been inflicted upon Theresa or Sally during those times in the afternoon when the accused had unsupervised visits to the house where the girls were?'

'Objection, Your Honour,' the defence counsel said.

'Overruled,' the judge said.

'Bobby never told me about any events that took place in the house on those afternoons.'

'Can you please tell the court what it was that you saw in support of the fact that Theresa was often alone with Mike Carlon?'

'From the treehouse there was a clear view into the yard next door, and I could easily see the entrance to Mike's flat down the backyard. There were many times when I saw Theresa, usually walking in front of Mike, go into the granny flat.' Ruby's chest pounded, her words bringing back the memories like they had just happened yesterday. 'On numerous occasions I saw him lead her by her hand, almost as if she didn't want to go into the flat. Sometimes it was clear that she was crying as she walked in front of him.'

'What did you think at the time? Why did you think she was going into the granny flat alone with him?'

'I was only a kid and I was also very naïve. Sometimes he carried a broom, or got her to carry the mop. I thought,' she said, gulping loudly, 'I just thought he was getting her to clean the flat.'

Although the courtroom had been silent throughout her statements, she felt the edge of silence, as if everyone had stopped breathing, the images obviously taking place in their minds.

'How long would you say each visit to the flat was for?'

'They would be in there for quite a long time. It wasn't very often that I'd see her leave. Usually once I'd seen them go in, I'd forget about them. I wouldn't bother looking over there again. After all, there wasn't much to watch. I just thought she was in there cleaning. I didn't really take much notice of when she came out.'

'And when exactly, Ms Bradley, did you become aware that there was more going on in the flat than just cleaning?'

'I can remember the day clearly.' She looked over at the jurors. 'I know I was only a kid, but I was pretty smart for a ten year old. Perhaps not streetwise, but I was a good listener and I remember Bobby's words exactly that day.'

'Please tell the court what he told you on the fifteenth of August 1972,' the prosecutor said.

'Objection, Your Honour,' the defence counsel said. 'I fail to see how a ten-year-old girl would know exactly the date that her friend told her a story.'

'Objection overruled,' the judge said.

Ruby stood tall, her eyes angry, her voice loud and clear. 'I remember the date clearly, because even at a young age I was a super-organised child. I kept a records book. I wrote down the sort of notes that kids keep when they have a club. Bobby and I called it the Silkworm Club. I wrote every detail in the records book each time we were in the treehouse. I never threw it out.'

'Exhibit F,' the prosecutor said.

'On the fifteenth of August, Bobby and I were in the treehouse with another friend. He told both of us what was happening to Theresa when his uncle took her down to the granny flat. Bobby broke down and told us what had been going on for years, the sexual abuse that Theresa suffered each time Mike led her down the backyard. Bobby said that Theresa was going to run away, that she couldn't take any more. He said that he hated his uncle because of what he'd done, and that his father knew what was going on and wouldn't do anything about it.'

Ruby took a sip of water, the cool liquid soothing her dry throat.

'And can you explain why you never told anyone about this?' the prosecutor said. 'Bobby has spoken about the fact that you liked to fix everything, solve everyone's problems. Why didn't you ever tell your family, or get help for Theresa?'

Ruby felt an ache in her chest. The words seemed harsh, and she now knew the consequences for hiding such hideous secrets from so long ago. She had, after all, questioned herself on the issue many times over the years.

'Bobby made me promise. Like I said earlier, we took an oath. He said if I told anyone he wouldn't be my friend and that he'd never see me again. He said that it would just make things worse, that his dad would beat him even worse, and then Theresa would cop it also—from her dad *and* her uncle. Bobby and I had a pact. We called our secrets, silkworm secrets.'

Feeling exhausted, Ruby was glad when the prosecutor indicated that she was finished for the day and could step down. She looked over at Mike Carlon. His head was down, his hands were wrapped around his balding head and his shoulders were slumped.

Closing her eyes briefly, she sent a silent prayer that he would be locked away once and for all. She looked over at the jurors and walked steadily through the crowded courtroom.

CHAPTER 41

It was another three days before Ruby was summoned back to present more evidence. During this time she stayed clear of anyone associated with the trial and remained cooped up at a friend's place, passing the days by reading and taking long walks in the suburban streets nearby. Francis rang a couple of times and she took solace from his reassuring words, both of them feeling the impact of what had taken place so near to them.

Today she could sense Mike Carlon's eyes on her as she confidently took her place in the witness dock. She knew that he was worried now, knowing that his movements had been observed so many years ago. Also, he knew that primary written evidence, documenting times and dates of his movements had been kept, hidden in a box that so many times had come close to being thrown out with each spring clean.

Now, as she listened to the words reminding her that

she was still under oath, she steeled herself for what lay ahead.

'Previous statements have allowed us to know,' the prosecutor said to Ruby, looking towards the jury, 'that you spent a lot of time in the treehouse in your backyard during the years that are under investigation. Would you say that's correct?'

'Yes.'

'And it has also been concluded that you had a clear view of the outside and doorway of the granny flat where Mike Carlon stayed when he visited the family next door, and you could also clearly view the yard without anyone seeing you.'

'Yes, that is correct.'

'Official evidence shows that in March of 1974, Bobby's mother Isobel Carlon was taken away and admitted under psychiatric care to Wolston Park Hospital, a hospital for the treatment of the mentally ill.' The prosecutor looked over his glasses at the jury before returning his attention to Ruby. 'Could you please relate to the court the events that took place on this day?'

'I didn't actually see what happened to Isobel, that is, Bobby's mother, or Sally, his younger sister. When I got home from school that day, my mother was waiting to take me out shopping for some shoes. So I didn't see Bobby like I normally would have straight after school.' She felt a lump forming in her throat and swallowed, clearing her throat. 'Late in the afternoon, after I got back from shopping, I rushed to the treehouse thinking he'd be waiting for me. But he wasn't there, and, well, he never came to the treehouse again.'

'Did anyone see you go up into the treehouse?'

'Not that I was aware of,' she said. 'I was small, and pretty nimble and quick. I didn't wear shoes, so I guess I was fairly silent when I climbed up the tree and then once I was in the treehouse.'

'What time do you think it was when you climbed up into the treehouse?'

'I would say it was around the six-thirty mark. The sun was getting quite low and I remember it being dim under the tree when I approached it.'

'What did you find in the treehouse?'

'Bobby had obviously been up in the tree earlier, probably when I was at the shops. He'd left me a small package and a note.'

'And can you please explain to the court what the package contained?'

'It … it was … well, it wasn't something that was his. It was something that belonged to Sally, an item that was her favourite possession. It was a red hairclip, a small clip that had a bright yellow butterfly on the end of it. She always used to wear two of them. She always had them on. They never came out of her hair, not even when she slept. The only time they came out was when Bobby brushed her hair and then she would hold them. She'd get agitated, angry, until Bobby put them back in her hair. She wouldn't go anywhere without them.'

'What did you think when you saw the clip?'

'I thought it was odd, strange, because she was uncontrollable unless she had both those clips in her hair.'

'And what did the note say, that is, the note that has been documented as exhibit H?'

'Bobby had written it quickly, I could tell that from the handwriting.'

The prosecutor passed the note to Ruby, beckoning her to read it out loud.

'"Dear Ruby Rose."' She took a huge breath, feeling like she was once again in the treehouse, back in another era, a small girl, confused and so upset that her best friend had left her. It was a strange note, and it still affected her, the emptiness, a sadness, like a part of her had been wrenched away.

Her voice echoed in the courtroom as she read. '"I'm going this time. I'll be gone by the time you read this and I've also left them a note saying not to look for me because I'm never coming back. Dad and Mike have locked Mum up and they reckon Sally as well, but I found this clip in her bed. You'd better have it. You're my best friend, but I have to go. Don't tell anyone, silkworm secret, that you have the clip or the note. Mike is evil. I can't take any more and I'm going where no one will find me, because there's nothing left for me. Don't look for me, you won't find me. I love Sally, but she's gone for good. Goodbye from Bobby."'

The prosecutor gave her a few moments to recover before continuing with his questioning. 'And what did you think when you read the note, Ms Bradley?'

'I was very upset. I read the note several times. I was so upset that Bobby had gone without seeing me and also that he hadn't let me know where he was going.'

'Can you tell us what happened next?'

'I lay on the floor of the treehouse. I just lay there staring at the note. I knew it was getting late but I couldn't move. I was so sad and I remember crying. The mosquitos started to get bad. I remember them biting my legs, so I sat up and that's when I noticed someone moving around the yard next door.'

'That would be the Carlons' yard?'

'Yes.'

'Can you please explain what it was you saw that afternoon?'

'It was still light, but the sky had started to darken and the yard next door was fairly closed off. There were sheds on either side so no one could see in from the side yards, and there was a farm at the back. The only place anyone could see into the yard was from up in our trees, in our treehouse.'

'Would you say that you could clearly see what was going on in the backyard? Or was it a bit too dark, perhaps not very clear?'

'No, I would say it was very clear. I could easily see what was happening.'

'Please tell us what it was you saw.'

'Bobby's dad and Mike Carlon were arguing. They weren't arguing loudly because I couldn't hear what they were saying, but I could see their gestures and it was obvious that they were arguing with each other. Bobby's dad was pacing, as though he was agitated, upset, and at first I thought it was because Bobby had left.'

'Did you think he might be upset because his wife and youngest daughter had also left?'

'No, I never thought that because I knew he didn't care about either of them. I'd spent so much time with Bobby and I knew his dad had wanted them both locked up for years. He used to tell Bobby that all the time.'

'Did you hear anything the two men said?'

'I do remember some words coming up to me. Mike

told Vincent that it was fine, no one would ever know what had happened. They were standing opposite each other, sort of facing each other, but quite a few feet apart. Both of them were looking at the ground. In fact, they looked at the ground quite a lot while they were arguing.'

Ruby felt the tension in the air intensify; it was as if the jurors all leant forward together, waiting for her next words. She didn't know what other facts Bobby had told them on previous days. There were many parts, missing pieces she didn't know about, memories that Bobby hadn't talked about back then and had still not shared with her to this day.

'Please continue, Ms Bradley.'

'Vincent, Bobby's father, kept looking around, back up to the house, as if he was waiting for someone. I clearly heard Mike Carlon say, "He's gone, he's not around, you're being paranoid." I didn't know what paranoid meant, but you can see it written in my records book. The spelling is wrong but it's plain to see what I heard.'

Ruby took a large sip of water before continuing. 'Mike Carlon grabbed a shovel from the side of the shed, right next to where he was standing. He scratched it across the earth, sort of flattening it. That was when I noticed that the ground had been dug up. Even though it was starting to get dark I could see. Where we lived there was really dark red soil, like clay red. I could see the red colour of the earth near where they were standing.'

'What was in that area, where the men were standing? What was the ground normally like in that area?'

'I never thought about it at the time. Later the vision nagged at me but I couldn't work out why.'

'The question was, what did the ground normally look like in that area?'

'It was usually a dusty brown colour on top. The grass grew over the brown soil, which I guess was like topsoil. Chooks always roamed around their yard, so it was always dusty because they constantly scratched it up. Usually the grass didn't grow very well in the back of the yard, that is, the section more down toward the back fence.'

'So why could you see red dirt?'

'Because when you dug down into the brown dirt, below that was bright red soil. We used to do it in our own backyard. The brown soil was on top, but just underneath was this beautiful rich red soil. That's why it was such a good farming area, you could grow anything in it.'

'What happened then?'

'I watched for a bit longer, but the light was fading fast and I knew my dad would come looking for me if I stayed any longer. I picked up my records book so I could write it up that night in my bedroom, and put the package and Sally's clip in my pocket.'

'Is there anything else you'd like to add?'

'I left the treehouse very quietly, being extra careful not to make any noise, and even though there was a torch up in the treehouse I never turned it on. I never took it with me the way I often did when I came down from the tree once the sun had set. Usually Bobby and I would use the torch, because there were often large snakes on the track under the tree. Neither of us liked snakes, so even though I was worried about the dark and the snakes, I didn't use the torch.'

'Why was that?' The prosecutor peered over the top of

his glasses, tilting his head to one side, emphasising his curiosity.

'Even though I was only twelve and naive about many things,' Ruby said, 'I had a terrible feeling about what I'd seen. Even today, as I tell this story, I feel nauseous. Even as a kid I knew that something bad had happened. I knew something wasn't right, that Mike Carlon and Bobby's dad were evil and that they were up to something.'

'And why have you never told anyone about this? Why didn't you report it or tell your family?'

'By the time I got back to the house, it was dark. I had so much to tell my parents over dinner. I told them Bobby had left, that Sally and her mother had been sent away to a mental home. When they asked how I knew, I just said that Bobby had left me a note. I never went into detail about what was in the note or what I had seen that afternoon. The next day Dad went to the police and they confirmed that yes, Bobby had run away, but he was nearly sixteen so there wasn't much they were going to do about it. Boys that age were always running away from home. And that yes, the woman and the little girl had indeed been sent to a home, it had been confirmed by Mr Carlon, and yes, they were better off in the home, they would be well cared for.'

'So over the next few years you never told anyone about what you had seen?'

'There wasn't really anything to tell. I knew the two men had been up to something, but I didn't put anything together.'

'What exactly do you mean by "put anything together"?'

'Well, the fact that a mother and her small daughter

had disappeared, apparently to a mental institution, and the two people who didn't want them living in the house had obviously just dug up the backyard. I didn't connect the two acts.'

'Are the two facts connected?'

'I feel quite strongly that they are.'

'Objection, Your Honour.'

'Objection overruled.'

'What makes you think they're connected, apart from the fact that you observed the two men on the same day that Sally disappeared and her mother was placed in a home.'

'Objection, Your Honour, the younger sister Sally did not disappear.'

The judge raised his voice. 'Objection overruled. There is no written or oral concrete evidence that the younger sister Sally was ever admitted to any mental institution anywhere in Australia during the years surrounding these events.'

There was a murmur from the public gallery and Ruby waited for everyone to settle before continuing.

'It never clicked to me as a child, but something has always niggled at me in later years. Something I've never been able to put my finger on. For a start, no one would've been able to put Sally in an ambulance without her screaming and yelling because that butterfly clip was not in her hair. My mother was home that day, and she saw the ambulance come and go. When I asked her years later she said there hadn't been any noise, the ambulance had come quietly and after a short while had driven away slowly. From our place we could often hear Sally when she was crying. She was a bit slow, what today we would call intellectually impaired. She was a beautiful little girl, though, and I would often stop and listen, as would my parents, when she was crying. We'd heard her yelling a few times over the years, and whenever I asked Bobby why he just said that she'd gone off about something. Often about the hairclips or someone taking her hairbrush from her. We could hear her clearly from our house, even in winter when all the windows and doors were shut. My mother heard no noise that day.'

Ruby took a large sip of water. The strain was starting to get to her and she stiffened her back, sitting up straight. 'The other strange thing was that after that last afternoon up in the treehouse, when I found Bobby's note, I only ever visited it rarely. I felt sad when I went there. I left food and drink there for Bobby just in case he returned, but he never did. After a while I stopped going there. One of the last times I went up there was just before they moved out, that is, Mike Carlon and Bobby's dad. I looked over into their yard and straightaway noticed the colour of the grass. From about half way down the yard all the way to the back fence, the grass was bright green and very neatly mowed. I thought it looked a bit like a bowling green, very neat and manicured. I remember trying to work out why they would do that. Was it because they were selling the place? But why only the back bit, and not the front yard, which was also dusty soil? The chooks were all gone, and there were a couple of new trees planted in the area where the two men had stood arguing that afternoon. That day there wasn't anybody around and I took one last look, and collected a few shells and cups hanging from the shelves before pulling the canvas door shut behind me and descending the tree for one last time.'

'Why do you think the backyard had been planted with grass so neatly?'

'I think someone was trying to cover up the fact that part of the backyard had been dug up.'

'Thank you, Ms Bradley, you're now dismissed.' The prosecutor gave Ruby a small smile and nodded, letting her know that she had spoken the way she should. She had told the truth and answered all the questions clearly. Hopefully her evidence would give weight to the earlier evidence from Theresa and Bobby.

CHAPTER 42

Ruby, Bobby and Theresa sat together on the final day. Days had turned into weeks and the trial had dragged on, fuelling the interest of both the media and the public. The bailiff approached the judge, who shuffled the papers in front of him, occasionally looking over the top of the glasses that hung precariously on the tip of his nose.

The accused sat emotionless, shifting occasionally in his chair, eyes focused firmly on the back wall. Ruby felt Theresa grab her hand and she turned to her, squeezing back, trying to give her some reassurance. Ruby was aware of others behind her—the curious public and some supporters from different organisations—all waiting to see if justice would be done.

Bobby sat motionless, his eyes fixed on the associate, who was asking the spokesperson for the jury if they had agreed upon their verdict.

For Ruby, the next few moments passed in a blur. Theresa squeezed her hand so tightly that at one stage

Ruby had to use her spare hand to unclench the trauma-tised woman's fingers from her own. She saw Bobby sit up straighter, knowing that it was all about to end.

The associate spoke clearly. 'Do you find the defendant Mike Carlon guilty or not guilty of indecent treatment of a child?'

The speaker replied, 'Guilty.'

'Do you find the defendant Mike Carlon guilty or not guilty of interfering with a corpse?'

The speaker replied, 'Guilty.'

'Do you find the defendant Mike Carlon guilty or not guilty of murder?'

The speaker replied, 'Guilty.'

Guilty, guilty, guilty: the words resounded in Ruby's head, and the next few moments passed in slow motion as the associate called upon the defendant. A few words travelled through the haze in her head. 'You have been convicted ... do you have anything to say ...'

Everything began to spin, and she felt Bobby's arm around her shoulder, tears streaming down his face. His other arm enveloped Theresa. There were more words spoken from the courtroom officials, a date set for sentencing, other words directed at the convicted. Before she knew it, Bobby had pulled her up and the three of them stood to exit the courtroom.

Ruby felt dizzy, an overwhelming need for fresh air and a panicky desire to get away from the crowded room motivating her feet to move. For a moment her eyes met Bobby's, the distress in his reflecting the sorrow, the pain of knowing that Mike Carlon had not only molested Theresa and Sally but had ultimately ended Sally's life and buried her body in the backyard.

Moving forward, Bobby grabbed both Theresa's and Ruby's arms, propelling them towards the side door of the courtroom out into the less crowded hallway where Theresa's support team guided the three of them into a room, shutting the door behind them, allowing them some privacy and calm, to take in everything that had just taken place. The three of them knew the respite was temporary, that this was just a quiet haven for a moment before they faced the barrage of journalists and cameramen outside the courthouse.

Ruby's legs stopped shaking and she composed her thoughts somewhat, concentrating instead on Theresa and Bobby. She filled up glasses from a nearby water jug and passed them to the other two, who only stared at each other, lost for words. Theresa kept shaking her head, an unlit cigarette in her hand while Bobby, an anguished look on his face, looked from Ruby to Theresa and back again.

Ruby was trying to take it all in, worried about the two of them, and she fussed over them, refilling their glasses with water and passing tissues. Her eyes met Bobby's. All of them shocked and angered, but relieved that it was over.

CHAPTER 43

It was late in the afternoon by the time the three of them returned to the inner-city hotel Ruby had booked for the night. They sat together on the small motel veranda, Bobby and Ruby both sipping from glasses filled with icy rum and Coke, the cool mixture of alcohol and soft drink soothing their dry throats as well as their nerves and emotions.

Theresa was perched on a stool, putting one cigarette after another in her mouth. She had drunk her rum in shots, slinging back the glass and downing the amber liquid straight. Now she was even more edgy and nervous than earlier and didn't want to hang around, instead telling them that she wanted to return to her family and house. Ruby wondered if she was hanging out for a hit of whatever substance she was obviously on.

The three of them stood on the pavement waiting for the taxi that would deliver Theresa safely home. Theresa said that now the case was over she just wanted to get on with her life, and was adamant that she needed to leave immediately. She had done her bit to put Mike Carlon behind bars, and said she didn't care how long he got locked up for. In her mind some justice had been served and she was just glad it was over with. Her voice was strained, her body agitated as she stood next to Bobby.

'The bastard got what was coming, but what does it matter anyway?' she said. 'You can't take it back, can you? My life's still fucked, has been for years. Just gotta get on with it. I got kids of my own to try and look after. I need to get back to my house.' She hugged the two of them, rushing the goodbyes.

Bobby and Ruby returned to the quiet of the hotel room, both exhausted but still with so many questions unanswered.

'Why did you leave me the hairclip, Bobby? Did you think I would work it out?'

'I don't know. I was so confused that day. I don't think I really knew what was going on, just that something wasn't right.' He pulled up a chair on the veranda, his back turned to Ruby.

'Oh no, you don't,' Ruby said. 'Don't turn away from me. I feel sick about what's happened. There's so much doubt and guilt. Talk to me, for God's sake. I know you're hurting but you need to talk to me.' Ruby felt her eyes welling up and she breathed deeply, gaining control so she didn't burst into tears. Her words were shaky. 'It didn't cross my mind that he'd killed Sally, not back then.'

Bobby turned and faced her, looking straight at her. 'I knew he had.' He put his head down, tears streaming down his face. 'I knew he'd molested her, the filthy bastard. I knew because I lay on her bed when I discovered she was gone. I wanted to keep her smell with me, so

I put my head into her pillow, burying my face.' He wiped his eyes with the back of his hand. 'When I testified in court, before you were called as a witness, I told them that when I put my head in the pillow all I could smell was him—Mike Carlon. That sickly aftershave he always wore. There was nothing of Sally, just his sickly odour on her sheets, over her pillow.'

'Oh, my god.' Ruby covered her mouth with her hand. She felt sick and put her glass down.

Bobby never spoke again until she returned from the bathroom, the sound of her vomiting upsetting him even more. 'You don't need to know anymore, Ruby Rose. It doesn't matter now. It's over.'

'I *do* need to know. I need all the facts or I'll just imagine all different sorts of things. You need to tell me. I've read bits and pieces in the newspapers, but I'd rather hear it from you.'

He turned to face her, his dark eyes looking straight into hers. 'The hairclip was under the pillow. There were a few strands of her hair still attached. I couldn't work it out at the time. It confused me because I knew she'd never have let them take her anywhere without it. It didn't matter because, as the evidence showed and by his own admission, he killed her there on the bed. He molested her then killed her. He panicked. He said he didn't want to kill her.' Bobby refilled his glass.

'Should I have worked it out? I mean, it's obvious now —the red soil in the backyard, the cover-up with the new grass. We all believed that she'd gone to the home with your mum. How blind were we?'

'Ruby Rose, we were kids. Well, you especially. How were we supposed to know how his evil mind worked?

Who would have investigated it anyway? Your dad told me he went to the police several times, that he had a bad feeling about it all. He even tried to contact the home to find out what had happened to both of them. It was all covered up. That bastard Mike had friends in high places, and my father was so caught up in it all that he just kept his mouth shut. He never cared about Sally anyway. He was probably relieved that we were all out of the way so he could move on and start a new life.'

'These last months have been torturous. When I think back to how it all started for me. Digging up the past, finding you and trying to help Theresa, one little girl's life taken and another's life destroyed ...'

Bobby's voice was calmer. 'I think a defining moment for me was the day we went back to the yard with the forensic guys and the detectives. It was like walking back into a nightmare. Even though the house was gone and the yards had changed, those sheds, still closeting secrets, hiding evils. You did well to pinpoint the area where they needed to dig.'

'At least now we can give her a proper burial, put her to rest.' Ruby reached into her purse. 'And we can put this one with her in the grave, next to the other hairclip that was still with her body.'

Bobby reached across and took it from her, the butterfly clip so tiny in his calloused, rough hands. 'I can't believe you kept this, this and your records book. I'm not sure we would've had such a sure case without your help.'

'Of course I kept it. You were my kindred spirit, my best friend. It was all I had to remember you by, that and a few tatty black-and-white photos.'

Bobby stood up, signalling the end of the conversation. She knew he was talked out. The conversation had been lengthy for him, and the past few weeks were catching up with them both, the shock and grief setting in.

He spoke firmly. 'I don't want to stay here. I know you've paid for the two rooms, but I feel claustrophobic, like I need to run, run away as far as I can go. Get out of this city.'

'You might feel better after a feed and a good night's sleep.'

He paced, agitated. 'Can you take me back to your place? I'd feel better sleeping in the cottage for the next few days. Once I've buried Sally I'll be going back out to work.'

'Of course we can. It doesn't matter about the rooms,' she said, 'money means nothing. I'll take you home.'

He picked up his bags, anxiety, even panic, written on his face, his body restless, shaky, as the feeling of being trapped between concrete walls in a big city overwhelmed him. 'Thank you,' he said. 'I do appreciate everything you've done, you know. I know, um, you know, that I don't always show it, but thank you, Ruby Rose.'

'It's okay Bobby, let's go home.'

* * *

Ruby spent the drive home going over the events of the previous months, facts and words tossing around in her head as she tried to put all the pieces together. As the bustle of the city faded into the distance and the highway turned into the familiar, windy hilly roads, she felt her load lighten.

She looked fondly at Bobby, who had fallen asleep before they were even out of the city, his long eyelashes stark against the dark tan of his face. She felt comforted by his company, even though he was asleep. For once he looked at peace; he was not arguing with her or going against everything she had planned.

How strange life could be. Who would ever have envisaged all of this so many years ago? So many secrets, clues, horrors occurring in a family home, right next door to hers. Now convicted, a man who had continued on a sick journey, exposed, not only as a child molester but also a murderer. Even though the sentencing was still to come, the worst was behind them.

As she looked at Bobby, she thought of Theresa. All three of them had felt the same: all that mattered was that the real story had been revealed and justice would be done. There would be no more silkworm secrets.

CHAPTER 44

*I*t took a full day for Bobby to talk again. Reverting to nods and short sentences, only speaking to her when she asked him something. He spent the days roaming across the property, inhaling the crisp mountain air, and often, Ruby noticed, gazing out across the valley.

'I never get sick of the view,' she said. She had come up behind him as he stood leaning on an old wooden fence, his beard long and unruly once more, his old tattered Akubra pushed down roughly on messy black curls that sprang out wildly from beneath the hat. 'What do you think of it?'

'It makes me calm. Probably because it's still,' he said, 'nothing moves. Well, only small things.'

They watched as the cows far in the distance formed a line, following an invisible path down the rolling hills to be milked.

'The council has given permission for Sally's remains to be buried in the local cemetery,' Ruby said. 'They just phoned and said the day after tomorrow everything would be ready.'

His continued to look across the valley. 'That's good. That'll be Friday. Theresa says she doesn't want to be there.'

'I would like to be there, Bobby. Dad said he would wait back here for us. We can have lunch together before I take him home.'

'That'd be good.'

'I'll let him know then.'

Their conversations over the previous days had been much the same, and she could feel that the wall, which had come down momentarily, had appeared again. The only thing he asked her about was if it was all right to work on the fences and gates that needed fixing. Ruby guessed that he liked being out in the paddocks, keeping himself busy and away from the house. Away from her and any conversation he might be forced to have with her.

* * *

Sunlight filtered in through Ruby's window, its warmth and brightness waking her, the curtains moving slowly with the soft breeze that drifted through the casement windows. Leaning on her elbow, she could see straight through the panes of glass to the house yard and over to the slopes that folded and melded down into the valley.

A distant figure walked across her view, stopping at the last piece of flat ground before the drop-off to the steeper paddocks below. Even from a distance she knew it was Bobby. The mist had started to lift from the valley floor and he was standing motionless, looking out beyond the slope. She wondered if he was trying to pick out the local cemetery.

Sitting up, she watched as he took a couple of steps to the north, peering higher, as if trying to pinpoint the grounds that were visible from where he was standing. The day before, she had tried to tell him that you could see the cemetery from the ridge where he was standing now. At the time he hadn't appeared interested, only giving her the customary nod to acknowledge he had heard her.

She rolled her eyes. Men, she thought, and particularly Bobby. Why did he shut her out so often, hardly speak to her? She tried to rid herself of frustrating thoughts. *Think positive*, she told herself as she got out of bed.

It wasn't going to be easy today. Although it would be another chapter of closure, the actual physical side of burying the remains of such a beautiful little girl was going to be very difficult, and she steeled herself for what the day would bring.

* * *

A CAR WOUND its way up the driveway, bringing Francis and his friend up to the veranda, where Ruby and Bobby sat eating their breakfast. There was always someone who jumped at the opportunity to drive him up the mountain, enticed by the prospect of not only a scenic drive, but also the chance to sit on the veranda and have a cup of tea before making their way back down to the coast.

This morning was no exception. Marion, a sprightly eighty-five year old, practically bounced out of the car and reached Francis, who was trying to get out of the passenger seat, well before Ruby or Bobby could get to the car.

Marion, who Ruby had met on several occasions, was, as usual, bubbly and chatty. She even managed to get a small smile out of Bobby, as he watched her fussing over Francis, making sure he was comfortable, checking that his cup of tea was exactly as he liked it.

'Marion and I will sit and enjoy the view while you two young ones go and do what you have to do,' Francis said, as he and Marion waved them off.

'Do you think they're a couple?' Bobby said as they drove away. He was behind the steering wheel today. With no threat of city traffic, he had taken up Ruby's request that he drive down to the cemetery.

'Who?' Ruby didn't know if she was more surprised that Bobby had actually shown interest in what was going on around him or that he had noticed the relationship between Marion and her dad.

'Francis and Marion.'

'What do you think?' she asked, trying to draw some more conversation out of him.

'Well, I hope you don't mind me saying so, but there seems to be some sort of chemistry between the two of them.'

'What sort of chemistry?' She was surprised at his choice of words, so different from his usual two-word sentences.

'Maybe more of a romantic connection.'

Ruby smiled and looked at him. 'I think it's been going on for a while. I asked him about it once, but he got all embarrassed and said something about just being friends.'

'Do you mind?'

'Mind? No, of course I don't. She's lovely, and I can see how she feels from the way she looks at him. He was so lonely after Mum died. Dad likes companionship, he likes to talk, play cards, go to bowls; he just loves being around people. Besides it's good for him to have the company of someone around his own age. They talk about different things than we do.'

'It's nice to see him so happy. I mean, he's always cheery, but he was glowing this morning, the way he looked at her.'

Ruby was shocked at the amount of words spoken. 'Well, you know what they say, Bobby, love makes the world go around.'

'Hmmph,' was the only reply, and she knew that the conversation had ended.

* * *

BOBBY STEERED the car in through the open gateway of the cemetery. The gates were flanked on either side by an old post-and-rail fence, the bulky wooden rails wrapped in colourful flowering creepers. Thick grass still wet with the dew, sparkled as the rays of sun pushed through the lifting mist. A freshly dug grave was visible under a massive jacaranda tree, its flowers coating the ground in a carpet of purple hues.

'How beautiful.' Ruby took a deep breath as she picked up the small bunch of flowers beside her.

Bobby came around to her side of the car and opened the door for her, his dark hair springy and wild without his hat. Already the tears were building and she would have to stay strong so as not to crumble into a useless weeping mess.

A celebrant and two men in dark suits stood beside the small grave and Ruby and Bobby shook hands with the three of them, exchanging a few words before Bobby indicated that the service could begin.

Previously they had both spent time with the celebrant, outlining what they wanted, and he spoke only briefly before gesturing to the two men to lower the tiny white casket into the ground. The song 'A Little Ray of Sunshine' played softly in the background.

Ruby closed her eyes, picturing the beautiful little girl from so long ago. Both hairclips were now with Sally. Ruby had asked that the clip she had kept for so many years be placed in the casket, along with the other hairclip that had been found with her remains.

Bobby tried to say something, but no words came out. Both of them stood silently as the rest of the ceremony proceeded. Breathing deeply, Ruby's chest ached as she watched the effect the small ceremony was having on Bobby.

AFTER THE OTHERS left it was just the two of them standing beside the mound of fresh dirt that covered the remains of tiny Sally Carlon.

'I'm sorry I couldn't protect you, my beautiful baby sister.' The tears streamed down Bobby's face as he finally spoke, his voice just audible. He bent down and smoothed the earth, resting one hand on the mound. 'I loved you and I will never forget you. You will always be my dark-haired baby. Rest in peace.' He kissed his fingers and held them to the dirt.

Ruby knelt down beside him, placing her small bunch of flowers on the mound, which was already sprinkled with purple flowers from the shady tree above.

'Rest in peace, you will always be in our hearts. We'll think of you with a smile.' Ruby smiled, remembering the vision of the little girl from so many years ago, sitting quietly while her hair was brushed, forever in her memory.

Bobby turned to Ruby, his voice shaky with emotion. 'It's right that she has the two hairclips with her and that she's buried in a beautiful place.' He picked up some of the purple flowers from the ground next to where they knelt and sprinkled them over the dirt mound.

Ruby's eyes filled with tears. For once she had nothing to say, nothing to add.

'It's fine, Ruby Rose,' Bobby said, 'we don't need to speak. Our thoughts are with her.'

The ceremony had given Ruby and Bobby a sense of closure, and although no words passed between them on the way home, both felt lighter. This had been the final act in a drawn-out series of events. It didn't matter how long the sentence was for Mike Carlon; for Theresa and Bobby, the effects would be for life.

The trauma of the abuse suffered by Theresa had already damaged her life beyond repair, causing her several times to try and take her own life, and leaving her in a life blurred and muddled, plagued with pain and drug abuse. She would survive, but the damage had been far-reaching and catastrophic.

Bobby would always carry the guilt. No matter how much he told himself it wasn't his fault, the edges of doubt often crept in and he suffered bouts of depression, and craved isolation to try and ward off the memories of years gone by. He had confided in Francis that the trial and subsequent discovery of Sally's body had eased his torment. It had laid to rest many of the demons that had plagued him over the years. There was, he said, a flicker of hope, a motivation for the years ahead, and a feeling he hadn't experienced for a very long time—that this was a new beginning.

Francis was waiting for them, leaning on his walking stick and sitting upright on the fallen log under the trees where he had been that first day Bobby had seen him again after so many years.

Marion's car was parked on the verge and she sat next to Francis. Ruby was sure she saw her dad's arm around Marion's shoulders, but he quickly removed it as they pulled up.

Watching the two of them sitting so innocently under the trees, Bobby chuckled. 'Do you think they were having a cuddle?' he said, turning towards Ruby.

'It looked a bit like it, didn't it? They look cute together.'

He chuckled again, and she thought how wonderful his light laughter sounded after the heavy grief of the morning.

Francis and Marion waved as they walked towards them, the coolness and shade beneath the trees providing a peaceful setting for the four of them to sit and talk before lunch.

'I need to keep moving,' said Marion, who could never sit still for long. 'I'm going to go for a walk further up the hill. Don't wait for me to start lunch.' She gave Francis a kiss on the cheek before she went.

'I can't keep up with her,' Francis said with a wide grin. 'She likes to keep on the move. She says it keeps her young.'

Ruby laughed. 'Well, I'm off also,' she said, 'to get lunch ready. I'll leave you two here, but don't talk for too long.'

Ruby knew that the two men would enjoy the opportunity to talk together and she walked up to the house slowly, enjoying the time to herself. The walk gave her time to think, to go over some of the events of the last couple of months.

She looked back at her dad and Bobby. Who knew what the two of them talked about? She was still miffed that Bobby had opened up so much to her dad, and that they discussed many things neither talked about with her. How long would Bobby stay now that the case was over and the burial completed? He had said he would go once they'd laid Sally to rest, but he hadn't actually set a date yet or asked if she could drive him to the airport.

The questions in her mind were interrupted by a group of fat dairy cows blocking the pathway.

'Shit,' she said out loud, before walking confidently through the middle of them, determined not to stop.

The cows only raised their heads momentarily to look at her, their large brown eyes blinking before returning to munch on the lush green grass. Another problem laid to rest, she thought.

* * *

THE TABLE WAS SET and the food waiting under the protection of the light fly netting when Ruby finally heard the car rattle into the house yard. Bobby and Francis were still talking as they walked up towards the house and she smiled, knowing they would be hungry and ready for a feed. Bobby's arm was firmly under her dad's, who shuffled slowly across the uneven ground, his face happy as he looked up at her waiting on the veranda.

'I thought you'd got lost,' she said. 'I was about to let the flies eat your lunch.'

'Aah.' Francis turned and looked at Bobby. 'We've upset her schedule, still little Miss Bossy.'

'I can hear you, Dad. I'm right here. Someone needs to be organised around here. You two would sit and yack until the cows came home.'

'Actually, we wondered how you managed to walk through the cows.' Bobby's mood was lighter when he spoke and he smiled at her.

'They know who's boss now. I'm not about to let a stupid cow block my path.'

Once the three of them were seated for lunch, Ruby made sure the two men had plenty to eat, fussing over both of them, filling their glasses and passing them everything they needed.

'I don't know what I'd do without you, Ruby Rose. You've always got everything under control,' Francis said as he winked at her.

'Well, I've become very good at looking after myself. I don't need to rely on anyone. I like it that way.'

'How about you, Bobby?' Francis asked.

'Yep, I'm a lone traveller. It's usually just me and the dogs.'

'How about you, Dad?' Ruby grinned, waving her fork in the air, pointing it at her father.

'Well, Ruby Rose, I can look after myself, with a little help from you of course.'

'I'm not talking about me. What about other friends?'

Francis looked at Bobby for support. 'Marion seems like a nice lady,' said Bobby.

'Of course she is. She's a great friend, although lately she's getting a bit forgetful. I'm not sure she'll be able to drive for much longer and I do need to have that conversation with her, sooner rather than later.'

"What do you mean forgetful?' Ruby asked Francis with concern.

'Oh, nothing too serious,' he said, 'we all forget things at this age. She does have a doctor's appointment coming up, though, and I'm going to go with her and see what he thinks. She doesn't mind me looking out for her. Marion and I talk about lots of things. I miss that since Mary died. It's nice to have someone to talk to, share time with and go for walks with. Speak of the devil.' Francis laughed and sat up straight in his chair.

They all turned to see Marion striding energetically up the driveway. Bobby and Ruby exchanged glances, observing Francis's eyes sparkling as he sat up tall, neatening his shirt.

'Right, you two,' the old man said to them both, 'watch what you say. I don't want her to think we've been talking about her. She's the boss, you know, and I don't want to upset her.'

The three of them laughed as they watched Marion walking towards them.

'Now, what are you all talking about?' Marion said, giving Francis a kiss on the cheek and sitting down next to him.

Ruby and Bobby laughed again as Francis's face went a deep crimson.

Ruby was surprised when Bobby raised his glass of orange juice. 'Here's to good friends.'

The four of them clinked their glasses, Francis grinning from ear to ear. His voice was emotional as he held his glass high. 'Good friends and life.'

That afternoon was one they would all remember for a long time afterwards. It was one of those days that Ruby wished would never end, and she soaked it in as the four of them sat around the old wooden table, lunch turning into afternoon tea as Marion and Francis kept them entertained with funny stories of years gone by.

Even Bobby had them all in stitches as he recalled the afternoon Daisy decided to make Ruby run for her life. Ruby enjoyed seeing him come to life, reminiscing about some of the happier moments of his childhood.

He went into great detail about the look on both the cow's and Ruby's faces. 'Your face nearly went purple, Ruby Rose. You had mud all over your legs and arms, and the saliva from the cow was dripping, hanging, from the barbed wire right in front of you.'

'I hated that cow,' Ruby said.

Francis sounded offended. 'Hey, that was my favourite

Jersey house cow. You drank her milk for all those years. She was a beaut cow. The best I ever had.'

'Whatever happened to her?' Marion was enjoying watching Francis reminisce as he recalled his beautiful Daisy.

'Ah, we had to put her down. She lived until she was about twenty, but then she became riddled with arthritis. It was a sad day. She used to love you, Bobby. I remember her rubbing up and down against you.'

'I remember her huge brown eyes,' Bobby said.

'She had issues, that stupid cow,' Ruby said. 'I seriously thought I was going to die that day. I think she had a split personality.'

The stories continued until late into the afternoon, all of them recalling incidents that had happened over the years. Bobby joined in with some hilarious tales from his life in the outback, causing Francis to laugh so much that tears streamed down his face.

Eventually Marion placed her hand on top of Francis's. 'I hate to break up such a great party,' she said, 'but it's getting late and I think we should be starting to make a move back down the mountain.'

Ruby helped her dad up, Marion taking his other arm as they walked him down to the car. The two women chatted closely while Bobby and Francis said their goodbyes. Ruby felt a strange twist in her stomach, watching the two of them together. They were the two men she cared for most. One she saw almost daily, and the other she would soon need to say goodbye to and probably never see again.

Bobby and Ruby stood apart, watching the last of the dust from Marion's little car disappear. It was evident to

Ruby that Bobby was struggling with his emotions as he pushed his hat further down on his head, his eyes watery.

Ruby finally spoke. 'It was a nice afternoon, the four of us all together like that.'

'Um, I'll, um …' Bobby's boots scuffed the dirt, his eyes still fixed on the empty driveway. 'I'll be leaving in the morning.' He finally looked up at Ruby.

'Oh, so soon, I, um, well, I thought you might stay around until the sentence is read. Or maybe even for a couple of extra days.'

'No, I, well, I've made up my mind. I'll go in the morning.'

'Oh. You're really leaving, then. What time do you need to go? I can drive you to the airport, or are you going by train?'

'I'll just make my own way. I don't need you to drive me anywhere.'

Ruby felt blocked out again, that familiar wall coming up now that they were alone. 'Fine then, do what you want. But I expect you up for dinner tonight. Come up at six, I'll see you then.' Turning around, she left him standing there, still staring down the driveway, scuffing the dirt with his worn leather boots.

CHAPTER 47

*P*ink hues blurred across the sky and the last of the sun's rays poked through the stand of giant trees as Bobby and Ruby sat down for dinner. He had arrived promptly at six, bringing a bottle of red wine with him. Ruby had prepared a special meal for tonight and they feasted on fresh king prawns.

As Bobby dipped the prawns in a homemade sauce that made him close his eyes and breathe in heavily, he said, 'This is something I never get out bush.'

'How good are they?' Ruby said. 'And just wait until you try the fish. Marion and Dad picked it up fresh from the wharf for me. I wanted to have a special dinner … after this morning. I hadn't counted on it being your last night.'

'You knew I'd go sooner or later.'

'I know. It's just, I guess, well, it's been nice you being here.'

The good food and red wine was filling, and they sat

relaxed, leaning back, their feet resting on the chairs in front of them.

Bobby spoke slowly. 'I wasn't going to come back with you, from out west you know. Right up until that morning we left, I still wasn't sure. It was tempting to just put it all behind me, like I always had, and disappear again. And if I wanted to disappear I could.' He looked straight at her, as if warning her. 'No one would ever find me.'

'So what made you come with me?'

'I think a lot of it was for Theresa. I figured if she could stand up and testify then so could I.'

'But that wasn't enough, was it? Theresa wasn't enough to make you come back?'

'No.'

'I honestly didn't think you were going to come back with me, either. I remember working out how the trip was going to feel by myself. What I was going to tell Theresa.'

'It's because of what you told me that final night. That is, what your husband had told you, the extra tip-off. '

'He's my ex-husband, Bobby. I'll tell you what, for once he didn't go by the book. Instead he stuck his neck out and passed that information onto me.'

'No one can ever know.'

'No one ever will. He won't ever tell anyone else. What were the chances? If he hadn't interviewed that particular prisoner and talked about politics, I don't think, well, I know no one would ever have looked into it.'

'How did you search? How did you find records from that long ago?'

'They archive everything, both government information and documents from the institutions. I searched through all the records of the homes that existed in Brisbane during those years. There were boxes and boxes of paperwork to go through, as well as some really old reels of archive I had to watch on a projector. Some of it had been transferred to computer files and they were the easier records to find. I found your mum's name, clearly written, the date, reason for admittance and place, even the time and the signature of the admitting clerk.'

'But you couldn't find anything on Sally.'

'There was nothing. Not in the home where your mum went, not in the children's homes, hospitals, hostels, halfway houses, adoption records, foster records. I checked school records, death certificates or photo records. You name it, I looked through it all.'

'That would've taken you a lot of time. Just as well you're stubborn.' He smiled, shaking his head.

'Well, you know me, I just don't give up, like a dog with a bone. I wasn't stopping until I found something. I'm not sure what I thought I'd find, but there wasn't anything. And I think that was when I knew for sure that there wasn't any use looking any further. Deep down I realised that Ben's tip-off related to Sally.'

'What you were looking for was actually the fact that there was nothing there.'

'That's right, and once I was sure I passed everything over to the legal team. I knew they'd do the rest,' she said, 'all they wanted was for me to find you.'

Bobby took the tattered hat off his head, resting it on his chest as he reclined in the chair. 'No one ever questioned it.'

'We were kids. Your uncle and father covered it up.

They told my family and the police that your mum and Sally were both put in the home. Who would ever ask or check? No one ever saw Sally. She didn't attend school, hardly went outside and didn't even get taken to the doctor. Who would notice she was missing? Your mum and Theresa were gone. '

'She barely existed, poor kid. How did your ex-husband connect the prisoner's story to you? How did he know that you knew Mike Carlon?'

'Years earlier, when we were really close, I'd talked to him about different cases at work. One night Mike Carlon was on the TV. I can't even remember what it was about, something to do with politics, supporting someone who was running for a federal seat in Brisbane perhaps. I felt sick when I saw his slimy face on the TV and I guess it brought a lot of memories to the surface. Ben and I talked and I told him what Mike had done to Theresa. I talked about you too, about our friendship, how much it had meant to me growing up as an only child to have a best friend who lived next door. Ben used to listen to all the stories about the treehouse and the silkworms. He obviously listened and remembered the names.'

'If he hadn't connected the names, the crim's story might not have meant much to him. I mean, they probably make up stories all the time, big-noting themselves.'

'That day we met for coffee, the day he told me everything, he said that one of the guys he'd interviewed a few weeks earlier had been talking about Mike Carlon. The conversation had been to do with cover-ups and the bribery that goes on in and out of jail. The crim, well, he'd seen Mike Carlon on TV and told Ben that he couldn't believe Mike was involved in politics again. He said that

Mike had been in jail with him years earlier and was always telling him about how he knew the right people and could get all the extras he needed.'

'Why do you think the guy repeated what Mike said to him? I mean, I thought they had some sort of code of secrecy in prison.'

'Oh, they like to brag sometimes, or perhaps he was trying to get a favour out of Ben. I don't know, I didn't ask too many questions. It was a bit of a rushed conversation because it was definitely a breach of confidentiality, Ben repeating anything one of his clients had told him. The fact is that if that tip-off had been revealed it could've thrown out the entire court proceedings.'

Ruby thought about Bobby's reaction that night she had sat in his small cabin, way out in the middle of the outback, talking to him, giving him the final push that would make him come with her the next day.

Tonight Bobby did not have that confused look anymore, just a resolute, determined attitude. He knew he'd done what he needed to do.

His voice was serious as he looked down into his glass, swirling the wine. 'It was the link, that crim telling someone that Mike Carlon bragged about molesting and then murdering a pretty little girl. If your ex-husband hadn't connected some of the facts, or if the businessman whose daughters were molested hadn't pursued any lead he could find ...' He shook his head, his voice shaky. 'The pieces might never have fallen into place and there wouldn't have been the charge of murder.'

'I know you were surprised when I first told you that night, but you also seemed to know it all made sense. I could tell from your face that a hundred pieces just fell into place. Was it because his smell was in the room? Did you always remember that?'

'I think that stench stayed in my nostrils for years afterwards. I loved it when the dust out west would clog everything up, get in my mouth, nose and ears. Then the stench would go, just for a while.'

Bobby lifted his feet down from the chair where they had been resting. 'It was the smell, but most of all, that day Sally went it was the red dirt, the mud. It was caked on Mike's boots, around the edges, and there were red footprints on the lino in the bedroom. I clearly remember staring at the prints from their boots when they both walked out that door, leaving me alone. I lay on the bed, my head spinning. But there was something … something was trying, pushing hard to get through to me. I kept looking at the lino, the red dirt mixing with the smell of the sickly aftershave on the bed. I was confused about what I was seeing; things didn't match up. But I was distraught. In my mind, Sally and mum had gone and there was only me left. The most terrifying part was that I was left alone with Mike and my dad.'

'And that's when you left?'

'Yep, I panicked. I didn't want to be there when they came back. I wanted to get as far away from everything as I possibly could. I pushed the sight of the mud to the back of my mind, like a kid blots out the really bad stuff that happens. I think I forgot about it. I didn't try and work it out, why there was red mud there when the yard was dusty and brown. The only time you got red mud was when you dug down.'

Bobby stopped talking and turned again to look at her, his tears spilling over, running down his face.

'It's all right, Bobby, it's so terribly sad.' She filled up his glass, trying to choose her words carefully. 'It's all clear to see in hindsight. I actually saw both of them on the newly dug-up ground, obviously nervous, arguing about something they had done or hadn't done to cover up their crime.'

Bobby lifted his glass to hers. 'To Sally.'

Their glasses clinked, the noise loud in the stillness of the night.

'You're welcome to stay. You can stay in the cabin for as long as you want. Have a bit of a holiday, or maybe even look at hanging around for a while. I'd love it if you were here for a bit longer.'

'I thought you'd like to get your own space back to yourself.'

'I am used to being by myself, but I also like the company. I have Dad here quite a lot and Marion often drives him up for a visit.'

Bobby was really opening up tonight. Ruby smiled at him. Was it the wine or the fact that he knew he was leaving tomorrow? She thought about how many times in the previous months she'd wished he would leave. She recalled her frustration at his short, often abrupt attempts at conversation and the fact that he still hadn't asked her about her life, what she had done since they were kids. Tonight, though, he seemed to be interested.

'I thought you always wanted to have kids. I remember you telling me that.'

'I did. I used to dream about it when I was little. I guess it was all I thought I really wanted. But it wasn't to be. We both wanted children, Ben and me. But I had a lot of problems, probably much the same as my mum had. That's why she could only ever have me, just the one.'

Bobby mumbled something and shuffled in his chair. 'Sorry, I didn't think before I asked. I don't need to know.'

Ruby laughed at how uncomfortable he was. It was obvious he hadn't taken part in too many conversations about female reproductive issues, and she could see he was nervous about her reaction or answers to his questions.

'I'm used to it now,' she said, 'it's been going on for so long. The tests were all done years ago, always with the same outcome. It's all right, Bobby, I've learnt to accept that I can't have kids.'

'I'm sorry to hear that. I always thought of you having lots of kids.'

'Shortly after Ben left, his new partner, who, um, was his partner also when he was married to me, well, almost immediately they had a family. They have a little boy and girl. They're really cute kids and he's a great dad. I know it's an odd thing to say, but I'm happy that he's had children of his own.'

Bobby's bushy eyebrows had shot up when Ruby mentioned the affair, and it was clear that he was lost for words, unsure of the appropriate reply.

'It doesn't upset me anymore. Actually, not much does upset me. I like to be in control and sort everything out.' Ruby chuckled. 'Plus, I'm very bloody good at it. Look how I organised getting you back here.'

'That's right, you don't get upset, do you, Ruby Rose? How come you never cry? How do you hold it together? I remember even when we were kids and you hurt yourself, you'd never cry. Me, I've become worse as I've got older.

Men aren't supposed to cry, but I tell you what, over the last couple of months I think I've cried more than I ever have.'

'You've been through so much, Bobby. And it's natural, you're grieving for the person you probably loved most in your life.'

'What about you?'

'I don't know. I do cry sometimes. I like to be in control, though, so I hold it all back. It's like I don't want to give in.' She thought about the fact that she had always told herself she would never cry in front of Bobby, and for some reason, even through the events of the last couple of months, she had managed to maintain that control. 'Would you consider staying?'

He shook his head. 'It's good of you to ask me, but I need to get back out there. It's where I belong. My dogs will be waiting for me.'

Ruby wanted to say so much, but she held her words back. She knew that apart from being able to see Sally's small grave down in the valley, there really wasn't anything to keep Bobby here. His life, as he told her, was out in the bush, riding along boundary fences with no one for company but his dogs and the cattle. Tomorrow he would leave and return to the isolation and remoteness he craved. This could be the last time she would ever see him.

'Will you keep in touch?'

'I'm not great with that sort of thing. I'm going to turn in, Ruby Rose. I want to get an early start in the morning. I'll probably leave just before dawn.'

'I'll get up to see you go.'

Together they cleared the table, neither speaking, just

going through the motions of putting everything away and neatening the table and chairs.

Bobby pulled a small item out of his pocket. 'I want you to have this. It was Sally's.' He passed Ruby a small fabric doll, the dress on it faded and worn. 'I took it the day I left and I've had it ever since. I want you to look after it for her.'

'Bobby, I can't take this, it's the only thing you have of hers.'

'I want you to have it.' And with that he turned and walked down the stairs, the sound of his steps fading into the darkness as he followed the pathway back to the cottage.

'Goodnight, Bobby.' Ruby held the little doll, watching him until she saw the cabin light come on, and then not long after, go off again.

'Goodbye, Bobby,' she whispered before going into the house.

CHAPTER 48

The air was crisp the next morning, a sure sign that winter was just around the corner. Soon the valley would be filled with smoky haze from wood-burners, filtering up from the chimneystacks of the houses below. Low clouds on the horizon blocked the sun's attempts to come over the hills, and the edges of the puffy white pillow clouds shone brightly, as though they were outlined in pen, yellow and vivid against the dark blue of the dawn sky.

Bobby watched Ruby walk down the steps towards him, her brown hair tousled from the warmth of the pillow she had just left. Her eyes were still sleepy and he wondered how much sleep she had actually had last night. Over the last couple of months he felt like he'd come to know her a little as an adult, and he knew that she would have gone over and over the events of the past months, analysing everything and working out what was going to happen in the days ahead.

He smiled to himself. She was still Little Miss Bossy;

organised and always in control. He was pleased that she was so independent and happy in her life, and he tried not to compare the way she looked to the hardened, haunted look of Theresa, who was much the same age.

She stifled a yawn and pulled her dressing gown tighter around her, the dawn air fresh and cool.

Smiling, Bobby jiggled his backpack and straightened his hat. His beard was long and scruffy, his hair, as usual, wild and untamed, poking out from under his torn hat in messy curls. 'You didn't need to get up.'

'I wish you'd let me drive you, at least to the train station.'

'I like to travel like this,' he said, 'I'll get there just the same.'

'I bought this for you as a goodbye gift,' Ruby said, holding out a brand-new Akubra hat.

He ran his hands over the smooth hide of the new hat, stumbling over his words. 'Thank you … thank you, but you didn't need to do that.'

'Well, I did, so take it and wear it. It's to say thank you for all the work you've done around here.'

'That was nothing.' He was lost for words, not sure how to say goodbye. When he eventually spoke, his words were slow, his voice shaky and emotional. 'Thank you, Ruby Rose,' he said, 'thank you from Sally, Theresa and me. Thank you for bringing me back, to face up to everything.'

'*We* put him away,' she said, 'we all did it together. At least he can't hurt anyone else if he's in prison.'

'And he'll be in there for a long time.' Bobby shuffled his feet.

Ruby knew he wanted to get moving. She stood in

front of him, looking up into those dark brown eyes, which hadn't changed that much over the years; they were still the same as when he was a kid.

Bobby's hand came up and stroked her arm. 'Goodbye, Ruby Rose.' He bent down and kissed her on the cheek, his scruffy beard rubbing against her soft skin.

Ruby watched him walk down the gravel driveway, the new hat sitting lopsided on his head. She watched him walk past the cottage, and open and close the gate. The clink of the chain was loud in the stillness of the morning.

Just before he reached the bend in the driveway, he stopped and turned, lifting his hand to give her one last wave. Ruby lifted her hand high in the air, waving slowly, stopping only when he was no longer visible. She stood in that position for a long time, staring down the driveway, waiting for what, she didn't know.

The sun crept over the clouds and faraway hills, throwing a hazy morning light over the paddocks below. Turning slowly, she returned to the flat piece of grass in front of the house as the rising sun brought warmth to the area.

Cows straggled up through the pastures in neat lines as they followed the worn narrow dirt paths to the higher, lush grasses. Roosters crowed their boasts, echoing out across the void, backed by the familiar and soothing laugh of what sounded like a hundred kookaburras perched high in the trees nearby. Dew that had sparkled freshly on the tips of the green grass had disappeared, and she heard the distant sound of a tractor chugging its way across a paddock.

Ruby let the sun soak into her skin, revelling in the

clear, fresh mountain air. She moved back to the house and sat on the top step, her dressing gown pulled around her, her arms wrapped around her knees. Looking down the driveway she gazed towards the huge trees where her dad liked to sit on the wooden log, where he had sat and waited for them to return just yesterday. The only movement was the slight breeze that rustled the leaves of the trees, swirling a little, the branches moving ever so slightly.

That's it, she thought. It's finally all over. Everyone had gone back to where they came from, Theresa, Bobby, Dad and Marion. The whole thing was finished. The accumulation of a year's work, done. Right, she told herself, I need to move on now.

Bobby had gone and she needed to concentrate on whatever it was she'd been doing before this all started. She would focus on her dad, and see him and Marion more often. Get back into work. Book in some more clients. Make some more money. Fix the place up a bit more. Maybe she'd go on a holiday. Where to, though, and who with?

Questions plagued her, but she liked that. It was time to get back into the swing of her life. She didn't need company. She had been happy before Bobby came back. It was just that she had become used to him being around. Even all those weeks when he wouldn't talk or open up, he had still been there. He was company at night on the veranda, and she enjoyed hearing him fixing fences, hammering in loose nails on the dusty floorboards, calling up the cows or herding them into the different paddocks. This feeling would pass. She pushed the doubts down; she was used to having just her dad and herself. Soon she would be back to her old self and stop thinking about Bobby.

Get organised, she told herself. Start the day. She would get changed right now and drive down to her dad's. Maybe he and Marion would like breakfast on the river. She would ring them, organise a time. Maybe pick up some groceries while she was there and call in at work.

Finally, a little motivation; she had a list in her mind, a stream of ideas and jobs that would fill her days, busy ideas that would make her forget.

Forget about what? Who? Just get back into the swing, she told herself. It'll all be good. She pushed her mind into control. Life would return to what it was before.

Slapping her hands on her knees, she jumped up off the step and said out loud, 'Get on with it, Ruby Rose.'

Francis and Marion had jumped at the invitation to have breakfast at one of the small pier cafes on the river, and now the three of them sat talking, waiting for the kitchen staff to cook up the first meals of the day. The smell of bacon cooking and coffee brewing, wafted out from the kitchen, mixing with the chatter of the staff catching up on the events of the night before.

It was one of those spectacular sunny Queensland days, where the sun shone brightly and the sky stretched out in an endless uninterrupted blue. The river wound its way slowly through the weeping paperbarks that lined its banks, its waters lapping gently against the pylons below.

Francis moved slowly, the arthritis that riddled his body keeping him in constant pain. But there were no complaints. 'What's the use of complaining?' he said. 'Hey, Marion, we're still here, so we can't complain.' He chattered away happily, always taking the positive approach to life.

'Oh, you're just a spring chicken, young Francis,' Marion replied as she picked at some loose threads on his shirt.

Since Marion was a couple of years older than Francis, there were always jokes about who was in charge, or who was the more responsible one.

'I just don't know how we got so old.' Marion sat upright, the cobalt-coloured shirt she wore accentuating her blue eyes. 'The years, they just fly by. It all just goes too fast. I feel like I'm putting the wheelie bin out every second day. Gosh, it was only yesterday that I was eighteen and trying to sort out my bridal gown. Now look at us, with nearly two hundred years of wisdom between us.'

'It's great that you have each other,' Ruby said. 'You sort of go together, you two.'

'It doesn't matter how old you are,' Francis said, 'love is ageless. Look at Marion, look at you both. An old man's lucky to have the company of two such beautiful women on a magnificent day.'

Francis smiled, grateful to see Ruby looking more like her old self and pleased that today Marion was getting her ideas and thoughts straight. She was becoming more and more forgetful and yesterday she had trouble remembering who Ruby was when he mentioned going to lunch with her.

'God, you're such a romantic, Francis,' Marion said. 'No wonder I let you hang out with me, even though you're so much younger and less wise than myself.'

Francis's hand closed over Marion's before he turned to Ruby. 'So, it's all done and dusted now. Life will get back to normal. What have you got planned, Ruby Rose?'

'Well, I'm not sure. You know me, I've already made a list in my head this morning of what's coming up next, what I need to get done, and what I want to do.'

'Well, don't forget to make time for some fun things in amongst all the other stuff.' Francis sipped at the cup of tea that Marion had poured from the small silver teapot in front of them.

'Will it be quiet back home without Bobby there?' Marion asked, leaning back, her white hair bright against the backdrop of the cloudless sky.

'It will be, Marion. I have to admit I've liked having Bobby there, even though he was fairly quiet sometimes and clammed up so much. It was nice to see him again, because as kids we were so close for so many years.'

'He's a nice fella, pretty wild and woolly, but underneath that rough exterior you could tell he was just a big softie.' Marion turned to Francis. 'He enjoyed the time with you. The two of you chat quite a lot. Did he open up to you?'

'He did. He did indeed. I guess it was good for him,' Francis said. 'We always got on, even when he was a kid. Bobby was always at our house, or up in that rickety old treehouse. The two of them'—he inclined his head towards Ruby—'they'd spend hours up there. He's still got quite a soft spot for you, Ruby Rose.'

'We shared a lot of secrets once. Well, he told me all his secrets. I don't think I ever really had much to tell him. My biggest secret was that I'd taken a cushion, or maybe a mug from the kitchen to furnish the treehouse. That was about as good as my secrets were.'

'Ah, but he had plenty, didn't he?' Francis soaked in the

warmth of the sun, now filtered by the bright restaurant umbrellas that shielded them from the full force of the heat.

Ruby nodded. 'He did, Dad. He really did. Those kids had it so tough. I feel guilty sometimes, that I was living right next door and didn't have to deal with anything really bad.'

'It's a wonder he turned out all right,' Francis said. 'It was probably the best thing for him, running away when he did, getting out and standing on his own two feet. He told me that the people out in the bush, they just took him in. No questions asked. They gave him work, paid him and provided him with somewhere to live.'

'He really opened up to you, didn't he, Dad?'

'Well, we talked about many things, although we didn't focus on his childhood. I mean, we did talk about the court case and the evidence he knew that would back up the murder charge. But most of all we talked, you know, about work, cattle, just the things we men like to talk about.'

Marion looked over her glasses at Francis. 'So, do you not like our conversation?'

'Now, I never said that, it's just that sometimes men talk about different things.'

Ruby laughed out loud at the sight of the two of them staring each other down, Francis trying to establish the fact that men liked the company of other men while Marion cheekily reminded him that he didn't seem to mind the time he spent with her, chatting for hours together.

The old man's eyes flitted from Ruby to Marion. 'We

like a good balance. It's lovely to talk with other men, but it's even better to have the company and chatter of women such as you two. I'm a very lucky man.'

Ruby snuggled in close to her dad, her head resting on his shoulder. 'No, we're lucky to have you, Dad.'

CHAPTER 50

Life for Ruby returned to normal after the trial. She threw herself back into her work, keeping busy while trying to push the events of the last year from her mind. Often on her way back from work she would stop at the cemetery and light a small candle on Sally's gravesite. As the months passed by, she watched as the falling flowers from the jacaranda tree once again covered the ground, the purple blooms carpeting the small burial mound.

At home she pushed herself to keep going, restoring the house room by room. Francis's visits to the farm slowed a little as the year wore on. A fall down some stairs had affected Marion considerably, her memory had deteriorated further and she could no longer drive or walk unaided. The old couple still liked to spend their time together, chatting, sitting hand in hand under the shady trees at the retirement village, swapping stories of so many years that had passed before them.

This morning Ruby arrived at the retirement village to find them sitting on a wooden bench seat, her dad leaning on his walking stick, Marion holding a large pink flower Francis had picked from the nearby garden. They both waved at Ruby as her car pulled up in front of them, her dad, as usual, delighted to see her.

'What a picture you two make.' Ruby was pleased to see them out in the fresh air, taking in the cool of the early morning. She noticed how slow Francis was as he tried to stand, sitting back down instead, waiting patiently until Ruby came over to them.

'My beautiful Ruby Rose,' he said, 'top of the morning to you. We're just sitting here taking in the warmth of the sun; at this age we have to appreciate every second we have.' He beamed even more broadly as Ruby bent down to give him a tender kiss on his weathered old cheek. 'Oh, you've made my day. I'm a lucky man.'

Ruby bent down to give Marion a kiss also and noticed something different about her usually sparkling eyes. Ruby looked more closely; something was missing, Marion's eyes were strange, watching but not really seeing.

'Marion, say hello,' Francis prompted, 'it's my daughter, Ruby Rose.'

Marion just looked at Ruby, a quizzical look on her lined face. She smiled a little, as one would at a stranger.

'Hello, Marion, it's Ruby. I'm Francis' daughter.'

But Marion just nodded, her bent, wrinkled fingers clutching tightly at the flower. She stared hard at Ruby, her eyes searching before looking down at her flower.

Ruby reached into her handbag, pulling out her

camera. 'Let me get a photo of both of you. What a peaceful morning, just the two of you sitting together.'

Francis leaned into Marion, who turned towards him. She straightened his collar and adjusted his sleeves. Then she faced Ruby and smiled, holding the flower as if it were a posy for a bride.

'Just two young lovers,' Francis said, winking at Ruby before waving to the nurse walking across the lawn towards them. 'I think this lovely young lady,' he said, nodding towards Marion, 'might be ready for her morning tea, or perhaps just a quiet sit inside.'

The nurse helped Marion into a nearby wheelchair, waiting while Francis gave Marion a peck on the cheek. Her hand reached up to touch his face, her eyes scanning his before looking suspiciously at Ruby and then back to Francis.

'Don't be long, Francis,' Marion said, 'and make sure you shut the flaming gate behind you or all those blasted cows will get out.' She looked straight ahead as the nurse wheeled her back inside.

Ruby sat on the bench seat beside him, her pale face betraying her shock at the decline in Marion's health over the last couple of months.

'Are you all right, love?' he said. 'Don't worry, she's happy as Larry. She thinks she's back on the farm when she was a kid. I'm not sure who she thinks I am. It's as if she's fitted me into her earlier life. Some days she knows me, but other times she just sits and stares at me and I can tell she's trying to work out who I am.'

'That's tough, Dad. And she really has no idea who I am. God, she's gone downhill so fast, ever since the fall. You can see it in her eyes. She looks lost.'

'It's a bastard of a thing, and hardest on those around her.' He looked down at his feet, both hands resting on the walking stick. 'Now, my love, enough sadness, what about you? What have you been up to?'

'Well, not much, really. The days just float by, one into the other. I've, well, I've, um, lost my drive, my motivation. I just feel a bit unsettled, although I keep busy, what with work and the house. It's like, well, some days it like I'm just going through the motions, like nothing's driving me. If it wasn't for you, Dad, I don't know what I'd do.'

'You were busy for so long, Ruby Rose, what with buying the farm and then looking for Bobby. And then the court case, that was all consuming. Now you've slowed down and stopped rushing. You're not looking forward, that's your problem.'

'I know, I'll climb out of it. It's just that nothing really excites me at the moment. It's one of the rare times in my life that I just don't have any drive. No real purpose.'

'What about Bobby?'

'What about Bobby, Dad?'

'Well, why don't you go out and pay him a visit? He'd probably like to see you again.'

'If he'd wanted to keep in touch or see me, he would have written, or even picked up a phone and rung me. He knows where I am. Not even one phone call over the last year. Nothing.'

'He's a real loner, isn't he?'

'Obviously he didn't feel any connection to me. Our friendship didn't mean anything.'

'I'm sure it did. In fact, I know it did. He told me so himself.'

'Well, he never told me. The day he left I wondered if

I'd ever see him again. I realised then that he'd probably just disappear, like he did when we were kids. He's always running from something.'

'You seem annoyed. Is he knocking around inside your head? I mean, if you're thinking about him maybe you should try to ring him.'

'I'm not thinking about him. I just would've liked our friendship to continue. Anyway, enough about Bobby, let's go and have some lunch. I've brought your favourite pickles and a nice little slab of silverside that I cooked up.'

'Did you happen to bring a couple of cold beers?' Francis was standing up now, eager for their regular lunch, followed by some icy-cold ales.

'I might've put in a couple.' Ruby gave him a teasing smile, loving the feel of his warm hand as it closed over hers. 'Lunch, beers and then, if we can put off the afternoon nap, there's a footy game on at two. I can't think of a better way to spend an afternoon.'

'You know how to make an old man very happy. That sounds like the perfect day.'

They walked together, Francis's hand leaning on Ruby's shoulder, his other arm pushing out on the walking stick as they made their way along the path to the little retirement unit that was home.

'Perfect indeed, Dad. This is when I am content and happy. When I'm with you.'

'We're kindred spirits, the two of us. Your mother used to always say that. She'd say, "You and that girl, it's like you even know what the other one's thinking. It's as if she's part of you." I'd tell her she was imagining things; that you were just as close to her as myself. But she wouldn't hear a bar of it. "I know the girl loves me, Francis," she would say, "but there's something about the two of you together."'

'She was right, Dad. You and I, we've always had that connection. I was close to Mum. We always did so much together, right up until she got sick, but it was different from what you and I have. Maybe it was always meant to be, because look at us now. It's just us left. Just as well we get on, you and I, because we're it.'

'I miss her, your mother. I miss her a lot, especially these days. She was my one great true love until you came along. And then it was shared. The day they first put you into my arms and I looked down at the most beautiful baby with the chubby pink cheeks and those darn big eyes looking straight into mine, I was lost. And then when you grabbed my finger straightaway—'

Ruby interrupted. 'All babies do that, Dad.'

'This was different. There was a tingling sensation when you squeezed my finger. You wouldn't let go and I couldn't move. I just sat gazing down at you, knowing I was going to look after you for the rest of my life. That I would look after you and your mother and do anything to make you both happy.'

'And you did, Dad. We had such a great life. I look back on my childhood, and those happy days, just carefree.'

Francis sighed. 'We never had a lot of money, and that little house with the worn lino and the rattling noisy plumbing … Remember how cold it was in winter because the windows never sealed up properly?'

'It was great. I loved that place. When you think about it, Dad, we were forced to live really closely together. We had to sit together for every meal, and to watch the TV. And the rooms were so close to each other; we were right next to each other when we slept. No wonder we were so content, we did everything together.'

'It was a very happy life. I love you, Ruby Rose.'

'I love you too, Dad.'

CHAPTER 51

That night, lightning, like forks of white electricity streaked across the sky. Ruby lay awake for hours, unsettled, tossing and turning, unable to sleep, instead watching the spectacle across the valley. Cracking thunder cut through the still air and flashes of bright light illuminated her room. Eventually the awaited torrential rain pounded down on the corrugated-tin roof.

Storms normally lulled her to sleep, but tonight the humidity and heaviness in the air stifled her, forcing her to move her pillow in different directions and stretch out her body, trying to find the best position. Her mind drifted, going over many of the events before Bobby came back and then after.

She wondered where he was. Had he returned to the property where they'd eventually met up? Or had he, as he had often hinted, gone where no one would find him again? Taken his dogs and swag and disappeared into the dust of the outback. Did he ever lie awake at night and think about her? Did he picture the final resting place for

Sally? Perhaps envisage a tiny mound covered in a purple carpet of flowers? Or had he pushed it all to the back of his mind and just continued with his life?

A window banged loudly, the wind that was picking up forcing it back and forth, the frosty glass shuddering with the collisions against the window frame. Ruby got up to shut it, her mind turning to Francis. Looking across the valley, she knew the storm would cross over the ridge before descending on the valley below. Eventually it would follow its usual path, finding its way to the coastline and bringing rain to his tiny garden before blowing itself out to sea.

Was her dad awake? He loved storms. Maybe he was also looking out the window, watching the lightning, pleased that the delicious life-bringing rain was falling heavily on the grounds around him. She smiled, knowing he would be thinking about her and the farm, estimating where the storm would have crossed the mountains before delivering its final downpour where he was. It would please him to know that her farm was copping a drenching, the water soaking into the rich soil, bringing life wherever it fell.

She wished her dad were with her now. When she was little he used to wake her up during the storms, get her out of bed and take her out to the back veranda, where they would sit together, their chairs pushed back against the stuccoed house wall so they wouldn't get wet. He would explain to her what made the thunder loud, and why the lightning zigzagged across the sky. Together they would count the seconds in between the light and the sound, working out the distance between their house and the storm.

Ruby went back to bed. She sat with her head resting on her bent knees, looking out at the driving rain that was visible every time lightning crisscrossed the sky.

She thought back to a special night, trying to work out how old she would have been. Francis had come to her room and gently shaken her shoulder. She could still remember his excitement as he whispered to her, 'Wake up, Ruby Rose. It's about to start.'

She had scrambled out of bed, instantly awake, her small feet tiptoeing across the cold lino floor and following him out the back door. In the middle of the small porch were two rattan chairs pushed together, and they had sat there, Francis making sure all the lights in the house were off.

'It's starting.' He had pointed up into the night sky.

'I can't see it. When will I see it?'

Francis laughed at her eagerness, excited to be watching her first lunar eclipse. 'Be patient, keep watching and you'll see parts of the moon disappear.'

'Why again? Tell me again, Dad, why the moon will disappear.'

'The earth, moon and sun are all lining up. They're forming a straight line.'

'But why will that make the moon go dark?'

'Because the sun will be behind the earth,' he explained, 'and its light will cast the earth's shadow on the moon. It's actually the shadow, see it there now.' They both looked in wonder at the dark shape moving in across one edge of the bright moon. 'That shadow, the shadow of the earth, will soon cover the entire moon. See it now? It'll move ever so slowly until it covers it all.'

'I can see it, I can see it happening.'

They sat together, Francis explaining to Ruby the different cycles of the moon and the way the earth moved on its axis. They were silent as the entire moon was blocked out and Earth seemed to stand still for a split second. The stars were bright, the Milky Way shone like thousands of tiny diamonds in the sky and the Southern Cross pointed its pathway down in the southern sky.

Her ploy was to keep her dad talking, asking question after question. Although she was curious about everything, she also wanted to drag out every last minute of the night. She wanted it to last forever, but once the shadow had passed over the moon and, little by little, the moon's brightness started shining back down on them, her dad had said it was time to go back to bed.

'There'll be plenty more to watch,' he said. 'It'll be our thing, we'll watch them together.'

And to this day they always had. Whenever there was an eclipse, whether lunar or solar, Francis and Ruby teamed up, meeting in different places to watch as the earth, sun and moon threw shadowed patterns across their surfaces.

Watching the rain tonight, Ruby felt like her father was with her now, talking to her about the driving rain, the patterns of the earth and why life was like it was. A shiver ran across her body and she wished, as she often did, that they still lived together, that she could always be with him.

A strange melancholy came over her and she thought again about that night so long ago: the night of that first lunar eclipse they had watched together. It was as if she could still feel the freshness of the night air, the shuffling sounds of the cow, which had come up near the back porch to see what they were up to, and the noise of the wind as it brushed through the leaves of the trees in their backyard.

When she was little she was scared to be outside in the dark, but when her dad was there nothing worried her. As long as he was by her side, she was never afraid.

Something worried her now, though, niggling at her, unsettling her usual calm. Was it the storm? She wasn't worried about the occasional thump or bang outside; she had grown to recognise the sounds of a loose piece of tin flapping in the wind or a large branch hitting the shed roof.

Her eyes flitted around the room, her heart thumping loudly at the overwhelming sensation that something was wrong. She walked around the house and checked the windows and doors, but all was secure and locked. What was it? Why did she have almost a panicky, frightened sensation inside her?

She pushed the fear aside and told herself not to let what was now a ferocious storm upset her. Get a grip, she told herself as she lay back down on the bed, willing herself to relax, to try and get some sleep. Finally her body felt heavy and she dozed off into a deep sleep, oblivious now to the torrential rain that drummed loudly on the corrugated roof.

Dreams filled her head as the storm strengthened, the old cottage creaking with the force of the wind against its walls. Childhood memories became muddled up with people and places of the present, swirling through her mind, vivid images that were all out of order.

In her dream Francis was there with her, standing by her bed, his body somehow moving around her, encircling the bed but not speaking. She couldn't see his face; there were no outlines, yet colours somehow made up the shape of his body. Lightning flashed as the images spun around her. His presence stayed very close to where she lay in her bed, and when her dream ended, he was gone. It was as if he had been trying to tell her something.

CHAPTER 52

Ruby's dream had ended, or rather, faded away, as a foreign noise became the background sound to the images that surrounded her. The noise became part of her dream, an incessant, continual sound that didn't fit at all with the colours and thoughts that filled her head. Forcing her heavy eyes open and ending the dream, she sat upright, dizzy from the interrupted sleep and the strange visions she had just experienced.

'Shit,' she said out loud when she realised the noise she had imagined in her dream was the sound of the phone, the shrill ring resonating through the house.

As she ran towards the kitchen she estimated the time, and felt sick to her stomach when she worked out it must be about four in the morning. *Please don't let it be Dad.* She snatched the phone from its receiver.

She barely heard the next words. She dropped to the floor, still clutching the handset, the rest of the phone falling heavily to the floor behind her.

'Are you still there?' came the matron's voice from the

retirement village. 'Did you hear what I said, Ruby? Is there someone there with you? Are you all right?'

'How? How? What happened?' Her voice sounded like it was in the distance, not coming from her mouth.

'We think it was a heart attack. He pulled the emergency cord,' the matron said. 'Perhaps he had some chest pains, a warning. Anyway, by the time we got in there he had gone. He was lying on his bed and he looked very peaceful.'

'Are you sure? Are you sure he's dead? I mean, I only saw him today and he was fine.'

'I know, love, that's how it happens. He was a good age and he'd been visiting the doctor lately about his heart.'

'He had? He what? He never told me. I can't believe it. I won't believe it until I see him. I'm coming now. I'll be there as soon as I can.' Ruby was trying to speak evenly, but the panic was spreading through her body, her chest tight, a hollow feeling, like someone had ripped something from inside her body.

'Please, Ruby, I know I can't stop you from coming, but it's really pouring down here. We've had a bad storm. Please drive carefully and take it slow. I know your father would want you to be careful. Are you sure you won't wait until it's light?'

'No, I'll be there soon. Thank you, I'm coming now.'

Ruby dropped the handset and stayed sitting on the floor, unaware of time passing. She put her head in her hands and drew her knees up to her face.

Outside, the remnants of the storm passed over the hillside, the odd bolt of lightning still flashing across the paddocks, the branches of the trees silhouetted against the scuttling clouds and the clearing sky. A full moon poked out its perfect roundness from behind a dark cloud that moved rapidly, following the line of clouds down across the valley. Golden light, a moonbeam, pointed across the paddocks and threw its light over the trees, coming to rest near the cottage on the hill.

Ruby had known this day would come. Francis had tried so many times to talk to her about the fact that he was now quite old. 'We can't live forever,' he would say, 'we've all got to go sometime.'

She had pretended to listen, nodding, smiling, but somehow thinking it would be years off and that he would live until he was one hundred. It had been bad enough when her mother died. But to lose her father … it was unbearable.

The room was spinning out of control. She sat on the kitchen floor, gulping for air, trying to breath in something that would make this all go away. To go back to yesterday, with its normality: the visits, hugs, chats, calmness, all the parts that made up her life, all those things, but most of all, her dad.

CHAPTER 53

All the necessary planning that goes with the death of a family member had been dealt with calmly. Once Ruby had sat beside her dad, held his hand, talked to him and stared for hours at his peaceful face, she felt more in control. They would have a ceremony at the local crematorium and, as Francis had wished, there would be no religious wording or prayers.

Ruby had chosen the songs; his favourite music. She organised native flowers, a solid timber casket, a book to be signed by those who attended and, most importantly, she had written his eulogy; the story of his life, his passions, and the kindness and love that had emanated from this wonderful man who had lived such a full, contented life.

His ashes would be scattered beside the small creek at the cemetery near Ruby's property, the same cemetery where Sally had been buried. Francis would be dressed in his favourite clothes, his shoes shiny and his beloved old cap atop his head.

Ruby had it all covered. The funeral notice had been put in the newspapers, all of Francis's friends and relatives had been contacted, accommodation was organised for those coming from afar, and arrangements had been made for drinks and food after the service.

Ruby had been to see Marion, who hadn't understood what Ruby was telling her. Firstly she had no idea who Ruby was, and when Ruby talked about Francis, Marion had tilted her head, as if trying to remember. Then she just smiled politely.

Ruby had also tried to ring the property where she thought Bobby might be working, but they didn't know where he was, saying only that he had left weeks ago for work a lot further out west. That was all he'd told them and they were terribly sorry, but they had no way of knowing where he was or contacting him.

Francis's younger brother, Tom, had arrived, along with Ruby's aunts, uncles and cousins, all whom had adored Francis. It cheered Ruby a little to see them all again, and to spend time talking about the many family events and get-togethers they had had over the years.

The afternoon before the funeral she sat sharing a drink with Tom on the veranda of the motel where the family was staying, not far from the retirement village.

'He had a good life, your dad,' Tom said. 'I used to love coming to your house when I was younger, before I was married myself.'

'I remember those parties like they were yesterday. We had so much fun in that backyard, all of us. I loved it when you came, Uncle Tom. You were the closest family I had, apart from Mum and Dad.'

'Francis was just so much fun, always laughing and

looking on the bright side of everything.' Tom wiped the tears from his face. 'Your mum and you were everything to him.'

Ruby smiled. She hadn't stopped since the phone call from the matron, and it was nice to sit quietly and talk to Tom.

'He always taught me to appreciate the simple things in life,' she said. 'It's hard to maintain that, particularly in this day and age, but I hope I can hang onto it somehow and live up to what he thought was important.'

'That was our era, Ruby. What mattered to us most were our families. Us men, we worked hard. Like your dad did. Life was so much simpler than today. We had small houses, old cars and not many possessions. Money all went on food and just living. There weren't any flash holidays; instead we just went to the beach with the kids, let them play in the sand and the water. It was all very simple.'

'I think we were lucky. Well, I was, I know that.'

'It's not just about luck, you know. They both worked hard, your dad with the concreting and your mum in the house. It's more than luck,' Tom said, 'you have to work hard at anything to make things right. Things do get tough sometimes, but you just have to keep going forward.'

'Thanks, Uncle Tom, I'm so glad you're all here with me.'

Ruby also thought about how hard it was to sit here and talk to her uncle without her dad. Not just because Francis was so obviously missing, but also because so many things Tom did reminded her of her father. Tom's hands were the same. The way he leaned forward when he talked, and the very same way his eyes scrunched up, the wrinkles joining at the corners when he laughed.

They hugged each other for a long time, neither wanting to let go of the other.

'It will get easier, Ruby,' Tom said. 'We will get through tomorrow.'

'I know. Everything's organised how he would've wanted it.'

Tom laughed, his hand on her shoulder. 'You were always so prepared, so in control. You're doing really well, Ruby, dealing with everything and everyone. Your dad would be proud of you.'

She smiled, pushing the thought of tomorrow from her mind. Pushing the aching dull feeling to the background, smiling again, steeling herself. Strong, I must be strong, she told herself, giving her uncle another long hug before waving goodbye.

CHAPTER 54

The morning of the funeral was finally here. The last few days had afforded Ruby little sleep and she reminded herself that she just had to get through the day, to be in control and make sure everything ran smoothly. She was, after all, the only one. There was no one else to do any of it. She just had to get on with. There's no option, she told herself. You can't run away like your legs are willing you to do.

The sun peeked over the top of the trees, the sunrise heralding another new day. Just like the sunsets, the arrival of the sun in the morning was usually a sight that stopped her doing whatever she was doing. But not today. She hardly glanced at the spectacular colours that were thrown across the valley, the pink-hued horizon topped by orange until it met the crisp blue of the morning sky.

There was a hollow sensation to it all, like nothing meant anything. The entire world felt empty; empty without her father.

The crematorium chapel filled up quickly. Ruby sat in

the front row, still shaken after saying her own private goodbyes to the body that now lay in the polished rosewood casket. Soft background music filtered through the chapel as people filed in, whispering as they greeted each other, nodding, kissing and embracing as the friends and family who had been part of Francis's life over the past years took their seats.

Tom sat next to Ruby. Out of the corner of her eye she could see him raising his pressed handkerchief, wiping his eyes. Two of her aunties sat next to him, their families sitting closely together in the rows behind.

Through the panelled side windows she glimpsed her ex-husband Ben and his wife Sue walking solemnly hand in hand. Perhaps they were sitting in the seats behind her. Her head tightened, and she felt her stomach churning. She concentrated hard on sitting upright, maintaining control as some of Francis's old friends approached her, nodding respectfully, offering their condolences briefly before placing flowers on the casket at the front of the chapel.

In the background she heard Tom asking her if she felt all right. She wasn't sure; her head was starting to spin, and everything seemed to be closing in on her, pressing on her body. An enormous urge to run almost overwhelmed her—to run out through the people behind her and keep running until she couldn't breathe anymore. Her legs started to shake uncontrollably and she looked down, willing herself to breathe evenly, her shallow breath making her chest heave and tighten until she felt like she was suffocating.

A firm hand grasped her arm and a familiar voice soothed her. 'It's okay, Ruby Rose, I've got you. I'm here.'

The words blurred and her vision dimmed. Her thoughts were muddled as she tried to sit up straight. There were only two people in the world who ever used her full name. Was she hearing her father? Lifting her head, she saw Tom move to the side and Bobby take a seat next to her. His hand held her arm firmly, and the sound of his reassuring voice cleared her head a little.

Her eyes narrowed, and her thoughts scrambled, as she looked up into the steady brown eyes she knew so well. 'You've cut your hair, and your beard, it's trimmed.' And then she couldn't speak anymore.

The music stopped and the celebrant started speaking, the words blurring for Ruby, who listened but didn't hear. She tried to concentrate but all she could think of was the body of the man she adored, the father who had been with her constantly throughout her life, who was now lying, not breathing, in the wooden casket covered in flowers in front of her.

Music, and more words, and then Bobby nudged her. 'The eulogy, Ruby Rose, it's time to read the eulogy.'

She fumbled in her bag, bringing out the pieces of paper, the words that she had taken so long to write over the last few days. She tried to stand but felt attached to the seat; her legs were not functioning, not moving.

'It's okay. You're going to read the eulogy.' Bobby's firm words and guiding hands compelled her to move.

Standing up slowly, she straightened her clothes and looked at him. He saw her eyes filled with grief, but strangely, he thought, no tears. Calmly she walked up to the pulpit, nodding politely at the celebrant as she took her place to deliver her father's eulogy. Thick brown hair curved around her face, which was paler than usual, and

Bobby noticed the elegance of her clothes, the way the floral dress hugged her body, the immaculately matched shoes and jewellery.

Always the same, he thought, envying the control she was able to show, the calm manner; just as in years gone by, a gentleness and kindness in amongst the chaos.

She cast her eyes across the crowd of friends and family who had come to pay their last respects to the man who was so well loved by so many.

Ruby's words came out clearly, as usual her words articulate and passionate, particularly when she started talking about the person who had been the central figure in her life. The words flowed and she had no trouble expressing her deep, true feelings. She talked easily about the previous years, the friends Francis had made in the retirement village, the people he bowled with each week, Marion, the staff who had grown to love and respect him, his family, brothers, sisters, nieces and nephews.

But when she began to talk about her mum and dad's love for each other, her own childhood, and what her dad had meant to her she began to stumble, the words at first choking in her throat and then coming out disjointed. She mumbled, trying to continue.

Bobby watched, concerned, listening to her shaky voice and disjointed words. Picking up the water bottle next to Ruby's seat, he stood up and strode to the front where he could stand beside her. He gestured for her to drink, then pushed her to drink a bit more. Leaning over her, he spoke quietly, flattening out the creased pieces of paper in front of her, talking again, reassuring, and waiting until she was able to look at him fully. He told her to continue reading and stood beside her.

Ruby was calmer now. The words came out lovingly and she was able to deliver the final and most important part of the eulogy.

Time blurred again, and before she knew what was happening Bobby was guiding her back to her seat, staying close, the tears streaming down his face as the coffin disappeared behind the heavy curtains that opened and then shut as Francis's body was forever taken from them all. The haunting strains of 'Amazing Grace' filled the room.

Bobby took her arm and helped her up, pointing her in the direction of the aisle that led out of the chapel. 'Stand up,' he said, 'you need to walk out. Hold yourself up straight.'

She heard his words through the fog of numbness, walking, one foot in front of the other, stopping only for a quick hug or handshake before he directed her out through the doors into the fresh air.

'Take a breath, a deep breath,' Bobby said, 'you're nearly there.'

The words found their mark, comforting her. For once someone was helping her, making the decisions, guiding her through the difficult parts.

Bobby hardly left her side again that afternoon. She noticed his concern, his worried looks when he bought her another drink, placed a sandwich in her hand, telling her to eat and drink again. He talked to her in between the conversations she was having with the many people who wanted to hug her, console her, talk about Francis, but he could see she wasn't hearing the words.

After a while the crowd thinned. Francis's family had

left and it was only his old-time buddies and bowling partners who were left drinking and reminiscing.

When Bobby told Ruby it was time for her to leave, she said, 'I can't go, it would be rude to go while they're still here.'

'You're exhausted,' Bobby said. 'They'll be here drinking all night. Let them be. C'mon on, I'm taking you home, now.'

For once she followed his instructions, not questioning him instead hopping into the passenger seat as he held the door open for her. The car wasn't even out of the street before her eyes closed, her head dropped back and she was asleep.

Bobby was also tired; the long trip from way out past Emerald was starting to catch up with him. Theresa had finally been able to contact him two days ago, after Lynette had rung her and told her the news.

'I only spoke to Francis last week, Theresa. He sounded so well,' Bobby had said.

'How come you spoke to him?'

'We've kept in touch since the trial. Not a week has gone by without me somehow managing to phone him, check up on him, see how he's going. He talked to me about his heart and told me a few things in case something happened to him.'

'Do you keep in contact with Ruby?' Theresa had asked.

'No.'

'Why not?'

'I don't know, I just haven't. I haven't seen or spoken to her since the trial, not since I left, just after we buried Sally.'

'So you kept in contact with the old man, but not your friend, Ruby? That's weird, Bobby.'

'I know, I don't know why. I loved seeing her again. I think I'm just scared.'

'About what?'

'I don't know. I get so mixed up around girls.'

'You're strange.'

Groups of wallabies, their eyes red in the gleam of the car's headlights, stared at Bobby as he drove the car up the winding dirt driveway to Ruby's house. The familiar archway of trees and the silence of the hilltop farm was a welcome embrace after the intensity of the day. Cows, gathered in groups, looked curiously at him as he got out to open the gate, the fresh country air causing him to stop and take a deep breath.

Ruby hadn't stirred, the effects of the last four days finally catching up with her. She slept solidly, her long legs tucked under her, her head uncomfortably positioned between the seat and the door.

'Ruby Rose, we're home. C'mon, wake up. I can't leave you here.' He jiggled her shoulder gently until she finally stirred. 'C'mon, you need to go to bed.' He helped her out of the car. Her eyes still heavy, she leaned on him as he took her up to the house.

'The key's under the mat,' she mumbled.

Bobby unlocked the door, propelling her like a sleep-walker into the kitchen, down the hallway and into her bedroom, where she collapsed onto the bed.

'Maybe you shouldn't have had that last wine.' He smiled as he leaned down and undid the small buckles on her sandals, tossing them onto the floor.

'Thanks, Bobby.' Her eyes were closed and she spoke just loudly enough for him to hear. 'Sleep in the spare bedroom. There're blankets in the cupboard.'

He pulled the doona over her, looking back once again before turning off the light and heading to the spare bedroom.

RUBY SLEPT until late the next day, and the sun was high in the sky by the time she joined Bobby, who was sitting out on the front veranda.

He greeted her with a smile. 'Good afternoon.' He pulled out a chair for her, noticing that she was still wearing the same dress she had worn yesterday— and slept in. 'Have a seat.'

'Thank you.'

'How about I make you a coffee and something to eat?'

'Just a coffee, thanks, I don't really feel like eating anything.'

He returned with some toast and her coffee, also placing a glass of freshly squeezed orange juice in front of her.

'Thanks.' She pushed the orange juice away, pulling the coffee over instead.

She watched him as he sat down at the end of the

table, a small pump from one of the tanks lying in pieces in front of him. He cleaned parts of it with a rag, manoeuvring other bits and clicking them into place.

'I meant to get that fixed.' Her voice was monotone, dull.

'It's fixed now,' he said, 'it just needed a bit of cleaning and a few pieces adjusted. I'll put it back in place once you've eaten that toast and drunk the juice.'

'I'm not hungry, but thanks.' She pushed the toast and juice away, looking up into his steady eyes.

'You need to eat. You're pale and you look like you haven't eaten in a week.'

'I haven't.'

They stared at each other until Ruby looked away.

'You've had your hair cut,' she said, 'and your beard is, well, it's much neater, shorter. You look so different. I can see your face.'

'Well, I thought I'd better clean up. It was a bit of a rush, but I wanted to get it right.'

'How did you hear about Dad? I tried to contact you but couldn't track you down.'

'Theresa let me know. But only two days ago. I hired a car and drove straight through. I just got here in time.'

'You keep in contact with Theresa?'

'Sure, only rarely, but yeah, I talk to her sometimes.' Bobby could feel her eyes on him as he continued to work on the pump. 'I used to ring your dad, you know, every so often.'

'He told me that.'

Bobby could sense that she was irritated with him, angry because he had kept in contact with Theresa and

Francis, but never, not once, had he ever rung her, or answered the messages she had left at various stations for him.

'You need to eat,' he said, 'you look terrible.' For a split second he caught the flash in her eyes before she looked away from him.

'Thanks for the compliment and the coffee. I'm going back to bed, make yourself at home.'

Bobby stood up, blocking her way as she headed for the doorway into the kitchen. 'I didn't mean it in a bad way. You just look really rundown and I can tell you haven't eaten. There's no sense making yourself sick.'

'Thanks, Bobby, but I don't need anyone looking after me. I can look after myself, always have and always will.' Ruby sidestepped him and continued into the house.

He watched her go, shaking his head as he heard the bedroom door slam. Just the same, he thought. Always wanting to show she was in charge and independent, trying to prove she was coping fine with everything. But perhaps she *was* that strong. Not once had he seen her cry since her dad died, not through the service, the gathering afterwards or back here at the house.

Ruby's uncle had taken Bobby to one side after the funeral. 'She's held up all week,' Tom said. 'She organised everything down to the colour of the napkins for the do afterwards. She contacted everyone, cleaned out his house, sorted out all his finances, reassured the family, and spent hours talking to all his old mates. Not once, not once, has she cried. I know her heart is breaking, Bobby. Can you watch her for me, please? Maybe she is that strong, but I doubt it.'

The strain Ruby was feeling was obvious to Bobby. He could see it in her face—the bewildered, lost look during the service and now the distant, confused responses.

* * *

Bobby stayed on for the next couple of months, watching Ruby sink further and further into herself. She never mentioned returning to work, and in fact hardly spoke to him. He stayed in the main house, sleeping in the spare bedroom.

He cornered Ruby when she ventured outside one day. 'I can move into the cottage where I stayed last time if you prefer.'

'Whatever, it doesn't make any difference to me. Do what you want.'

'I want you to sit down here and have something to eat. I want you to stop sleeping all day, and I want you to start getting back to doing the things you normally do.'

Ruby raised her eyebrows, stopping in her tracks, startled at his words. 'Wow, so many words from one who normally says so little, and tell me, what are the things I normally do? What difference is it going to make to anyone what I do? Who really cares, Bobby?'

'Your dad would have cared.' He spoke softly, cautiously. He watched her straighten up at his reference to Francis.

'How would you know what Dad wanted, and seriously, what do you care anyway? How long are you going to stay? Long enough to feel like you've done your duty to me? Actually, I don't really think it is about me. Is it a duty to Dad? Do you feel like you owe him something because he was so good to you?'

'He was worried about you, concerned about how you'd go if anything happened to him.'

'Is that so?' she said. 'Well, he needn't have worried, because I'm fine. Everything of his is in order and everyone can just go back to doing what they were doing before.'

'I don't think you're doing fine.' Bobby stared hard, his eyebrows lifting a little as he met her glare.

'Really.'

'Well, I mean …' He struggled with his thoughts, trying to make sure he chose the correct words. 'You've done an amazing job organising everything and looking after everyone else.' He looked at her. 'But what about you?'

'I told you, Bobby, I'm just fine. Everything is good with me.'

His eyes followed her as she strode up towards the house, taking the stairs two at a time. Feeling frustrated, he walked towards the sheds, determined to get on with the jobs that needed doing around the place.

* * *

THE SUN WAS low in the sky when he finally put the tools back in the shed and made his way up to the house. No lights shone from the darkened interior and he walked inside to the same quietness that had pervaded the house since the funeral. Making his way into the kitchen and through to his room, he walked softly, knowing that, just the same as other days, Ruby would be in bed, sleeping, closing her mind to all the sadness, the grief that he knew she was going through.

He ate dinner alone, and was clearing away the dishes and cleaning the kitchen when Ruby made an appearance.

'There's a plate in the fridge for you, chicken and salad.'

'Thanks, but you didn't have to do that.' She walked slowly outside to the veranda.

Bobby walked out behind her, putting a plate full of food in front of her before pouring them both a glass of wine.

She ate a tiny morsel of salad before pushing the rest of her food around the plate. 'Did he ask you to come back if something happened to him?' Ruby stared hard at him, suspicious, taking in the beard that had obviously been trimmed again, and his still unruly but much shorter hair.

'What do you mean?' Bobby sat down opposite her, determined to ensure that she ate the dinner he had prepared for her.

'Did Dad ask you to come back if he died?' She put down her fork and took a huge gulp of wine. 'Did he ask you to come back and watch me until I was okay? Because if that's what he did, then you don't need to be here.'

'He didn't ever ask me to come back.' Bobby was trying to be patient, but Ruby's attitude towards him was not helping. 'But he did ask if I ever would.'

'And what did you tell him?'

There was a long silence. Bobby looked off towards the paddocks, his eyes following the cows make their way across the ridge down to the warmer areas beneath the protective trees. 'We talked about a lot of things.'

'Why would he ask you if you'd ever come back? He never talked to me about you. I didn't even know that you talked so regularly to each other until now. I want to know what was said.'

'I think he was hoping that I'd come back and be around, maybe to help out, support you. But he never outright asked me to. And we talked about a lot of different things.'

Ruby stared out at the night sky, the stars like thousand of flickering diamonds spread out across the expanse of black. Bobby waited for her to talk more about Francis, but there was nothing. They both sat watching the empty space in front of them, lost in their separate thoughts.

Finally Ruby broke the silence. 'I know you must want to go back out bush. It's been great that you came to say farewell to Dad, but it's probably time for you to go back home.'

'Well, we'll see. Unless you're going to kick me out, there are a few things I still need to do while I'm here. Actually, could you be ready early tomorrow morning? There's somewhere I want to go.'

'Where?'

'You'll see. It's just somewhere I've often wanted to visit and you can come with me tomorrow morning.'

'I've got some things to do here.'

'Like what? You've got nothing to do. All you've done for the last two months is mope around and sleep. You've hardly set foot off this property since the funeral. Tomorrow you're coming with me.' He held his hand up to stop her protests. 'I'm not listening. You're coming with me. Be ready about seven and wear something you can swim in.'

With that, Bobby walked back inside, Ruby's excuses lost on him as he went into the spare bedroom and shut the door.

CHAPTER 56

Ruby rose early the next morning, and Bobby found her sitting in her usual spot on the front stairs, gazing intently into the valley below. Although she replied to his cheery 'Morning', she didn't look up and only turned towards him after he pushed a plate with toast onto her lap.

'I've had coffee, thanks,' she said.

'Eat, will you? You're going to need some energy today.' His glance took in her dull eyes, encircled by large dark rings, and her hair, which was scruffy and needed brushing. 'I want to get going.' His voice sounded gruff, his words impatient. 'And make sure you have something on you can swim in.'

'I don't really want to go anywhere. Do I have to come?' she said quietly, with no expression in her voice.

'Yes, you do. If you're not in the car in ten minutes, I'll lift you up and put you in there myself.'

Ruby was unsure of herself. Bobby sounded cranky and serious about making her go. Who knew where they were going? She didn't know, and couldn't be bothered asking. Her body felt numb, as if the life had been drained from her. She realised that she didn't actually feel anything. Nothing mattered anymore.

Inside the house, Bobby was busy, banging cupboard doors, cleaning up the kitchen, which was always in a mess lately, and getting his things ready. Maybe she should ask him to leave, go back out west and just leave her alone. She heard his footsteps coming back through the kitchen.

'You haven't moved. C'mon, up you get.' He grabbed her hand and pulled her to her feet. 'Where are your togs or bathers, or whatever you call them?' Bobby propelled her inside, guiding her to her room. 'That's it. Open the drawers. You need something to swim in.'

'Why, where are we going?' She pulled a pair of togs out of the overflowing messy drawer, stuffing everything back in before slamming the drawer shut.

'Never mind.' He grabbed her shoulders, pushing her towards the bathroom. 'Get changed. I'm telling you, I'll throw you in that car if you're not ready. I'm really running out of patience with you, Ruby Rose.' The bathroom door slammed shut in his face. 'I know there's no lock on that door. If you're not out at the car in five minutes I'll be back to get you.'

He strode to the spare room, picked up what he had packed for the day and headed out to the car.

Before long he heard the front door shut and the key turning as Ruby locked the door behind her. He could see her in the rear-vision mirror, barely lifting one foot in front of the other as she slowly walked towards the car.

'Christ almighty,' he called out, 'pick your feet up, girl. Look, it's a beautiful day.' There was no reply.

Once in the car, Ruby kept her head turned toward the window, away from him, her face resolute, showing no emotion as the car wound its way down to the bottom of the hill.

'Can we stop at the cemetery?' she asked.

'How about we stop on the way back?'

'I'd like to stop now.' She continued to stare out the side window.

'I guess we can stop.' Bobby gave in, not knowing what else he could do to snap Ruby back to reality.

He watched as Ruby bent over Sally's grave and placed a small bunch of flowers in the glass jar that sat atop the mound. Moving on, she stood for a long while in front of Francis's plaque, which was attached to a large rock just behind Sally's grave.

Bobby felt like he was fighting a losing battle. How could one woman be so obstinate, so drawn down into her misery and unable to lift herself out?

She looked so thin. Dark circles had gathered under her eyes and her face looked gaunt, hollow and unemotional. The floral shift dress she had thrown on was crumpled and hung loosely on her tiny figure. Her eyes had lost their sparkle and her words were monotone. She was uninterested in most of the conversations he tried to strike up with her.

He started the car as she headed back towards him.

Once again, she looked out the side window rather than at Bobby as they drove away. 'Why didn't you get out?'

'Jesus, Ruby Rose, we were only here two days ago. I

don't think your dad would've wanted you to spend so much time at his grave. I think he would've liked to know that you would get on with life. I mean, he had a great life and lived until a ripe old age.'

She turned and looked at him, a dull, hollow look in her eyes, before turning back to look out the window again.

Bobby turned on the radio for something to fill the awkward silence. Her manner reminded him of how she had been when they'd both gone to visit Marion the week before. It had been his idea. When he suggested it to Ruby, she answered mechanically, saying she'd let the nursing home know they were coming.

Marion had been propped up on a comfy chair, surrounded by cushions, a fluffy teddy bear on her lap. She spent most of their visit tying and untying the tartan bows that were wrapped around the bear's ears and neck. Her health had deteriorated significantly over the last couple of months, and she no longer recognised them or showed any sign that she knew either of them.

Every once in a while she stopped her chatter about the ways the bows should be tied and what a lovely bear she was holding and looked up at them. Once she squinted at Ruby, as if something deep in her mind was being triggered. Then her bottom lip came up over her top and once again she concentrated on the bear.

It had been too much for Bobby. He gave Ruby a look, letting her know he needed to leave. He strode through the hallways, breathing heavily, suffocated by the enclosing walls and distressed at the sight of a once intelligent woman's mind being reduced to the conversational level of a tiny child.

Eventually Ruby followed, once again like a methodical robot, with no emotion, just the same blank look that was always on her face these days.

'It's only sad for us,' she said to Bobby. 'Marion doesn't know anything else, so she's happy enough. Could you please unlock the car? I need to post some letters and pick up milk before we go home.'

'I can't come back here again. That'll have to be the last time I see Marion. I can't do that again, it's heart-wrenching.'

Ruby pulled out a notepad and began making a list of food they needed, waiting patiently for Bobby to get in the driver's side.

He spoke slowly, trying to gain control of his emotions. 'She was such a clever lady, always so happy and up for a chat.'

'Do we have any bread left?' Ruby seemed oblivious to the torment Bobby was feeling after visiting someone who no longer recognised anyone, or had the same sense of purpose in life that others had.

'Listen to yourself. For God's sake, how can you not be affected by that visit?' Bobby's voice showed his anger.

'Can we get going, please?' She looked at her watch. 'I'll drive if you're not up to it.'

He took a moment to breath deeply, angry at Ruby as well as upset over the visit.

It had taken him days to get the vision out of his head: Marion sitting in the chair with the bear on her lap. He hadn't felt so affected by anything since he was a kid, apart from reliving the events of the past at the trial.

Tears had come easily to him at Francis's funeral. There had been a feeling of great loss, a heavy grief, but also a sensation of wonder, of happiness that he had been a friend to Francis, both as a child and then later in life. They had spoken many times over the phone since the trial, mostly talking about farming, the weather and the day-to-day things that happened on the huge properties where Bobby worked.

Sometimes, however, the conversations had run a lot deeper. Bobby had been able to let go of many of the hurts of the past, simply by listening to Francis's practical ideas for putting many of the horrors of the past behind him.

At other times the conversation would turn to Ruby, and Bobby had assured Francis that he would come and see her if anything happened to the old man. Francis hadn't asked for that, but Bobby knew that his reassurance had comforted the old man, who was worried that Ruby would be completely on her own once he was gone.

The conversations had continued over the months.

'I thought you two might have clicked,' Francis said one day, 'maybe a little romance in the air.'

'Not likely, I'm not real good with women. Besides, no doubt she'll meet someone, she has a lot of friends.'

'Friends, yeah, and a lot of them have asked her out. But, you know, she goes out once or twice and then she's not interested. I'm not sure what she's looking for.'

'Maybe she's not looking for anyone. A beautiful woman like her can make her own choices.'

'So you think she's beautiful. I've never heard you say that before, Bobby. Did you ever tell her that?'

'Now, Francis, there's no use matchmaking, Ruby Rose and I are completely different people. I don't think I'm the sort of person she'd be interested in.'

'Hmmph, that girl, always too busy sorting out other people's lives to worry about her own.'

Lately Francis had often referred to his health and how he could feel that something was not quite right. 'I've been to the doctor again,' he told Bobby. 'They're going to run more tests on my heart. I don't think it'll be good. I don't really feel myself.'

'Have you mentioned this to Ruby Rose?'

'Good lord, no. She'd be in a panic, bossing me around, making me go to all sorts of doctors.'

Not long after that conversation, the phone call had come through from Theresa. He rang his sister every so often, and either Theresa or Francis always knew where he was, which was a huge change from the years previous to the trial.

He had wanted to come back to see Ruby before now, but something always stopped him. She had her own life —a busy, organised lifestyle mixing with people who were much like herself, professional types, academic young men and women who spoke with big words and wore flash clothes. He had met some of them when he stayed with her during the trial.

Ruby had dragged him to a few gatherings, and his scruffy beard and long unruly hair had made him feel completely out of place with her smartly dressed friends. She had been so happy back then, always laughing and encouraging him, staying by his side when he felt out of place and lost for conversation among her friends, who seemed to love talking about investments, their properties and where they were flying for their next holiday.

Some of the neighbours had been a bit more compatible,

and a few times he found himself deep in conversation with some of the farmers who lived near Ruby. He was interested in hearing what they grew, in particular the organic farming that many of them had adopted, and the different methods they were using to get the most out of their crops. In return, they had wanted to hear about his life and his work out west. A couple of times he had actually found himself enjoying the company of other like-minded people.

Ruby had been delighted one night when Bobby came with her to help out at a local charity function. A single woman, Bettina, had attached herself to him, talking and laughing loudly as she tried to get more than a few sentences from him. Bettina's heavy perfume and thick gold jewellery had amused Bobby, who frantically tried to catch Ruby's attention as she roamed around the room serving food and drinks.

Bettina had hung off his arm, talking incessantly, oblivious to the fact that his nodding wasn't a sign that he was interested; instead her words were starting to blur together and make his head spin. But he clearly heard her ask him to come home with her. Her house was empty and the night could be theirs, together, she said. The woman had been persistent, and in the end he had to speak gruffly to get the point across that he was not interested.

Ruby had laughed when he repeated the full conversation the next day. 'You're a good-looking man, Bobby. She wasn't the only one eyeing you off last night. You want to watch out, two of my young single friends have been asking about you also.'

He'd mumbled into his beard at the time, not sure how

he felt about the attention of city women, who were very different to those he had met out west.

The same two young friends had been at Francis's service and the wake afterwards, two young women who had not held back in targeting Bobby. Once they started talking, he hardly had a chance to get a word in.

'Wow, you look fantastic,' one of the women said. 'We love your new look, Bobby. Listen, after this is all finished we want you to come back with us to our place. Ruby's not great at entertaining; she's a bit of a homebody.'

'Yes,' said the other. 'You need to come and have a look around with us. We'll definitely show you a good time. We go everywhere together. Like *everywhere*.'

They had giggled together, leaving him in no doubt about their intentions.

Bobby nearly spat out his drink. He could hardly believe it. Were they serious, propositioning him so openly, together, and at a funeral? They were stunning looking, both of them, in their tiny, short black dresses, the plunging necklines revealing breasts that were barely covered. Who dresses like that for a funeral, he thought. He averted his eyes, aware that they were waiting for his answer.

He had put down his glass and removed the taller girl's hand, which was wrapped firmly around his arm. 'Thanks, but no thanks.' He moved away quickly, relieved when he saw Ruby coming through the crowd towards him, not noticing the attention the girls were giving him.

'You have some interesting friends.' He looked over towards the two girls, who were still watching him.

'Oh yeah, those two often ask me about you. I don't mind if you want to go with them.'

'As if I want to do that,' he said. 'And besides, I'm going to take you home, when you're ready, that is.'

As Bobby thought about the encounter now, he wished Francis could have been there to laugh about it with him. What would the old man have thought about two scantily clad women turning up to his funeral and propositioning Bobby? He thought of Francis fondly, remembering the laughs they had shared. He knew the old man would have loved chatting to everyone and enjoying a drink at his own party.

CHAPTER 57

Now as they drove down through the valley, he turned his mind back to the present. In front of them the mist covered the bottom of the valley floor like a fluffy white blanket, with the peaks of the volcanic plugs rising sharply through the thick cloud.

He thought Ruby would comment on the fog or the groups of kangaroos that looked up as they drove past, at least show a little interest. But she didn't ask about anything lately, not how long he was staying, what he was up to when he went out into the paddocks, or even where they were headed today. She had let herself sink into a deep hole of sadness and loneliness, and nothing he did seemed to awaken her from wherever her mind had turned to.

He gave up trying to make conversation and concentrated instead on the increasing traffic as they neared the beaches that were not far from where Francis had lived.

'Put your walking shoes on and bring your swimmers because we're going around the headland,' he said as he stood in the carpark waiting for Ruby to join him. He was starting to feel like he wanted to shake her. Never had he seen her so lethargic, slow moving and not in the least bit interested in anything around her.

The day was hot, and he pushed an old straw hat down on her head, annoyed that she hadn't bothered with her usual fastidious rules around hats and sunscreen. 'C'mon, we're going to walk around the point and then go for a swim.'

They followed a concrete footpath that soon narrowed down to a small dirt path, winding its way through the rainforest. It was cool under the shade of the trees and eventually the path opened up to reveal the ocean that pounded incessantly on the rocks far below.

Ruby walked in front of him, her pace slow, devoid of enthusiasm or spring. She was just going through the motions, putting one foot in front of the other.

An opening in the trees provided Bobby with a gap to look out, and he watched in amazement at the waves that rose up further out. Swells moved across the ocean, building up, rising, pushing upwards until the tops curled over into white foamy heads before smashing down onto the rocks below.

'Hey, stop for a minute,' he called out to Ruby, who was disappearing around the next corner in the path. 'Wait up.' He waved at her to come back to where he was standing. 'Let's just sit for a minute.'

He pulled on her arm, forcing her to sit down on a log bench, situated to take in the amazing view. The ocean stretched out in front of them, sparkling diamonds flickering on its surface as far as the eye could see.

'I don't get to see this very often,' he said. 'It's a bit different from the dusty red dirt.'

Ruby sat next to him, looking at the waves.

Bobby stood up, his voice animated. 'There are dolphins out there. Look, Ruby Rose, there must be about ten of them. Can you see them? They're dancing in the waves.' He pointed excitedly to the waves that were breaking just beyond the rocks. 'Can you see them? They're just there.'

'I can see them.'

It had been so long since he'd seen the ocean, never mind the beauty of a group of dolphins frolicking in the waves so close to where he was standing. Closing his eyes, he let the salty spray of the ocean float across him, breathing in deeply, the fresh sea air making him feel alive, healthy and, best of all, at peace. His mind became clear and he wanted the moment to go on and on.

'I'm going to keep walking. You can catch up if you like.' Ruby was up and already starting to walk off further down the track.

Bobby waited for a minute and then followed her, looking back over his shoulder to get one last glimpse at the playful dolphins. When he caught up with her, she was standing very close to the edge of a rocky cliff edge that dropped down sharply to the ocean below. He let her stand alone for a moment, watching her as she peered down onto the jagged rocks and pounding waves far below.

'Righto,' he said, as she turned and came towards him, 'the next beach is where we're going. There's a track further along here that'll take us down to one of the bays. It's supposed to be calm and good for swimming.'

Following the windy path through the bush to the swimming beach involved walking down a multitude of steps, and they were both sweaty and hot by the time they reached the bottom. The beach was secluded and there were only a few other people, probably due to the steps that led up and down the steep climb.

Bobby took off his shirt and shoes and stood in his board shorts, ready to go in the water.

'I think I'll just watch you. The water will be cold.' Ruby sat down and took off her shoes and socks, wriggling her feet in the sand.

'Right, here's the go, Ruby Rose,' Bobby said, looking her straight at her. 'If you don't come in by yourself I'm going to carry you down in your clothes and throw you in.' His dark eyes held hers.

She had no doubt that he meant what he said. She also took in the fact that he was a lot bigger and stronger than she was, and his body was muscled and fit from years spent doing physical work.

She was annoyed that he was ordering her around, telling her what she should be doing. The water would be cold, and she'd looked forward to putting her head down on the sand and going to sleep. When she was asleep she didn't think about anything; there was numbness, a nice feeling of hiding away under her eyelids, the way kids shut their eyes and think no one can see them.

Bobby took a step towards her.

'I will come in.'

'I'm waiting. You know I'll throw you in.' He pulled her up by her hands, surprised at how light she was to drag up from the sand.

'Okay, okay, I'm coming.' Ruby took off her shorts and T-shirt, her swimmers accentuating her thinness.

Bobby looked her up and down, his face showing surprise.

'I know. I look like shit. I've lost a bit of weight.'

'You have lost weight, but you definitely don't look like shit, let me tell you.' A broad smile lit up his face. The admiring look on his face was lost on Ruby as she followed him down to the water.

Bobby was quick to get in, diving under the waves until he reached the calm waters just beyond the breakers. Lying on his back, he let the cool saltwater wash freely over his body, feeling like every inch of dust from the past years was being washed away. He dived under, swimming easily, his strong arms propelling him through the sea, the surge of the water rushing against his body.

Looking back towards the shore, he saw Ruby standing on the beach, the water lapping at her ankles, her eyes down as she made patterns in the sand with her feet. Eventually she looked up and he waved at her to join him, annoyed when she looked down again at the sand.

Ruby didn't notice Bobby catching a wave in; her mind had closed off again and she was lost in the pattern of her feet and the water.

'The water is amazing out further. Come on.' He took her hand and pulled her gently out through the waves, wading knee deep through the first couple of small breakers before guiding her out deeper. 'There's a big one coming, hold your breath, we'll duck under it.'

Both of them dived under the oncoming foam of a breaking wave, surfacing only to look straight up into another one coming quickly in behind.

'And again.' He held her hand as they both bobbed down together, letting the wave pass easily over the top of both of them. 'Just a bit further and we'll be past the breakers.'

Bobby let go of her hand and waded out into the deeper water just as a set of waves pummelled in. Ruby wasn't far behind him, but he realised he should have grabbed her hand to make sure she was in the same spot as him. As he ducked under the wave, he could see she wasn't prepared for a much bigger one to follow so closely behind the one before.

Ruby was still getting up from the last wave and concentrating on adjusting her bikini when the next wave struck. The breaker curled around and twisted her with its force. Moving quickly, Bobby came up the other side of the wave and watched as the water barrelled her, throwing her roughly towards the shoreline. She had only just stood up, her back to the waves, when another large wave struck her from behind. As he swam towards her he could see her thrown around again, her arms and legs going every which way, like a piece of seaweed caught in the power of the wave and then spat out the other side.

Dragged by the force of the wave back into the shallows, she stood knee-deep in water, the waves that had dumped her panning out in front of her before reaching the shoreline. Bobby reached her just as she turned around; water was coming out of her nose and mouth, her face was covered in sand and tangled hair stuck out in every direction.

'Are you all right?' he said. 'I tried to warn you.'

Her hands flapped wildly over her face as she tried to get the sand and saltwater out of her eyes. The waves were calm for a moment, rolling in as small undulating swells, and Bobby grabbed her arm, pulling her back out into the deeper water.

She finally spoke. 'I nearly drowned. Where were you? I turned around and you weren't there.' A laugh escaped her lips as she adjusted her bikini, which was skew-whiff. 'Bloody hell, I think I have sand and shells in every orifice of my body. I feel like I've been in a washing machine.'

'You look like it, too.' Bobby grinned broadly, laughing out loud as he looked at her. 'You remind me of a drowned rat. You should see your hair.'

Suddenly they were both laughing.

Ruby tried to flatten her sandy hair, which rose up like a curling wave on top of her head. 'Seriously, you would not believe how much sand is up my nose. I think the whole beach is there.' Bobby's deep chuckles of laughter caused her to laugh even more, and she splashed water at him.

He took her hand and led her back towards the incoming waves. 'This time I won't let go of you. Now watch the waves. I'm the desert dweller, you should be better at this than me.'

'I don't like cold water so I rarely swim. Oh no, there's a big wave coming.'

'Duck down.' He pulled her down, hanging onto her hand and then bringing her up with him so they were positioned behind the wave.

Ruby laughed each time they surfaced, excited once they had reached the calm, still water that lay beyond the breakers. 'I don't normally go out this deep.'

'You'll be fine. There's a sandbar out further, see?

Where the other swimmers are. We're safe here. Just enjoy. Look, lie on your back and watch the clouds float by. It's the best feeling.'

Soon she was floating, nervous at first and struggling to maintain a stable position that would allow her to float effortlessly. Then, finding the balance, she relaxed, a smile on her face as she shut her eyes and let the warmth of the sun soak into her skin.

The two of them bobbed up and down on the water, floating, rising up and down with the gentle swells that continuously rolled in.

'We'd better go in,' Bobby said finally. 'We've been out here for ages, I can tell by the wrinkles on my hands.'

Ruby looked at her hands, also wrinkled from the time spent in the water. 'Remember when we were kids and our feet and hands would go wrinkly from the hours we spent in the pool?'

'I loved swimming in that pool.' Bobby bobbed near her. 'At the time it seemed huge, but it was just a cut-off corrugated water tank. It can't have been that big.'

'Remember the jagged edges on it? You had to be careful getting in and out. How many times did we cut ourselves on it?'

'Your mum would bring us ice blocks. We'd sit in that pool all day in summer, sucking on lemonade ice blocks. Sometimes your dad would sit on the grass and have one too. Remember how he'd sit there and talk to us about the silkworms? He used to ask me about school. How come he never swam in that pool, Ruby? Did he swim in the ocean here?'

'You're right, I don't ever remember him getting in

that pool. Not even in summer to cool off. He used to put the hose over his head sometimes and let the water run all over his work clothes.'

'But you lived so close to the beach. Did he swim in the surf?'

'No. He used to like to walk along the edge, and dip his feet in. He couldn't swim well because he'd never learnt how to, so he was a bit scared of the water. Mum could swim, though. She'd been to the beach a bit when she was a kid, but she only ever went out to her knees. That's probably why I'm not very confident in the water.'

'You did look pretty funny today. Sort of like a crab in a dilly pot, arms and legs going every each way.'

'Very funny,' she said. 'I can't believe you nearly let me drown.'

'I told you to duck down. You were too busy fixing your bathers.'

Ruby laughed. 'Well, now you need to get me back to the beach, past these waves.'

'If I get you in safely, can we go for lunch somewhere? I'm starving. I need something to eat.'

'That would be fun, let's do that.'

They stood facing each other, Bobby so happy to see her smiling again, and some of the lightness coming back into her eyes. 'You look so much better. It must've been good for you when your face was ground into the ocean floor.'

'The water is amazing. It's so clear and refreshing. Actually, I do feel quite good.'

Bobby took her hand, ready for them to leave the calm swells and make their way back through the breakers to the shoreline. 'Okay, this time when I say "duck", that means go *under* the wave.'

Ruby squeezed his hand and laughed, happy and having fun for the first time in many months.

CHAPTER 58

'I love that sensation of dried salt on my skin.' Ruby ran her hand along her arm, enjoying the tight, tingling feeling of salty skin.

'How good does this feel? That washed off every bit of outback dust that was ever on my body,' Bobby said as he pulled out a chair for Ruby to sit on.

They settled in at the small café, ordering large plates laden with local prawns and mud crabs. Bobby laughed as he tried to master the art of peeling the huge prawns that filled the bowl in front of them.

Ruby enjoyed the fact that she knew how to do something that Bobby wasn't sure of. 'Take the head off first, that's it, now peel the rest and then wiggle the tail off. Don't leave any shell on there.' She laughed as she poured a delicious glass of cold white wine for both of them, raising her glass to meet Bobby's.

Springy curls of dark hair framed his rugged face, the well-trimmed beard so different to what it had been a year before. 'You look really healthy,' Ruby said. 'The surf and beach agree with you.'

'We should come down for a swim more often. You need to get a bit of sun and have some fun.'

'Drowning is not fun.'

'You didn't drown, you were only in two feet of water.' He chuckled. 'If only you could've seen yourself. Arms and legs, bikinis going everywhere.'

'Very funny, I'm glad you can laugh at my expense.' She raised her glass again, clinking it against Bobby's. 'Here's to Dad.'

'To Francis, and to getting on with life, Ruby Rose,' he added.

'Thank you, Bobby.' She took a big gulp. 'I hope you're driving, because this wine is going down way too nicely.'

'Have as many as you want, this one will do me. I want to do some work this afternoon. There's a fence down in the back paddock, the cows have been just stepping over it and going next door for the past week or so.'

'Really? I didn't notice. I mean, well, I guess I haven't been out there much to see what's going on.'

'You should really start to think about what you're going to do with some of the paddocks. The place up the back of yours, the Thompsons', they've just planted a paddock full of olives. He was telling me all about them. They take a while to fruit, but it sounds like the outcome would be worth waiting for.'

'I know I do need to do some thinking about where I'm headed. I just don't have any motivation anymore. I'm not going anywhere, there's nothing to aim for and I really don't care.'

'That's great, but you've got a property to look after. You can't just let it get rundown.'

She wanted to ask him how long he intended staying. Was he getting ready to head off again? But she pushed the questions aside, not wanting to spoil the beautiful lunch, the fun day that this had turned out to be.

* * *

THEY WERE both quiet on the way home. Ruby was relaxed and although neither spoke much there was an air of calm and a peaceful connection with each other.

Glancing over at her, Bobby was reminded of when she had travelled back with him from out west, after she had tracked him down and persuaded him to face up to his demons. So much had changed since then. Mike Carlon was locked up behind bars, where he belonged. Theresa was much the same as usual, battling the drink and drugs, but she was managing to hang in there and grab some snippets of life with her kids. The biggest change was that Francis was gone and only fond memories and a melancholic sadness remained, a reminder of a long life well lived. Marion, well, Bobby could hardly bear to think about her, and he tried to ensure that the picture in his mind was of her sitting on the veranda when she had been well, laughing and holding Francis's hand.

And then there was Ruby Rose. Today she had pulled herself out of the great black hole she had let herself slide into, at least for a while. The water and the dumping had woken her up. He watched over lunch as the life came back into her eyes.

Was it time for him to go back out west? Was it too

soon? There was a lot to get done around her farm and he wanted to finish the fencing he'd started. It was also time to spray the cattle again, and one of the sheds needing fixing after the last string of storms. As soon as that was all finished, well, it would be time to head back out west.

Ruby would manage. She always had before. Her friends would rally around, help her out, and hopefully she'd get back into her work; find the rhythm, motivation, and her usual desire to organise. He wouldn't say anything about going back just yet. Maybe he'd just enjoy the next few days and then decide when would be the best time to leave.

He wondered how she would feel about him leaving again. This time he would stay in touch. Leave her his number, or even ring her sometimes. He didn't want to lose contact now; he wanted to see and talk to her again.

I'll stay a week, he thought. Everything should be done by then.

* * *

A WEEK TURNED INTO A MONTH, and Bobby was still spending every day working around the property, where there was something to fix or attend to at every turn. He kept looking at the maintenance that needed doing on the house, but he couldn't get to it with the cattle to see to and the work in the paddocks.

Ruby went up and down. Some days she would begin the day fresh and start some sort of small project. The veggie patch had been weeded and the dirt turned over, but that was where it stopped.

'Were you going to plant it out?' Bobby asked, looking at the vegetable garden.

Ruby was leaning on the shovel, aimlessly turning over the same pile of mulch she had been at the day before. 'Oh, yeah, I guess so. I don't really feel like it. I'm not that interested in it at the moment.'

Other days she woke late, dragging herself out of bed and sitting for hours on the veranda with a cup of tea before tackling the mess inside the house, which seemed to be increasing with each passing day. Sometimes she drove down to the coast and did some work at the counselling agency, where she was much in demand. When she was in work mode, she was able to switch off from everyday life. She could focus on organising her appointments and complete any work that needed to be done.

'Are you coping, honey?' her boss said, cornering her one day. 'You don't appear to be your usual self.'

She was immediately on the defensive. 'I'm sorry, Gus, are you not happy with the way I'm working?'

'No, it's all good,' he said. 'You know we appreciate any appointments you take. The feedback from the clients is always positive. You just don't have your usual get-up-and-go attitude. It's almost like you're going through the motions but your heart's not in it.'

'I'm fine, everything's good. Thanks for asking, but honestly I'm fine.'

Gus left it at that, gauging from her tone and the look on her face that she didn't want the conversation to go any further. He didn't want to put her off; any time she could give them for appointments was appreciated. She was and always had been one of their best workers, and it was usually Ruby that clients requested. Maybe the Easter break would do her the world of good, he thought.

* * *

On Good Friday Bobby rose, as usual, just before the sun. It was his favourite time of the day, and he enjoyed his routine of making a cup of tea before going to sit on the veranda.

He watched from the kitchen doorway as heavy fog lifted from the valley floor and the sun broke through over the top of the hills, throwing the first morning rays of sunshine down on the hillside where the farm was situated. The sounds of different birds filtered through the trees. His favourites were the kookaburras and he closed his eyes for a moment soaking in their laughter as it echoed from far across the valley, the birds' chortles bouncing from hill to hill.

The sun rose slowly and the impressive peaks of the craggy Glasshouse Mountains pushed through the barrier of mist, their crests lit by the sunlight that soon filled the expanse in front of him.

It was as if the world opened up. This was his time each morning, when he felt at peace, his body and mind relaxed as he settled into the tranquillity of the day, planning what he was going to get done in the hours ahead.

This morning, however, Ruby was up before him. When he came outside to the veranda she was sitting forlornly on the very spot where he usually sat.

'Morning, Ruby Rose. What brings you out so early this morning?'

'Oh, hi. I, well, I just couldn't sleep. I've been up for a while.'

Her dull voice told him that this was not going to be a good day for her and he noted once again the dark rings around her eyes and the paleness of her face. He breathed in deeply, trying to find the inner patience to deal with these moods that darkened her on so many days. He had tried to talk to her, tried to make her see what Francis would have wanted her to be doing and not doing, after he was gone. But nothing made any difference. For a couple of hours he would get a glimpse of the Ruby of old, and then she would sink back into that dark deep hole where he just couldn't reach her.

Aware that she was in the spot where he usually sat, she got up. 'I think I'll go back to bed for a while.'

'Why don't you sit with me and watch the sun come up?'

'I'm going back to bed.'

He stood in front of her, frustrated, not knowing what else he could do to help her. When he had suggested she got some help, she had reacted badly. She had practically sneered at him. 'What, like counselling?' Her tone had been sarcastic, abrupt.

'I think you probably need to talk to someone,' he had said, 'get some help to lift yourself out of wherever you are.'

As usual, she had walked away from him, the conversation ending with nothing resolved and nothing changed.

She walked past him now towards the door, then stopped and stared in shock at the object propped up beside the doorway. 'Where did that come from?' She picked up Francis's old walking stick, turning it over in her hands, one hand running over the smooth gnarled timber.

'I found it yesterday in the boot of your car. You must've left it there after you cleaned out your dad's house.'

'It's like his hands are still on it,' she said as she caressed the wood, bringing it up to rub it against her cheek, the smell of the timber reminding her of her dad and the way he had held this stick in his hands. In her mind, she could see his wrinkled hands wrapped around it as he leant on it or pushed it forward to steady himself. She slumped into the nearest cane chair, the walking stick falling noisily to the wooden floorboards, her head down in her hands, her hair sprawled across her face and shoulders.

Bobby was unsure what to do. He moved towards her, but stopped when he heard the sound of muffled crying. He hesitated. Should he just leave her and let her have her own space, or should he comfort her? He was annoyed with himself for not knowing how to respond, but perhaps it was best to give her some space.

He turned to walk away, but the sound of her heart-wrenching sobs stopped him and he went back to where she sat.

The events of the past months overwhelmed Ruby and her body shook with emotion. Sitting down next to her, he put his arm around her, waiting for her to push him away, to tell him she was okay. But for the first time he could remember, she turned towards him, her face wet as tears streamed down her face, mumbling words about her dad, her life without him, questions spilling out, her eyes searching Bobby's for an answer.

When she tried to talk her words came out between gulps, shudders of grief making her body shake. Pulling her chair towards him so they faced each other he tried to console her, but she was too distraught to listen. Bobby continued to talk quietly, his words slow and even, but no matter what he said, nothing had any effect.

Apart from his shock at seeing her cry like this, he was also starting to break down a bit himself, both at the thought of her grief and the loss of Francis. Hold it together, he told himself.

This was the first time he had seen Ruby like this. She was always the stoic, practical one. She was the one who had held it together when they were kids, never letting him see her cry. Throughout the trial and the presentation of horrific evidence, she had not cried. It had been Ruby who had kept everyone going, Ruby who held everyone together.

This morning, she had collapsed. It was as if every part of her had given in and surrendered to the deep sorrow she had been trying to deal with in her own ever-efficient way. Now she needed help from him.

Leaning forward, he pulled her towards him, his huge arms wrapping around her. Her face pressed into his chest, the tears rolling down her face, wetting his shirt. Words came out between the sobs, the meaning jumbled as she tried to talk.

'Let it all out, Ruby Rose. I've got you,' Bobby said.

He wasn't sure how long he held her for. Eventually he felt her relax, the sobs lessening, only occasionally her body shaking with the after-effects of crying for so long.

'Come here.' He pulled her up and guided her down into the hammock that hung in the corner of the veranda. She followed like a child, her eyes sad, the sobs starting up again.

The hammock swung slowly, the world quiet around them as they lay together, Bobby's arms wrapped tightly around her, wiping her tears and stroking her hair. Speaking softly, the words seemed to come out right for once. He told her that everything was going to be all right, the pain would get easier, and that he knew how hard it was for her to lose Francis.

Enfolded as if in a cocoon, she fell asleep, tiny shivers of sobs still emanating from her even as she slumbered. Bobby's arm went numb, and pins and needles set in as her body lay against him and on top of his arm. But he didn't move.

After a while she became quiet and slipped into a more peaceful sleep, exhausted from the hours of crying and also the effect of not having slept properly over the last months. The warmth of her body pressed against him and he looked closely at her face. Dark eyelashes wet from her tears highlighted her face and he saw how beautiful she was this close up.

Even when he was a young boy, he always thought she was the most beautiful girl he had ever seen. As an adult, he watched the way she moved, the way her long slender hands poured a cup of tea or how her cheeks lifted up when she smiled. Those lips … he looked down at her.

One of her legs was thrown over his, and he lowered his head and kissed her forehead, silently admonishing himself. What the hell was he thinking? This was not the time to be taking advantage of her, just because she was upset and clinging to him. Well, wrapping herself around him actually and—he looked down—with her body pressed firmly up against his. Her breathing was light and he could tell she was fast asleep; she obviously felt secure and comfortable with him in the slowly swinging hammock.

He knew the only reason they were so close physically was because she had become so upset. All the time they had spent together, she had never once shown that sort of interest in him. She loved him as a friend, a childhood friend, and that was all. It was stupid of him to think anything else. Just like he had so many times before, he had to recognise that it was never going to happen for them.

Relationships just didn't work for him, and just like previous times, he had to get out of this situation. Leave, so Ruby could get on with her life.

He gently manoeuvred himself out of the hammock, trying not to disturb her sleep. The warmth of her body had been comforting beside his, and he closed his eyes, trying to retain the feel and smell. He looked down at her for a long time as she slept, his mind reeling with emotions and confused thoughts. He battled with his emotions, knowing he had to leave, to get as far away as possible and let her get on with her life without him.

CHAPTER 59

$\mathcal{M}$ost of that day she slept in the hammock, turning from side to side, trying sometimes to open her eyes before falling back into a deep slumber. Checking on her throughout the day, Bobby tried to control his mind, working out how long it would take him to get through the jobs he wanted finished before he left. Then he would find himself thinking back to the events of the day.

* * *

THE HOUSE WAS quiet when Ruby finally woke up. She lay gently swinging, thinking, exhausted from all the crying, her body empty, hollow from the months of grieving. There was also lightness, though, a definite change. It was as if there was a future that she wanted to get on with.

Different ideas of what she wanted to do bounced around in her head as she lay in the hammock. She closed her eyes for a long time, the scent of Bobby lingering, the warmth of his body next to hers still tingling on her skin. Although he had moved quietly without disturbing her, she had known when he left, and now she knew that he would be thinking hard, that what had happened would confuse him. In her sleep she had felt his hands stroking her face and hair, and his lips brush across her forehead. How would his mind be working? How far would he run this time? Would he leave again without a trace?

She gathered energy and lifted herself out, feeling sure that he would already be planning when he would leave. It was inevitable; she knew him too well. He wouldn't want to stick around; the intimacy would push him away. He would want her to get on with her life, back to the routine she had had before Francis died.

The walking stick still lay on the veranda. She picked it up and propped it against the wall near the door, positioning it, moving it slightly until it sat exactly where she wanted it.

'Righto, Dad, I need to get on with it.' Determined words, spoken out loud, as she walked inside the house, looking at the mess that abounded in every room, working out where to start and how to get the place cleaned up.

She was back. The dark melancholy had been left behind; she had swum through the murky sadness and climbed out the other side. She started to sing, the banging dishes and cupboard doors shutting and closing creating a noisy background to her cleaning and, once again, the organising of the household.

* * *

IT WAS NEARLY dark when Bobby returned to the house, his clothes covered in dirt, his heavy work boots caked in mud. Large wads of mud flicked off his boots as he stomped heavily on the concrete path that led up to the stairs.

'That pump's broken down in the bottom paddock,' he said. 'I'll need to order the parts tomorrow. Your troughs haven't been filling up, so I've moved the cattle up to the higher ground.'

'Thanks for that. It's only a new pump, that'll be the second time its broken since I bought it.'

His eyes flitted around the kitchen and he looked into the other rooms, noticing straightaway the difference Ruby's tidying up had made. 'Wow, you've been busy,' he said. 'I can actually see the kitchen bench. Is that a cake I smell baking?'

'I need to get this place back into some sort of order. I really appreciate that you've kept it tidy for me, and, well, thanks so much, Bobby. I know you haven't stopped working outside, either.'

'I enjoy it. You look a bit better, Ruby Rose. It's good to see some colour in your face.'

They looked at each other and Ruby's heart pounded hard as she tried to choose her words carefully. 'Would you consider doing some paid work for me? There's so much that needs to be done and I just thought if you're going to stay a bit longer, well, I'm going to have to pay someone, so maybe you'd like the work. I know it's not what you normally do, but, well, the option's there if you want.'

'No, I couldn't take money from you. Paul next door has offered me work also.'

Unsaid and unanswered questions hung in the awkwardness between them, until finally Ruby blurted out, 'You're going to leave soon, aren't you?'

Bobby did not reply as he disappeared into his room.

* * *

OVER DINNER that night he finally answered her question. 'I'm probably going to get moving in about a week. I figure I'll have the fencing complete and the pumps fixed by then.'

'A week?' She looked down at her plate, her appetite suddenly disappearing.

As usual, Bobby had cleaned up everything on his plate, the steak and vegies disappearing just like all food that was put in front of him. Francis had commented on this once to Ruby. 'He's like one of those bins,' Francis had said, 'you just step on his foot and his mouth opens. He'll eat anything.'

Now Bobby was reaching for the bread. 'Yeah, I'll let you get your life back to normal.' He looked up at her. 'Once you're back into work a bit more you'll be really busy.'

'Uh-huh.' She pushed the food around her plate, getting up suddenly as she felt the tears start, her voice shaky as she tried to give a steady reply. 'I might start to clean up.'

She was unable to hide the tears on her face and left the room quickly, unused to not being in control of her emotions.

* * *

LATER THAT EVENING Bobby came looking for her. He was confused as to why she'd been upset at dinner. He thought today had been a turning point for her, when she could finally accept that Francis was gone. Hopefully, she would now grieve properly; let it all out and get on with her normal life. He expected to see her busying herself in the kitchen, but the room was empty. The sound of the shower running could be heard from the bathroom and he guessed she was getting ready to turn in for the night.

Surely she wasn't upset about him going. Was it a good idea to keep in contact with her after he left? Perhaps it would be better not to. The question rattled him.

Bobby was also confused about the way he had let go of his own feelings this morning, thankful that she had been asleep in the hammock and unaware of how he had let down his guard. He knew his thoughts had changed towards her. When they were chatting on the veranda, or driving somewhere together in the car, he felt a closeness now, an attachment. The way he felt about Ruby Rose had developed into something a lot more than friendship.

That's why he knew he had to leave. There was no way it would work. For a start, he imagined that her feelings for him were more like for an older brother or a friend she had shared so much with many years ago.

They were from different worlds. He had lived in isolation for so long. And all of his relationships over the years had ended disastrously, often through his own fault. The moods, the mistrust and then the dark days of depression, like insurmountable obstacles that punched at him for days, sometimes even weeks. The few partners he had had over the years had not had the patience or the understanding to deal with any of it. It always ended in huge arguments, accusations that he was cold, hostile and uncaring.

Had any of that changed now that he'd faced up to the past? Now that he'd let go of many of those past hurts and the guilt? He thought not. If he stuck around and tried to see if his feelings were reciprocated, he would no doubt, at some stage, mess it all up. It would end with him hurting Ruby. She would turn away from him.

Jumbled thoughts bounced around in his head. Deep down he knew this was not a practical way to think, that perhaps they did have something, even a lot, in common. Francis had often tried to point this out to Bobby when the older man had sometimes quizzed him, in a round-about way, about his feelings for Ruby.

'She's not really from a different world than you, Bobby,' Francis had said to him over the phone one night. 'What is her world, anyway? She only goes to work, spends time with me, and potters around that farm of hers. Is that so different from what you do?'

For once, Bobby had opened up. 'I've got nothing much to offer anyone, Francis. I don't talk that much. I'm really bad at communicating, you know, talking about my emotions. Particularly with women.'

'Yes, Bobby, but you can talk to Ruby Rose. And you and her, well, she knows how you feel about so many things.'

'She'll meet someone one day, Francis, some hand-some, rich fella who'll be able to keep her happy. Me, what have I got? A few stockman skills and a shitload of baggage from a bloody terrible childhood. I wouldn't wish those problems on anyone. I need to be by myself to deal with it all. Truly, it's better for me to just look after myself.'

Bobby recalled that conversation now as he sat on the veranda by himself. He heard Ruby's door shut and watched the yellow glow from her window disappear as she turned off the light in her bedroom. She hadn't even said goodnight.

The smell of bacon cooking and coffee brewing wafted into Bobby's bedroom the following morning. The table was set, and Ruby was serving eggs and bacon, along with his favourite, fried tomato and mushrooms, topped with what he jokingly called 'that pretentious green stuff' she liked to scatter over the top of the eggs. 'They wouldn't dare put rocket on top of a breakfast where I come from,' he always teased her. 'Jeez, that would be rabbit food out west, all pretty and decorative on top of a big breakfast.'

'I knew you'd smell the food,' she said, putting a third egg on his plate.

'Smells great,' he said. 'Wow, you've got the sauce ready and everything, coffee, orange juice. I'm impressed.'

'Well, you've cooked a lot of meals for me recently, so I thought I'd better get some in before you go back home.'

Bobby was thankful to see her in a better mood. He decided that she had most likely thought about him going back out west and, from her smiling face this morning, had obviously come to terms with it. His chest felt heavy as he listened to her chatting happily, clearly not worried now about him leaving.

'You look much more like your old self,' he said, enjoying the hearty breakfast.

He glanced up. The colour had returned to her face and her hair was brushed and shiny, the brown waves falling softly onto her shoulders. She's just so beautiful, he thought, wanting so much to tell her, but forcing himself to drag his eyes away from her, concentrating instead on the food in front of him.

'I thought we should go to the beach today,' she said. 'We could go back to where you took me last time.'

'You mean where you ate sand?' Bobby chuckled, the vision of her being tossed around, legs and arms going everywhere, still vivid in his mind. 'We could do that. That would be good.'

For some reason he felt lost for words, as if something was being taken away from him. How easy it would be just to stay. That was his problem, he realised. That was why he was starting to experience waves of sadness, melancholy, seeping through his body. He didn't want to leave. He wanted to stay and see her every day. To eat breakfast with her, swim in the ocean, work together on the farm and, most of all, to recapture the feeling he had had yesterday. He wanted to feel her body next to his again.

Startling himself with his thoughts, he realised that he was staring at her lips.

'Bobby, are you listening to me?'

'Yes, I'm listening, and that sounds good. I'll finish up here and then we can get going.'

CHAPTER 61

This time Ruby walked alongside Bobby, a spring in her step as they followed the narrow dirt path that wound around the mountainside. Dark clouds hovered on the horizon and threw shadows over the ocean, which were broken by rays of sunshine lighting up different sections of the water. Sets of waves rolled in across the bay in front of where they stood.

They watched the board riders sitting patiently waiting for that perfect wave. Once in a while a rider would paddle briskly, riding the crest of a wave before standing up, balanced, arms positioned, feet strong and firm on the board as they rode towards the shore. Eventually the surge propelling them would dwindle and they would dive under before paddling back out, their boards rising up and over the swells and spray.

'They stay out there for hours,' Ruby said. There was something fascinating and calming about watching the distant riders who sat and waited, turning only when they had carefully chosen the perfect wave.

'I wouldn't mind trying that one day.' Bobby observed the skills and techniques required to get the board to slide down the front of the large waves that relentlessly pounded in from the north.

'You should. You're a strong swimmer and you don't have any fear. Why don't you have a go at it? I think there might even be an old board out the back in one of the sheds.'

He laughed, shielding his eyes so he could look at the ocean, the sun glaring as it rose higher in the sky. 'I'm probably too old to learn now.'

'That's rubbish. You're not that old, and besides, people learn all sorts of different skills, regardless of their age. That's just an excuse.'

'When I was younger I used to listen to the kids at school talk about riding their boards. I always wished I could go to the beach, just for one holiday, or even just one day on the weekend. I always wanted to experience standing on a board and riding down the crest of a huge wave.'

'You missed out on so much. You never really had a childhood, did you?'

'Nope, lucky I was friends with you. I was always happy when we were together, especially up in the tree-house in amongst all those silkworms. It was the one place I could go. Your mum and dad and you—you three were the only ones I could talk to, and feel safe spending time with.'

They sat quietly staring out across the ocean, each with their own separate thoughts.

Bobby smiled. 'How much fun did we have in that backyard? I was very lucky to have had you there, Ruby

Rose. Those times are the one good thing I can look back on.'

Ruby went to speak but stopped, thinking hard as she watched the board riders. 'Let's get going. You need to take me for a swim.'

They descended through the bush to the bay where they had swum previously. Ruby remembered how miserable she had felt the last time they were here: the emptiness and the feeling that nothing mattered, that there was nothing to aim for. This time she felt different. There was so much that she knew mattered now. She had so many different, new thoughts and an excitement, an appreciation for the warmth of the sun on her skin. An entire ocean sparkled in front of them.

She pointed to the waves. 'Look, Bobby, your dolphins are just out there. Look, just near the breakers.'

'Wow, they're so close in. Look at them go, they just dance through the waves.'

The dolphins weaved and plunged through the clear water, their bodies easily visible as they rode the waves, twisting and jumping into the air as they frolicked together. Bobby was transfixed, unable to take his eyes off the scene in front of him. He looked at the pristine beach, the rocky headland that jutted out at the far end of the bay and the dolphins that played in the waves just in front of them.

'Can it get any more beautiful?' When he spoke, his voice was husky.

'The water looks amazing.' Ruby had stripped off and stood next to him, a tiny dotted bikini accentuating every curve of her body. He blinked rapidly, lost for words. 'Come on,' she said, 'I'll need you to get me out over those waves today.' She noticed that he was unable to take his eyes off her and he didn't speak as she handed him the sunscreen. 'Just a bit on my back, if you don't mind. I can't reach around there.'

'You want me to rub it on for you?'

'For God's sake, Bobby, just get a bit and rub it on. Hurry up, I want to get in the water.'

His hands felt nice on her skin, and she was glad she had kept her body in reasonable shape over the years. All that yoga and walking, she thought. At least I still look somewhat decent.

'I'll have to start exercising again.' She twisted around, looking at him. 'I'm thirty-eight this year, and it's getting easier to put on weight. I think I've let myself go a bit since Dad died.'

'You look just fine to me.' His eyes met hers and he hoped she couldn't read his mind.

'Oh, it's easy for you. Look at you, all muscle. I suppose you keep so fit because you're always on the move.'

'I like to be busy.' The words were getting stuck in his throat. He concentrated on trying to sound calm, ignoring the electric feeling that was tingling through his hands from touching her skin.

'Let's go. I'm dying to get that saltwater on my skin. It makes me feel so alive.'

Ruby strode out in front, making her way down to the water. Bobby followed, trying to avert his eyes from her, trying not to notice the way her body moved as her long legs strode out, that tiny dotted bikini that covered so little of her body.

CHAPTER 62

The day at the beach was amazing. They stayed in the water for hours, floating on their backs, watching the fluffy white clouds pass over them as if racing to be somewhere else.

'It reminds me of when we used to lie together and look at the clouds through the holes in the roof of the treehouse,' Ruby said, glancing over at Bobby, noticing how the lines on his face didn't appear so harsh any more. His forehead had smoothed, as if the worries of the past had gone, or at least been pushed away, hidden under a rock in some deep recess of his mind.

'That treehouse seemed so big at the time.' Bobby looked over at her, watching her hair floating out like a mermaid's, her long arms moving slightly to keep her afloat. 'I wonder how big it would be to us now. I mean, we only just fitted across the floorboards and we weren't as tall as we are now.'

'Everything seems so big when you're a kid,' she said, 'buildings, people, toys. Then when you see the same thing as an adult, you realise it's only small and often not that impressive.'

'You were always so little on that bike, Ruby Rose. You looked so small when you couldn't reach the pedals and had to stand up to ride.'

'I know, how funny. When I sat on the seat I couldn't reach anything. That's why I fell off so many times.' She thought about how Bobby had always been there to pick her up, to fix the bike and take her home so her mum could put that smelly yellow stuff on her cuts.

'You never cried,' Bobby said. 'I never saw you cry. You must've seen me cry so many times and I was supposed to be tough, boys weren't supposed to cry.'

'I had a thing about it. I promised myself that I'd never cry in front of you. I used to be able to stop the tears, because it would've been so embarrassing if you saw me cry. I was always trying to be the strong one.'

'Well, sometimes you need to let go. You're always telling me to let go, to let my feelings out. You really made up for it the other day, I've never seen anyone cry so much.' He prodded her in the ribs.

'Hey, don't drown me. I need to concentrate when I'm floating.' She moved her body so that once again she was balancing on top of the water. 'I needed that release. I really needed it.'

The two of them floated silently, both lost in their own thoughts, oblivious to what the other was thinking, yet both remembering the warmth of lying together in the hammock, the softness of their skin touching and the feeling of being together.

'Right,' Bobby said, breaking the silence, 'time to go in.'

'Are you hungry?' Ruby asked as they walked up the

beach, her skin fresh from the saltwater. He raised his eyebrows at her. 'Right,' she said,' Stupid question, I know. Well, you can take me to the little cafe on the river again.'

'Oh my God, I can taste the food already.' Bobby walked faster. The prospect of great food and wine beckoned, and he knew it would top off such a special day. I feel so good, he thought to himself. Alive. Happy, really happy.

'What are you smiling about? Are you already tasting those prawns?' Ruby asked.

'I just feel good.' He moved closer to her, their eyes meeting. 'I feel really good. Like I could take on the world. I don't remember being like this, not ever. It must be the saltwater.' He averted his eyes, his arms aching. He had nearly reached out for her, could imagine his arms wrapping around her. 'Food, that's what we need.'

He moved away, picking up their towels and leading the way up the winding path. Ruby followed behind, stopping every so often to look back at the ocean, to get that final glimpse. In the end she had to tear her eyes away. The sparkles of the ocean, the clear water and the cool spray and salt air drifting across them were stored in her memory. She closed her eyes and let it all soak over her. Bobby was right: it was a really good day. One she would always remember. She turned and followed him slowly up the pathway.

* * *

THE NEXT FEW days blurred together as they both kept busy. Bobby was trying to sort out everything that needed fixing before he left. He had pulled his clothes out of the old wooden drawers and stacked them on top of his bag, his few possessions tied up in a smaller bag beside it.

He had written her a list of other items that needed fixing and given her instructions on how to go about getting them seen to. But he became exasperated when he started to give her details about moving around some of the feeding stacks, remembering other jobs that would need to be done at the same time.

'Shit,' he said, pushing his hat hard onto his head. 'I'll just go and do it now. By the time I explain it to you I could have it done.'

He's a bit cranky, she thought, watching him stride through the grass towards the shed where he would get his tools out to fix whatever it was, which was obviously at the forefront of his mind.

Later she went outside to look for him, and after not being able to find him walked some distance down the driveway. She stopped suddenly, stepping backwards, allowing the shed to screen her. Bobby was sitting under the grove of majestic trees. I wonder what he's thinking about, Ruby thought, watching him.

It was the same spot where Francis had often rested, trying to work out the ways of the world and working over the issues confronting him. Often, while leaning on his walking stick, Francis would just sit and look, taking in the beauty of the valley below and the tranquillity of the cows chewing peacefully on the lush green grass.

Bobby sat there now, in the coolness of the shade, like a statue, his back to her as he gazed out across the valley and the nearby cemetery. Maybe he's saying his goodbyes to Sally and Francis, she thought.

She turned and walked back up the hill, not wanting to

disturb his peace, knowing that sometimes Bobby needed to be alone, to sit by himself in quietness so he could think freely and counsel himself on whatever might be bothering him.

* * *

THE AIR WAS cool under the trees, the worn timber of the homemade log seat a comfort, a familiarity, reminding Bobby of Francis. There was a picture in his mind of the old man sitting there leaning on his stick, looking down, just as he was now, breathing in the beauty of the valley below.

He wondered if Francis would have understood why he was leaving, why he was walking away from someone who he now knew he felt so strongly about. But what good would it do to stay? He didn't want to stay if all Ruby wanted was help around the place, and company. They did get on well together, but now he had different feelings for her and that was all the more reason to go the other way.

Let her be, he told himself, don't complicate her life. His own had been muddled enough. One day, hopefully, she would meet someone she really loved, not like the friendship kind of love she had for him. His mind was made up. Just a few more jobs to do and then no looking back, just walk away. Let her get on with her life.

He stood up, the breeze blowing softly across his face, cool against the tears that were running down his face. As always, his emotions were close to the surface. Years ago he had fought the tears, trying hard to stop them as soon as he felt them welling up. He had cried so much as a kid, but at other times there had been no tears because life had been so horrendous, so terrifying, that the shock of what happened, or what he saw, rendered him tearless. As a child, the tears would come afterwards, perhaps when he told Ruby about something that had happened, or at night when he lay awake, stiff with fear, listening, straining to hear in case anyone was walking towards where he and Sally slept.

Years spent on the properties out west had hardened him, and he had learned to control his feelings, only letting go when he was alone. But when he had met up with Ruby again, and then Theresa and Francis, his emotions had pushed to the surface and now it didn't take much to set him off.

Life had changed drastically over the past couple of years. He thought about how far he'd come since the day he had arrived here on Ruby's farm. Running his hands through his hair, he smiled at the thought of how long and scraggy it and his beard had once been. Both had once been unkempt and tangled, but now he kept them neat and short.

Best of all, he felt he was so much better at communicating. Conversations with others were not something to be feared anymore. He had ideas, opinions, and a newfound confidence that he did actually know what he was talking about. Strangers he met warmed to him, were friendly and actually enjoyed his conversation.

The new me! He laughed out loud, pleased with the transformation that had taken place.

Most of all, he had a closeness with Ruby. They had opened up to each other, and hopefully she would stay in contact. He just needed to get rid of that niggling, lost feeling. She would never feel the same way about him, and he had to accept it.

He dusted his hat against his jeans and closed his eyes. Immediately he had a vision of her in that tiny bikini, the softness of her body next to his, the way she sometimes looked him straight in the eye. His stomach flipped as he thought of her green eyes, often looking as if they were reaching deep into his soul, reading his mind, just like she'd done when she was a kid. There was an aching in his body as he accepted that he was going away, that he needed to say goodbye in the next couple of days and put her behind him.

CHAPTER 63

*B*obby was quiet the rest of that day, although Ruby chatted away, seemingly oblivious to his deep thoughts and pensiveness about leaving. He talked only a little, instead enjoying listening to her conversation without contributing himself.

When he had first returned from out west his silence had made her angry, and several times he'd seen her face go red with frustration. His gruff replies and short answers, when she used to try and talk to him before the trial often forcing her to walk away from him in frustration.

This evening he soaked in the sound of her voice, storing it permanently in his mind so he could imagine the sound of it when he was lying by himself in his swag, way out in the dusty red dirt in the middle of nowhere. Finally Bobby spoke. 'I'm going to turn in for the night. That was a pretty long day today, but I've nearly finished everything. The jobs are just about all up to date.'

'You just keep going all day. I've never seen someone work so hard.'

'I've worked like that since I left home as a kid. I love it,' he said, 'the harder, dirtier and hotter the better. It's what I like. The best part is fixing something or being with the cattle or horses. It's part of me. Goodnight, Ruby Rose.'

''Night, Bobby.'

* * *

As he drifted off to sleep, Bobby could hear Ruby pottering in the kitchen and knew exactly what she would be doing: that final cup of tea before bedtime, warming her hands on the mug as she positioned herself on the front stairs; looking down across the valley, watching the stars flickering in the sky, thinking. She was always thinking. His mind drifted, listening to the shower running and then the sound of her bed squeaking as she got into it. Tonight his eyes were heavy and he had no problem drifting off into a deep sleep.

* * *

Bobby didn't know what time it was, but he felt that he'd been in a sound sleep for a couple of hours. The floorboards creaked, and he forced himself to open his eyes. The sound had come from near him, maybe even in his room. The light from the moon beamed in through the coloured glass windows, allowing him to see shapes, silhouettes of the furniture and walls in the room. Had he imagined the sound or perhaps been dreaming.

His eyes opened wide as he realised there was someone moving towards his bed.

'Bobby, are you awake?'

'Jesus, Ruby Rose, you scared the hell out of me. What's up? What's wrong?' He could see her now, her body outlined in the darkness, standing next to his bed.

'I wanted to talk to you.'

'What time is it?'

'It's about three o'clock. This can't wait. I want to talk to you now.'

'Well, hang on. Let me wake up properly, and Jesus, I'll get up, hang on a minute.' He could see her moving closer to him.

'Don't get up. You don't need to get up.'

Bobby was confused. He shook his head to make sure he wasn't dreaming. But no, he could see her clearly now, standing right beside where he lay. She had on that flimsy nightie he'd sometimes caught a glimpse of. Once or twice they'd got up at the same time to get a drink or use the bathroom and had nearly fallen over each other. He had tried not to look but it was a light, flowing nightie that barely covered her, revealing her legs and arms ... and now she stood there in the same nightie. What the hell was she doing?

'Did you hear someone outside?' Bobby propped himself up on one elbow. 'Do you think there's someone prowling around or something?'

'No. I said I want to talk to you. Are you awake?'

'Well, yes, I am now. What's the matter? Are you sick?'

'I need to tell you something before you go this week. I'm not going to let you go without saying it, and if it makes you run further and faster, then so be it. But at least I will have said it and got it off my chest.'

She sat down on the edge of the bed, turning around, tucking one leg under her so she was looking straight at him. In the moonlight he could clearly see her eyes, her face, so serious. She spoke softly. 'It's a silkworm secret.'

'Ruby Rose, it's the middle of the night. What's the matter?'

She started off slowly, her words clear. 'I'm in love with you. It's not a friend love, it's not an I-need-some-one-I'm-lonely love, it's a definite I've-fallen-in-love-with-you love.'

Bobby froze, unable to move, staring at her, not blinking. Outside, crickets chirped, highlighting the silence that pervaded the room.

'I don't care if you think I'm crazy. I just wanted to tell you before you leave. Just in case you feel even a little bit the same.'

Silence. Bobby finally blinked. The words stuck in his throat. She was still sitting there, staring at him, waiting for him to say something. Her words echoed in his head as he tried to take in the situation and what she had just said. They stared hard at each other.

Finally Bobby's hand reached up and stroked her face, tracing his finger across her lips. Ruby moved slowly, pulling the sheet back and sliding her body in next to his, his strong arms wrapping around her as the warmth of their bodies joined.

* * *

A GENTLE BREEZE ruffled the leaves of the massive trees that threw their shadows over the paddocks. The air rustled the leaves and wove its way through the grasses before reaching the trees that stood tall on the grassy slopes. The breeze rested briefly as it flickered across a gravestone in the cemetery, slowing as it brushed lightly over a plaque that was just visible in the moonlight. The wind picked up speed, gathering a few dry leaves, moving through the delicate flowers of the towering jacaranda tree that stood guard. Further on it gathered small sticks, throwing them back to the earth before swirling around the sacred mountains. Finally it made its way back up the slopes, following the well-worn paths of the cows, causing the cattle lying together under a tree to lift their heads, watching as the hurtling breeze raced back up the hillside.

The crickets and cicadas joined together, the noise filling the night air with life as the golden moon eased gently behind a cloud, darkening the valley, the paddocks and the rooms of the farmhouse perched high on the hill.

* * *

'WHEN I'M UP HERE, it's like I'm floating. Like everything else has been left below. My mind settles as I climb the mountain and I feel at peace. The ancient trees with their rough bark wrap around me like silk cocoons. Their solid trunks and tendril roots grip the ground as if to say, I will hold you, I will not let go. My life with Ruby Rose is balanced and steady. The air is clear, not sticky or musty, and there's a breeze that wings its way through the branches, the leaves and across my face. The world below sometimes ceases to exist. If I close my eyes I float above the surface of the earth and ... I am calm.' Bobby Carlon

ABOUT THE AUTHOR

 Rhonda Forrest is an Australian author who juggles writing and publishing, alongside teaching high school students. She writes captivating contemporary and historical/romance fiction about relationships, family life and social issues, set amidst beautiful and uniquely Australian landscapes.

After bringing up three daughters and traversing several careers, Rhonda went on to teach creative writing, English and history. Her passion for literacy, history and travelling around Australia fuels her novels. Along with her husband, she divides her time between Tamborine Mountain and a century-old cottage with a rambling garden overlooking the waters of the Whitsundays.

***If you enjoyed this book or any of Rhonda's other books, you can make a big difference by writing a review, or leaving a star rating on Amazon, Goodreads or Bookbub. A personal recommendation to family, friends, libraries and book clubs is another great way to share the books with others. You can also follow Rhonda on Facebook, Instagram, Goodreads and Bookbub. Website - https://www.rhondaforrest.com/

FOREVER MORE - Silkworm Secrets Series Book 2

The days pass for Ruby and Bobby just how they like: slow and peaceful with plenty of time for the two of them. The dark secrets they once shared have faded into the past, and their life in the Sunshine Coast Hinterland is full of activity as they build their new business. A few head of cattle, a couple of horses, and their dog Rusty complete their family. It's hard to imagine that anyone could want anything more.

However, when family connections from long ago surface, Ruby and Bobby face responsibilities they hadn't anticipated. Bobby is reminded of his own tumultuous upbringing and the two of them make decisions that will change the paths of everyone involved.

Forever More, continues the story of Bobby and Ruby and reminds us of the good and bad in people and that, a loving family can come in many different forms.

BOOK 1 - *'A dingo howls, a star falls.*

Don't worry for me, I'll be home soon.'

Based on actual events, *Elizabeth's Star* begins the story of Michael and Joanie, unfolding the lives of their families and friends while following the life of Gracie, a little girl left behind when her father went to war. A moving tale of love, loss, and separation.

BOOK 2 - *'When you go home, tell them of us and say, for your tomorrow, we gave our today.' John Maxwell Edmonds 1918*

Until We Meet is an epic war saga based on actual events that continues the story of Elizabeth's Star. A tale of survival, love and family, set amidst the backdrop of World War II.

BOOK 3 - *My troubles are all over, and I am at home; and often before I am quite awake, I fancy I am still in the orchard at Birtwick, standing with my friends under the apple trees.' (Black Beauty)*

We'll Meet Again is a story of devotion and family, a connection between those who suffered loss and separation and a sweeping tale of hope, chance and love.

TWO HEARTBEATS

When Jess heads west for a fresh start in a small mining town, the dusty, outback plains are a far cry from her former life in the city. Despite having no knowledge of country life, she finds herself loving the isolation and local people who she lives with. All she has to do is keep her head down and work hard to create a better life for herself and Johnno, the only person she has ever truly cared about.

Happy Valley BooksRead —

Amazing authentic relatable characters, the harsh but beautiful Australian country settings and a storyline of realness that you can connect to. This wonderful Australian writer knows how to pull her reader into the plot and bring all the feelings bubbling to the top!

Chapter Ichi Book Reviewer - *I could not put 'Two Heartbeats' down. Rhonda Forrest has such a beautiful style and describes the Australian land in a way that makes me feel a closer connection and appreciation of the country I live in. The scenery described is breathtakingly realistic.*

TIME WILL TELL - Sequel to TWO HEARTBEATS

A rural love story, where friendship, romance and hearts entwine.

When Jess discovered love with Daniel in the tiny outback town of Gowrie, her previous troubled life was cast aside. However, differences in their backgrounds, her doubts about real love and the urge to return and support her twin brother Johnno, forced her to make a decision to leave.

A new home in the small community of Tamborine Mountain provides an opportunity to contemplate how she really feels and what is important. Johnno lives nearby and new friends and a romantic encounter give her a fresh start, but is this what she really wants? And if it isn't, will Daniel welcome her back with open arms?

The tranquil setting of Tamborine Mountain joins forces with the outback of Queensland to continue the story of *Two Heartbeats*. Will the decision be taken out of Jess's hands, pushing her further away, or will her heart lead her to where she will find true happiness?

When I read Rhonda's work, I think "authentic". There is no pretense. Just raw, honest and beautifully crafted characters and dialogue. The Mad Hatter – Book Reviews

Rhonda writes with such emotion and compassion that it oozes from the pages, very raw and honest. Happy Valley Books Read

KICK THE DUST

'If I close my eyes, it's easier to hold onto a memory. When I open them, I think it might really be there in front of me.'

After three tours of duty in Afghanistan, Liam Andrews is home safe in Queensland. His weekly life drawing class, full of colourful local artists, helps him manage his post-traumatic stress disorder. But he's struggling to open up about a past that still haunts him.

Belourine 'Billy' is an Afghan refugee who lost everything before arriving in Australia as a child. She finds joy in her daily swims in the lake. After years of upheaval, she's still searching for a place to call home. But her past makes it hard to trust people.When Liam and Billy meet, they form an instant connection. But will they ever overcome the past? And will it be together?

***

Rhonda Forrest's books always captivate and touch my heart, and this one did too, just as much as all her other books. Her story telling style is unique, full of emotion, and her characters come to life instantly. This book deals with themes of: war, refugees, immigration, PTSD, friendship, and art. Telma Rocha - Canadian Author

THE SHACK BY THE BAY - by Rhonda Forrest

An isolated fishing shack on a beautiful bay in the Whitsundays provides Luke with a retreat where he can find peace and solitude. However, the discovery of family war relics, and a developing relationship with the beautiful Lily, connects family histories and reveals a story that threatens to destroy his chance at real happiness.

Will the wartime secrets prove to be the breaking point for a beautiful romance? Or can two families put the deeds of the past behind them?

Romantic and purely Australian, The Shack by the Bay captures the pristine beauty of the Whitsundays and the wartime memories of older Australians while introducing an eclectic blend of friends and family.

***

Review comments - *An intriguing mix of historical romance, a coming of age, love and its complications against the backdrop of World War II.*

Praise for The Shack by the Bay - *A novel that offers a linkage between the present and past while showcasing the natural beauty of a spectacular slice of Australia.*